Eye Contact

Novels by Michael Craft

FLIGHT DREAMS
EYE CONTACT

Published by Kensington Publishing Corporation

EYE CONTACT

MICHAEL CRAFT

Kensington Books
http://www.kensingtonbooks.com

KENSINGTON BOOKS are published by

Kensington Publishing Corp.
850 Third Avenue
New York, NY 10022

Library of Congress Card Catalog Number: 97-074365
ISBN 1-57566-292-2

First Printing: June, 1998
10   9   8   7   6   5   4   3   2   1

Printed in the United States of America

The author wishes to thank a circle of friends and trusted readers who acted as an informal "brainstorming committee" in developing the core idea for this story. They are Michael Gudbaur, Mari Higgins-Frost, Leon Pascucci, Tim Radigan-Brophy, and Brian Schend. For their assistance in lending technical credence to various aspects of the plot, the author also thanks Bill Althaus, Roxanne Decyk, Frank Gerlits, and Andris Kursietis. Finally, he expresses his ongoing gratitude to Mitchell Waters and John Scognamiglio for nurturing this series in print.

—M.C.

Seulement, toujours
à Léon

Contents

PART ONE

DISCOVERY

CELESTIAL SHAKEUP!

Astronomer claims discovery of a long-sought tenth planet

❖

by Mark Manning
Journal Investigative Reporter

June 22, 1999, Chicago, IL— Dr. Pavo Zarnik, the renowned astrophysicist who was named director of Chicago's Civic Planetarium just three weeks ago, stunned the scientific world late yesterday when he announced his discovery of a tenth planet in Earth's solar system.

Issuing a prepared statement, he told the press, "This tiny, remote body is of course not directly observable, but its existence has been verified by a computer model that accounts for minute anomalies, or perturbations, in the gravitational fields of Neptune and Pluto."

Planet Zarnik is said to orbit the sun at a distance of 7 billion miles, roughly twice the distance of Pluto, with the Zarnikal year lasting more than 600 Earth years. But because its equatorial diameter is less than 1,000 miles, compared to Earth's 8,000 miles, it spins through a day in about two Earth hours. The planet is said to be solid, not gaseous.

Reaction from other experts came quickly. A spokesman said that NASA would not recognize the new planet until Dr. Zarnik's claims have been independently verified. Replicating Zarnik's complex computer model would take months under ideal circumstances, but because of funding setbacks, the research could take much longer.

Although news of the discovery has been met with broad skepticism, none of the critics has questioned Dr. Zarnik's professional integrity in making the claim. The NASA spokesman conceded, "The man's credentials are impeccable."

Zarnik, 56, took up residence in Switzerland several years ago, fleeing the civil war that still ravages his Eastern European homeland. His recent appointment as director of the Civic Planetarium was arranged, with help from the State Department, as part of the city's Celebration 2000, marking the millennium with a yearlong festival of arts and sciences, to open July 3. ❏

Wednesday, June 23

Mark Manning gazes across the expanse of the *Chicago Journal* city room, then lowers the newspaper to his lap. This morning's article, repeated from yesterday's late editions, wasn't exactly his best work, certainly not typical of the in-depth investigations that have marked his career and secured his reputation among the city's top journalists. But then, this particular assignment didn't qualify as "reporting" at all—not in his book.

Yesterday afternoon, the paper's managing editor, Gordon Smith, nabbed Manning in the hallway and thrust a copy of a one-page press release into his hand, telling him, "Cobble something together for the next edition. This might be big, and we've got squat."

Manning skimmed a couple of paragraphs—something about an astronomical discovery. He asked Smith, "Shouldn't this go to Cliff Nolan?"—referring to the *Journal*'s science editor.

"It *did*, Marko. Nolan was supposed to interview this Zarnik character and write up the discovery in layman's terms, but he never delivered." Smith was already backing away from Manning, taking a turn down another aisle. "I'm late for the daily editorial meeting," he explained. "Just piece something together and get it into the system. We need to have *something* in ink, or we'll be playing catch-up to the *Post.*"

"What happened to Cliff?" asked Manning, but Smith was already rushing away toward his meeting. So Manning got to work. Even though he was more than qualified to rewrite a press release for print, he still felt qualms about putting his byline on a science story that was out of his realm and, to his way of thinking, not very interesting. There was nothing in this claimed discovery that roused his curiosity. Other than the skepticism of Zarnik's peers, which might well be dismissed as professional jealousy, there was no *conflict* in this story. Manning would simply relay the known facts, like some talking-head TV anchorman. Grousing, he told himself, This story has no element of mystery—does it?

Now he leans back in his chair, folds the paper, and sets it squarely on his clutter-free desk, which accommodates only the essential telephone, appointment book, steno pads, pencil mug— and a framed photo of a handsome man of thirty-three who stares at the reporter with a fixed, worshiping smile. Half-walls surround the desk on three sides, demarcating the limits of Manning's work space. A babble of organized confusion, intensified by an approaching deadline, fills the vast room, but he does not hear it, immersed in thoughts about a promising story he's eager to begin drafting. There's a ghost-payroll scandal at the local water utility that's about to burst wide open, ripe for a round of investigative journalism.

He switches on his computer terminal and begins transcribing notes, originally written, as always, in the blue-black ink of an antique Montblanc, his pet fountain pen. His right leg pumps autonomically, burning off energy not consumed by the action of his fingers on the keyboard. The heel of his spit-polished cordovan shoe taps the hard carpeting. A summer-weight blazer, only recently brought out of storage, drapes the back of his chair.

He stops typing and leans forward to check his words, searching for a tighter phrase. He squints, unsatisfied, and the clean, strong features of his face turn momentarily comical. If a stranger were to glimpse him at work and guess his age, he might be pegged for thirty-something, but in fact, he's forty-two now, fit and trim—the waist size of his khaki slacks hasn't changed in years. His eyes, uncommonly green, appear even more so, their color amplified by the background hue glowing from the screen. Finding his phrase, he resumes typing, then uncaps his pen and checks off several items on a page of his steno book.

"Say, Mark. Got a minute?"

Manning swivels from his computer to find Gordon Smith standing behind him with a cub reporter, David Bosch, in tow.

The eager kid was a newsroom intern from Northwestern until a year ago, when he finished his journalism degree and was kept on full-time. His broad shoulders and owlish glasses give him the air of a boyish Clark Kent—a likeness that has not escaped Manning, who has taken care to keep their chummy relationship strictly professional.

"Of course, Gordon," Manning answers while standing. "What's up?" As a casual aside, he adds, "Hi, David."

"A few minutes ago," the editor says, "I got a call from Nathan Cain. . . ."

"Oh?" asks Manning, a hint of caution coloring his voice. A phone call from the *Journal*'s legendary publisher may be an everyday occurrence for Gordon Smith, but others in the newsroom rarely see the man, let alone speak to him. As the result of this call from on high, Smith is now standing at Manning's desk. "And . . . ?"

Smith laughs, scratching the back of his head. "It's the damnedest thing, Marko, but Nathan was really knocked out by your Zarnik piece this morning. He told me to keep you on the story, and he wants to make a splash with a page-one follow-up on Sunday. We'll be promoting it for the rest of the week— broadcast *and* print."

Manning opens his mouth to protest, intending to tell his editor that the story was nothing, a rehash of a press release. If Cain wants it taken further, Cliff Nolan is clearly the best writer for the job. Besides, Manning is itching to get started on that waterworks story.

But before Manning can voice the first syllable, Smith tells him, "I *know* how you feel about it, and between you and me, I agree. But Nathan gave a direct order, and *I'm* not inclined to tell him he's wrong." Again Smith chuckles—his customary technique for dispelling tension. "It's just a couple of days' work, then you can get back to whatever steamy exposé you're cooking up. And to sweeten this story, Nathan suggested that I assign you an assistant."

Peering over Smith's shoulder, David Bosch waggles the fingers of one hand as if to say, That's me.

Lord, Manning tells himself. All I need. If there's no way to get out of this nowhere story, I'd rather work it alone. But now we're going to turn it into a "learning experience" for some rookie.

Resigned to the inevitable, he forces a smile and tells Smith, "Okay, Gordon, we'll have it wrapped up within forty-eight hours."

"That'a boy, Marko." Beaming, Smith pats Manning's back, then strides off toward the city desk, leaving the cadences of yet another chuckle in his wake.

Manning shakes his head and sits. David steps into the cubicle, telling him, "Sorry, Mark. I know you've got better things to do. The whole setup sounds goofy to me too—but the truth is, I'll be honored to work with the best in the business."

There now, Manning thinks, this may not be so terrible after all. In spite of the kid's limited reporting experience, he's already a pro at pushing the right buttons. And he's certainly not hard on the eyes.

Manning gestures that David should sit, telling him, "Actually, I'm a bit rusty at 'team reporting,' so it may turn out that you're just along for the ride."

"You're the boss," David assures him. "And I'll try to keep out of your way." As he perches on the edge of the desk, Manning can't help but notice the long, knotted muscles of David's thighs— he's clearly invested some time at the gym.

"And *I'll* try to make you feel useful," Manning tells him. Glimpsing at his desk calendar, he asks, "Is your schedule open this afternoon?"

"*Now* it is."

"Let me give Zarnik a call and see if he has time for us to visit him later." He pulls a file from a drawer, retrieves Zarnik's original press release, and makes note of a phone number, telling David, "In all honesty, I shouldn't grumble about this. With Celebration Two Thousand set to open in less than two weeks, we're both lucky not to be writing sidebars for the 'Arts' section."

With a laugh, David nudges his glasses, which have crept down his nose. "That's exactly what I was doing five minutes ago when

Mr. Smith rescued me. I know the festival is a big deal and all—
it seems the whole world is pouring into the city these days—
but I think it's being blown way out of proportion."

"Tell me!" Manning flumps back in his chair, eyeing the
framed picture on his desk. "I have more than a passing interest
in seeing this festival up and running." Indicating the photo, he
asks, "You know Neil Waite, don't you? My, uh . . . loftmate?"
Not that Manning would ever deny his relationship with Neil—
these have been the happiest, most liberating two years of his
life. But he just doesn't care for the term "lover," finding it
entirely too earthy for most contexts. The language is full of
other descriptors—roommate, companion, partner, husband,
friend—all of them borrowed from other settings, none of them
le mot juste. "Loftmate" will suffice.

"Sure," answers David. "You introduced us when he dropped
by the office one day. He seems like a great guy—an architect,
right?"

"Right. And that's what got Neil involved with the festival.
He's really got his hands full with the architecture committee—
so involved that most of his building projects have been back-
burnered till after the Fourth. And now he's tied up with another
committee that's planning the human-rights conference."

David hesitates, uncomfortable with the topic. "That's like,
gay rights, right?"

Manning stands. "It sure is." He closes Zarnik's folder. "And
it's got a lot of people upset. The Christian Family Crusade
wasted no time announcing they'd stage a counterdemonstration
at the opening."

David stands to look Manning in the eye. "Don't mind them.
They're just a bunch of crazies."

Manning exhales an odd noise, something between a sigh and
a laugh. "That's what makes me nervous."

From the aisle, a lilting voice interrupts their discussion. "Here
you go, darlin'. A fresh supply of bedside reading." Into the
cubicle sidles Daryl, a gay black copy kid, still a student at Northwestern, who has never made a secret of his general interest in
men—or his particular interest in Manning. He carries a hefty

stack of oversize books, foxed and musty-smelling, just plucked from the reference section of the paper's morgue. He nudges between the two reporters—" 'Scuse me, David"—and drops the books onto the desk with a dusty thud.

Manning looks askance at Daryl. "What's this?"

"Basic astronomy, hon. Time to brush up on the cosmos."

"How'd you know?"

Daryl's gaze glides first over one shoulder, then the other. Coyly, he responds, "My ear's to the rail."

Manning flips through the titles, recognizing that Daryl has chosen well. "I suppose I should thank you for your efficiency."

Daryl purses his lips, cooing, "You owe me one, Mark."

David smirks at the comment, but Manning lets it pass, picking one of the books from the pile, a thin primer of astronomical theory and vocabulary. He hands it to David, telling his new assistant, "Spend some time with this over lunch. It'll be helpful background if we get to meet Zarnik this afternoon."

David tucks the little book under one arm. "Will do, sir," he tells Manning, cuffing him on the shoulder with his massive fist—a playful gesture typical of his jock-friendly manner. Then he turns and leaves the cubicle, heading toward his own desk at the far side of the newsroom.

"Unh-unh-unh," croaks Daryl. "Remember, gorgeous—you're 'married.' "

Manning sits. "What's *that* suppose to mean?"

"I saw you watching David's sweet derrière strutting down the aisle." He plants himself on the edge of Manning's desk and looks down at the reporter with an accusing grin. "If you're entertaining a dip in the company inkwell, I've got first dibs."

"Christ, Daryl, there's no harm in looking. I confess, you caught me—David's an eyeful. But he's off-limits. I'm happily coupled, and he's happily straight."

"*Ha!*" Daryl's reaction is so explosive that it briefly quells the surrounding hubbub. He leans into Manning's face to say, "That four-eyed muscle-boy may *look* like a big butch stud, but I'm telling you, honey, when the lights go out, his feet hit the ceiling."

Manning's blank stare conveys disbelief.

"It's true," Daryl assures him. "We were in school together. Not that I've had the pleasure, mind you, but I know plenty of others who have."

"I had no idea," says Manning. "He's worked here almost two years. . . ."

"He's a *closet case*, Mark. Or would it be more charitable to call him 'guarded'?" Daryl's tone turns confidential. "In any event, if you're interested, he's makable."

Manning laughs at the idea, pointing out, "I'm old enough to be his father."

Daryl tells him, "He's twenty-four; you're forty-two. That would make you one very young, very attractive daddy."

"Get off it. He'd never be interested in me."

"I happen to know otherwise." Daryl gives him a lascivious wink.

"Besides"—Manning's voice rises a register—"*I'm* not available."

"Uh-huh," says Daryl, sounding unconvinced.

"Now hold on," says Manning, dead serious, needing to sort this out. "Neil and I are committed to each other. I changed my whole lifestyle, my very self-identity, in order to build a life, a *home* with him. And he moved cross-country, walked away from an established career in Phoenix, in order to be here with me. We love each other, Daryl. We're happy. Why would I jeopardize that?"

Equally serious, Daryl tells him, "Because you're human, Mark. You're a man. You're curious. Neil brought you out— God bless him—and I can see why you were bowled over. But that was two years ago, and you've never played the field. Neil has."

"Before I came along, sure."

"Sure." Insinuation hangs in the air.

They eye each other warily for a few long seconds, then, as if responding to some unspoken signal, they each break the stare. They have often sparred like this, though always over trivial matters, office chat. Daryl has never strayed into such intimate territory, and he has gone too far. "Sorry," he says, removing his butt from Manning's desk, "I oughta keep my yap shut. You and Neil are great together. Keep it that way."

Manning smiles. "Coming Saturday night?" He and Neil have just finished an extensive renovation of their loft on the city's Near North Side, and they've invited Daryl to a housewarming party.

Sheepishly, he answers, "If I'm still welcome."

"Of course," Manning assures him. "Now, if you'll excuse me, I need to get hold of Dr. Pavo Zarnik." As Daryl turns to leave the reporter alone with his work, Manning mutters into the messy pile of books strewn on his desk, "I still think Cliff Nolan would be a far better choice for this assignment."

"He probably would be"—Daryl turns back—"if we could find him."

Manning looks up. "What?"

"Smith expected him to interview Zarnik and file his story by Monday night, but he didn't. Then Tuesday—yesterday—he didn't show up at all, so Smith reassigned the story to you."

"And this morning?" asks Manning, guessing the answer.

Daryl shrugs. "Still no Cliffy-poo. Smith told me to start phoning his apartment every hour, but I haven't been able to reach him."

Manning wrings his brows. Clifford Nolan is a dedicated and intelligent writer—with a Partridge Prize to prove it. Manning has always admired the man's refined tastes and astute mind. He's at least fifty now and not much fun, but he's certainly dependable, and it's not like him to fail on a story. Even so, Manning considers, Cliff is still single, with an adolescent appetite for women. And though he rarely drinks, when he does, he binges. Manning has seen him out of control at a party or two. So the unexplained absence may not be such a mystery after all.

Manning tells Daryl, "When you hear from Cliff, let me know."

Driving south from the Journal Building along the lake toward Civic Planetarium, Manning reflexively checks his pockets, confirming that he is equipped with pen, notebook, cell phone, and pager. Seated to his right is David Bosch, who has turned in the passenger seat to face Manning, speaking with animated gestures that cause his owlish glasses to inch down his nose.

"When Gordon Smith took me aside this morning to say that I'd just been assigned to assist *Mark Manning* with the Zarnik story, I was blown away. I mean, J-school was one thing, and the internship was another, but there's nothing like on-the-job experience to really *learn* a field—and now they've placed me at the feet of the master." He mimics an elaborate bow to the sultan. "What is your will, O Great One? I am here to do your bidding." His glasses have slipped down his nose again. He cuts the act and pushes them back. "Really"—his beefy hand now rests on Manning's shoulder—"this is awesome."

Manning glances at the hand on his shoulder, then returns his gaze to the road.

"Oh, sorry." David plants his hands in his lap, looking absurdly prim.

Manning isn't sure how much more flattery he can stand. When they left the office this afternoon, David couldn't stop gushing about Manning's car, which pleased him greatly—to a point. But now this personal-hero routine leaves Manning ready to reopen the discussion of his "plus one" wheel upgrade. He decides to shift the topic back to business, asking David, "In what capacity does Gordon expect you to function as my assistant? Any clues?"

"Guy Friday, I guess." He laughs. "It's up to you, sir. Anything goes."

"Please, don't call me 'sir.'" He tries to keep his sense of humor, but doesn't find this especially funny. David's subservient attitude makes Manning feel older than he'd prefer. Even more unsettling, in light of Daryl's recent revelation, it hints that David has plans for an after-hours slave-and-master romp with the boss. This is nuts, Manning tells himself. Laughing at his overvivid imagination, he tells David, "Don't call me Marko, either."

"Right. Mark."

"Hey," says Manning, "I almost forgot. Neil and I are having a party Saturday—no big deal, sort of a housewarming at the loft. Care to come?"

"You bet!" Then his enthusiasm drains. "Sorry, but I'm booked. My uncle and a friend are arriving from New York on Friday. They're involved with the theater festival as part of Celebration Two Thousand."

"Oh?" Manning turns to David. "Who are they?"

"My uncle's name is Hector Bosch. He's a—"

"My God," Manning interrupts, "he's the most influential theater critic in New York. He's one *hell* of a writer. The name never clicked—Hector Bosch is your *uncle?*"

"One and the same," replies David with a shrug. "Maybe you've heard of his friend, too. She's Claire Gray, a director. Supposed to be pretty good."

"Well, *sure,*" says Manning, amazed that David seems unaware of her celebrity status. "Claire Gray is not only one of Broadway's best directors, but also a superb playwright. Her first script, *Traders*, ended up as a movie a few years ago."

"Yeah," says David. "I saw it. That's her."

"That is *she*," Manning dryly corrects him. Then, lightening up, "Why don't you invite *them* to the party? Neil would be thrilled to meet them—so would I."

Big smile. "Sounds like a plan."

Spotting the planetarium ahead, Manning reins the conversation back to business. "Did you get very far with your astronomy lesson?"

"I read all I could, but I'm not sure how much I absorbed." He knocks on his skull. "In grade school, I memorized the planets in order from the sun, and I can still recite them, but the rest is way beyond me."

"Ditto. And Zarnik is among the elite, the most knowledgeable in his field. He seemed friendly enough on the phone when I called—in fact, he sounded inexplicably eager to meet me—but I simply don't feel qualified to question the man. We'll just have to wing it, and that makes me uncomfortable."

Manning turns the car off the road and onto the grounds of the planetarium, parking at the farthest reaches of the lot to minimize the possibility of door dings. The Bavarian V-8 is new enough that its interior still smells of leather and its exterior has not yet been baptized to the ravages of city driving. It's slick. It's black. It's perfect.

As they leave the car and Manning sets its alarm with the fob button, David glances back with a gleam in his eye. "Sweet rims."

Once inside the building, Manning is surprised to find Zarnik himself waiting for him and David at a circular receptionist's desk in the noisy, echoing lobby. Manning recognizes the scientist from file photos, but Zarnik cannot identify the two reporters among the crowd. Manning approaches him and extends his hand. With a smile he asks, "Dr. Zarnik, I presume?"

"Ah!" says the scientist, checking his watch, "I *knew* that you would be prompt. Welcome to my domain." His English is fluent, though colored by a nonnative stiffness, spoken with an indefinite accent.

"Thank you, Professor, and welcome to Chicago." Manning introduces David, and they all exchange pleasantries. The fusty astronomer then leads the two reporters through the back hallways of the planetarium, away from the yattering clumps of children, away from the meteor exhibits and the circular theater with its sky show, up a metal stairway, and down another hall.

"Monday's announcement was timed, Mr. Manning, to coincide with the summer solstice. I do hope such punctilio was not wasted on your readers." Zarnik skitters along with quick, short steps, stopping at a locked door that bears a red plastic sign: *Observatory. Authorized Personnel Only.* He examines each of several keys hanging from a chain over his white lab coat like baubles on a necklace. A hefty chrome police whistle rattles among the keys.

With a laugh, David asks, "What's that for, Professor? Expecting trouble?"

"Ah, *pfroobst!*" He shrugs. "One never knows. Where I come from, everyone believes that Chicago is yet riddled by gangsters. Now that I have come to know your city, I am happy that this seems not true. Nonetheless—as you Americans are fond to say—

better safe than sorry." He gives his whistle a toot, unlocks the door, and waves David and Manning inside.

Arcane electronic hardware clutters the fluorescent-lit room, whirring constantly, blinking randomly. A dusty chalkboard runs the length of one wall, but instead of mind-boggling formulas, it bears only a grocery list, a stray phone number. Computer screens stare blindly at the new visitors. Manning, in turn, absorbs the visual details of the laboratory, uncapping his Montblanc and scribbling a few hasty notes.

Dr. Zarnik asks, "Is something amiss, Mr. Manning? You appear perplexed."

"Your observatory isn't what I expected," he explains. "I was hoping for a giant telescope—it would have made a great backdrop for a photo."

Zarnik clucks as though Manning should know better. "No telescope could possibly fathom such depths of space to view so small a planet, a dead speck of cosmic sand spinning wildly in the darkness. No, Mr. Manning, this"—he pats the top of a computer monitor—"*this* is my window to the universe."

David asks, "How does it work?"

As Zarnik begins explaining some of the intricacies of his research, David stands listening and Manning sits at a desk to take notes. The professor rambles on about vector points, magnetic fields, and polar wobble. Manning struggles to follow, dutifully transcribing Zarnik's verbal minutiae, but his mind begins to drift, and his eyes are soon exploring the room again. There's a fire cabinet in a wall near the door, stocked with an ax, extinguisher, and folded hose. On the floor, a foot-thick bundle of cables snakes between the towering racks of high-tech electronic gear. From the desktop where Manning writes, a stack of greenbar printout spills over the edge and into a wastebasket. He pushes aside a half-eaten peanut butter sandwich to make more room for his notebook, and at the corner of the desk, he notices a no-frills Radio Shack VCR.

Finding it difficult to concentrate, Manning loosens his tie. "Excuse me, Professor, but let me bring this discussion back to planet Earth for now. I'd like to cover a few basic facts and figures.

For instance, the theoretical basis of your research—Who has been your key influence? Which methodology have you followed?"

For the first time, the astronomer's tone shows signs of annoyance, as if perturbed by this direction of the interview. "I would be loath to sound egotistical in such matters, and I hope you will afford me the courtesy of not printing these words, but my research is truly revolutionary, grossly more sophisticated than methods of radio astronomy employed in the past. There is no precedent for what has been accomplished in this room. If you insist upon labeling my method, however, it should rightly be termed the Zarnikal Model."

Both Manning and David are now making copious notes. Manning asks, "Can you tell me how much computer power is at work here?"

"*Pfroobst!*" says Zarnik, waving both arms about the room, as though the answer should be self-evident. "*All* of it."

"No," says Manning with a laugh, "I'm talking about gigabytes and such."

Zarnik pauses, weighing his words. "I am ashamed to admit that I do not know. The battery of computers was installed in phases, designed as we progressed. We are charting new territory here—unknown worlds—and to devise a comprehensive plan at the outset would be rash. So the computer power required by this project has been left as an open-ended variable. I have no accurate numbers at this moment, but if you care to check back, I shall compile them for you."

"Thank you. Yes, I'll do that."

Zarnik dons a pair of reading glasses and makes a note of his own. The easy manner of his pencil strokes shows his satisfaction in having successfully dodged the question. Just when he's feeling off the hook, though, Manning asks, "And what about funding?"

Zarnik's pencil stumbles on the pad. "Funding?"

Manning borrows Zarnik's earlier gesture encompassing the entire room. "This stuff doesn't come cheap. What did it cost, and who paid for it?"

"I am a scientist"—he clears phlegm from his throat—"not

a bookkeeper. The pursuit of science, the gleaning of knowledge purely for its own sake, is among man's highest callings. Man's curiosity, his thirst to *know*, defines his very humanity. My role in this noble endeavor is to supply the vision and, I daresay, the brains. What it costs and where it comes from is of no concern to me. I find myself in the happy position of—what is the expression?—not losing sleep over it."

"You came to Chicago from Switzerland with the help of our State Department. Can we assume that your work here is backed by federal dollars?"

Zarnik takes off his glasses, thinking. "I presume so, yes."

"Which agency do you presume provides the funding?"

Zarnik chews the ends of his glasses. "I do not know."

"The funding for this project must amount to many millions of dollars. Can you hazard a guess as to how many?"

Zarnik tucks the glasses into a pocket. "No, I cannot."

Manning says, "Excuse me, Professor, if this question sounds too personal, but who signs your paycheck?"

Zarnik tells him, "I am paid by the Chicago Civic Planetarium. I do not recall that anyone signs it—a computer spits it out."

Sensing that he has pushed as far as he dare, Manning says, "Thank you, Dr. Zarnik. This has been helpful. Please understand that I didn't intend to 'grill' you this afternoon. By the nature of my job, I need to dig for hard facts—you can surely appreciate that, being a man of science. We'll let these issues slide for now in favor of the central question."

Zarnik asks. "That being what?"

"I write for a very general readership, what we used to call, in less peevish times, 'the common man.' Those readers don't care about vectors. They just want an answer: Is there really a tenth planet out there? If you can prove your claim to my satisfaction, I'll let them know."

Zarnik sighs, clapping his palms to his cheeks. "Ah, thank you, Mr. Manning. You are truly a godsend." He plants himself in a chair to face Manning squarely, rolling so close that their knees touch. He explains, "Though I am new here, your repute has spread far beyond this city. You are known to be scrupulous, insightful, and fair"—Zarnik punctuates each adjective by tapping his index finger on Manning's khaki-clad leg. "It is important that you understand this discovery, that you *know* it, *believe* it. Then you can tell the world."

"You mentioned on the phone that you've developed a simple demonstration that makes the validity of your discovery apparent to any layman. I believe you called it"—Manning checks his notes—"a 'graphic realization.' "

David interjects, "Cool."

Zarnik stands and turns toward David. Smiling, he tells him, "Indeed it is, my young friend. But alas, it is now too late. The demonstration, which depends on the simultaneous gathering and comparison of data transmissions, can be made only during a narrow astronomical oculus, for a few fleeting moments at noon."

David frowns, "I wish we'd seen it."

"And you surely shall," Zarnik tells him. He explains, "There will be another prime oculus in two days, Friday at noon. Can you return then?"

David turns to Manning, who stands, answering, "Absolutely, Professor. I'll need to see the demonstration before I can draw any conclusions in print." He notes the appointment in his date book. "That will leave me just enough time to finish the story for the weekend editions."

Zarnik reaches to shake Manning's hand. "Thank you so much. That is all I ask. You will not be disappointed. But please take care to arrive a few minutes early, or the opportunity may be missed." He also extends his hand to David, escorting both report-ers to the door, which he opens for them.

Preparing to leave the lab, Manning turns and says, "Excuse me, Professor, but something's troubling me. You've just announced the biggest astronomical news since the thirties, when Pluto was discovered, and your claim has been met by the skepti-cism of your peers. Reporters everywhere, including the scientific press, are now clamoring to get to you. But when I phoned earlier, you said that you were eager to speak to me alone. I appreciate the exclusive—but why me?"

Zarnik answers flatly, "Because you are known to be the best in your field."

David concurs, nudging Manning with his elbow, flashing him a thumbs-up.

"I'm flattered," Manning tells Zarnik, "but any science writer would be far better qualified to judge your research and interpret it for the public."

"Those hacks are mere leeches on the carcass of science, sucking the blood of knowledge from the work of others. Besides, they are read by no one, excepting other—how do you say?—eggheads."

Manning laughs. "You have a point, Professor. Even so, I'd be much more comfortable if Clifford Nolan, the *Journal*'s science editor, could witness your demonstration as well. He's far more qualified than I."

"To the contrary," scoffs Zarnik, "he struck me as a mere dilettante whose mind is ruled by crude skepticism."

Manning blinks. "You've met him?"

"Of course," Zarnik answers, as if Manning should have known. "He came here on Monday, shortly after my press release was issued. We discussed my discovery at length, but he left unconvinced. Fortunately, your paper had both the taste not to print his worthless words and the intelligence to remove him from this story."

Manning assures him, "The *Journal* did nothing of the kind. Cliff Nolan never delivered a story—that's the only reason I'm on this assignment now."

The astronomer shrugs. "It matters not. As the great bard of your native tongue so aptly observed: 'All is well which ends well.' " With a curt nod of his head, he dismisses the two reporters from his lab, closing the door with a thump.

Working at home that evening on his notes for the Zarnik story, Manning taps a code into his laptop computer, sending the file by modem to his directory at the *Journal*. He wants to get a fresh start on a draft tomorrow, Thursday, even though he must wait till Friday to see the graphic realization of Zarnik's discovery. The story will first run in the Saturday-afternoon "bulldog" edition of the Sunday paper.

Manning closes the laptop, disconnects it from the modem, and begins stowing it in a carryall case. He turns in his chair to face Neil, continuing their conversation. "Nathan Cain is so hepped up about this story, they're promoting it with a TV blitz."

Neil is on a step stool, barefoot, wearing only running shorts, pulling liquor bottles from a corrugated box and arranging them in glass-doored cupboards above a granite-topped bar. He says to Manning, "Here's an idea. Why don't you invite the big cheese himself to our shindig?"

Manning contemplates the unthinkable. "Nathan Cain—*in our home?*" Then he breaks into a grin. "Hell, why not? All he can do is say no."

Neil plucks the last bottle from the box. "I didn't think Cain took much interest in day-to-day stuff at the paper."

"He *doesn't*, which makes this assignment all the more intriguing. Maybe he's a closet astronomy buff."

"Speaking of closets, could you put this carton away, please, and bring me the next? God—seventy-two hours, and we'll have *guests* pounding on the door."

"Everything will be fine," says Manning, rising from the desk and crossing to him. "I, for one, can't *wait* till the guests arrive. You've done a magnificent job with this place—people won't recognize it—and I'm eager to show off your talents." He hugs Neil's legs, nuzzling his hips, then grabs the empty box and carries it toward the storeroom.

The loft was little more than raw space three years ago when Manning bought it, one huge room with concrete floors and a semblance of a kitchen along the back wall. While the urban aesthetic had a certain appeal, it was anything but comfortable, and Manning's challenge to "fix things up" became an uncharacteristic exercise in procrastination. Every attempt to sketch his ideas on paper ended in mindless doodles or fretful crosshatching.

Then he met Neil, an architect who would eventually fill the void of Manning's unfinished loft. He would also fill the void of

Manning's confusion, his long-repressed need to love another man.

Neil's detailed plans for the loft, a surprise Christmas gift a few weeks after they met, first struck Manning as overly ambitious, well beyond his reporter's means. But Neil also surprised him by noting on the plans, "Together, I'll bet we could swing it." And so both of their lives, to say nothing of the loft, changed.

They had met while Manning was embroiled in a high-profile investigation that brought a measure of celebrity to his career. His efforts were further recognized with a half-million-dollar reward for solving the case.

Within months, his good fortune more than doubled when a gay uncle, whom he barely knew, met his demise and left to his handsome nephew a magnificent Prairie School house in central Wisconsin. Manning cherished childhood memories of the place, but he didn't think twice about selling it.

Acknowledging to Neil that "a million doesn't go as far as it used to," he was nonetheless able to forge ahead with the loft project, buy exactly the car he had always wanted (that big Bavarian V-8), and still have plenty left earning interest—monthly bills don't seem to matter anymore.

Now, after more than a year's upheaval, the loft is finished, transformed into a sculptural network of platforms and balconies, a complex interplay of masses and voids. While the overall composition of the room is boldly artful, it is also functional, divided into distinct areas for conversation and reading, cooking and eating, sleeping and bathing. The aesthetic is modern but not sterile. To the contrary, rich detailing and Neil's playful allusions to styles of the past lend an inviting, livable atmosphere to the design.

Manning carries the empty box past the outer wall of the loft, where a double-high row of windows looks east onto a still-bright summer evening. The loft's shadow rises like a black slab against brick walls glowing orange across the street. Between the other buildings, green wedges of Lincoln Park swarm with the after-office games of earnest young professionals. Beyond, Lake Michigan spills to the horizon.

"Let's take a run along the lake," says Manning. "I'll help with the bar later."

Neil protests, "Mark, I . . ."

"Get your shoes," Manning tells him. "It'll take me only a minute to change."

Outdoors, along the concrete embankment at the water's edge, Manning and Neil find their stride and fall into a comfortable gait, side by side. Their arms brush. Their breathing adjusts to the pace. In this shared act, a nightly habit during decent weather, there is a physical communion, vaguely erotic—often sufficient to inspire lovemaking upon their return home, though not recently. The pressures of finishing the loft, to say nothing of Neil's various commitments to Celebration Two Thousand, have taken a temporary toll on their passions. During these runs, they usually pass the miles in silence. Sometimes they talk.

"Cain told Gordon Smith to assign me an 'assistant' for this story," says Manning. "Can you imagine?"

The question has a rhetorical ring, and Neil doesn't answer.

Manning continues, "So guess who I got. David Bosch."

"Oh?" says Neil. He muses, ". . . sweet David." Neil and Manning have shared fantasies starring the cub reporter. "We ought to invite him to the party."

"I'm way ahead of you," Manning tells him. "Guess who else is coming."

A wary pause. "Who?"

"None other than David's uncle, Hector Bosch, the critic. And director Claire Gray. They're coming to town for the theater festival."

Neil stops in his tracks. "Hector Bosch is David's *uncle?*" He seems agitated. "I never made the connection."

Manning stops running, turns, and walks back to face Neil. "Neither did I. But they're coming to town. And I thought I should invite them—sorry I didn't clear it with you."

"No, that's fine," says Neil. "Of course they should be invited. But I wasn't expecting them. I had no idea. . . ."

"Calm down, kiddo," Manning tells him, placing both hands on Neil's shoulders. "They're just people—they just happen to be famous."

Their run is finished, so they begin the trek home at a pace barely faster than a stroll. Neil seems lost in anxious thoughts. Manning affects a casual tone to tell him, "Daryl—you know, the copy kid who'll be at the party—dropped an interesting morsel of information today." Then the bombshell. "David Bosch is gay."

"Right." The news has not had its intended effect. Neil isn't buying it.

"No, really," says Manning. "Daryl was serious. They were in college together. He *knows*. David's butch act is just a cover."

"Oh?" Neil is now fully attentive. "And . . . ?"

"And . . . I thought you'd want to know." Manning doesn't mention that he's high on David's "most wanted" list. Such a detail would cause more trouble than the momentary ego-boost would be worth.

"God," says Neil, "if he ever gropes his way out of the closet, it'll be open season. With that face—*and* body—he could bag any prey in his sights."

"Think so?" asks Manning, detached, now lost in his own thoughts. He doesn't hear Neil's answer.

Back at their building, climbing the stairs behind Neil, Manning recalls a similar view of Neil's body when they first ran together on a winter morning in Phoenix some two years ago. They had met in Chicago in the fall during a business trip of Neil's. Manning recognized at once that their budding friendship carried carnal overtones that he both welcomed and suppressed. Confused but determined to resolve the issue, he accepted Neil's invitation to spend a long holiday weekend with him at his home in the desert. They went running that first morning—it was Christmas. All was quiet as they wound their way along a mountain road that took them back to the house. Neil led the way, and Manning watched, mesmerized by the movement of his younger friend's body, the clenching of his calf muscles, the trickle of sweat that soaked the crack of his shorts. When they arrived at the house, they walked without discussion to a concealed courtyard in back, where they made love under a pristine blue sky. Their drive was so urgent, they didn't take time to remove their running shoes. They later joked about the kinkiness of that first torrid mating, but the memory—the images of it—remained etched in their minds. To this day, they have indulged in the private celebration of a mutual fetish.

Arriving at the door to their loft, Neil inserts the key. There in the hallway, Manning nuzzles up behind Neil, pressing his nylon shorts against Neil's rump. He grabs a shock of Neil's hair and turns his head, speaking point-blank into his ear: "Let's horse around."

Neil opens the door. "We've got *work* to do, pal."

But it's a mild protest, and as soon as the door closes behind them, they're at it—on the floor. It's been a while, and both quickly succumb to the lure of impromptu sex. Their shorts are off by now, but neither has bothered to remove his shoes. They are transported to a warm Christmas morning when their lives first merged.

Just as their senses begin to cloud, their frenzy is penetrated by the beep of a pager—it's an arm's length away, clipped to the waistband of Manning's shorts.

Neil catches his breath. "That better be important."

"Sorry, kiddo." Manning rolls over and peers at the gadget. "It's Gordon. I'd better return the call."

Neil lies watching, grinning, as Manning rises and crosses to the phone, his treaded soles squeaking on the polished wood floor. Manning dials and waits. "Hello, Gordon," he says. "You beeped?"

"Yeah, Marko," the editor's voice buzzes over the phone, "sorry to bother you at home, but Nathan just phoned. He wants to see both of us upstairs tomorrow—early."

"Hmm," says Manning, impressed that he would be summoned to the top-floor office of the *Journal*'s publisher. Few lowly reporters have ever set foot in Nathan Cain's penthouse lair—though tales of the walnut-paneled "inner sanctum" abound. Manning asks Smith, "Do you know what he wants?"

"I assume it relates to Zarnik, but who knows? I wish Cliff Nolan had delivered that story as planned—we'd be *done* with it now."

"That reminds me," says Manning. "Are you aware that Cliff actually interviewed Zarnik? They met on Monday afternoon."

Smith pauses. *"What?"* He's incredulous. "Just wait till I talk to that guy. . . ."

"You mean you still haven't reached him?"

"Hell no—he's missed two full days at the office."

Manning bites his lip, thinking. "Gordon, his apartment is only a few blocks from here. Why don't I run over there and take a look?"

From across the room, Neil rolls on the floor, laughing. He calls to Manning, "You'd better put some pants on first!"

Five minutes later, Manning is on the street, walking through his Near North neighborhood toward Clifford Nolan's apartment building. The long summer evening is a warm one, and the urgency of Manning's stride has caused him to break into a sweat. He tells himself to slow down. Nothing is wrong.

After all, Cliff Nolan has pulled these brief disappearances before. When he won the Partridge Prize a few years back, there was the traditional Friday-afternoon champagne toast in the newsroom. With uncharacteristic spontaneity, Nolan invited everyone to his apartment to continue the celebration that night. Manning was inclined not to go, but dismissed his reticence as base jealousy of Nolan's award (known among reporters as "the coveted Brass Bird"), so he joined the festivities later that evening. Funky dance music was blasting from the apartment, and Manning laughed in astonishment as he climbed the stairs—at the office, Nolan never missed an opportunity to flaunt his ballet-and-opera tastes. Inside the apartment, the party was in full swing, and so was Nolan. His usual abstemiousness, which only rarely allowed a glass of port or an exceptionally fine Armagnac, was out the window that night, and he raced through the crowded rooms half-naked in pursuit of female coworkers who laughed hysterically at his metamorphosis. The next week, he didn't show up at the office for several days, and when he did arrive back, he offered no explanation for his absence. Whether he was drying out somewhere, or shacked up with someone, or simply embarrassed into hiding was never known.

The incident reminds Manning that there has been newsroom gossip of other parties, not attended by Manning, that also led Nolan to miss work. In the course of Nolan's career, however, these aberrations have been rare, and Manning is willing to dismiss his colleague's current disappearance as merely another brief escape from a repressed personality.

Manning has reached his destination, standing now at the canopied entrance to the other reporter's building. He tries the door, knowing that it will be locked, and indeed it is. He presses the buzzer to Nolan's apartment, and predictably there is no response after several tries. Stymied, he stands there in the shade of the awning, wondering what other options he has. Perhaps he could try to reach the building's superintendent. Then he notices an older resident approaching the building, a woman with two bags of groceries, packed high. As she steps up to the door, she struggles with her purse, fishing for her key.

"May I be of help?" asks Manning, reaching for one of the bags.

"Thank you so much," she gasps, handing him the groceries. "Every day, it seems that life just gets more *complicated.*" She laughs at her futile complaint.

When she unlocks the outer door, Manning opens it for her, steps inside with her, then opens the inner door. Inside the lobby, when she has recomposed herself, he hands back her groceries. She thanks him again and hobbles off toward her own apartment. Manning is already up the first flight of stairs.

Arriving on the top floor, he walks past several doors to the one he knows to be Nolan's. He pauses, listening. There's a television playing somewhere, but it comes from another apartment. Otherwise, silence. He knocks. There is no response. So he knocks louder, calling, "Cliff? It's Mark Manning. Are you in there?"

Down the hallway, the door to the next apartment cracks

open, emitting the sound of the television he heard—someone is preaching about moral decay. Through the narrow opening, a face peers out, wondering who's in the hall. Manning turns to get a glimpse of the woman, and the door snaps shut.

Returning his attention to Nolan's door, Manning knocks louder still. *"Clifford?"* And still there is no response. So he tries the knob, knowing that it will be locked. But in fact, it clicks open, and Manning swings the door wide before him.

Stepping inside, he remembers entering the living room on the night of the party. Even then, crowded as it was, the place struck him as lavishly furnished, expensively decorated. This return visit confirms that impression—the apartment is serene and tasteful, all velvet and crystal and dark hardwood, with framed old art *(real* art) on every wall. Air-conditioning wafts through the chilled but stuffy rooms, carrying the slightest whiff of something rotten. Then he notices that all the lights are on. The sun won't set for another hour, and daylight streams in through west windows. So the lamps have been left on since at least last night.

In the hush of the apartment, he senses that his ears are ringing—but no, it's not that—it's a different sort of noise. What he hears is a low electronic hum. It comes from the next room, which he knows to be Nolan's study. Manning again calls, "Clifford?" but this time his voice is colored with apprehension. He crosses the room to the doorway of the study and looks inside.

There in a chair sits Clifford Nolan, his body slumped forward onto the desk. Manning steps closer. "Good God," he mumbles. "Cliff?" But he knows that his colleague will not answer. The underside of the reporter's face has turned purple, swollen against the surface of the desk. Bullet wounds, several of them, pierce his back. Blackened blood has caked down his shirt, disappearing into his pants. He's starting to stink. He's been here awhile.

Manning stands at his side for a moment, head bowed, then heaves a sigh of resignation to this grim discovery. Carefully, he nudges Nolan's shoulder. As he suspected, the body is limp and flaccid—it has been here for at least a full day.

Aware again of his surroundings, Manning notices that the hum he heard is still sounding from a stereo system housed on shelving along the wall opposite the desk. Stepping over to it, he sees that the volume has been turned to its upper limit. The lights on the amplifier indicate that a CD was playing and has finished. There are many CD cases stacked in the vicinity, and it is not apparent which one contained the disc that's inside the machine. He's tempted to tap the button that will open the drawer and give him a look—but no, he reminds himself, don't touch *anything*. He shouldn't even switch off the amplifier, even though it's running very warm.

He returns to the desk and studies the articles atop it, which seem to radiate from Nolan's lifeless body. There's a phone, of course, pencils and pens, a few pictures and other personal mementos—including the coveted Brass Bird, shoved unceremoniously into a dark corner behind the lit desk lamp. There are several reporter's notebooks, some of them open to blank pages, all of them sprouting shreds of missing pages from their spiral bindings. At the edge of the desk sits Nolan's modem, identical to the one issued to Manning by the *Journal*. It's plugged in, and its standby light indicates that it's ready to transmit over the phone line. Missing from this tableau is Nolan's laptop computer.

Manning checks. It's not hidden beneath the hunched body. It doesn't seem to be anywhere in the room, although its carryall case is plopped next to the desk on the floor, zipped open and empty. Glancing around the carpet, Manning also notices that no shell casings were left behind—they'd be conspicuous within the tidy confines of Nolan's study.

Manning reaches for the phone, then stops himself before touching it. Instead, he pulls his own phone from his hip pocket, flips it open, and punches in the code of a programmed number. When someone answers on the other end, Manning asks, "Is Jim in?" He waits. Jim is a high-ranking Chicago police detective who has become Manning's principal contact at headquarters. "Evening, Jim. It's Manning from the *Journal*. Glad I caught you in."

"Always good to hear from you, Mark—but I assume this is no social call."

Manning allows himself a short laugh. "No, Jim, it's not. I'm at the apartment of a fellow reporter, Cliff Nolan." He gives the address. "He's missed some work, and I just found him shot to death, multiple wounds to the back."

"Ouch. Any signs of break-in or struggle?"

"No. He was working at his desk. His computer may have been stolen, but robbery isn't a likely motive—his place is full of pricey stuff. All the lights were left on, so it must have happened at night."

"Is he stiff?"

"Beyond stiff," answers Manning. "The rigor is resolved."

Jim can be heard scratching notes. "Then the corpse should be at least thirty-six hours old. If he was shot at night, it couldn't have been yesterday, Tuesday."

"Right," says Manning. "And he was alive on Monday afternoon—he conducted an interview at Civic Planetarium. So Clifford Nolan was murdered Monday night, sometime after dark, while working on something at his desk."

Thursday, June 24

The next morning, Gordon Smith leads Manning past a *Journal* security guard and into a small elevator. He fidgets with a seldom-used key, inserting it into the control panel. With a twist of his wrist, the elevator begins to rise. Under the black gaze of a video lens, Smith turns to tell Manning, "Nathan Cain looked upon Cliff Nolan as an intellectual equal—few reporters can make *that* claim. I haven't talked to Nathan since yesterday, but I'm sure he's devastated by the news of Cliff's murder."

Manning shakes his head in recognition of the tragedy. "Nathan didn't know about the murder when he called this meeting. I wonder if there'll be a change of agenda."

"He's the boss," Smith says with a shrug. "I'm sure he *intended* to discuss the Zarnik story. Did you bring your notes?"

Manning answers by patting the breast pocket of his jacket, which contains a notebook. He asks his editor, "Do you spend much time up here?"

"Where, the inner sanctum? My fair share, I guess. But it still never fails to impress. Prepare to be wowed, Marko."

Throughout his life, Manning has been grateful that his given name is one of those that don't lend themselves to nicknames—but his editor has managed to invent one. Though older than Manning by only ten years or so, Gordon Smith has grown increasingly paternal toward his star reporter, showing signs of proud, manly affection that are altogether new to Manning, who never really knew his own father. Mark Manning, Senior, died when his son was only three, leaving the boy to grow up without his influence—or the tag of "Junior." He's always been Mark, just Mark, to his mother, his friends, his coworkers, even Neil. Now this "Marko" business. . . .

The elevator stops, opens. Manning and Smith step into a small lobby that leads to a single door, wide and heavy, constructed of rich walnut panels, bearing a plaque with gold lettering: *Colonel Nathan Cain, Publisher.* Cain's military days are long past, but the title has stuck. A security guard, seated at a ridiculously petite desk, rises, nods to Smith, and swings the massive door open.

Manning and Smith enter an outer office, a windowless room with walls covered in the same walnut paneling. The dark wood, combined with the deep carpeting underfoot, creates a hushed atmosphere, churchlike. Manning's throat tickles, but he stifles the urge to cough. The room's sole occupant is a receptionist at an oversize desk, atop which there is only a fresh arrangement of flowers, a telephone, and a computer terminal—no pictures, papers, or clutter. A bundle of cords slithers down the side of the desk and disappears into a slit in the carpeting—a clumsy installation, notes Manning, inconsistent with the impeccable fit-and-finish of these posh quarters. The computer is clearly a recent addition, never envisioned by the architect who won the international competition for design of the Journal Building back in the twenties.

The receptionist rises, greets Smith, is happy to meet Manning, bemoans Nolan's murder, then ushers them down a hall. They pass through another windowless room, which houses Cain's secretarial pool, four well-dressed women, all on the high side of middle age, who tap away at their computers. Cords and cables again spoil the finesse of the room's decorating.

They pass file rooms, a lounge, and several closed doors, arriving at last in Cain's outer office where they meet his special assistant, Lucille Haring. She's a tall woman, lean and mannish, with carrot-red hair worn short and parted. She speaks and moves with military precision, an impression that is reinforced by her olive-colored gabardine suit. She wears no makeup or jewelry, just a Swiss Army watch, a no-nonsense timepiece with a large, readable dial.

Manning can tell by her conversation with Smith that they

have not met before, so she is apparently a recent addition to Cain's staff. She makes no mention of Cliff Nolan, whose murder has been all over the news this morning, and Manning concludes that the woman never met the late science editor. As they continue to talk, the receptionist who escorted them from the front office excuses herself, and Manning turns to acknowledge her departure from the room. Doing so, he notices that this office has windows, and his glimpse of the skyline confirms that they are at the top of the *Journal*'s landmark tower. He also notes that Cain's outer office, now Lucille Haring's domain, is cluttered with even more computer hardware. Racks of electronics line one of the walls, covering part of a window—a hasty, makeshift setup.

"This way, gentlemen," Miss Haring tells them. "The Colonel is expecting you." Manning could swear he heard her heels click. She leads them through an imposing doorway, and Manning gets his first glimpse of the fabled inner sanctum. He fully expected the publisher's office to be grand, even lavish, but he wasn't even remotely prepared for *this*.

If the outer offices seemed churchy, this room is more like a cathedral. Indeed, the curved wall at the far end of the room, two stories high, resembles an apse, replete with Gothic arched windows overlooking carved limestone gargoyles and the city beyond. The high altar enshrined by this vaulted space is the desk of Nathan Cain, which lacks only candlesticks to complete the image. The computer terminal on the desk seems not only anachronistic to this setting, but baldly offensive to it.

Cain is not at his desk, so Smith and Manning feel free to explore a bit. Manning gapes at the timbered ceiling, the stone and paneled walls, as Smith explains, "There's more beyond that door, an entire *living* quarters. Nathan can hole up in here for weeks on end if he wants—and occasionally he does." The main room contains not only the desk, but a large conference table, a glass-doored cabinet that displays a collection of rare firearms, a sitting area furnished with a tufted-leather chesterfield suite, a fireplace big enough to barbecue a steer, a fully stocked bar, and a circular stair that corkscrews its way up to a library loft overlooking the room below. The library is no mere display for decorative volumes, but a serious research center, with books arranged on shelving that protrudes at perpendiculars from the wall. Some of these shelving units, Manning notes, have been replaced by vented metal cabinets, the type that often houses electronics.

From behind these cabinets, a voice announces, "Good morning, Gordon."

Smith and Manning turn to see Nathan Cain appear on the balcony. Smith sweats with the knowledge that their boss has overheard their conversation. Trying to remember exactly what has been said, he concludes that he has made no fatal slip, but nonetheless resents the fact that Cain would allow Smith to put himself in jeopardy.

The publisher descends the circular stairs, telling them, "In light of last evening's disturbing developments and the grievous loss to all of us within the *Journal* family, I'm especially pleased to see both of you today. It's good to be together at times like these." His tone lightens momentarily as a thought occurs to him. He asks, "I don't believe you've been up here before, Mr. Manning?"

"No, sir. It's . . . beautiful."

"*Hngh,*" grunts Cain. Wryly, he adds, "Thanks. We like it." Then he laughs at his little joke.

A tall man of rigid bearing, Cain takes the stairs slowly. He's sixty-four, but will never retire. His heaps of *Journal* stock, his years of deferred compensation, his seven-digit salary—it all means nothing to him. Like his ever-present black silk pocket handkerchief and his custom suits, his wealth is simply a fact of life, another quirk that defines him to himself and to others. He has never married, and the ultimate disposition of his fortune has become, with the passing of years, a popular subject of speculation. He doesn't give much thought to his material rewards because his greater pleasure, an obsessive pleasure, derives from power.

He has focused that power on only two goals: building the *Journal* and serving his country. A war injury (a wound to one of his thighs) sustained in Korea (he was too young for the Big One) left him with a bad leg. He has since walked with difficulty, bearing his pain silently, too proud to use a cane, which would in fact suit his style to a tee. With one hand he grips the railing; in the other he holds a book.

Arriving at the bottom stair, he again speaks in a somber tone, quoting: " 'Day of wrath and day of mourning. See fulfilled the prophets' warning.' "

Smith smiles awkwardly, not knowing what to make of this verse.

Manning recognizes Cain's words. "Aren't those the opening lines of a medieval dirge, sir?"

"Bravo, Manning. Very good. I intend to use them at the top of Clifford's obit."

Manning finds the lines overly morose and melodramatic, a throwback to his own Catholic upbringing. Though he has renounced the theology of his youth, he is still fascinated by its trappings. As an altar boy, way back when he still believed, he was sometimes sprung from school to serve at funeral Masses. He remembers the melody of that dirge well. Chanted in Latin, it was grimly exciting, the perfect aural counterpart to the nostril-sting of incense, to the flicker of huge orange candles in their black-lacquered bases flanking a coffin in the center aisle. That was thirty years ago, when words of godly wrath still held power over him.

Today, he would never invoke such sentiments to eulogize the passing of a friend. He knows, though, that he's in no position to express these thoughts to Cain, so he simply nods, acknowledging that Cain's intentions are understood.

In contrast to Manning's passive acquiescence, Smith effuses, "That's *brilliant*, Nathan! Do you mean to tell us that you're writing Cliff's obituary *yourself?* I'm sure he'd be honored by such a send-off."

"Noblesse oblige," Cain tells him dryly. "I owe him that much."

Manning says, "We'll all miss him. He was one of the most cultured and intelligent writers I've ever worked with."

Cain approaches Manning and rests a hand on his shoulder.

"And to think—you were the one to discover his body. It must have been terrible for you."

"I've seen the aftermath of murder before, but you're never prepared to find a friend with bullets in his back."

"Ughh," Cain breathes a shudder, "bullets again." He grips the area of his thigh where fragments of lead still abrade nerves and rob sleep. With measured steps, he crosses the vast office toward the case that displays his gun collection. He gestures toward the weapons behind the glass. "In light of Clifford's tragic demise, I'm sorely tempted to issue an editorial calling for a broader ban on handguns—they've become tools of such wanton violence."

Smith and Manning have followed him to the showcase. "Gosh," says Smith, "I never thought I'd see the day when the *Journal* jumped on *that* bandwagon. Not that I disagree—there are strong arguments on both sides of the debate—but this paper has always been a staunch defender of the Second Amendment."

"I haven't *decided,*" Cain reminds him. "I said that I'm tempted. We'll see." He notices Manning peering close at a jade-handled pistol enshrined within the display. Cain chortles. "It didn't take you long to zero in on the centerpiece of my collection, Mr. Manning."

"I have no great knowledge of guns," Manning responds, "but that one certainly seems . . . unique."

"Indeed it is," Cain assures him with grave understatement. "That gun has a remarkable history that, one day, I may share with you. Suffice it to say, that rarest of Nambu pistols has been used solely to defend honor, never to commit treachery."

There is a pause. Enticed by Cain's statement, Gordon Smith eagerly says to him, "Well, come on, Gordon—tell us the story!"

"Patience," commands Cain, one hand raised to fend off further inquiry, the other still grasping the book he carried down from the balcony. "That can wait. We have important *business* to conduct this morning. First, the most urgent question, one that must be answered quickly: Who killed Clifford Nolan?"

Smith stammers, "The police, well, they're working on it even as we speak."

"The hell with them," snaps Cain, "and damn their bureaucratic bumbling." He repeats, louder, "Who killed Clifford? And why?" He's a powerful man, and he expects answers.

Flustered, Smith suggests, "The *Journal* could undertake its own investigation."

Cain smiles, silently thanking Smith for not forcing him to make the suggestion himself. Watching this exchange, Manning can predict with near certainty that Smith will later assign the investigation to him. That's what he hopes, anyway—and there's a good chance that someone else may now inherit the Zarnik story.

Content that a Nolan investigation will soon be under way, Cain waves Smith and Manning toward the grouping of leather sofas. As the three of them walk across the room, Cain continues, "I've been brushing up on my textbook astronomy"—he hefts the book he has been carrying—"and I can't decide if this Zarnik character is a crackpot or if he's actually *on* to something. What have you learned?" He drops the book onto a low table. The thud actually echoes in the cavernous room.

Sitting, Manning consults his notebook. "In a nutshell, Zarnik's credentials are solid and his research seems sound, but I was put off by his inability to answer some straightforward questions of fact. He promised me a video demonstration—he calls it a 'graphic realization'—that he claims will prove the existence of his tenth planet unequivocally."

"Yes," says Cain, "Miss Haring showed me the notes you sent in last night."

Manning stops short, unaware that his computer stories were accessible to anyone while still being drafted, before being filed in the editorial pipeline.

Cain continues. "If Zarnik's claims are fraudulent, he talks a damn good story—I'll grant him that." He settles against a long credenza that faces the sofas. Its top is cluttered with two television sets, a computer monitor, a rack of black-box hardware, and a pedestrian-looking VCR, its clock flashing midnight.

"His technical mumbo-jumbo is way beyond me," Manning admits, "but for some reason, he trusts me. I told him that any science writer would be better qualified to report this, but he insists that I alone tell his story to the world."

Gordon Smith beams. "Now *that's* an exclusive! Don't look a gift-horse in the mouth, Marko. If the professor wants you to write it, we'll run every word."

"Indeed," says Cain, seizing the reins of the conversation. "If Dr. Zarnik feels some sort of allegiance either to Mr. Manning or to the *Journal,* we'd be foolish not to take advantage of it— our summer circulation can always use a little goosing. But there are other considerations, too, with ramifications beyond the selling of newspapers."

Smith's normally jovial visage turns quizzical. He glances at Manning, then peers at Cain. "What do you mean, Nathan?"

"That's why I originally called you here today, gentlemen. May I get you a little something first?" He hoists himself from the credenza and crosses to the bar. A flick of his index finger signals that Smith and Manning should follow.

"Bit early for me," says Smith, chuckling.

Manning tells Cain, "Club soda, if you have it."

"*Hngh.*" Cain nods, pours Manning's drink, then a stiff snifterful of cognac for himself. He tips the glass to his lips, breathes deeply from it to savor the foretaste, then drinks. He closes his eyes, finally swallows, and sighs.

Manning lifts his glass in a silent toast, then drinks the soda.

Cain indicates by the direction of his glance that they should sit again, and he begins leading them back across the room to the sofas. Manning and Smith measure their steps so as not to outpace their boss. When they have settled in again, with Cain seated on the sofa across from his underlings, Manning produces his notebook and uncaps his pen.

With a wag of his finger, Cain tells him, "No notes this morning, Mr. Manning. What I'm about to tell you is strictly between us."

The reporter obliges by closing his steno pad. With elbows planted on his knees, he stares at Cain, at full attention.

"Ever since its founding," says Cain, "the *Journal* has been widely perceived as a conservative paper. Whether in terms of the political philosophy promoted on its editorial page, or in terms of the prudent fiscal management that has allowed JournalCorp to thrive and reward its shareholders—this paper, this *tower*, and all that it represents has been guided for more than a century by the tenets of conservative capitalism. The pendulum of public opinion has swung erratically from generation to generation, but the *Journal* has stood tall as a bastion of time-honored values. We have been alternately lionized or vilified, depending on the mood of the day."

He swallows again from his snifter before continuing, "I realize that the *Journal's* guiding principles are not shared by everyone within its corporate family. Today's journalists, in particular, seem to be of a decidedly liberal stripe. That's fine, that's healthy. Society is always enriched by debate, never endangered by it, and this paper exists, at its very core, to defend freedom of speech and diversity of ideas. I tell you this not to impress you with my open-mindedness, not to enlighten you with a history already known to you, but to prepare you for a glimpse of things to come."

Cain leans forward, ready to share a secret. "Gentlemen, when I made the decision to leave military life and turn my attentions to the private sector, I never dreamed that I would one day be entrusted at the helm of the most venerable newspaper in the Midwest. With such miracles behind us, though, our vision has been greatly expanded. The *Journal* is now poised to become the centerpiece of a communications empire that will rival anything in New York"—Cain's eyes bug as he spits a single, explosive breath of laughter—"let alone *Atlanta.*"

Smith and Manning, seated next to each other, exchange a reticent glance, unsure if they should share Cain's mirth or be awed by his ambition. Smith says, "That's wonderful, Nathan. I didn't realize there were plans—"

"Gordon," says Cain, nostrils flaring as he sniffs at his glass, "of *course* you didn't know. I hate to sound secretive, but the Pentagon's involved here—they're making it *happen* for us."

Smith and Manning again exchange a glance, but this time there is no option of mirth. Nathan Cain has long been known for both the perversity and dryness of his humor—what there is of it. For him to make the Pentagon the subject of a fib, though, would be the moral equivalent of flag-burning.

Cain continues. "You're well aware that our broadcasting division has been developing a new communications satellite. Greater capacity, higher output, blah blah blah, all the bells and whistles. But you're *not* aware that the satellite employs a whole new technology that will enable JournalCorp to take a commanding lead in integrating broadcast functions with print journalism, telecommunications, cable, the Internet, you name it. It becomes one big ball of wax. And, gentlemen"—with a decisive *clack*, he sets his snifter on a marble-topped end table—"it's *ours*."

Smith and Manning don't even look at each other. They're speechless.

"But," says Cain, "there's no way in hell we can accomplish this on our own. The military sees the potential value in all this— who wouldn't?—and thanks to old friends and unforgotten favors, the *Journal* and the Pentagon have gone to bed together. They're helping us enhance our computer power, and they're bumping us up to the next shuttle launch. Strings have been *pulled*, my friends. They have *cooperated*. And now they expect a little cooperation—a minor accommodation—from us."

Manning clears his throat before asking, "What do they want?"

"It's Dr. Zarnik. They need to know more about him."

"Ah," says Manning. "But why come to us? They've got the whole State Department at their disposal."

Smith turns from Manning to tell Cain, "That's a good point, Nathan."

Cain tells them, "They've got plenty of background on Zarnik, which is all that the State Department can provide. What they *need* to check is the man's science, his research. As I understand it, the military has no particular interest in the tenth planet itself, but in the methods employed by Zarnik in documenting his discovery."

"I'm no scientist," Manning reminds them. "I can't possibly explain Zarnik's methods on a level that would be useful to the scientific community."

"That's not what they're after," Cain tells him, sounding impatient. "They need to take this in steps. And the first step is simply to determine whether Zarnik is on the level. In other words, is his claim genuine, and if not, why not? The Pentagon seems to think there's something peculiar about the timing of all this. As you know, Manning, it would take months for NASA to replicate Zarnik's research. The military feels that that period of uncertainty may present a window of opportunity for . . . God knows what."

Resigned to the fact that the Zarnik story is his for keeps, Manning asks, "What would you like me to do?"

"Go back," says Cain, "talk to the professor, and put him through his song and dance again. Your story is slated for page one, so the follow-up interview is a reasonable backup anyway."

"No problem," Manning tells him. "I still need to see his video demonstration. David Bosch and I have an appointment with him tomorrow."

"That's all I ask," says Cain, rising. "I hope Zarnik *is* shooting straight. It's a great story—everybody loves that interplanetary stuff. It expands our horizons. And even though it tells us we're a smaller part of the big picture than we thought, it makes us feel a little bigger for having figured it out."

Smith always knows when the conversation could use some lightening. "I'm glad *somebody's* able to figure it out. I think we were born a little early, Nathan, to fully grasp the technology that now surrounds us. As for me, I'm a Neanderthal from the Dark Ages, when computers were just fancy typewriters. Look at this place," he says, rising. "They've got you wired for just about everything now."

"Did you notice the mess they've made of the outer offices?" Cain asks. "That's just the tip of it."

"I wondered about that," Manning muses while rising, stuffing his hands in his pockets.

"And who's that new assistant?" Smith asks. "Lucy . . . ?"

"Lucille Haring," Cain obliges. "She's part of the whole package. I don't know what to make of her. She's on JournalCorp's payroll, but the Pentagon dug her up for us, security clearance

and all. She's a model of efficiency, but God, what a stiff woman—
like talking to a board." He laughs, but it's more of a grunt. "I've
come to depend on her, though. She knows computers inside out,
and I'm older than you are, Gordon, so I've got some catching-up
to do. Every day, I spend an hour or so with her in remedial
training."

Smith says, "My hat's off to you, Nathan, if you're actually
able to master these gizmos." He waves at all the equipment on
the sideboard. "I wouldn't know where to begin. Well, on second
thought, I could probably figure out how to turn on the TV. And
the VCR doesn't look too intimidating—don't ask me to set its
clock or program it to record, but any idiot can hit the 'play'
button."

"Yes, Gordon," says Cain, sounding ready to wrap up the
meeting. "Mr. Manning, you'll be in touch with Dr. Zarnik soon?"

"I'll phone him this morning to reconfirm tomorrow's
meeting."

"Excellent." Cain claps Manning on the shoulder, a bonhom-
ous gesture unnatural to him.

As they begin strolling toward the door to the outer offices,
Manning says, "I *thought* I was forgetting something, Mr. Cain.
There's a party this Saturday. Neil and I—that is, my loftmate,
Neil Waite—"

"I *know* about Neil," says Cain. "He's done committee work
for the celebration, correct? Commendable. You see, Mr. Manning, the *Journal*'s management is not totally unenlightened and
Victorian—although I'm still convinced that the military's 'don't
ask, don't tell' policy is probably the wisest. It's certainly the most
comfortable."

"A lot of folks take issue with that, sir," Manning tells him.

Smith cringes.

"Indeed," says Cain.

With a smile that defuses the tension of the moment, Manning
says, "Societal issues aside, Mr. Cain—Neil and I have just finished fixing up our place, and we're throwing sort of a housewarming Saturday night, and we'd be honored if you'd care to attend.
You too, Gordon—and bring Molly, of course."

"Thanks, Marko," says Smith. "We'll be there."

Cain draws his brows together. "Sorry, Manning. It just won't work. Other commitments, you know. There are some labor issues pending at a subsidiary, and I'll be tied up late with lawyers that night."

"Certainly. Very short notice—"

Manning's words are cut short by Lucille Haring, who raps once, sharply, on the door and enters the office. "Excuse me, Mr. Cain," she says, "but there's a call from Washington I think you'll want to take."

"Thank you, Miss Haring. We were just finishing up. I'll take it inside." He begins crossing toward the door to his private quarters, waving a perfunctory farewell to Smith and Manning, when he stops and turns, having thought of something. "Mr. Manning, if it's quite all right with you and your friend, why don't I send Miss Haring in my stead Saturday evening? Miss Haring," he says to her with a bent smile, "you strike me as the sort of gal who's always up for a good party."

David asks, "So now they have you working *both* stories?"

Manning pulls his car to the curb, lucky to find a space so close to Cliff Nolan's apartment building. "That's right." Manning wags his head, recognizing the irony of this turn of events. "Cain insists that I investigate Zarnik's planet, and Smith wants me working on Nolan's murder."

"If anyone can handle it"—David cuffs Manning's shoulder, that jock gesture of his—"Mark Manning can. Besides, he's got an assistant now."

Manning laughs. "Good thing, too. He *needs* an assistant now."

They get out of the car, and because of the heat (it is midafternoon during a week that has turned sultry) they leave their jackets locked inside. Manning feeds the meter and double-checks that his bumper isn't hanging into a yellow zone—the very thought of a police wrecker towing the car is enough to make him cringe.

As they walk the few yards to the door of the building, Manning tells David, "Actually, now that I've given it some thought, I'm sort of glad they've assigned me both stories. What if they're related?"

David looks at him with blank astonishment.

Manning stops in the shade of the building's canopy and turns to face David, their eyes only a few inches apart. Speaking softly, as though someone might overhear, he says, "Think about it: Cliff was murdered mere hours after meeting with Zarnik. Zarnik made it plain to us that he was miffed that Cliff was skeptical of his discovery. Cliff was killed while working on something at his desk, which might have been a story debunking Zarnik's planet."

David is wide-eyed. "Professor Zarnik is a *suspect?*"

Manning shrugs. "A *potential* suspect. It's a stretch, I admit, but at this point, I'm at a loss to think of anyone else who had even the slightest reason to want Cliff dead." He steps up to the row of door buzzers. "That's why we're here."

He squints at the labels above the buttons, but other than Nolan's, the names mean nothing to him. They seem to be arranged by floor, in the order of each apartment along the hall, and Manning locates the button that would logically belong to Nolan's nosy neighbor, the one who opened her door to check on Manning in the hall last night. The label above the buzzer reads, *D. L. Fields.* Manning presses the button, then waits.

"Who's there?" croaks a voice through a small, raspy speaker in the wall.

"Hello, Miss Fields?" asks Manning.

"*Mrs.* Fields," she corrects him.

"Mrs. Fields, my name is Mark Manning. I'm a reporter for the *Journal.* I wonder if you could spare a few minutes to talk about your neighbor, Cliff Nolan."

"Police were here already. Here all night. Talked to ever'-body."

"I understand, Mrs. Fields, but Cliff was a friend of mine. You might say I have a personal interest in this case. Would you mind?"

There's a pause. "What the hell. Come on up." The door lock is already buzzing.

Manning grabs the knob before she changes her mind, then

opens the door and enters with David. Manning tells him, "Top floor," and they start up, David bounding ahead, taking the stairs by twos.

When Manning meets him at the top, he first notices that the door to Nolan's apartment has been yellow-taped off-limits by the police. There's been a lot of activity up here, and the hallway furniture looks askew. The dim lighting has been replaced with brighter bulbs, there are carpet tracks from the door to the stairs, and the floor is generally littered with scraps of the investigation. Manning just stands there, taking it all in—it seems so different from the scene he stumbled into last night. Then he notices that the neighbor's door is cracked open, just an inch or two, so she can spy on him as she did last night.

Her burly voice tells him through the crack, "Didn't say there was two of you."

"Sorry," he says, stepping quickly to the door, hoping it won't snap shut on him. "I should have mentioned that my colleague, David Bosch, is with me."

The door opens a bit wider so she can get a better look at David. " 'Nother reporter? Damn fine specimen, I'll say that!" She belts out a laugh, but it's aborted by a coughing spasm. She tells Manning, "You were alone last night. You find him?"

"Yes."

"Thought it was mighty quiet over there. Not that I didn't enjoy it—for a change." She swings the door wide open. "Come on in, boys."

They enter the apartment, and Manning is struck by the contrast to Cliff Nolan's place. It's hard to believe the two dwellings are in the same building. While Clifford's apartment was a show-place of genteel refinement, these digs are packed with a hodge-podge of junk furniture and gaudy bric-a-brac. Cheap gilt-framed Bible scenes are centered high on nicotine-beiged walls, and a spangled jumpsuit—it looks for all the world like an Elvis costume—hangs from a hook on the door to a bedroom. The television Manning heard last night is still on, still tuned to a religious channel. A preacher drawls, "With God's help, and with your support, my dear friends, we plan to expand the television ministry of the Christian Family Crusade, bringing the good news of Jesus, twenty-four hours a day, to every nook and cranny of this great land of ours, now riddled, as it is, by the forces of perversion."

As for Mrs. Fields herself, she's a husky woman, but not fat—in fact, she wears a kimono-style bathrobe cinched tight at the waist, strutting a good figure. She has a big, lacquered hairdo, but wears no makeup at this hour. Her years of smoking have taken their toll on her face, and Manning would guess she's fifty-five. She asks, "Won't you sit down?"—affecting an air of decorum. Then she laughs at her feigned manners. The laugh triggers another coughing jag. "Excuse me." She primps.

Manning and David sit, taking chairs that flank a small table, facing the TV. Mrs. Fields mutes the evangelist, but leaves the picture on. Though there are several other chairs in the crowded room, she remains standing, planting both palms on her broad hips. "Now what can I do for you gents? Getcha something?"

"No, thank you, Mrs. Fields," says Manning.

She tells him, "You can call me Dora Lee. You said your name was Mark, right, honey? And David—my, what a sweet child."

David is accustomed to flattery, but not from the likes of Dora Lee. He blushes, telling her, "Thank you, ma'am."

"Dora Lee," says Manning, pulling out his notebook and uncapping his pen, "may I ask how long you've lived here?"

She screws her face in thought. " 'Bout a year."

"Is there a Mr. Fields?"

"*Pfff,*" she dismisses the memory with a jerk of her head. "Dead. Long dead. Packed my bags and moved north from Memphis. Not sure why—bored, I guess."

"So you live here alone?"

She beads him with a get-real stare that asks, Do you see anyone else?

Manning grins, jotting something in his notes. He asks, "Were you and Cliff Nolan . . . friendly?"

She smirks. "Let's just say we traveled in different circles."

Manning crosses his legs at the knee and leans forward in thought, searching for his next question. "Did you think of him as a good neighbor?"

"Hell no!" Her coy manner has evaporated. Her eyes are fierce. She's ready to unload something. "Snotty little tea-drinker didn't give a shit for his neighbors. All that damn music at all hours—canons and gongs, all that yelpin' they call singin'—I warned him more than once!" She needs a smoke now and fidgets in her pockets for cigarettes and lighter. But the pack is empty, so she scrunches it in her hand and hurls it to the floor.

Manning and David eye each other, unprepared for the outburst, trying not to laugh. Then she stamps to the table between them and yanks open a drawer. She snatches out a fresh pack of Camels and zips open the cellophane. As Manning glances down at the clutter within the drawer, she slams it shut.

Fuming, Dora Lee lights a cigarette, draws a long drag from it, and paces across the room. When she turns back, smoke shoots from her nose as she tells them, "He always played that highbrow music way too loud, and it was even louder than usual that night." She throws up her arms in exasperation. "I'm glad he's dead! I coulda killed him myself!"

Manning's brows instinctively rise. Seeing this, she stammers, "I . . . prob'ly shouldn't say that, Mark." She snorts. "I mean, just wanted to have a little peace and quiet. I was *mad* enough to kill the little weasel, but of course I didn't."

He lets it pass. Rising from the chair, he turns a page of his notebook and says to her, "When I was in the hall last night, I noticed that you opened your door to see who was out there. Do you try to keep an eye on things up here?"

Happy to shift the discussion away from the murder, she tells him, "A woman's got to look out for herself. Can't be too careful these days."

"That's true," Manning mumbles, "so true." He takes a step closer to her. "I'm wondering, Dora Lee, if perhaps you noticed anyone in the hall on the night Cliff was killed. Did you see anyone enter his apartment?"

She takes a puff. "Sure did."

David, sensing pay dirt, pulls out his pad to take a few notes of his own as Manning continues, "Do you know who it was?"

"Never saw him before. Sort of tall—well, taller than Clifford, but that ain't sayin' much. Only saw him from behind, never got a look at the face."

Now Manning is pacing. "That's not much to go on. Did you hear what he sounded like? Can you remember any conversation?"

"Over that 'music'—you nuts?"

Manning stops pacing and turns to her. "How was he dressed? I mean, shabby like a bum, sporty like a college kid . . . ?"

"No," she steps toward Manning, wagging the cigarette in front of him, "he was more like a salesman. Dark suit, maybe."

"This was Monday night, right? Do you recall what time?"

She sucks her Camel, thinking. "Right around ten. The news was on."

Manning nods. "That would fit. What time did he leave?"

"That damn music was blarin'!" She's getting worked up again. "Louder than I ever heard it. It was bangin' so loud, I never even heard the shots. I pounded on the wall and made a few choice threats, but it did no good. That caterwaulin' didn't stop for over an hour. The caller was prob'ly gone by then. Didn't hear anything else that night"—she snorts—"or ever again, for that matter."

Manning pauses, looking at his notes. He stabs a period with his pen. "Have you told all this to the police?"

"Yes." She exhales wearily. Then she leans close to Manning and tells him, under her smoky breath, "All except that part about how I coulda killed him myself, if you know what I mean."

He nods confidentially. "This has been helpful, Dora Lee. I only wish you'd seen more." Then he nods to David, signaling that they're ready to leave.

As David rises and pockets his notes, Dora Lee says, "Awful sorry, Mark, but there wasn't much *to* see. There was nothin' special about the man at Clifford's door—except, of course, that there was a *man* at Clifford's door."

Huh? Manning looks at David, who asks, "What do you mean, Dora Lee?"

She laughs. "Well," she explains, coughing, "most of Clifford's callers were of the female persuasion. Especially at that hour. Especially when the music got loud."

Manning and David again look at each other, exchanging a shrug. It's time to go. "Thank you," Manning tells the woman, "we appreciate your taking time for us."

"Hell, Mark"—she extends her hand, a big, beefy mitt of a hand, crunching his knuckles—"anytime." She walks both men to the door and opens it. "If you think of more questions, just ask."

David glances over his shoulder into the apartment. There's a quizzical look on his face. "Actually, Dora Lee, I've been sort of curious . . ."

"Yeah, sweetie? What?"

His glasses flash toward the bedroom. "It's that, uh . . ."

"Elvis?" She laughs, coughs. "Why, that's my *costume*—for my *act*. See, I do this impersonation? And folks seem to think it's pretty good, and I been workin' a lot of church fund-raisers lately. Maybe you heard, the Christian Family Crusade is openin' a fancy new hotel here in Chicago, the Gethsemane Arms, and I'm booked for a nightly show there next month."

"Really?" says Manning, struggling to appear interested. "We'll try to catch it."

Dora Lee beams. "You just let me know when, and I'll getcha a good table."

"Thanks," the guys tell her. "We'll let you know."

As they pass by her on their way through the door, she takes aim at David's plump, muscular rear and gives it a hearty slap. He stops and turns to her, stunned. She leans, croaking into his ear, "Feel free to pop back up and see me anytime!" She breaks into laughter and thumps the door closed. Then the apartment reverberates with the explosive hack of another coughing jag.

The two reporters retreat down the stairs, David trying not to laugh. Manning lags behind him by a couple of steps, immersed in his thoughts, sorting through what he has seen and heard. When they at last pass through the vestibule and emerge into the hot shade of the building's canopy, David blurts, "She's *nuts!*" He has found the whole experience uproarious, but he's had to restrain himself till this moment. "Did you see that Elvis getup?"

"That's not all I saw." Manning smiles, but he's too preoccupied to fully appreciate David's hilarity. "When Dora Lee opened that drawer for cigarettes, I noticed something peeking from a batch of old Christmas cards and other junk—it was the muzzle of a pistol."

Friday, June 25

It's a planet—not in theory, not in virtual reality, not in digitized projection—but in itself, in all its density and roundness, anchoring a rose-colored atmosphere that resembles the Day-Glo haze airbrushed on a psychedelic poster that a college roommate once taped to the cement-block walls of Manning's dorm room.

Manning grinds his feet in the Zarnikal dirt, ready to run. He breathes the strange vapor, filling his lungs with galactic fog. At first he attributes his light-headedness to the gas he has inhaled, but then he discovers that it is not his brain that has been buoyed, but his body. The mass of this distant world is so slight that it generates barely enough gravity to keep his feet in touch with the surface. The horizon before him arcs like a world in miniature, a dusty landscape through a fish-eye lens. The globe spins so rapidly—its day, he remembers, is equivalent to two Earth hours—that his hair is tousled by never-ending winds blown by coral-fingered clouds.

He feels neither hot nor cold in the dim sunlight that radiates from a moving pinpoint in the farthest reaches of the sky. He is alone and without inhibition, so he bends to remove his running shorts. He kicks free of them and sends the ball of yellow nylon hurtling before him. It disappears beyond the horizon, and as he contemplates the laws of physics rewritten for this strange terrain, his shorts reappear—from behind, in the sky above him, fixed in an eternal orbit. The pink planet now has a little yellow moon. Dr. Zarnik got to name the planet he discovered, but Manning can take credit for its moon. "Eros," he names it aloud.

Intrigued by his newfound power to launch projectiles into

space, he looks about for something else to fling into the cosmos. But there is nothing—no rocks, no plants, no birds or lizards— just the perfect, untrampled stretch of talc-fine dirt that surrounds him, the rosy tendrils of clouds that streak with geometric precision overhead. The only other objects, he concludes, in his entire new world are the shoes on his feet—white leather running shoes, his favorite pair, the ones he wore the morning when he first had sex with Neil, the ones that have taken on the power of a fetish, their laces crusty with the spatters of uncounted orgasms. The thought of losing them to the heavens is unspeakably painful. The shoes, he decides, must stay.

Manning has been running since high school, at times escaping something, at other times pursuing. He ran on a cross-country team because he was told it was required. Later, in college, he ran for the enjoyment of it. In adult life, in the real world, he rediscovered it and hoped it might forestall middle age. But the revelation he expected least was the hedonistic pleasure of running, the erotic element that scratches his consciousness every time he laces up those shoes. He has run on cinder tracks, on city streets, on the shore of Lake Michigan, and on a mountain road one Christmas morning in Phoenix. He has run in his dreams as well, a recurring dream in which he returns to a hometown where he never grew up. Running there, he has flown, taken flight, soared above a fluttering tunnel of elms and convulsed in midair, shooting semen into a pristine blue sky.

But this is different. Neither blue sky nor fluttering elms are here to conjure memories of a childhood never known. There is no cinder track, no lakeshore, no mountainside—there is only the compacted vastness of an empty world.

Manning moves. He steps forward, and the entire globe turns beneath his feet, as if riding on frictionless ball bearings. He walks faster, and the rotation of the planet increases. The pinprick sun moves faster overhead and begins to set behind him, stretching his infinitely long shadow beyond the horizon. Night falls instantly. Manning quickens his pace, knowing that the rosy tinge of morning can be only a few strides ahead.

And there it is. The sun pops into view again and begins another ascent toward Zarnikal noon.

Manning shifts to a faster pace and achieves a running stride. Both feet momentarily leave the ground. His toes tap the surface, sending him forward with longer and longer leaps, nearly weightless. His breathing adjusts to the greater exertion; his lungs are fueled by the clouds. He circumnavigates the planet so quickly now that the sun rises and sets with dizzying regularity. He could run like this forever. And although he has already traversed great distances, he realizes that all his efforts have moved him nowhere—planet Zarnik spins beneath the worn treads of his shoes, but he's still seven billion miles from home.

It's as if he's running in place, yet he's unquestionably in motion. The minimal landscape rushes past him. The sun continues to circle. And the endless long-fingered clouds streak overhead in perpetual winds. Their sagging tendrils of vapor whip past him, through his hair, around his body, sliding across his skin, invading every pore, picking at each follicle. The relentless gusts turn playful, scrambling between his legs, licking at his testicles, caressing his penis, which swells at the touch.

He slows his pace to savor these sensations and clears his mind of the frettings that clutter his waking hours—time, distance, speed, goals. His head tilts back and his mouth gapes open so he can gulp at the clouds and feel their presence within him. Strands of his hair (it has grown quickly here) tickle his shoulders. His pace has slowed to a walk. A shuffle. He stops.

He squats, resting in the powdery sand, still breathing deep, not from exertion but with excitement. With the tips of his fingers, he feels his hardened nipples. He slides his hands to let his palms rub his buttocks. But just when his senses are shuttering themselves, blinded to every stimulation but pleasure, Manning notices his shoes. One of them has come untied, its laces drooping in a loose, sloppy knot.

Manning exhales. The erotic moment is held at bay as Manning's mind snaps back to reality. He plants one knee in the dust and brings his other foot forward to examine the offending laces.

He unties the shoe, tugs the lace tighter through the series of eyelets, then ties a new bow—just so. It's perfect.

He sits, brings the other shoe forward, and touches up its bow as well. With knees bent, he leans to place both hands at the sides of his feet. He pets the white leather, feeling the laces with his thumbs and the rough-treaded soles with his index finger. He draws his hands up his legs, past his hips, to rest again over his nipples. Then he places his hands behind him and leans backward to lie fully on the ground. The dot of sun halts at the apogee of its path, directly overhead. Its pencil beam cuts through the drifting clouds like a pink laser with Manning felled at the bull's-eye of a glowing circle projected on the desert floor.

Manning writhes in the dim noon-light, closing his eyes so that his mind may freely explore the uncharted fantasies that now flicker about him. The dull pink glow from his eyelids blackens for an instant. Something has cast its shadow over him. He looks into the sky and spots the craggy yellow ball of Eros in its lunar path, which has just eclipsed the sun. Manning laughs, grinds his hair in the dirt, and grabs his penis. Again his eyelids close as his mind drifts out of his body so that all his senses may focus on his groin. And again a shadow blurs over him. Eros, he thinks, has intruded once more on the sunbeam that bathes his nakedness. He glances into the sky, but the wad of yellow nylon is not there. His breathing stops. His pulse quickens. Something has darkened his noon. Something has invaded his private world.

Neil laughs. Manning rolls onto his left side to find his loftmate crouching there, inches away, wearing only the track shoes he wore on the morning when they first made love. Manning breathes. He smiles with relief. "Hello there, kiddo. Care to help me with this?" Neil shares the smile and bends forward to kiss Manning, sliding his tongue over Manning's lips and across his cheek, planting it in his ear. Manning groans, closing his eyes.

Once again, the hazy light goes momentarily dark. His eyelids spring open to confirm that Neil is still at his side—the shadow was not his. Nor was it the shadow of Eros—his shorts are nowhere in the midday sky. He flops his head, looking to the right, and there he sees another man standing near him in the dust, younger, more muscular, wearing nothing, not even shoes. Manning's gaze climbs the sculpted body and is riveted at last by the dual image of himself reflected in the lenses of owlish glasses worn by a boyish Clark Kent. Manning quickly turns to see if Neil has spotted the intruder, but he has not—his face is now buried under Manning's arm.

The one with glasses smiles, then kneels at Manning's side. Leaning close, he touches Manning's lips, generating a tiny white-hot spark that crackles in the explosive atmosphere. The one with glasses laughs, then drives his tongue into Manning's right ear. Manning groans.

Hearing the groans, Neil again puts his tongue into Manning's left ear. The tongues wag within Manning's head—he's sure they must be touching. They slide and thrust like pistons, creating a deafening racket of suction noises. Lost in this din, Manning extends his hands to explore the bodies of his partners, who hunker at both sides of him. His hands find their groins, cupping their balls. He flicks his middle fingers across the two anuses; the tongues push deeper into his ears.

Someone's hand now holds Manning's penis and begins to stroke it. "My God," he breathes. The stimulation is so intense, he fears that he may simply black out and fade away before reaching an orgasm, retaining nothing of the sensual memories that would pack his brain if he could think straight. But his wits have vanished.

And there's more. Someone's fingers begin to pinch his nipples, twisting just to the verge of pain.

That does it—his back arches as he raises his head from the ground. The tongues slip away, the suction noises cease, and his world is suddenly silent. The moment of orgasm approaches, then grips him. He watches his weightless semen pump out of his body and into the black sky. Backlit by the sun, which moves again along its path toward evening, the sticky strands glisten and tumble in the darkness. Then they break apart, congealing into beads that dance and shudder and finally come to rest, a new constellation of milky jewels in the farthest reaches of an imaginary universe.

"Hey," says Neil, "are you okay?"

Manning's eyes open. His face is half buried in the sheets, but he can see the clock on the nightstand, which isn't set to go off for another twenty minutes. He turns onto his left side to find Neil sitting up in bed.

"You were moaning. Pain or pleasure?"

Manning tosses back the sheet to give Neil a gander. "Pleasure."

Late that morning, Manning arrives with David at the planetarium for their appointment with Dr. Zarnik to see the "graphic realization," which the astronomer has claimed will prove the existence of his newly discovered planet. Today is Friday, and the parking lot is jammed. The weekend has begun early for hordes of families on vacation, and the sky show is a popular attraction.

Once inside the building, Manning knows his way, telling the receptionist that Dr. Zarnik needn't come downstairs to escort them up to the lab. He leads David around a doubled-back queue of visitors, down a rear hallway, and up the metal stairs. Walking through the hall toward the door to the observatory, Manning says, "Play along with me, David. I hate to sound devious, but something's been troubling me about Zarnik's lab. I want to take a closer look at things while he's not watching. I doubt we'll be lucky enough to get him out of the room, but if we can get him involved with *you*, that may give me sufficient leeway to do some snooping. So I want you to assume the role of a green rookie—all wide-eyed, young and eager."

As David nods with unbridled enthusiasm, Manning feels foolish, realizing that in fact the kid *is* young and eager.

David tells him, "You can count on me. I've *dreamed* of opportunities like this."

Manning assumes that David has spoken of his dreams figuratively. A strained smile contorts his lips as he deadpans, "So have I, David."

They stop at the door with the red sign. There is no knob,

only the keyhole for the lock, and no doorbell. Manning shrugs, then knocks.

After waiting a full minute, David whispers, "Are you sure we were expected?"

"I *thought* we were," says Manning. "He said to be here before noon."

"Ah, gentlemen!" says Dr. Zarnik, skittering toward them from the opposite end of the hall. "Sorry to make you wait, but— clumsy me—I forgot something, as usual." Wedged under his arm is a folded newspaper and a black plastic box, the size of a book or a videotape. Fumbling with the whistle and the keys chained around his neck, he manages to open the door. "Do step inside, please."

He escorts them toward the middle of the room, tossing the paper and the plastic box—it's a videocassette—onto the desk. He turns to face his visitors, standing in a clearing amid the electronic hodgepodge. Checking his watch, he tells them, "Several minutes remain until the graphic realization can be presented."

Manning says, "That should give us enough time for a few more questions, Professor. As I told you on the phone, I'd like to clear up some details before finishing my story."

"I am at your service. I want you to be absolutely confident of the veracity of my claim. Any questions you might have— please, fire away."

"Thank you. Do you mind if I sit?" As he speaks, Manning sits at Zarnik's desk, opening a steno pad and uncapping his Montblanc.

"Make yourself comfortable," says Zarnik. "You too, Mr. Bosch."

David pulls a chair to a corner of the desk and takes out his own notebook, uncapping a ballpoint with his teeth.

Manning says, "Dr. Zarnik, I wonder if you'd be willing to speculate about the physical characteristics of this new planet. I want my readers to feel that this story 'takes them there,' that they have actually set foot on planet Zarnik. For instance, if I were standing on its surface, what would I see looking up to the sky as the Zarnikal day reaches high noon?"

The astronomer looks at him with a blank expression, as though he's never tried to visualize the environment of the far-flung world he has found. With hands behind his back, he paces to the center of the room, suggesting, "It would not really matter whether it were day or night. The sky would be black, punctured everywhere by an intense display of stars."

"If the sky is black, that implies there is no atmosphere. Is that the case—no clouds, no vapors, nothing?"

Zarnik crosses his arms, then brings the fingers of one hand to his chin. "That would be pure speculation, Mr. Manning, although I appreciate your attempt to draw a more vivid picture for your readers."

The disappointment in Manning's voice is unmistakable as he reads aloud the note he has written: "Black sky, just stars, nothing else."

Zarnik shrugs. "If you're looking for a little excitement, you could throw in some meteorites, an asteroid belt."

Manning perks up. "Asteroids?"

"Cosmic litter. Hunks of something that blew up in eons past." He simulates an explosion with his hands. "Pesky space rocks." His fingers waggle like falling debris. "Unpredictable complications that could spoil one's day out there." A chipper laugh reveals that he has enjoyed this brief foray into the more poetic aspects of his science.

David eyes Manning with a glance of approval while making a note.

Zarnik taps his wrist. "It is almost noon, gentlemen. Please position your chairs in front of the desk, facing the large computer monitor. I shall take care of the rest."

Manning and David move their chairs as instructed, while Zarnik dashes about the room firing up his equipment, adjusting its settings, twiddling dials, taking care not to trip over the fat bundle of cables. David follows every movement with rapt attention, pen poised over his notepad, ready to record details of the demonstration.

Manning sits back pensively in his chair, watching Zarnik fuss. He reaches back to stretch an arm on the desk, drumming his fingers while waiting for Zarnik to finish. His hand brushes the edge of an appointment calendar, the ubiquitous style with the date appearing as a big red number at the top of each page. Manning peers over his shoulder at it. Noted there on the line just before noon are the initials *MM*. As Zarnik disappears behind some equipment, Manning pulls the calendar to himself, flips back through several pages, and finds that all of Zarnik's notations are short and cryptic, usually consisting of initials. There, Wednesday afternoon, is another *MM*, and late Monday there's a *CN*, the meeting with Cliff Nolan.

Manning slides the calendar back to its original spot and stares idly at the desktop. There's a brown paper lunch bag; he recalls the sandwich he moved aside on Wednesday. The messy stack of computer printout has swelled a few inches. The morning edition of the *Journal* carries Nathan Cain's page-one tribute to the slain Clifford Nolan, headlined, "Day of Wrath." The cheap VCR still sits at the far corner, winking midnight with the blue digits of its display. The arrangement of the desk has not changed since his first visit, yet something seems to be missing.

"All is nearly ready," says Zarnik, reappearing from behind a cabinet, his hair looking frizzier than ever. Manning chuckles to himself, wondering if Mr. Wizard got his finger stuck in a socket back there. "With a little patience," says Zarnik, "you will both soon join the exclusive ranks of a handful of witnesses to the motion of a new planet." He directs them to look forward at a large dark computer screen. He explains, "Data are being constantly collected from numerous antennae, then systematically compared in order to detect infinitesimal perturbations in the polar wobble of Pluto. Digitized, the data from these coordinated observations can be translated into a television image, a graphic realization." He switches on the monitor, then skitters behind Manning and David to the back of the desk, where he sits.

His voice is now hushed. "The image you see before you is a bitsy slice of our solar system, a view as if through the eye of a needle, extending billions of miles into the dead cold darkness."

"There's nothing there," says David, squinting. "Just the crosshairs through the center of the screen."

"So it seems. So it seems. But I tell you, my young friend, there is indeed something there, hidden beneath the intersection of those lines. It is a tiny planet, a wanderer in the far reaches of space."

" 'Wanderer,' " repeats Manning. "That's what 'planet' means, doesn't it?"

"Precisely. That is what the ancients called those bodies that wandered through the seemingly fixed constellations. Stars do not move; planets do. And with patience, *you* will see one move—in real time—before your very eyes."

The two reporters peer closer. Then, from under the white lines, into the blackness, emerges a speck of pink. A few moments later, it nudges farther from center, and the computer begins tracing its path along the arc of a giant ellipse. Zarnik tells them, "Behold the tenth planet."

"It's awesome," says David, "that an abstract theory can be proved by such concrete means."

"That is the elegance of this demonstration," says Zarnik. "Even the most casual observer, untutored in the rudiments of scientific method, can clearly grasp the evidence of this graphic realization. Not everyone can matriculate in advanced astrophysics, but any idiot can watch TV—no offense, gentlemen."

Laughing, Manning is reminded of Gordon Smith's comment in Cain's office yesterday: Any idiot can push the "play" button on a VCR.

Manning's laughter stops short. He turns to smile at Zarnik, and while doing so, confirms that something *has* changed about the desktop—the videocassette that Zarnik plopped there when they arrived is nowhere to be seen. As Manning returns his gaze to the screen, his eyes dip for a blinking instant to glimpse the display panel of the VCR. The clock still flashes midnight, but it has been joined by another symbol, an icon of a rolling tape.

Manning quickly turns toward the monitor again so that Zarnik cannot read the suspicion and mounting anger in his eyes. "Amazing," he observes. "It truly is a mechanical universe."

"Truly," affirms Zarnik.

"Awesome," says David.

Manning turns to him. "You're wearing out that word, David. You're a *writer*, for God's sake."

Taken off-guard by Manning's sour tone, David tells him, "Sorry, Mark. Thanks for the tip."

Remembering that he had asked David to act like a kid, he reaches over to pat his knee, a gesture of apology. He wants to lean over and whisper, "I'll explain later," but he can't, not with Zarnik watching, barely two feet behind them. Manning sits as if frozen there, resisting the temptation to steal a glimpse of Zarnik's hand movements. He strains to hear the mechanism of the tape player disengage the cassette, but the hum of other equipment in the room makes it impossible to detect any telltale clicks.

At that moment, the image of the planet and its ellipse vanishes, leaving only the crosshairs on the screen. "Ah," says Zarnik, tapping his watch, "we have overstayed our welcome in that pertinent slice of the cosmos. Our transmission is kaput."

Manning rises from his chair, capping his pen. He looks at the VCR; predictably, its tape icon is no longer lit. He tells Zarnik, "Thank you so much, Professor. That was enlightening—probably more than you realize. And I think it's safe to say my young assistant was impressed."

David chimes in. "*I'll* say. It was totally aw—impressive. I can't thank you enough, Professor." Still seated, David makes some quick additions to his notes.

The astronomer rises from his own chair, approaches Manning, and shakes his hand. "Do please let me know if there is anything else I can do for you."

Manning looks to David for a moment, then back at Zarnik. He says, "Actually, Professor, there *is* something you could help us with. Young David here has never been assigned a story of this scope and has never had the opportunity to interview a celebrity of your stature. If you have the time, could he ask you a few questions and cover the basics of this story on his own?"

Without hesitation, Zarnik says, "My pleasure, Mr. Manning."

Turning to David, he asks, "Well, my friend, how may I help you?"

Standing behind Zarnik, Manning indicates with a jerk of his head that David should get the professor to sit in the chair Manning has just vacated.

David says, "Thanks for your time, Dr. Zarnik. Why not get comfortable?" He gestures toward the chair.

With a bow of assent, Zarnik seats himself, facing David across the corner of the desk, giving Manning free reign to explore the portion of the room behind Zarnik's back. David asks the astronomer, "What first led you to suspect the existence of a planet beyond Pluto?"

Manning recognizes that David has asked an intelligent opening question, but he doesn't listen for the answer. Instead, he studies the racks of computer hardware, the fat bundles of cables, the vented metal cabinets, the seemingly purposeless array of video monitors that clutter the cement-floored room. It looks like a movie set—a mad scientist's laboratory—but what's the purpose of this sham?

Baffled, he rubs the back of his neck, as if to stimulate clearer thinking. Twisting his head sideways, he notices the chalkboard covering the length of a wall. He remembers that on his first visit, he was disappointed to find no mile-long calculations, only a grocery list and a phone number. The list has grown some— Zarnik must visit the supermarket on weekends. And the phone number has been mostly rubbed out to accommodate the longer list.

Manning removes the pen and notebook from his jacket. He copies the shopping list: *TP, PT, TVG, milk, bread, PB, diet, munchies, JD-2L, bowl cleaner, Ban unscented, blades.* The first three digits of the phone number are still legible, and Manning notes that they match the *Journal*'s private exchange. He thinks that the number might have been his own, since he gave it to Zarnik when he first phoned on Wednesday. But then he notices the last two digits, sevens, peeking through the bowl cleaner—it's not Manning's number.

Manning eyes his notebook for a moment, glances at the

chalkboard, then notices Zarnik, who is rising from his chair. David, also rising, says to him, "Thanks so much, Professor. It's been a great honor to spend this time with you."

"Nonsense," says Zarnik with an air of modesty, nonetheless enjoying the praise. "It is I who must thank you two gentlemen for your efforts on behalf of promoting this momentous discovery." He has turned and begins escorting both reporters toward the door.

"I almost forgot," says Manning. "The party Saturday. My . . . *loftmate* and I have just finished fixing up our place, and we're throwing sort of a housewarming tomorrow night—David will be there. I wonder if you'd care to join us, Dr. Zarnik?"

"Perfection!" says the astronomer. "I have the good fortune to be at liberty."

Manning recalls from his peek at Zarnik's calendar that there was nothing initialed for Saturday night. He says, "Anytime after seven. Would you care to make note of the address?" He folds open his steno pad and offers it to Zarnik.

"Thank you, yes." Zarnik picks one of several mechanical pencils from his lab coat's pocket protector, clicks out a length of lead, and transcribes the directions.

"That was seven o'clock," Manning reminds him, watching as he writes.

"Yes, seven." Zarnik makes note of the time, removes the page, folds it, and returns the pad to Manning.

"We'll look forward to seeing you," says Manning, extending his hand, which Zarnik shakes.

David extends his own hand. "Good luck with your research, Professor."

"*Pfroobst!*" says Zarnik, recoiling a step, raising his hands as if at gunpoint. He explains, "In my homeland, it is considered a curse to wish one luck while shaking hands. Instead, offer me your little finger." David does so. "Now hook it with mine." They do. "And shake. There. Good luck for both of us, fully protected, no curses." He laughs. "Mr. Manning?"

Manning obliges, engaging Zarnik in the pinkie-shake. "Not very scientific, Professor."

"No," he admits. "But hey—whatever works."

They all share a laugh as Zarnik opens the door for them and ushers them into the hall. While walking toward the stairs with Manning, David turns back to say, "Till tomorrow, Professor."

"Farewell, my friends!" Zarnik waves, toots his chrome police whistle, then disappears behind the security door. It closes with a thud, locks with a clank.

Making their way out of the building and through the parking lot toward the car, Manning doesn't say a word. He doesn't need to—David gabs on and on, still heady from his taste of big-time journalism. "God, this is exactly the kind of assignment I've been hoping for, but I never dreamed it would come this quickly. What a rush! Thank you, Mark."

Manning opens the car, and they get in. From the passenger seat, David says, "You know what would make this day complete? Getting behind that wheel."

"Dream on," says Manning. As they pull out of the lot and into traffic, he asks David, "Could you grab that file from the backseat?"

David reaches for the manila folder and opens it in his lap. Flipping through the pile of photos, he says, "It's Zarnik—from the *Journal*'s morgue."

"Look closely at them. Notice anything?"

David adjusts his glasses and lifts the pictures one by one, scrutinizing them at varying distances from his face. "It's him. So what?"

Manning's eyes are focused on the road, his brows wrung in thought. He can't examine the pictures while he's driving, so he's left with David's appraisal of them. "Hmm." Lost in this musing, he doesn't notice that David has returned the file to the backseat. Nor does he notice that David has reached across the console to put his hand on Manning's knee.

Then David gives a little squeeze, catching Manning's attention fast.

"David," says Manning through a nervous laugh, "when I touched you back at the observatory, it was meant as an apology—

for my brusque reaction to your overuse of 'awesome.' I don't know what *you're* doing, but it doesn't feel like an apology."

"No, *sir.*" His voice has an unmistakably suggestive lilt.

Manning grips the wheel with both hands. "David, don't. Not now. We've got other issues to deal with. There's work to do—digging."

"What do you mean?" asks David, unwilling to remove his hand. "Your story's all but written. You're sitting on a page-one exclusive detailing the biggest scientific news of the year, maybe the decade."

"*David,*" says Manning, brushing away the kid's hand, "Zarnik's a fraud."

"Huh?"

"While you were running him through your interview—"

David interrupts, "I got some really great quotes, too. You may want to work them in."

Manning glances sideways to tell David, "Listen to me. The planet's a sham."

"But he *proved* it. You saw it yourself."

Manning explains, "He was playing a videotape for us. It was a baby-simple setup. I should have seen it coming."

Dumbstruck, David asks, "But why would he try to fake something like that? Even if he could manage to jerk *us* around, he'd be proven wrong eventually."

"I have no idea what he's up to, but the deception runs deeper. Not only is his planet bunk, but the man himself is phony. *That's* not Zarnik."

"Whoa, Mark," says David, edging to the far side of his seat. "Don't blow me away here. That *has* to be Zarnik."

"He doesn't add up," insists Manning, pulling the notepad from his jacket. "Look at this. I copied a grocery list he was keeping on the blackboard."

David reads through it, then turns to Manning with a quizzical look. "Doesn't cook much, does he?"

"That's not the point. The man who made this list is *not* from Eastern Europe. He's a homegrown corn-fed American."

Incredulous, David asks, "How can you tell that? I can't even make *sense* of this. For instance, what's *TP, PT, TVG?*"

"Toilet paper, paper towels, *TV Guide*—simple."

"How'd you figure *that* out?"

"Don't you keep a grocery list? The stuff you need every week ends up at the top, usually in some sort of shorthand. Everybody does it that way. Well, I do."

"Okay," says David, "makes sense. *Milk, bread*—weekly stuff. What's *PB?*"

"Peanut butter."

David's eyes widen with astonishment.

Manning explains, "It goes with bread, and there was a sandwich on his desk the other day. Even then, it struck me as odd. Europeans don't eat peanut butter for lunch—no more than we'd eat kippers for breakfast."

David runs his finger down the list. "Next items, *diet* and *munchies.*"

"Vernacular," says Manning. "American vernacular. I have no idea how much Diet Coke and Cheetos is consumed in Eastern Europe—very little, I imagine—but I'll bet a week's pay they wouldn't refer to it as *diet* and *munchies.*"

"Here's a good one. What's *JD-2L?*"

Manning frowns. "That one's got me stumped."

"Then it ends up with *bowl cleaner, Ban unscented, blades.* Last-aisle stuff."

"Right. This guy's awfully tidy, and while I hate to cast aspersions on the personal hygiene of an entire continent, it's a fact that I've known few if any European men of Zarnik's generation who use deodorant."

"Fine," says David, handing the notepad back to Manning, "this is an American shopping list. But how can you be sure that Zarnik wrote it?"

Manning tucks away the pad, explaining, "I looked at his desk calendar. His appointments were written in the same hand, usually noted with no more than initials. Then I had him copy the directions to tomorrow's party, and I watched. He didn't write in that tortured style Europeans take such pride in. It was Palmer Method all the way. And here's the corker: He didn't cross his sevens. David, that man has either managed to change a heap of lifelong habits in the last three weeks, or he's not who he claims to be."

David flumps back in his seat, exhaling a heavy sigh, convinced by Manning's argument. "Who *is* he, then?"

"Beats me. But the State Department helped bring him here, and I doubt if he could bluff *them*. What's more, he didn't even *mention* Cliff Nolan's murder, which has been all over the headlines for the past two days. He met Cliff, remember, only hours before the murder, and he made no secret of not liking the man. I smell something very fishy here."

David tells Manning, "I smell a major exposé."

PART TWO

ASTEROIDS

PFROOBST POSITIVE!

Zarnik's computers demonstrate that his far-flung planet exists

❖

by Mark Manning
Journal Investigative Reporter

June 26, 1999, Chicago IL— Dr. Pavo Zarnik, the renowned Eastern European astrophysicist who stunned the scientific world on Monday with his claimed discovery of a tenth planet in the Earth's solar system, has demonstrated the verity of his claim by means of a sophisticated "graphic realization," a computer-generated television image.

Meeting with this reporter in his observatory at Civic Planctarium on Wednesday, Zarnik explained that while the planet cannot be seen, its existence is deduced from its movement, which in turn is calculated from its measurable effect upon the polar wobble of Pluto as well as perturbations (disturbances) in the gravitational fields of both Neptune and Pluto.

To track the movement of the new planet, data are collected from both satellite-borne and earthbound antennae, then systematically compared in real time to produce a "live" image on a computer monitor. In the tele-vision picture, planet Zarnik appears as a pink speck in the black cosmos, traveling along a giant elliptical path, an estimated distance of 7 billion miles from the sun. The video demonstration was exhibited to this writer and a colleague on Friday, during a brief period described by Zarnik as an "astronomical oculus."

The methods employed in Dr. Zarnik's research are unprecedented in radio astronomy. How much computer power is required to accomplish this near-magical feat? *"Pfroobst,"* replied Zarnik, lapsing into his native dialect, "I do not know. The computers were installed in phases, designed as an open-ended variable."

Zarnik came to Chicago via Switzerland less than a month ago with help from the State Department, and his revolutionary methods have drawn recent interest from the Pentagon. The source of the funding that backs Zarnik's research project was not determined at press time. ❏

Saturday, June 26

"**W**hat the hell is *this?*" snorts Neil, flopping the late-Saturday edition of Sunday's paper onto the kitchen counter next to Manning, who turns from the last-minute clutter he's washing in the sink. Neil has been out to get a few forgotten items needed for tonight's party. He begins unloading them from a supermarket bag. "You told me Zarnik was a quack. I thought you'd rake him over the coals. Instead, you've sent him a valentine."

Manning turns off the water. "I need a little time," he tells Neil, wiping his hands on a dish towel. "I'm buying time."

Neil stacks several cans of Sterno and turns to face Manning. His accusing tone is softened by its underlying jest. "Is that fair to your readers, Mr. Ethical?"

Aware that Neil has targeted the core issue, Manning tells him, "I had to print *something*, and I don't yet have sufficient facts to tell the whole story, the real story. I hope the public's 'right to know' will ultimately be better served by my temporary willingness to play along with Zarnik. It was a tough call—one I'm not entirely comfortable with—but the decision's made, so I have to run with it."

"How?" asks Neil, folding the paper bag.

Manning stows the newly washed utensils in a drawer. "I'm not sure. That's why I invited Zarnik here tonight. Till now, I've met him only on his own turf, in his lab, where he's secure in his act. This'll be different." He looks out from the kitchen into the main space of the loft. "This is *our* territory, which may allow me to catch him off-guard. With any luck, he might enjoy a drink or two. Maybe he'll let something slip."

"Shame on you," says Neil, mocking disapproval, "getting that kindly old man liquored-up—a foreigner, no less—so you can have your way with him."

"Don't forget," says Manning, "that 'kindly old man' is a liar to the core who had an ax to grind with Cliff Nolan. What's more, he's no foreigner."

"Regardless of what he isn't, I know what he *is*." Neil steps across the kitchen aisle and drapes his forearms over Manning's shoulders. "He's a celebrity, at least for now, till you blow his cover. He'll add a certain—what . . . cachet? star quality?—to our big evening. Thanks for snagging him." Neil gives Manning a genial peck on the lips.

"You're welcome." Manning pecks back. "But *you're* center stage tonight, kiddo. We're unveiling our new home. It's a show-case of your talents, and I couldn't be prouder." Manning pulls Neil tight, and their casual embrace turns serious. As their lips press together, Manning's passions rise, but his thoughts of impromptu lovemaking are dashed by the door buzzer.

"Curses," says Neil, "foiled again." He gives Manning's crotch a gentle squeeze, then reacts to what he finds there. "Good heavens—save that thought."

"Count on it," Manning tells him, pulling him close for a last hug.

Neil glances toward the door. "That should be the caterers. You go put yourself together. I need to review some details with the boys from Happy Happenings."

"Don't forget to tell them about the peanut butter."

"Yes, Mark." Neil rolls his eyes—Manning's plot to bait Zar-nik with peanut butter seems far-fetched at best.

Manning gives him a thumbs-up, then crosses to the far end of the loft and climbs an open stairway that leads to their sleeping area and the bath beyond.

Neil buzzes open the lobby lock. A minute later, a crew of buffed young men files through the door bearing an array of chafing dishes, cooler chests, and racks of glassware. Their white polo shirts sport the *Happy Happenings* logo. Their uniforms are finished off with baggy tan shorts and black combat boots with an inch of white socks protruding from the tops. The procession winds its way toward the kitchen, punctuated by laughter, hoots, and occasional shrieks that belie the paramilitary look of its ranks.

"Hi there, hon," one of them calls to Neil. He's older than the others and far from lean. It's the boss.

"Hello, Henry," says Neil. "Your troops are looking better than ever. Where do you *find* these guys?"

"Hah!" says Henry with a toss of his head. "Wouldn't *you* like to know." He shoos a couple of straggling beauties from the hall toward their clones in the kitchen.

Upstairs in the bathroom, Manning steps from the shower— no molded plastic stall, but a room in itself, tiled with black Carrara glass—and pauses while toweling himself dry. The man reflected in a wall-high mirror looks back at him, then winks. In spite of the sobering events of this past week, the man in the mirror seems pleased with life, pleased with himself.

Though not at all religious—Manning lost the faith when he was twenty-something—he feels moved at this unlikely moment to count his blessings. He's healthy. He's attractive, not only for a man in his middle years, but judged against any standard. These thoughts make him wonder, Am I that vain? Narcissistic? Maybe. But objective. If I refuse to delude myself with denial of my foibles, denial of reality, why should I deny my own virtues?

Virtue—funny word for a physical trait, a blessing. *Blessing*— funny word for dumb luck. Amazing how the God-folk have managed to claim a lexicon of their own, restricting a rational society in the use of its native tongue.

Manning recognizes that he enjoys other blessings that are not the booty of luck, but the reward of his own efforts. The success of his career is the most obvious of these blessings, attested to by the respect of his peers and the growth of his readership. With it has come material blessings—the marble-floored bath is a good example. The car. The comfortable lifestyle. What he wants, he buys.

His affluence, he knows, is not entirely the result of his reporting skills and his *Journal* paycheck. There was the cash reward for his work on that high-profile missing-person case—

but he "earned" that, didn't he? There was the inheritance from his uncle in Wisconsin—okay, that was dumb luck. And there has been the pooling of resources with Neil, an architect with a thriving career of his own.

Ah yes, Neil—the greatest of Manning's blessings. Did he earn such a gift? Was it chance? How can he account for the affections of another human being, for the melding of two minds, for their mutual past and their planned future, for the proprietary right they have granted each other to share their bodies in bed, or after a run, or whenever they feel the spark. How can he account for love?

It *was* luck. He might never have met Neil, who turned out to be the right man at the right time. But Manning also earned their love. He willed it. The accumulated frustrations of his heterosexual life before Neil, while disturbing, were not sufficient to nudge him into the arms of the first willing man who came along. Manning's frustrations were accompanied by the emotional baggage of a lifetime, by definitions he had set for and of himself, by a gut-deep fear of *queer* and *faggot* and all those other labels. There were mind-dragons to fight, demons to conquer before he could banish uncertainty and redefine himself. But he did it. And he has never looked back.

The man in the mirror has an erection. Manning laughs, wraps the towel around his waist, and works his fingers through his hair, deciding that a wind-tossed look will suit the evening's festivities better than his usual comb-and-brush style. He says to his reflection, "Lots of blessings, ample sunshine. No clouds on the horizon?"

The man in the mirror frowns. What about the clouds of his dreams? The pretty pink clouds of planet Zarnik are not what they seem. Their playful tendrils are wisps of unknown gases that might sear the lungs if swallowed. Caution. Manning reminds himself that tonight's celebration will be tempered by the arrival of a mystery guest, the man who claims to be Pavo Zarnik. And there is still the great looming question of Cliff Nolan's murder.

"What's wrong?" asks Neil, reacting to Manning's frown as he enters the bathroom. Ready for his own shower, he wears only lounge shorts. "A Happy Happening is in the works—and Henry has assembled a crew of first-class eye candy."

Manning smiles. Hugging Neil, he tells him, "You're all the eye candy I'll ever need. I'm a lucky man—who just happens to be momentarily put-off by his work."

Neil peers at him. "Don't let this get to you, Mark, at least not tonight."

"Nope," says Manning, tracing his thumbs along Neil's pectorals, "tonight's a celebration. If I happen to glean a stray tidbit from Zarnik, all the better." He crooks his head to lick one of Neil's nipples, then kisses the other.

Neil says into his ear, "Get dressed. Our guests are due. But save that thought."

A few minutes later, Manning stands in the dressing area of the balcony, deciding on an outfit for the evening. Pleated khaki slacks—no surprise, though these are gabardine, a dressier version of the twill variety he always wears to the office, an easy decision. But the top half vexes him. Jacket and tie? That's what he'd normally wear, but Neil won't, not at home—too stuffy. Then he thinks, Why not try a T-shirt with a vest? He's seen younger guys wear such outfits. Hell, why not?

"That looks great," says Neil, padding out from the bath.

"Think so?" asks Manning, needing reassurance. "I'm not . . . too old for it?"

"Hardly," says Neil. "You'll be the hottest man in the room."

"What about the catering boys?" Manning asks.

Neil pauses. "They don't count. They're paid to be here."

A few minutes later, Neil is dressed, and he and Manning head downstairs to await their first arrival. As they cross the main room toward the kitchen, a voice from behind asks, "Can I get you guys a drink?" Manning turns to find one of the Happy Happenings waiters standing there with a tray. He wears an engraved plastic name tag, *Justin*, not on his shirt, but below his belt, on his hip. Neil was right—this kid's a knockout. "Something before your guests arrive?"

Manning and Neil eye each other with a look that asks, Should we? Neil tells the waiter, "We'll both have vodka on the rocks—the Japanese brand—with a twist of orange, just the peel."

Manning nods his agreement and watches the waiter strut away to fill their order. The knotty muscles of Justin's calves bulge from the top of his boots.

Music is playing now, and it sounds great—a familiar, nameless cocktail tune—but there's some sort of commotion in the kitchen. "I'd better keep an eye on things," says Neil, following Justin.

Manning stands alone in the center of the room, telling himself that all is ready, that he looks just fine—when the buzzer yelps, shattering his fragile confidence. He looks about, wondering who'll answer the door, then realizes that the task has fallen to him. He assumes that all the staff has arrived, that whoever has buzzed must be the first guest. Manning swallows, crosses to the door, and swings it open.

"Happy new home, gorgeous!" says Daryl, flinging his arms around Manning for a full-body hug. A herd of other copy kids and *Journal* interns piles in behind him—the party has begun.

Justin nudges through the crowd with his little silver tray balanced overhead on the prongs of his fingertips. "Your cocktail, Mr. Manning."

"Thank you." Manning takes the drink—needing it—having managed to disentangle himself from Daryl, who now stares at the waiter with wide, unbelieving eyes, like a lucky cat who has stumbled upon a fat, fated mouse.

Justin asks the guests, "What can I get you?"

"Honey," says Daryl, brushing up next to him, "you've got it all backwards. What can *I* do for *you?*" In the same breath, he has his arm around Justin's shoulder and walks him away from the group to explore the loft.

Manning takes a gulp of the vodka. "Come on in, gang." With a shrug, he tells them, "There's plenty more where that came from," knowing, as the words leave his lips, how insipid they sound. He's certain he's blown it—doomed the whole evening by his lack of social finesse.

But his young guests aren't fazed. Indeed, they laugh at his comment as if hearing it newly coined. They gape and coo at the artful transformation of the loft, wishing him happiness amid interjections of "Congrats" and "Way cool." Their enthusiasm, he can tell, is genuine, and he wants to share it with Neil, whose creativity has shaped these surroundings. As if summoned by Manning's thoughts, Neil appears.

Manning asks him, "You know everyone, don't you? We were just singing your praises."

The arrivals number about a dozen, college-age or so, both men and women. Neil has met most of them at previous gatherings or in the city room of the *Journal*, where he sometimes meets Manning for a lunch date.

While newsroom attire is generally conservative, the trend toward the casual has been evinced even there, especially by these journalists in training. A copyboy can wear jeans to the office without thinking twice, but he knows instinctively that tank tops are beyond the limit. Tonight is different, though—it's a party. And while it's hosted by the paper's star reporter, there's a general consensus that he and Neil are "totally rad," so these guests have dressed as they please.

It's been a hot week in the city, and the younger crowd has responded by baring some flesh. Some of the girls wear tube tops with skirts that remind Manning of his youth in the liberated sixties. Some of the guys wear shorts and sandals. One of them wears a vest—like Manning's—but without a T-shirt underneath, displaying shifting glimpses of his tanned torso. He also shows a tattoo, and he's not the only one.

This is a trend that Manning has noticed, bewildered. No longer the blue-collar insignia that were once limited to anchors, eagles, or hearts with ribbons bearing *Mother* or the name of an erstwhile gal, these new tattoos are much smaller, worn by well-educated youngsters of both sexes in unexpected places—on the ankle, for instance, or the shoulder blade, or God-knows-where. They are tributes neither to patriotism nor to love, but to beer brands, cartoon characters, and pop-music fads.

It's another sign of growing older, Manning tells himself, when you can't figure out why kids do what they do. Try to keep an open mind.

Neil says, "Hey, guys, the bar's in the kitchen. Have fun." And they will. They pass around Neil, offering pats on the back, making a beeline for the booze. Neil tells Manning, "That's what I like about youth. Aside from their obvious visual charms, they're so easily amused."

Again the buzzer. "Your turn," says Manning, sweeping his hand from Neil toward the door.

Neil opens it, and in steps David Bosch with his two out-of-town guests. David wears an outfit similar to the uniforms of the catering staff, but with preppy loafers instead of boots. His shorts and knit shirt confirm that a fantasy body has lurked all along beneath his office attire. Neil gives Manning a private Groucho-twitch of his eyebrows, a silent allusion to David's "obvious visual charms."

Pink clouds. Manning realizes that his earlier tally of clouds on the horizon failed to include David, whose newly revealed doting is a sticky, unexpected development.

"Hi, David," says Neil, shaking his hand. "Welcome to our humble home."

"Awesome," says David, who then cringes at the word. Then he turns to his older companions for a round of introductions. The woman is fifty-something, fashionable and handsome, not quite pretty; she wears tailored slacks and a vibrant red silk blouse. The man is in his sixties, balding, slim, and dapper; he wears a dark silk suit, lightened for the occasion by a jaunty yellow necktie with matching pocket handkerchief.

David says, "Claire and Hector, I'd like you to meet Mark Manning of the *Journal*." David beams with pride, then adds sheepishly, "I don't have to tell you—Mark's the best in the business."

Manning rolls his eyes, saying, "David, please. . . ."

David continues. "And this is Mark's friend, Neil Waite, an architect who's involved with the planning of Celebration Two Thousand." Then turning to Neil and Manning, David says, "Gentlemen, please meet Claire Gray and my uncle, Hector Bosch."

They all shake hands, honored to know one another. Manning

concludes by telling David's guests, "Welcome to Chicago. We're delighted to have you in town."

Claire tells him, "The theater committee was kind enough to invite us for the opening ceremonies during Fourth of July weekend. We were thrilled to be asked."

Hector says, "And since I've spent no time whatever with my favorite nephew (my one and only, actually) since his earlier salad days in college, this trip provides me a perfect opportunity to scrutinize his new life among the Second City's fourth estate. So I'm prepared to be impressed, Mr. Manning. Naturally, I'll be filing reviews of the theater festival."

"I should have guessed," says Manning, recognizing the mannered prose that is a hallmark of Hector's columns. He adds, "And please—call me Mark."

Hector and Claire invite Manning and Neil to use their own first names as well.

Manning offers, "Let me get you a drink." Hector and Claire both decide on kir. Manning asks for help from David, who gladly tails him to the bar, leaving Neil to get acquainted with the New Yorkers.

He says, "It's a shame, Claire, that your schedule won't allow you to direct part of the theater festival."

"I feel terrible about it, darling, but my commitments back East were chiseled in stone, they tell me, so I'll be watching the efforts of others for a change—which is really quite a nice idea, when you think about it." She flips her palms in the air. "I'm on vacation!"

"Yes, my dearest," says Hector. "So I've noticed—especially while I've been chained to that damned modem in our hotel room."

"Poor baby. Man may work from sun to sun, but Hector's work is never done."

Dryly, Hector tells her, "Your sympathy is appreciated more than you know." Then he asks Neil, "What can we expect at the opening ceremonies next weekend at the stadium?"

Neil ushers them away from the door toward a furniture grouping that anchors the central space of the loft. With a gesture, he invites them to sit. He tells Hector, "The plans are changing daily, but it ought to be spectacular. The nation's top talent, from pop to opera, will be there doing snippets for a capacity crowd and a worldwide TV audience. But the festival isn't only about the performing arts. We'll also put the visual arts, the practical arts, and the sciences center stage. And then there's the whole political aspect—the human-rights rally and the president's address, assuming he decides to accept the committee's invitation."

"Bravo," Claire tells him. "That's exactly the sort of coordinated effort that stands a chance to make a meaningful difference to society. When the brightest minds come together, not only to entertain but to inspire, then we can all begin to move ahead. For the first time in memory, I'm actually looking forward to a presidential election, to say nothing of the broad public debate that will precede it."

"You needn't wait till the election," Neil tells her. "The 'broad public debate' has already begun. The Christian Family Crusade has announced plans to stage a rally of its own, countering the event at the stadium. They're mounting a protest march as part of the grand opening of that luxury hotel they've built on the North Side—the Gethsemane Arms—have you ever heard anything so ludicrous?"

Hector admonishes Neil. "I wouldn't be so quick to judge. The CFC has flourished under the prudent financial management of its current leadership. Even more important, they stand for principles held dear by a great many Americans."

"Like what?" asks Claire. "Intolerance and bigotry? They've been in the limelight too long already, and with any luck, they'll find their influence has waned. It should be a wide-open race next year, and maybe this country will at last engage itself in a rational exchange of ideas."

"I hope so," says Neil, sitting back, crossing his arms. "That's why we've invited presidential hopefuls from both parties, as well as that upstart Libertarian, to take part in the ceremonies. If we can begin to establish common ground on only one issue—human rights, which of course includes gay rights, a topic that's near and dear to me—our efforts will be proven worthwhile."

Attempting to shift the topic, Hector says, "I understand where the arts and politics fit into all this, but how do you plan to include the sciences?"

Neil's eyes gleam. He leans forward to say, "That's the best part. It hasn't been publicized, but arrangements have been made for a state-of-the-art sky show. A laser spectacle will appear over the whole Loop and Near North Side, with the new stadium at its center. As the president concludes his speech—in effect, a changing of the guard, an ushering-in of the new age—the sky above the city will burst alive with the light of a laser show, a giant floating pink triangle."

"Good Lord," says Claire. "How does it work?"

"It will be projected from masts atop three tall buildings—Sears Tower, MidAmerica Oil, and the Journal Building—forming the points of the triangle. It'll blow people's minds. And the show will be repeated each night of the celebration, into the year two thousand."

"Sounds like a marvelous spectacle," says Hector. "But why pink?"

Claire eyes him as though he should know better. "Really, Hector. The pink triangle symbolizes gay liberation."

"Ah, yes," he says, "an allusion to the paper badges of Nazi death camps. Odd choice for the graphic identity of a progressive social movement—rather grim, isn't it?"

"It *was*, certainly," says Neil. "Symbols can be powerful weapons, and the pink triangle originated as a symbol of hate. But by claiming it as our own, we have not only defanged it—we've been empowered by it. Such a metamorphosis may sound like voodoo, I know, but it truly happens. In the same way, much of the gay community has embraced the term *queer*."

Hector winces.

Noting his discomfort with the direction their conversation has taken, Neil asks, "Is something wrong, Hector?"

"Not in the least." His tone is curt and unconvincing.

Claire offers, "Hector has been a tad uneasy with gay issues of late."

"Sorry," says Neil, the accommodating host. "I presumed . . . Well, you're from New York, involved with theater."

"I have many gay friends," Hector assures him. "A person's sexual preference—or orientation, or identity, or whatever the correct buzz-of-the-day happens to be—is of no concern to me at all."

"Unless," interjects Claire, "that person happens to be your nephew."

"*Claire*," Hector admonishes her, as though she has betrayed a confidence.

"Hey, no problem," Neil says offhandedly, trying to ease the tension. "I already know about David. I've . . . had vibes." Although it would be more precise to say he's "heard rumors," he assumes that Hector would not appreciate such wording.

Claire leans to tell Neil, "Hector has always felt protective of David. This unexpected turn in his life has left Hector feeling unable to guide the boy."

Resigned to the fact that he will not be able to sidetrack this discussion, Hector decides that Neil should hear details from the source. "I hope not to sound mawkish," he says, "but I've always thought of David as more of a son than a nephew. Though I've been married—briefly, more than once—I have no children of my own. And now, of course, it's too late to begin a family, even if Claire would consent to be my bride. I've asked her on occasion, by the way, yet she seems obstinately determined to enter her latter years still single—with no pretense, I might add, of maiden-hood." He casts her a visual jab. She responds with an exasperated look that says they've covered this ground before.

He continues, "So David, my brother's son, has been lent to me from time to time over the years, a little boy I could help rear in life's finer ways. His parents are good people, hardworking midwesterners who've given him the security and love any child deserves. And they've had the common sense to recognize that David's upbringing could be enriched by a sophisticated uncle in Manhattan—none other than yours truly. I've introduced him not only to theater, but to music. I've shown him the world, at least the parts that count: Paris one Easter, Rome for Christmas, theater trips to London whenever possible. During his high-school years, he spent entire summers with me, enjoying life from a penthouse overlooking Central Park, taking advantage of the best the city has to offer."

Hector pauses, touches up the knot of his necktie, and settles farther into the sofa, one arm draped elegantly along its back. Unmistakable pride colors his voice as he continues, "It was also during those summers that David got a firsthand look at my day-to-day life as a writer, which nurtured his own budding interest in journalism. I was as thrilled as his parents when he was accepted at Northwestern, and I'm overjoyed that he's now launching his career at the *Journal*. Who knows? Maybe one day he'll be ready for the *Times*." Hector again pauses, savoring the prospect of his nephew's advancement, without needing to clarify that the *Times* on his mind is the one in New York.

Returning to his story, he says, "I had become his Auntie Mame. We'd joke about it—Claire too—'Life is a banquet' and all that. But after David entered college, his summers got busy, so his visits became shorter and less frequent. He was growing up, developing into his own person, acquiring new interests—such as bodybuilding, which I've never understood." Hector shudders at the thought of David's incessant weight training.

He tenses, leans forward. "Then, during the semester break of his senior year, he came to spend a couple of weeks with me. I found it unusual because he seemed especially eager to visit New York, which is anything but pleasant in January. His first night there, while we were at dinner, he told me he had big news—the *Chicago Journal* was taking him on as an intern. He mentioned that he'd visited the newsroom earlier that week and had met Mark Manning, whom he had long held in high esteem. He judged the experience to be an omen of great things to come, explaining that the *Journal*'s cub reporters are typically hired from the pool of interns who are finishing college. So we celebrated his good fortune that night amid toasts to the future."

The smile that has reflected Hector's happy remembrance

fades as he tells them, "Surprised as I was by the news he delivered, I was even less prepared for the *other* morsel he would soon divulge to me. We spent most of our evenings together at the theater, then at dinner, which could last till past midnight. Instead of returning with me to the apartment to retire, David began staying out on his own, telling me he wanted to explore the nightlife. This seemed reasonable for a man of his age, and I didn't give it much thought. He was always up and about the next morning before I was, fixing breakfast, over which he'd share tales of the previous night's exploits. I marveled at his energy, which seemed boundless."

Hector again fixes the knot of his tie, but there's no need—it's still perfect. "One morning, however, David hadn't returned. While making coffee, I heard the front door. A few moments later, he stood in the hallway to the kitchen. I told him, 'I may not be your mother, but I deserve an explanation.' He asked me to sit down and joined me at the table. He poured coffee for us both. As I reached to pick up the cup, he took my hand into his and looked me in the eye. 'I have something to tell you,' he said. I'm sure you can guess what it was."

Neil coughs. "I have an inkling."

"He'd been hitting the bars that week—gay bars, it turned out—and on that last night, he went home with someone. 'Why?' I asked him. 'Are you sure?' I stuttered through the predictable litany of questions. Calmly, David explained that he'd been wrestling with this for several years, since the start of college, that he'd had no satisfaction from his flings with women. The previous summer, he'd stayed on at the apartment he kept near school, and during those months, less pressured by the demands of classes and the expectations of friends, he 'found himself,' he said, and became comfortable with his self-awareness as a homosexual."

Hector's discourse has grown agitated, and he starts to rise from the sofa, as if he needs to pace. But he stops short of standing, plops back into his seat, and gestures with both palms open, as if beseeching Claire and Neil to understand.

"Flustered, I suggested that his comfort level should end right there. 'Keep this to yourself,' I warned him. 'If you take this any further, if you spread the news, it will probably kill your parents and will certainly thwart your career.' In truth, David's parents are open-minded and tolerant, but I was afraid to predict how my brother might react to learning that his son had 'gone gay' during one of his visits to dear, worldly Uncle Hector."

Claire crosses her arms. She eyes Hector with an accusing stare. "Wouldn't it be more accurate to say that you were afraid your brother might think it was *you* who turned David gay?"

"That's bullshit," says Hector, in no mood for honesty.

But Claire persists. "Come on, Hector. Theater, ballet, opera? French lessons in *third grade* so the kid might find his way around a menu? The costume parties and opening nights and weekend excursions to Provincetown? Of *course* David's parents would conclude that you'd dangled a tantalizing plum before their baby. But the point is, Hector: you've done that all along, and they've known it. They've known that you live in a milieu that might appeal to their son, and they've never denied him the opportunity to be with you. In fact, they've encouraged it. So I don't understand . . ." She stops short, having thought of something. "My God. Do you think they'd suspect you'd *slept* with David?"

"For Christ's sake, Claire, they'd know better. They've often razzed me about the effete company I keep, and I admit that I project something of an affected persona, but they understand, as I'm sure you do, that I'm playing a role. I'm a theater critic— New York based, nationally syndicated, with a public that likes to imagine me as a glib socialite. I have no problem with that. Indeed, I enjoy it. But I am not gay, which you know better than anyone. David's parents know it too. I would never take advantage of their son, under *any* circumstances."

Neil clears his throat and wonders aloud, "Where are Mark and David with those drinks?" The party is filling in with other guests, and there's a crowd at the bar near the kitchen. Neil spots Victor Uttley, someone from the mayor's office who's had his fingers in much of the committee work for Celebration Two Thousand.

Returning his attention to Claire and Hector's discourse, Neil cautiously enters the conversation. "I'm sure you're right," he tells Hector. "Intelligent people no longer fear gay 'recruiting.' Gays have always known instinctively what is now accepted as fact: Sexual orientation is *in* you. It's genetic, and it's there from day one."

"Okay," says Claire, conceding the issue, "but then I'm all the more bewildered, Hector. Why are you so uncomfortable with David's homosexuality? You *are* glib—I've rarely seen you frenzied by anything more serious than a sluggish first act. What could possibly concern you about something so pedestrian as your nephew's sex life? It's not rational."

"I never claimed it was 'rational.' But it troubles me. I'm worried."

Neil asks him, "It's AIDS, isn't it?"

Hector looks from Neil to Claire, whose eyes ask, Well, is it?

Hector exhales, then he lays the issue bare. "Of course it's AIDS. The worry wrenches my gut. I don't give a damn what David does with his dick—do excuse my rather crude indulgence in alliteration—but I don't want him to *die* doing it. He's at exactly the age when he should explore life to its fullest, tasting from the 'banquet,' but in historical terms, this is exactly the wrong age to belly up to *that* smorgasbord."

He pauses to clear his mind, then sums up his concerns: "If David became infected, his parents would never forgive me for introducing him to a world turned deadly. Worse yet, I could never forgive myself."

The tenderness of Claire's smile declares a truce in their squabbling, revealing that her affection for Hector is deepened by the knowledge that his displeasure with David's gayness is ultimately selfless and loving. She pats his hand. Then she turns to Neil. "Where *are* Mark and David with those drinks?"

The music has kept pace with the changing tempo of the party, and the tasteful cocktail tunes have segued to jazzier selections that sound a tad nasty. Some of the guests have started dancing. Others graze at the buffet. But most are clumped near the bar— reaching for drinks, greeting acquaintances, marveling at the loft, flirting with the boys from Happy Happenings.

"*Kir*," Manning tells the bartender over the din, "nor kirsch."

He passes back the two snifters. "Put a spoonful of cassis in white wine."

David says, "Leave it to Uncle Hector to stump the help. He'd never *think* to ask for gin and tonic, your basic hot-weather standby." He shrugs, as if to offer a lame apology for his uncle's refined tastes. David downs the last of his drink, the second gin and tonic he has managed to procure during the confusion over the kir. He orders a third.

"Easy there," Manning tells him. "The night is young."

David smirks. "Promises, promises. . . ."

God help me. Manning tells David, "Take this, will you?" It's one of the kirs. Manning carries the other, along with his own drink.

Jostling through the crowd, David spots one of the *Journal*'s new interns, just hired for the summer. There's a splotch on the back of his hand, and he's showing it off. "Tough tatt," says David, leaning to admire a little portrait of Beavis.

"Thanks, dude."

As they move onward with the drinks, Manning says, "I hate to sound like an old fart, but what's with these tattoos?"

David gives him a vacant I-dunno look. "Lots of kids are doing it. Just a trend."

"I mean," Manning grapples for the words, "it's so . . . permanent. Trends are fine. They're fun. By definition, fashion is fleeting, but an entire generation will go to their graves wearing those."

"I imagine we will," says David, agreeing but not caring.

" 'We'?" says Manning, stopping right there. "You mean . . . ?" Now he's truly curious. "Where?"

David laughs. "Relax, Mark. My 'we' merely acknowledged membership in generation X—isn't that what you call us? I'm not into tattoos. That's kids' stuff."

"Thank God," says Manning, visibly relieved.

"Not so fast," David sounds a note of warning. "I'm into something else entirely." He fixes Manning in his stare.

Manning returns the stare, half smiling, half sure that David isn't serious. "Okay, *what?*"

"Not telling. Not yet."

"Smart-ass."

"I love it when you talk like that."

"*David,*" says Manning through clenched teeth, "behave."

They've arrived to deliver drinks to Hector and Claire, who seem involved in a serious discussion with Neil. "Sorry for the delay," Manning tells them, handing out glasses. "There was a bit of mayhem at the bar."

"Thank you, dear," says Claire. "It's rare that I *need* hooch, but frankly, my tongue was hanging out." She drinks.

"Really, Claire." Hector doesn't quite approve of his companion's hearty thirst, but succumbing to his own, he joins her, downing half the glass.

Manning says, "It looked as though you were all having a fairly heavy talk."

"Just party chat," says Neil. "Comparing notes on some of the guests."

"Oh?" says Manning. "Anyone I know?"

Hector tells him, "One of your colleagues—nothing important."

Claire says to Manning, "On the topic of your colleagues, that was dreadful news this week about the *Journal*'s science editor."

"We all feel terrible about Cliff Nolan," says Manning. "David and I have been assigned to work on an investigation of his murder—our publisher, Nathan Cain, thinks that the police could use some help."

Looking up from where he sits, Neil asks, "How's it going? Any suspects?"

"Several," Manning answers, "but nothing firm yet." He's unwilling to say more.

Seating himself next to Claire, David tells Manning, "As long as we're into shop talk, I have some questions about your big weekend story on Professor Zarnik."

"I'm sure," says Manning. He sits next to Neil, completing the circle. "As I explained to Neil earlier, I'm not ready to expose Zarnik yet. Everyone knew the story was slated, so I had to stall."

Manning notices Hector and Claire exchanging a quizzical glance. He asks David, "Haven't you filled them in?"

David mimes a zipped lip.

Manning tells David, "I admire your restraint, but I think we can take them into our confidence. In fact, I'd find an outside perspective helpful."

Manning tells them the background of the story, then he and David recount details of their visits to the planetarium. Manning concludes, "So even though I'm reasonably sure that Dr. Zarnik's an impostor, I haven't a clue as to who he really is or why he has faked this 'discovery.' What's more"—Manning hesitates— "there's a possibility that he's somehow related to Cliff Nolan's murder. That's why I invited him here tonight. Maybe I'll catch him from another angle."

Hector and Claire have listened to every word, astonished that the man who claims to be Zarnik might be involved in a murder plot, not to mention that he would attempt to pull off such a large-scale ruse. Claire says, "He surely doesn't think he can get away with it, at least not for long."

Manning agrees, "It's nuts. I don't care how remote and tiny he claims his planet to be—if it's not where he says it is, people are going to figure it out. My God, he's even piqued the curiosity of the Department of Defense."

"Maybe they're not so dumb," says Neil. "Maybe they're behind it."

"Yeah," says David.

"A reasonable theory," Manning concurs, "but why would the Pentagon have an interest in deceiving the public about an astronomical discovery? Look, I was an adolescent during Vietnam, which was lesson enough. I still harbor a healthy disdain for the military and most of what it does, including their 'blood pinnings' and their double-standard adultery trials. They're certainly not above deception—they'll justify anything in the name of 'national security.' But *this* doesn't make sense. I may not trust them, but I don't think they're stupid."

Hector has been silent since the start of this discussion, but now he asks Manning, "Your publisher, Nathan Cain—what's his role in the Zarnik story?"

"He has military connections from way back," says Manning, "and he used his pull to strike a deal that will give the *Journal* a huge advantage in satellite communications. The Pentagon is even helping him with computer power and staff. But now they've called in the favor. For some reason, Zarnik is set on using me as his mouthpiece, so Cain's been instructed to have me do some digging. On the surface, it would appear that Zarnik's deception is meant to be conveyed from me, through Cain, to the Pentagon. But that doesn't wash if the Pentagon itself is involved."

Hector asks, "What about Cain?"

Manning sips his drink, then answers, "He's a man of supreme integrity. I don't agree with all of his politics, and I don't even find him especially likable, but I do respect him. Yes, he's an odd man, a powerful man whose behavior is sometimes quirky, but he's a consummate journalist and businessman—and a patriot to his very marrow. He *loves* this country. If in fact the Pentagon is tinkering with a conspiracy, they've involved Nathan Cain unwittingly, and it offends me to think he could be used as a patsy. If *that's* the case, he could be in danger, which is why I wrote the story you've all read. I can't tip my hand yet. We don't know what's at stake."

Neil whistles pensively. "Heavy-duty. I don't know about the rest of you, but I could use another drink."

Just as the others are voicing their assent and Neil turns to search for a waiter in the crowd, someone taps him on the shoulder, telling him with dry enthusiasm, "*Neil.* The place is *fab*-ulous. Congratu-*lations.*"

"Victor," says Neil, rising, "I *thought* I spotted you over at the bar." The man would be hard to miss, well over six feet tall. "Let me introduce you to some people."

Neil tells the others that Victor Uttley was appointed by the mayor a few months ago as the city's new cultural liaison to the world. Uttley interjects, "Whatever *that* means!" The group laughs with him. Neil explains that Uttley has been involved in coordinating many of the committees that are planning Celebration Two Thousand. Then Neil asks him to meet Manning, David, Hector Bosch, and Claire Gray.

Uttley's languid manner becomes suddenly animated, "My *God*, Miss *Gray*. I had no i-*dea* you'd be *here* tonight!" He crosses from Neil to her, eager to shake her hand, but his progress is impeded by a severe limp.

Noticing this, Neil says, "Victor! What happened?"

"Silly *me*," he tells Neil. "Rollerblading at *my* age. Lucky not to break a *knee*." Then he returns his attention to Claire, whom he obviously holds in great esteem.

Watching, Manning decides that Uttley is perhaps thirty years old. His fop-wristed gushing over the Broadway director, coupled with the lilting cadence of his speech, fits an over-the-edge stereotype that Manning can't help finding laughable. Completing the picture, Uttley sports a lean dark suit of fashion-forward Italian design, worn over a gauzy crew-neck sweater. He babbles at Claire, who politely responds to his questions and flattery.

At last he tells her, "I don't want to intrude any further, Miss Gray. Perhaps later this evening, we could chat again. Meanwhile, I need to step outside for a ciggy break. Ta, all. It's been a hoot."

As they watch Uttley limp away through the crowd, Justin, the Happy Happenings waiter, swaggers by with an empty tray. "*There* you are," says Neil, realizing that the waiter hasn't been seen since disappearing with Daryl, the copy kid. "What happened to Daryl?"

Justin looks about vacantly. "Oh, he's . . . making the rounds."

Claire says, "Since you mention 'rounds,' darling—could you, please?"

David offers, "Let me give you a hand with that, Justin."

Hector is about to suggest that David should stay put, but he's already on his feet, sauntering away with Justin, his beefy arm draped across the waiter's shoulders.

As they pass near the front door, another waiter opens it to admit a new arrival. Seeing who it is, Manning crosses the room to greet her. "Welcome, Roxanne. Glad you could come." He kisses her cheek, just at the corner of her lips. "Where's Carl?"

"He's late at a meeting—I doubt if he'll make it at all. God, Mark, this is gorgeous."

"Thanks to you-know-who." Manning begins guiding her through the crowd, saying, "He's over here with some people I'd like you to meet."

When they arrive where the others are seated, Neil bounces up to give Roxanne a hug. "Hi there, Rox. You look great!" She does look great—mid-thirties, mature bearing, fit body, strictly professional but highly stylish linen suit, streaked blond hair in a perfect new bob. "Love the do," he tells her. "Very handsome. I daresay, mannish." He growls his approval.

"Thank you," she says dryly.

"It seems I saw more of you before I moved to Chicago—it's not fair."

"The practice is thriving, so my life's not my own."

"Lawyers," says Neil—that sums it up. "Claire and Hector, I'd like you to meet Roxanne Exner, a dear friend, token female partner at Kendall Creighton Yoshihara, an esteemed Chicago law firm. Rox, it's my pleasure to introduce you to none other than Claire Gray and Hector Bosch."

They all shake hands. Roxanne compliments Claire on her latest production, Hector on his column, while welcoming them to the city. Referring to the loft, she tells them, "I saw the plans, but the guys wouldn't let me near the place while things were torn up. I'm amazed—isn't it wonderful?"

"Indeed," agrees Claire. "Tell me, Miss Exner, how do you happen to know these gentlemen? Do you cross paths professionally?"

"With Mark, yes," she answers. "I did some work for the estate of a woman who was missing a while back. We compared notes from time to time, as we did on an earlier story. We became friends." Standing next to Manning, she hugs his waist.

"Hell," says Manning, "we had a fling."

Neil volunteers, "That was before *I* came along."

Hector smiles uncomfortably.

"Actually," says Roxanne, "I knew Neil much earlier, in college. We were both involved in a local political campaign. I was a senior; he was a freshman. We hit it off right away—you can still see what drew me to him."

Neil smirks, then tells the others, "We kept in touch, and I used to stay with Roxanne from time to time when I came here on business from Phoenix. I met Mark at a party she threw for me."

Roxanne asks rhetorically, "How's that for a twist of fate? The two men I was most interested in, I brought together."

"It was meant to be," Manning tells her. Then he adds, "By the way—thanks." He kisses her cheek again.

"Besides," Neil tells her, "you did fine in the man department. Carl's hot."

"For a father figure," she concedes.

Neil tells her, "He's not *that* old."

Roxanne reminds him, "He's a senior partner."

Neil persists, "Carl Creighton is what—ten years older than you?"

"Twelve."

"Close enough," says Neil. "Point is, you're obviously satisfied, or you wouldn't be dropping hints about the *m*-word."

"*Marriage* is not a dirty word," she says. "The time may be right. Or maybe not. We'll see." She pauses, then says, "The next few days could be revealing. Carl and I are driving up to Door County tomorrow. He bought a new convertible for the trip, some high-end roadster—that's why I cut my hair."

"Door County?" asks Neil, still not totally at home in the Midwest.

Manning tells him, "Up in Wisconsin, a resort area on a peninsula."

"Oh?" Neil's brows arch. "Sharing a cabin in the north woods?"

"As a matter of fact, yes, we are."

Justin and David arrive with a trayload of drinks. Justin holds the tray while David distributes the glasses.

Manning asks Roxanne, "What would you like?" He leans close. "Mineral water?"

"Yup," she says, not thrilled with the choice. "Still on the wagon."

"Good girl," says Neil.

"Don't be patronizing," she tells him. "It's been over two years, and I still think about it every day."

Manning hugs her shoulder. "I know how you feel. I quit smoking about the same time you swore off liquor. It's a bitch, but it beats the alternative."

"I know," she says, resigned to a new life, a better life, one that she still doesn't find appealing.

Softly, Manning tells her, "Come on, let's get you fixed up." He excuses himself from the group and leads Roxanne off toward the bar. Once lost in the crowd, he asks her, "Everything okay?"

"Yes." There's an uncertainty in her voice that elicits a probing gaze from Manning. She tells him, "Really, Mark, everything's fine. Carl and I are on the right track, you and Neil have built your dream home, and I'm coping with sobriety." She concludes, "Nothing could be finer." She shifts gears. "How's *your* life these days?"

He sighs. "Hectic. We've been under the gun getting ready for tonight. Neil's up to his neck with Celebration Two Thousand. And now I'm embroiled in *two* stories that have raised more questions than answers. I'm not only losing sleep over them— I'm *dreaming* about one of them. Planet Zarnik."

She halts their progress toward the kitchen. "I meant to talk to you about that piece of yours in the early edition. Hardly up to snuff, Mark."

He hesitates. "Can I take you into my confidence? This may sound nutty, but it's top secret, at least for now."

"You know you can trust me."

He knows he can. Strolling her to a quieter corner, he tells the story.

When he has finished, she says, "I'd ask if there's any way I can help, but it seems you're on your own."

"I know, Roxanne, but thanks for lending an attentive ear. I've always admired your logical thinking, to say nothing of your more . . . *corporeal* assets. So please, keep my predicament in mind. Maybe something will click."

"I'll let you know," she says. "Now, do you suppose we might find a Pellegrino?"

"Will club soda suffice?"

"In a pinch."

Wending his way with her toward the kitchen, Manning again notices the entry of new arrivals. It's editor Gordon Smith and his wife. Manning asks Roxanne, "Could you possibly fend for yourself at the bar? It's the boss—I'd better say hi."

"Good luck." Her mouth curls into an ominous smile, then she turns, in search of bottled water.

Manning nudges through the crowd and arrives at the door just as the Smiths have ordered their drinks. "Gordon," he says— big smile—"and Polly! Glad you could come." They all shake hands.

"It's *Molly*," the woman tells Manning, tittering at his gaffe.

"Of course, Molly. Sorry," he says, "it's been a while."

"*Whew.*" Smith is wide-eyed. "Quite a pad you've got here, Marko."

"Thanks, Gordon. It's Neil's braindchild—I just sign the checks."

Smith reminds him, "Never underestimate the power of the pen." They chuckle. Then Smith frowns. "Uh, Mark"—he doesn't use the nickname this time—"speaking of 'the power of the pen,' your bulldog story wasn't quite what I expected."

Manning gulps. "Gordon, I—"

Molly interrupts, "Time for me to bow out. If you boys are talking business already, I'll just do a little mingling." She kisses her husband, waggles her fingers at Manning, and disappears into the crowd.

Smith says, "We've been promoting that story for three days as an in-depth page-one Sunday blockbuster. What happened, Mark? Other than the hoo-ha about Zarnik's computers, the story was little more than a rehash of old news."

"Listen, Gordon." Manning pulls him aside from the clump of people near the door and leans close to be heard over the noise. "Something's up. Something big. There is no tenth planet, the guy at the observatory isn't Zarnik, and this may all be related to Cliff Nolan's murder."

"What are you *talking* about?"

Manning details his suspicions, then tells his editor, "The timing isn't right to print any of this, but because of the *Journal*'s broadcast blitz, I had to deliver something, however feeble."

Smith asks, "Why *not* blow the whistle on him? Even though the story's not complete, it would make a sensational Sunday headline."

"Because I can't *prove* anything yet." Manning rivets him with a stare. "And there's more, Gordon. Nathan Cain may be in danger. This is only a hunch, but his Pentagon pals may have set him up for something."

"Christ," mutters Smith, trying to sort through Manning's news. "Should we tell Nathan? We could phone right now—I can have him paged."

"Not yet," says Manning. "Frankly, I don't think he'd buy my theory, and I have nothing to back it up. I suggest we tread water a little longer. Give me a few days to try to piece this together."

Smith's lower lip is pinched between his teeth. He opens his mouth to speak, hesitates, then says, "Okay, Marko, you can call the shots for a while." He breaks into his customary grin, makes a fist, and cuffs Manning below the shoulder. "Be careful, huh? We wouldn't want to lose our jobs over this."

They both laugh, but without much gusto, realizing that the joked-about consequences are indeed a possibility, however remote.

Smith asks, "When do you plan to get going on this?"

"Is tonight soon enough? I invited Zarnik to the party. He said he'd come."

"Good move," says Smith. Pondering the mystery, he says, "Nathan's one of the smartest guys I know. If they're planning to make a stooge out of him, they don't know him very well. Even though you never see Nathan in the newsroom, I assure you: he's a hands-on micromanager. Nothing gets past him. If they think they can get around him to use the *Journal* for clandestine purposes, they're in for a surprise."

"What if they planted someone to help make it happen?"

"Come on," says Smith, "This is starting to sound way too cloak-and-dagger. There's no way they could . . ." Gordon stops, nearly choking on the thought. *"Lucy?"* He breaks into laughter. "That redhead?"

Without expression, Manning waits for Smith's mirth to subside. He tells his editor, "Consider this: Not only does she have Pentagon connections, but she also has access to electronic drafts of reporters' stories. I never knew that. Did you? There's good reason to assume that Cliff was filing a story exposing Zarnik at the time he was shot. Lucille Haring could have been watching from her own monitor as he typed every word of it. And I'm willing to bet she's been trained in the use of guns."

Smith ponders all this. "Maybe. Hey—she's supposed to be here tonight. Nathan all but *ordered* her to put in an appearance."

"Exactly," says Manning. "Let's see what develops."

"Any other suspects?"

"Zarnik himself, of course, whose obvious motivation would be to avoid exposure. I've also got something of a wild card, Cliff's nosy neighbor—she struck me as someone who might be nutty enough to kill for some peace and quiet. I thought I'd go talk to her again tomorrow."

"Good idea," says Smith, nodding. Then he thinks of something. "Say, Marko, as long as you plan on doing some work tomorrow, maybe you could drop by the newsroom and clean out Nolan's desk. Sundays are quiet there, and you won't be interrupted. You might pick up a clue."

Manning is surprised by Smith's suggestion. "You mean the police haven't gone through his stuff yet? They sure tore apart his apartment."

The editor shrugs. "I guess they're stretched thin by all this festival stuff. There's talk that the president is coming." He snorts. "Nathan was right—the police do need some help on this case."

The music that has been playing now ends, and after a short pause, the space begins to pulse with a remix of last winter's chart-topper. The stretch of open floor where some younger guests have been dancing now fills to capacity with partygoers of all ages.

"Mark," says Claire, approaching from behind, "I'm in search of a partner. Hector's a skilled dancer—his tango's truly wicked—but this isn't quite his style."

"I'd be delighted," Manning tells her. "But first, have you met Gordon Smith? He's managing editor of the *Journal.*"

After an exchange of pleasantries, Smith says, "I seem to need a drink, so I'll leave you two to boogie. If we don't talk later, Mark, let's meet first thing Monday at the office." And he's gone.

Manning tells Claire, "Be forewarned: I'm not too current with dance trends, but I can probably muster something more timely than a fox-trot."

"Whatever," says Claire. "I just enjoy moving to the music. More important, I hoped we could talk by ourselves."

"Oh?" Manning lifts his hands. Claire does likewise. They touch, palms to palms, and sway their bodies—a restrained interpretation of the frenetic beat that has other dancers whirling and stomping, flapping their elbows like wounded birds. Manning tells her, "I've never been much for the club scene, and to be honest, I haven't danced with a woman for a while. Hope you're not disappointed."

"Don't be so modest, dear. You move naturally and with self-assurance. You're a splendid dancer, to say nothing of a perfect host."

Not expecting such flattery, Manning says, "I've never been told *that* before."

She squeezes his fingers. "Ah, gay men . . ." she trails off. "I do enjoy your company."

Manning says wryly, "I'll bet Hector doesn't quite approve."

"No," she admits, "but it's my life to live, and I like it that way. I love Hector, but I could never marry him. Isn't that curious? We're so different, but in many ways, we're too much alike."

"The mysteries of human chemistry."

She laughs. "I shouldn't burden you with my emotional musings, not when you're wrapped up in mysteries of your own.

Persevere, Mark. You'll unravel it. You're good at this—probably the best. When you solved that missing-person case, it wasn't for sloppy reporting that they handed you a Partridge Prize."

An uncomfortable grin falls across Manning's face. He tells her, "They *didn't* hand me a Partridge."

"Oh dear, I'm sorry," she says. "I remember reading something about it. I assumed you had it sewn up."

"I assumed so too—most everyone did—but the awards committee saw it differently. There was a problem with the fact that I had delayed announcing my find until the last minute, at a public inquest. There was a feeling that I had unduly sensationalized the story, and it didn't help matters that I accepted a half-million-dollar reward from the estate. Some of the committee felt that I had already gotten my prize." He pauses, weighing the possibility that these concerns of the committee might be justified.

Then he tells the rest. "But the deciding factor, I've since learned, was sheer politics, if not outright prejudice. The *Chicago Post*, our competitor, has some contacts on the committee, and they managed to sway a vote or two. Their objection—get this—had nothing to do with the method or ethics of my reporting."

The pace of their dancing slows to a shuffle as Manning explains to Claire, "Shortly after breaking that story, I came out in print. It was no big deal. I worked it in as an aside where it was relevant to another interview. I still feel it was the honest, responsible thing to do. But there are still a lot of people, sophisticated people, who have trouble with gay issues. So the bottom line is that I wasn't deemed quite worthy of the Brass Bird."

Claire has listened quietly. "I'm stunned. I had no idea that such prejudice could still exist at an official level."

"The Partridge Prize is handed out by a private foundation," Manning reminds her. "They can set any standards they please, and I defend their right to do so."

"Under the circumstances, you're more understanding than I'd be."

"Intellectual honesty is a path that sometimes leads to unexpected conclusions."

She eyes him askance. "Did you just make that up, or did you cop it from a fortune cookie?"

"I'm not sure," he tells her with a laugh that acknowledges the heavy-handedness of his dictum. "You can quibble with the rhetoric, but the notion is sound. Whenever we're willing to abandon self-evident principles for the sake of a quick fix, we indulge in the irrational. And when we forsake reason, choosing to disregard logic and the evidence of our senses, we toss away our very *humanity*, our innate tools for survival. We lay the groundwork for self-destruction."

They no longer dance, but their hands still touch. Claire says, "Thank you, Mark. It's easy to lose sight of objectivity. We're tempted at every turn, often in the name of so-called 'higher ideals' that are rooted in little more than mysticism. I needed a reminder. Keep doing what you've always done, and eventually the skeptics will notice the inescapable." She ponders their discussion for a moment, then asks, "In light of what you've told me, do you even *want* a Partridge?"

"Of course I do," he tells her. "There'd be some money, sure, and the flash of fame would feel good, but most important, it's an affirmation. The Brass Bird may look like a cheap trophy, but it happens to be investigative journalism's highest award. It would tell me that I haven't been wasting my time. In short, it would prove that I was right."

Claire draws their hands together, holding his between hers. "You *were* right," she assures him, "but you were robbed. Fortunately, your attitude is not only philosophical, but practical. You'll have other shots at the prize."

"That's the beauty of this business," he tells her. "You never know what's next—when opportunity might knock."

Right on cue, someone answers the front door, and in walks Dr. Zarnik. He has been in the news so much lately, he is recognized by many in the crowd as Chicago's reigning celebrity. But he's a scientist, not a pop-cult hero, so he's greeted not by a giddy mob, but by a round of whispers and sidelong glances.

Claire tells Manning, "Better get cracking."

"Come with me," he says. "I'll introduce you."

Across the room, David has also noticed Zarnik's entrance. He sets down the remnants of another cocktail. "Come on," he says to Neil. "I'll introduce you."

Manning, Claire, David, and Neil converge upon Zarnik as he finishes ordering a drink. The waiter turns to fetch it, but Zarnik reconsiders and tells him, "With *diet* cola, please, if you have it."

The guy from Happy Happenings nods and disappears.

"Ah, Mr. Manning," says Zarnik, spotting his host. "I hope you will forgive my tardy arrival, but your story in this afternoon's paper prompted numerous telephone calls. There were many requests for interviews, which of course I would not grant. These interruptions not only prevented my timely departure from the laboratory, but diverted me from a crucial phase of my research there. Such, alas, is the downside of public recognition." He punctuates the thought with a playful toot of the whistle that hangs, as always, with keys on the chain around his neck.

His white lab coat has been left behind, replaced for the evening by a dark tweed jacket, years out of style as well as wrong for the season. He wears the same necktie that Manning has already seen twice this week, but its knot is now pulled tight under Zarnik's chin, where the collar of his shirt bunches, unbuttoned. Manning notices, in fact, that the button is missing. The edge of the collar has not yet frayed, but has pilled, abraded by the stubble of neck-beard that escaped Zarnik's razor.

Manning shakes his hand. "Better late than never, Professor. We're delighted you could come. You haven't met Neil Waite yet, have you?"

"No, I haven't," says Zarnik. He turns to Neil and extends his hand. "It's my pleasure, Mr. Waite."

Neil tells Zarnik, "We're honored to have you in our home . . . *Professor.*" The word is spoken with hesitation, as Neil doesn't know the man's true identity, and he's not as adept as Manning at acting out the charade.

Zarnik says, "I understand that congratulations are in order. May you enjoy many years of happiness here." Then he notices

David. "And Mr. Bosch. It is good to see you again. I hope that yesterday's visit to the planetarium proved gratifying."

With wide, innocent, boozy eyes, David overplays the dumb kid, telling Zarnik, "More than you'll ever know, Professor." Finding the insinuation clever, he tries to suppress a sloppy laugh.

Manning grabs Zarnik's shoulder and whirls him away from David. "Claire," he says, "permit me to introduce Dr. Pavo Zarnik, the astrophysicist I told you about." He says to Zarnik, "I doubt if you keep tabs on American theater in your country, Professor, but I'd like you to meet one of our most respected directors and playwrights—"

"Ah, *pfroobst!*" he interrupts. "Introductions are hardly necessary, not for the illustrious Claire Gray. Even in my homeland, we have quickly become fans of—how is it called in English?— *Barterers.*"

"*Traders,*" she corrects him.

"Of course. Forgive me. I am humbled by your presence, dear lady." He bows.

Claire smirks at Manning, who makes a silent appeal for her to play along. She extends her hand to Zarnik, who kisses her fingers.

Manning asks, "So, Professor, were you satisfied with the story verifying your discovery?"

"Entirely," says Zarnik, beaming. "However, recognition for one's work, which I daresay we all crave, seems to bring with it an abrupt lack of privacy. Would that we might achieve the one without the other."

"Good luck," says Claire. Her wistful tone suggests that she has long abandoned such futile wishes.

"Whoa," says David, stepping forward, a bit unbalanced, shaking his head as if Claire should know better. "That's *bad* luck— right, Professor?" David crooks his pinkie and displays it to the group, explaining, "You've gotta hook 'em."

Zarnik laughs. "Mr. Manning's young colleague is referring to a custom of my people. It surely appears silly to an outsider, but like most traditions, it has taken on meaning for us through the momentum of repetition. Miss Gray?" He offers her his little finger.

Claire happily obliges, offering her own pinkie. They shake. She pauses in thought for a moment, as if something has dawned upon her.

She asks Zarnik a question about his research, but finds that he is far more interested in discussing her opinions of the current Broadway season. They both lament that New York's theatrical scene has become dominated by revivals. Claire observes, "Some of the best original theater in the country is coming out of Chicago these days, and I plan to get a healthy dose of it during my visit."

Bowing out of their conversation, Manning summons David with a finger-wag, signaling that they need to talk. He leads David a few yards away, out of Zarnik's earshot. Neil follows.

"David," says Manning, "you'd better shape up. There could be a lot at stake this evening. You want to blow it?"

David leans close to Manning's ear so that Neil won't hear him. "I'd love to."

But Neil has heard, and he looks at Manning with blank astonishment.

"Cut it *out*," says Manning. He's losing his temper, and David can tell, drunk as he is, that he's gone too far. "If you want to stay on this story, you'd better clean up your act—and fast."

"Sorry, Mark." He turns to Neil. "Sorry, Neil. I've had way too much to drink."

"It's okay," says Neil, relieved that David's tone has taken a new turn. He offers, "Can I get you something—Coffee? A sandwich maybe?"

"Thanks. You're a bud."

Manning gives Neil a quick hug and sends him off to feed David. He notices Roxanne standing alone near the door, sipping a tall cool one—ice water. He makes his way through the crowd and asks her, "Having a good time?"

"I am," she tells him. "You've collected a colorful circle of friends lately."

"Are you talking about the *Journal* folks," he asks, "or the gay contingent?"

"Both. I spend *my* days, and many nights, with lawyers."

Manning thinks he's heard a rap at the door. The music and the yammering now make it impossible to hear the buzzer, so most new arrivals simply walk in. Again he hears it—someone *is* knocking—patiently, methodically, waiting to be admitted. Manning shrugs an apology to Roxanne, then reaches to turn the knob and swing open the door.

There stands Lucille Haring, Nathan Cain's assistant. She wears a colorless suit, similar to the one she wore at the office on Thursday, except that it has pants instead of a skirt. The tuft of cropped red hair blazes atop her head, a conspicuous exception to her otherwise featureless appearance. Even tonight, stepping out for a party, she wears no jewelry, no frills, nothing that acknowledges the festivity of the occasion, let alone her womanhood. She stands stiff in the doorway.

"Hello, Mr. Manning," she tells him. "I'm here. Reporting as instructed."

"Good of you to come," says Manning, not at all sure what to think of this guest who was not invited, but ordered to attend. "Do come in."

She crosses the threshold, and Manning closes the door, telling her, "Miss Haring, let me introduce a great friend of mine, Roxanne Exner."

Lucille Haring pumps Roxanne's hand with a firm grasp, all business. The ladies exchange a few comments about the summer weather, about their jobs, about the loft. Roxanne mentions, "Over the years, I've seen most of Neil's design projects, at least photos of them, and I can tell you without hesitation that this is his best work to date. Isn't it marvelous?"

The redhead glimpses about, jabbing the air with her nose as if sniffing a fire—but she's just looking, absorbing the room with a series of quick mental snapshots, giving no facial clue as to whether she likes the place or not. "Very nice," she tells Roxanne without a trace of enthusiasm. Then she turns to Manning and in the same flat tone tells him, "Congratulations." She grips his hand and shakes it smartly, once.

"Can we get you something?" he asks her, snagging the arm of a waiter who is brushing past.

"Scotch, please. Neat." She dismisses the waiter with a sharp nod, then pivots to face Roxanne again, asking, "Your law work— do you ever see the inside of a courtroom, or is it all paper-pushing?"

Roxanne laughs. "Both, but mostly the latter."

To Manning's surprise, it seems the ladies have connected. There's actually a spark of rapport between the two, whom he presumed would have nothing in common. This may work out just fine, he tells himself. Roxanne has already broken the ice, so she stands a chance of gaining Lucille Haring's confidence and getting into her head. Deciding that Roxanne can best work this situation alone, Manning excuses himself and forays into the crowd to mingle with other guests.

But the party is beyond mingling now. The hour has grown late, liquor flows freely, and the music is cranked high. David Bosch slumps semiconscious on a sofa, where Uncle Hector ministers to him and Neil attempts to hand-feed him a meatball. All the other guests—as well as most of the staff—are on their feet, jostling to the electronic beat.

At the center of the action, Claire Gray and Pavo Zarnik flail about in the vortex of chest-pounding sound. Younger dancers, impressed, have backed off, giving the couple more space. Claire's index fingers jab at the ceiling à la Travolta; Zarnik adds to the din with shrill disco-blasts of his police whistle.

Manning shakes his head in mild astonishment and sideslips around the room, arriving at the sofa where David sips coffee from a cup that wobbles in an unsteady hand. Neil has spread an oversize napkin on David's lap, hoping to protect the kid's bare legs, as well as the new furniture, from spills. Hector sits with a vacant stare, watching Claire's performance with the astronomer. Manning places a hand on Hector's shoulder and leans to ask, almost shouting in his ear, "Enjoying the party?"

"Oh my, yes indeed," Hector responds politely, though insincerely. "If the success of an evening can be judged by the level of energy expended by one's guests, I'd have to say you've mounted a smashing entertainment."

Manning pats Hector's shoulder, a silent thank-you for the critic's gracious review. He asks Neil, "How's David doing?"

"He'll be fine," says Neil.

"I'll be fine," echoes David, slurring.

Neil continues, "He just needed a little nourishment."

Manning steps behind the sofa and places both hands on Neil's shoulders. "Congratulations, kiddo." He kisses the top of Neil's head. "The party's a success, and your loft is a hit."

"*Our* loft," Neil corrects him.

"Our *home*," says Manning, squeezing Neil's shoulders.

More alert than before, David twists his neck to gaze up at Manning. "Sure, guys, the party's a blast, but have you gotten any dirt on Zarnik?"

Manning is about to respond when the music stops. A moment later, a new song begins, much more sedate than the previous one. The disappointed dance crowd begins to disperse, in search of misplaced cocktails. Manning moves to the front of the sofa and crouches before it, facing Hector, David, and Neil. He tells them, "Zarnik seems to have hit it off with Claire, so I left her to do a little digging on my behalf—it's less conspicuous. Ditto for Lucille Haring and Roxanne—they're over by the door talking."

"My dears," says Claire, approaching from behind Manning with Zarnik, "what an extraordinary event you've staged tonight!"

Manning rises to face her. "Quite a compliment, considering the source."

A waiter appears in their midst and asks, "Anyone for another drink?"

David raises a finger, opening his mouth to ask for something, but Hector cuts him off with a slicing motion of his hand. Manning, Neil, and Claire all dismiss the offer, but Zarnik says, "I don't suppose another Jack-and-Coke would hurt." He blots sweat from his brow with a rumpled handkerchief, once white, now gray.

The waiter asks, "Diet Coke, right?"

"Please," says Zarnik. "You'll find me at the buffet. I do hope there are more of those clever peanut butter–and–celery hors d'oeuvres." He thanks Claire for their time on the dance floor, bids farewell to the others, and wanders off.

Mystified, Hector asks the group, "Jack and Coke—what in blazes is that?" His lips buckle as he imagines the unsavory concoction.

"Jack Daniel's," Manning tells him, "good old Tennessee sour mash, which I would bet is virtually unknown in Zarnik's 'war-torn homeland.' " Then he asks David, "*JD-2L*, remember? He had two liters of American whiskey on his weekly shopping list."

Neil snorts. "If he puts away that much of the stuff, why bother saving calories on diet pop?"

The others glance at one another and laugh, shrugging a wordless reply to Neil's query. The anemic recording that has been playing now ends, and no one bothers to play something else. The party is winding down.

Claire pulls Manning aside to tell him, "You were right about Zarnik, Mark. He's a fraud. That pinkie-shake of his, supposedly an Eastern European tradition, is nothing of the kind. I *thought* it seemed familiar, and it finally came back to me. In the theater world, there are many backstage superstitions—for instance, one never wishes a fellow actor good luck. Instead, many alternate rituals have taken hold, including the pinkie-shake. So I can tell you with reasonable certainty that this 'Zarnik' character is no astronomer, but an actor, probably a pro. . . ."

Crashing glass interrupts the conversation, silencing the room. Heads turn, seeking the source of the noise. A cocktail has been dropped, near the door, Manning notices, and he's relieved that it was only rented barware—they'll be billed for any breakage, but it's cheap. Then he realizes that it was Lucille Haring who dropped the glass. Her face is red with either rage or embarrassment—Manning can't tell. She turns her back to Roxanne, opens the door, marches out, and slams it shut.

Stunned, Roxanne glances about for a moment, crosses to the door with hesitant steps, opens it, steps out, and peers down the hall.

Amid the murmur of other guests, Manning wends his way

through the crowd and passes through the open doorway to join Roxanne in the hall. "What happened?"

Roxanne stares down the hallway in the direction of Lucille Haring's abrupt departure. Then she turns to Manning, blinks. "She's a lesbian."

"Yeah?" Manning blinks. "I figured. So?"

"And she, uh . . ." Roxanne pauses before continuing. "She thought I was, too. She *came on* to me, and when she realized her mistake, she freaked. I think my haircut threw her."

Wide-eyed, Manning stares at Roxanne's newly cropped hair, trying not to snigger. Then he crows with laughter.

Exasperated, she closes the door to the loft, leaving them alone in the hall. "There's more," she says. "And it's not funny."

He catches his breath, calms himself. Warily he asks, "Yes?"

"Sensing I was . . . *simpatico*, she did a bit of soul-baring. She really needed to talk to someone, and I got elected. Sometime after her arrival at the *Journal*, she ran into Cliff Nolan. He took a liking to her and began to pursue her, but of course she showed no interest in him. Ultimately, there was an after-hours encounter, and he actively tried to seduce her—not quite rape, but he tried. From what she told me, Nolan was sort of a squirrelly little guy, and she had no trouble fending him off. This cold response led Nolan to correctly deduce her homosexuality, and he threatened to spite her by exposing her gayness to the military brass. For weeks, she lived in mortal fear of losing her career. Then Clifford Nolan met his untimely demise. Needless to say, Lucille Haring shed no tears."

Sunday, June 27

Immersed in thought, Manning ambles through his neighborhood. On Sunday morning, just past ten, there is little activity on the streets, save for a few tardy souls who hurry up the stairs of a corner church, its old foundation crumbling from the toll of a hundred winters-turned-summer.

Last night was a late one for Manning and Neil. When their last guests said good-bye sometime after one, they stayed up and cleaned the loft, agreeing that they couldn't face a mess in the morning. The whole experience left Neil exhausted, but Manning rose early today, refreshed by the few hours' sleep he had, and he was outdoors for a run not long after sunrise. Preparing for the party had been stressful, and he was glad to have it over, secure in the knowledge that everyone (everyone, that is, with the apparent exception of Lucille Haring) had enjoyed the evening.

That run was several hours ago, when the morning air along the lakeshore was still cool—he actually felt goose bumps on his bare legs while working through his warm-up stretches. But now the heat has set in, and Manning's lightweight chinos feel tight and clammy around his legs as he walks at a leisurely pace toward Clifford Nolan's apartment building.

He hopes to find Dora Lee Fields at home—it seems she's always there to keep an eye on things, but she's the type who might be at church today. Since his conversation with Roxanne in the hall last night, his mind has been busy weighing possibilities suggested by Lucille Haring's revelation. He needs to ask Dora Lee a few follow-up questions.

For instance, she told him she had seen a tall man in a dark suit at Cliff Nolan's door on the night he was killed. That's a slim lead at best. After all, there must be a million men in Chicago fitting that description. He noticed several at his own party last night—Hector Bosch and Victor Uttley come to mind. But he also noticed that Lucille Haring was wearing a suit last night. She's tall and mannish. And he now knows that she had a compelling reason to silence Cliff Nolan at any cost. What's more, because of her computer savvy, she knew exactly where to find him that night—in his apartment, at his desk, filing a story through his modem. So the question is: Might Dora Lee have mistaken Lucille Haring for a man?

He has arrived at the building. Locating the buzzer marked *D. L. Fields*, he presses the button. A few moments later, the tinny speaker in the wall asks, "Who's there?" There's a lot of background noise. The Christian Family Network is cranked high, and someone's praising Jesus with a vengeance. Dora Lee is a surprisingly modern woman, Manning concludes—with all the electronic amenities, she needn't even leave the house for salvation on Sunday.

"Hello, Dora Lee," he tells her. "It's Mark Manning again. I wonder if you could spare a few minutes to talk."

She asks, "Bring along that young-buck helper of yours?"

"Not today, I'm afraid. I suspect he's nursing a hangover."

"Shit." She laughs. Coughs. "Come on up."

The door lock buzzes anemically. Manning enters the building and climbs the stairs, arriving in a sweat at the top floor. Dora Lee's door is already open, and the woman peers out at him. She asks, "Hot one, huh?"

He answers with a nod, mopping his brow as he walks down the hall to her.

"Come on in," she tells him, swinging the door wide. "It's cooler inside."

And it is. An ancient window air-conditioner is churning away, and the sun hasn't hit her side of the building yet. She has already muted the television; a robed choir now mouths silent hallelujahs. As they sit in the two chairs facing the TV, she offers, "Getcha something? Glass of water? Shot of something stronger?"

He shakes his head. "Thanks, Dora Lee, but no." He slips a steno pad out of his hip pocket and flips through several pages of notes. "If you don't mind, I'd like to pick up a few loose ends from our interview on Thursday."

She crosses her arms. "Go ahead," she tells him. "Shoot."

He takes the Montblanc from his shirt pocket and uncaps it, poising it over a page. Mustering a quiet laugh, he tells her, "It's funny you should use that expression, because I wanted to ask you about the gun in this drawer." He glances down at the table between them.

She looks vacantly toward the ceiling. "Saw it, huh? Thought maybe you did."

He leans toward her. "Dora Lee, do the police know you keep a gun? Do you have a permit for it?"

She looks at him as if he's crazy. "Hell, no. Wasn't brought up to ask nobody permission to keep a gun." She grunts. "Ain't the only one, either."

"What do you mean? Do you have more than one gun here?"

Again she eyes him as if he's from Mars. "Of *course*. A woman's not safe without one—or three, or whatever. I forget."

With blank astonishment, he asks, "You keep three guns in the apartment?"

She pauses for some mental math, then nods. "Wait," she says, "there's four."

"Have any of them been fired in the last week?"

"Nah. No need."

He persists, "Would police tests prove it?"

"Mark," she says, leaning toward him and sliding open the drawer, "honestly can't remember the last time that thing was used. Be my guest. Take a sniff."

As on Thursday, he sees the pistol among the Christmas cards, cigarettes, and other drawer-junk. He's tempted to take her up on her suggestion, but decides it's best not to touch the gun. He tells her, "I'll take you at your word, Dora Lee, but *I'm* not the one who needs to be convinced. Would the police buy your story?"

"The police haven't *heard* this story, and I don't intend to tell 'em. If you tattle, that's your business, but it would just stir things up for nothin'.'"

"Dora Lee"—Manning's tone is growing exasperated—"you told me on Thursday that you 'could have killed him' yourself, and now you tell me that you own enough firepower to arm a small militia. What would you *expect* a person to think?"

"That was just an *expression*," she insists, pulling a fresh pack of Camels from the drawer and lighting one. "People *say* things when they're riled. You're smart—you know that." She smacks the drawer closed with the back of her hand.

Yes, he does understand that her "slip" may have been nothing more than a poor choice of words, but when those words are considered along with her stash of guns, her threats to Nolan, and her general nuttiness—well, who knows?

Sensing that he's hit a dead end with the issue of guns, he decides to switch topics. He leans back in his chair and flips his notebook closed, a gesture meant to ease the tension that has mounted between them. He says, "I'm intrigued with your story of the person you saw at Cliff's door on Monday night. You told me he was tall and wore a dark suit. Think back, Dora Lee. Think hard. Is there anything else you can remember about this person, anything unusual that might help us identify him?"

"Like what?" she asks, exhaling her first drag of smoke. It drifts toward the air conditioner then blasts toward the ceiling on a stream of chilled air. She reminds him, "Lights in the hall were dim till the police changed the bulbs. Wasn't much you *could* see."

"I understand," says Manning, coaxing her along, "but I'm curious if you noticed anything that was at all distinctive, a feature like, well . . . red hair."

She thinks, shakes her head. "Nah," she tells him, blowing smoke, "don't recall his hair." Then something clicks. "Guess you might say his limp was peculiar."

Manning freezes. He asks, "The man at the door *limped?*"

"Yeah." Dora Lee whirls her cigarette—like Bette Davis—thinking. "Him and Clifford were talking at the door for a minute, then Clifford stood back and let the other guy in. He walked through the door with a bad limp. Or maybe he just had shit on his shoes and didn't want to track it on Clifford's pretty rugs!" She roars with laughter and smoke. Coughing, she wipes a tear from her eye. "Then the door shut. Never saw him again."

Manning has opened his notebook, scribbling to keep up with her story. He tells her, "This could be an important new detail." At the same time, he reminds himself that this could also be an invention of hers, a too-obvious "clue" intended to cast suspicion away from herself. He asks, "Why didn't you mention this before?"

She shrugs. "Just thought of it."

Exactly, he tells himself. Even so, it's an intriguing detail that he cannot blithely dismiss. If she's not lying about the limp, he needs to get to work and find a suspect matching her description— Victor Uttley, for example, but there is no reason to think that Chicago's swishy, Rollerblading cultural liaison to the world would have any connection to Cliff Nolan or any interest in Zarnik's claimed discovery. If, on the other hand, Dora Lee is not lying but merely mistaken about the limp, the "man" at the door could still be Lucille Haring or Zarnik himself. And finally, if Dora Lee is lying about having seen *anyone* at the door, she herself may be Nolan's killer.

He caps his pen, checks his watch, rises from the chair. "Thank you, Dora Lee. I've got some thinking to do."

He's also got some housekeeping to do—cleaning out Cliff Nolan's desk downtown in the *Journal*'s newsroom.

Arriving at the Journal Building around noon, Manning enters the editorial offices and walks the halls toward his own cubicle, noting the eerie weekend calm, the scarcity of staff, the anemic ring of a distant phone. Stopping at his desk to check for messages, finding none, he walks another aisle that takes him to Cliff Nolan's desk.

Predictably, Nolan's cubicle seems disarrayed. He hasn't sat here in nearly a week, and there's the clutter of messages and other memos that continued to accumulate until the news broke that he would not be returning. Gordon Smith must have phoned this morning to alert someone that Manning would be cleaning out the desk—a neat stack of corrugated boxes has been delivered to the cubicle, along with packing tape, labels, and a fat black marker. So Manning sets to work, quickly clearing the desktop, sorting its unremarkable contents into various boxes, labeling them *trash, morgue, office property, personal,* and such.

Moving onward to the desk drawers, he finds, as expected, that all but the center pencil drawer are locked, so he strolls out to the center of the newsroom, hoping there might be someone at the metro desk who knows where to find a key. Nothing is happening at this hour, and one of the city editors actually dozes in front of his terminal. Manning snags a copy kid (one he's never seen before—the new ones get broken in during slow shifts) and explains his predicament. After a bit of confused searching and a few phone calls to God-knows-where, Manning is surprised that the kid manages to produce a master key.

Back at Nolan's desk, Manning unlocks the drawers, excited by the prospect that they may contain clues to the reporter's murder. Manning also wonders if maybe, just maybe, Nolan's missing laptop computer has been stored here in the desk all along. But this anticipation proves for naught, as the drawers contain nothing more than office supplies, morgue folders, files of Nolan's own past stories, and the inconsequential junk that spawns in the dark recesses of any desk over the years.

With all of this properly sorted into appropriate cartons, Manning is ready to leave, sliding the drawers closed in sequence. The last of these, however, the big lower file drawer, slides with more difficulty than the others. Curious, Manning kneels and peers into it. Empty. But then he realizes that the drawer is deeper than it first appeared—there's an adjustable metal divider closing off the back section of it, and there must be something heavy back there. Is it the laptop?

He extends the drawer fully, removes the divider, and finds— to his disappointment—just another stack of morgue folders, perhaps a foot thick. Grousing, he stands, closes the drawer with his foot, and carries these files to the carton that will be returned to the morgue. Placing them in the box, he is about to tape it shut when he notices that these last files are different from the others. The manila folders themselves are identical, but their labels are handwritten, not typed.

Retrieving the folders from the box, he sits in Nolan's chair and begins flipping through the files in his lap. They contain a few photographs, copious handwritten notes (conspicuously, nothing is typed or printed by computer), and copies of old news stories, some from the *Journal*, but many from other sources. Each file pertains to a different person. "Oh Jesus, Cliff," Manning mutters aloud, realizing that his colleague has been collecting the sort of unsavory information that typically serves a single purpose—extortion. Sure enough, there's a slim, recent file on Lucille Haring. There's another name he knows, too.

Manning feels his stomach turn, and he wonders for a moment if he might vomit. But the sensation passes, and he rises. Once he has sealed the various labeled cartons he has filled, he places them in the aisle for removal. Then he flumps Nolan's secret files into another box, unlabeled, and carries it out of the newsroom.

Monday, June 28

Monday morning has dawned hot and sticky in the city. Chilled air gushes from vents in the loft where east windows brighten with a white sky. There are no telltale signs that a mob partied here Saturday night—all is in order for the start of a new week. It will be a busy one for both Neil and Manning.

The opening of Celebration Two Thousand on Saturday is now only five days away, and Neil is up to his neck in last-minute committee work. The little time he's spent at the office lately has been occupied by preparations for the festival, and he's had to rely on other architects in the firm to pick up some of his work. But there's a big project, a corporate headquarters, that's been back-burnered too long, needing his attention before it can proceed. He decided to arrive early at the office today in order to spend some time working on it uninterrupted. So he's up with the sun this morning, showered and dressed already, brewing coffee in the kitchen.

Manning is due for a challenging week as well. In contrast to Neil, who knows exactly what he must accomplish during the next few days (Neil has a clipboard with a checklist that keeps getting longer, not shorter), Manning is faced with the uncertainties of not one, but two vexing stories. He knows that Professor Zarnik's claimed discovery is a fraud, as is the actor who claims to be Zarnik. He fears that Nathan Cain has been unwittingly drawn into some far-reaching conspiracy, but he hasn't a clue as to the nature of the plot or the motive behind it. Further, all his instincts suggest that the Zarnik plot is somehow related to Cliff Nolan's murder, and yesterday, while going through Nolan's desk, he discovered to his utter dismay that the esteemed science editor had a dark side, a taste for "dirt." Worst of all, Manning has knowingly misled his readership—and that, more than anything, goads him to get some answers fast and set the record straight.

Like Neil, Manning has risen earlier than usual this morning. He appears from the shower wearing a pair of linen shorts, then pads down the stairs to find Neil pouring coffee. He gives Neil a kiss, stands back to look at him, and steps near again to tweak the knot of his tie. "You *are* the early bird today. No time for . . . ?"

" 'Fraid not," Neil tells him, patting Manning's thigh. "If I can just get through this week, we'll get our lives back—I promise." He hands Manning a mug of coffee and sits at the breakfast table to review his clipboard.

"Is the paper here yet?" Manning asks while rummaging inside the refrigerator.

"You won't find it in *there*. Want me to check?"

"No thanks, kiddo. I'll go look." Crossing to the door, he notices Neil studying the list. "Nose to the grindstone already, eh?"

Immersed in thoughts of the chores that await him, Neil doesn't answer.

Manning joins him at the table, spreads open the freshly delivered *Journal*, and slurps from his mug as he glances over page one. Nothing earthshaking—Sunday, as usual, was a slow news day.

Manning sips from his mug again and swallows; Neil does the same. Manning turns a page of the *Journal*; Neil turns a page of his checklist. Sip, swallow, turn. Sip, swallow, turn. "Even the letters are nowhere," Manning mumbles.

"Hmm?" Neil isn't listening.

Sip, swallow, turn—then something catches Manning's eye. "*What?*"

Neil looks up. "Hot story?"

"No," says Manning, "it's this ad." He slides the paper across the table so Neil can get a look at it.

It's a full-page ad, full-color too, congratulating Pavo Zarnik on his momentous discovery. "You've done Chicago proud!" it trumpets. "The City of Big Shoulders welcomes you with open arms!" There's a picture of Zarnik, another of the mayor, and a drawing of little planets playing hide-and-seek in a benign star-dusted universe. The ad concludes, "The Office of the Mayor salutes one of Chicago's favorite sons."

Neil looks up from the paper. "Pretty lame."

"Yeah," Manning snorts his agreement. "It's also a waste of tax dollars. Do you have any idea what that page cost?"

Neil shrugs. "Thousands."

Manning rises, stands behind Neil, and looks over his shoulder at the ad. "If you ask me, it's an overly generous gesture if it's simply intended to make Zarnik 'feel good.' Other than that, what's the point?"

Neil shrugs again, then notices something on the page. He peers close. "*Aha!*" He taps his finger on a line of agate type buried at the bottom of the ad.

Manning strains to focus. "It's a bit early for that, babe. What does it say?"

Neil reads, " 'Paid for by the Office of the Mayor, City of Chicago, Victor Uttley, Cultural Liaison to the World.' "

"You're kidding," says Manning.

Neil tells him, "Until last night, I'll bet you didn't even know we *had* a cultural liaison to the world. Point is, it's been sort of hush-hush. It's a patronage job, naturally. Victor Uttley is related to someone who must have had a favor coming. The position was dreamed up a few months ago, and Victor fits it to a tee. He's an ineffectual bureaucrat whose job is on the line."

"What does he actually do?"

"Good question. Basically he just bugs the festival committees. I don't think he *means* to be intrusive—he's looking for something to justify his paycheck."

Manning circles the table and faces Neil from across the newspaper. "So this ad is meant both to congratulate Zarnik and to pump up the esteem of Uttley's office."

"Exactly."

"God. . . ." Manning takes his coffee from the table and crosses the room, rising several steps to a platform area in front of the big east windows. He gazes vacantly at the sky, squinting through the sunlight, thinking.

Neil moves the paper aside and returns to the perusal of his checklist.

Manning turns, backlit by the white haze, and asks, "Victor Uttley—who *is* this guy? Does he have any qualifications as a cultural ambassador?"

More amused than annoyed by the repeated interruptions, Neil closes the pad on his clipboard and shoves his chair back a few inches, sitting sideways to face Manning. "He's no Alistair Cooke, but he seems well versed in the arts. Mostly theater. He was an out-of-work actor waiting tables somewhere before he lucked into the mayoral appointment—good thing his uncle's a ward boss." Neil winks.

Manning raises the mug to his lips and drinks. With his other hand, he scratches his scalp, then rubs the back of his neck. Thinking aloud, he says, "It's curious that Uttley would make such a hoopla about Zarnik. Uttley's job security would seem to depend more upon the success and prestige of Celebration Two Thousand. What interest would a 'cultural liaison' have in astronomy? It doesn't fit. Does it?"

Manning's question was rhetorical, and Neil doesn't bother to answer. Instead, he simply watches Manning as he poses in thought, nearly naked, on the platform that displays him as if on a stage. Gaping windows give the world a glimpse of the profoundly beautiful man whose intimacy has been Neil's alone to savor for the past two years. Something stirs between Neil's legs. He grins. I'd take you here and now, he telepaths, but I'm ready for the office, and duty calls. No time to linger. Sorry.

Manning says, "Too weird. Just yesterday, Cliff Nolan's neighbor told me that the man she saw at Cliff's door had a limp, and I'm still not sure if I should believe her. When she told me this, Victor Uttley sprang to mind—he fits the description perfectly—but I couldn't imagine that he would have any connection to either Pavo Zarnik or Cliff. Now this splashy ad. Who knows?"

"He doesn't strike me as a killer, if that's what you're driving at." Neil is talking about Victor Uttley, but he's thinking about Manning. Damn, what a hot man, right there in front of him, his for the asking. "By the way, don't be thrown by his fey manner—he's straight, thank God."

"He's *straight?*"

"Sure is." Neil steps up to the platform, and drapes his arms over Manning's shoulders. "But guess what—I'm not."

"I'd heard rumors to that effect."

Neil presses his mouth to Manning's. Their tongues meet, and they taste each other's coffee—Neil likes that amaretto-flavored cream, while Manning takes it black.

Manning's passions quickly rise. So does the lump in his shorts. He tells Neil, "Take your clothes off."

"Can't. No time." He drops to his knees, takes the coffee from Manning's hand, sets the mug down, and hooks his thumbs in the waistband of Manning's shorts. "There's time for this, though." And he shucks them to the floor.

Manning's head lolls backward as Neil's face nuzzles his crotch. There they are—one naked, the other fully dressed—onstage before an anonymous city. Thousands of waking eyes may be watching. More likely, none at all. Manning's arms hang limp, his fingers tracing lazy circles on the temples of the man who loves him. Manning's eyelids flutter, revealing strobe-flash glimpses of the ceiling of the room where he is worshipped by the man who kneels before him. As if dreaming, Manning feels himself slipping down Neil's throat. He's needed this. *They've* needed this.

The phone rings. Neil's teeth clench; Manning's eyes pop. "Sorry," Neil tries to mumble, but it sounds more like "thawgy." They attempt to ignore the intrusion and get back to business, but it's impossible—the moment has passed.

"Thanks anyway," says Manning, bending over to plant a kiss on Neil's head. "It might be important."

Manning trots to the kitchen and answers the phone. "Oh. Hello, Gordon."

Neil, satisfied that the unwelcome call is not for him, rises from his knees, checking his watch. He whisks his hair and clothes with his hands, picks up Manning's shorts and coffee, and heads for the kitchen.

Gordon Smith's voice tells Manning, "Sorry to bother you so early, Marko."

"No bother at all," Manning lies. He and Neil roll their eyes at each other.

The editor continues. "Nathan Cain just phoned me."

"Oh?"

Neil has rinsed their cups and put the clipboard in his briefcase. He's ready to head out, but he still has Manning's shorts shoved under one arm.

Smith says, "He wants to see us in the inner sanctum again. Thirty minutes."

Neil approaches, flips the shorts onto Manning's head like a big floppy beret, then gives Manning's penis a jaunty good-bye tug—it's still wet with Neil's spit, but has shrunken fast in the air-conditioning. Seconds later, Neil is out the door.

There's a touch of nervousness to Smith's chuckle as he suggests, "Better get cracking, Marko."

Resigned to a morning that just isn't working out right, Manning tells him, "No problem, Gordon."

Half an hour later, riding the private elevator to the top of the Journal Building, Manning asks Smith, "Did Cain say what he wanted?"

Smith shakes his head. "I assume he wants an update on Cliff Nolan or an account of your meeting with Zarnik."

"Either that," says Manning, "or he wants to know how his star reporter managed to screw up the Sunday lead."

Bingo. "I doubt that," Smith says.

The door slides open, the security guard nods—he's been expecting them—and they are admitted without comment into Cain's outer offices. The receptionist rises, also without comment, and escorts them down the hall past the secretarial pool, where the four desks are not yet occupied, since it's barely eight o'clock. When they arrive in Lucille Haring's office, the receptionist gives

Manning and Smith a half-smile, then turns and retreats to her desk.

The office seems empty. Manning and Smith exchange a look that asks, Now what? Then, someone rises from a desk behind a file cabinet. Their first glimpse of short-cropped carrot-colored hair confirms that Lucille Haring also got an early start this morning.

"Gentlemen," she says. It's a greeting without inflection that merely acknowledges their presence. She's busy shuffling paperwork. Her eyes do not meet theirs. "The Colonel is expecting you." She crosses to the arched door that leads to Cain's office, reaches for the knob, and turns back toward Manning and Smith. She at last looks Manning in the eye, but her face seems utterly featureless, even more so than before. The slightest cock of her head signals that they should enter.

The situation is entirely too weird for Gordon Smith's down-home nature. As he passes Haring on his way into Cain's office with Manning, he tells her, "Cheer up, Lucy. I don't much care for Monday mornings, either."

She looks at him as if he's out of his mind.

Awkwardly, he adds, "It was sure nice to see you at Marko's party Saturday. Too bad you had to skedaddle."

She looks from Smith to Manning with a panicky expression that asks, How much do you know? What did you tell him?

Manning opens his mouth, searching for something to say, but before he can muster any words, she slips back into her office, closing the door behind her.

Standing just inside the inner sanctum, Smith lowers his voice to ask Manning, "What got into her?"

Beats me, Manning shrugs silently.

A pervasive quiet fills the vast room, and Cain does not seem to be present. Last Thursday, however, Cain was lurking, listening, somewhere in the library stacks. This time, Smith won't give his publisher the opportunity to eavesdrop, so he stifles his loquacious tendencies and prudently decides to zip it. He and Manning aren't sure what they should do, where they should go, but they feel silly standing there by the door. Side by side, they walk with measured steps toward the high altar of Cain's desk, like timid Munchkins approaching Oz. They look about. Smith clears his throat and calls out, "Nathan?"

No response.

From the side of his mouth, Smith tells Manning, "Must be in the crapper."

With a clank of heavy brass hardware, the door to the publisher's private quarters opens, and Nathan Cain appears. He apparently spent the night here in the tower, for he still wears pajamas— silk, of course, the color of deepest burgundy. Over them he wears a copious robe—also silk, of royal blue that's almost black. If he wore a stovepipe hat, he'd look like a smoked Uncle Sam.

"Good morning, Gordon," he says dryly, then adds, "Mr. Manning," nodding to each of them. He guides a pair of ostrich-leather slippers across the parquet floor, moving toward the bar. "Can I get you something?"

Manning's had his coffee, but wouldn't mind some orange juice. Then he sees Cain pour himself a generous snifter of cognac. "No, thank you, sir."

Smith asks, "Do you have any coffee, Nathan?"

"I'll send for some," he offers, then crosses to his desk. He presses a button there, telling the gadget, "Coffee."

He walks toward the seating area where they had their last discussion and flumps himself with difficulty onto one of the sofas, sloshing some cognac over the edge of his snifter. He wipes the side of the glass with his index finger, which he then licks. With his finger still in his mouth, he motions with his eyes that Smith and Manning should sit on the sofa across from him.

Smith says, "I was surprised to get your call so early, Nathan. What's up?"

" 'Up'?" Nathan Cain doesn't need a reason to call underlings to his office, day or night. Maybe he felt like talking. Maybe he wanted company. "I thought Mr. Manning might appreciate my take on Sunday's Zarnik piece."

Uh-oh. "Mr. Cain," Manning begins.

But Cain cuts him off with a flick of his hand. "The story seemed a little . . . thin. Not quite as much meat as I expected."

Manning glances sideways toward Smith, who looks toward him with a nervous smile. Manning isn't sure how he can justify the story to Cain—he's buying time, and for Cain's own good, but he's not yet prepared to reveal his suspicions. Cain would expect proof, and Manning doesn't have it.

"However," Cain continues, "on balance, I felt you did a commendable job of making a complex topic accessible to the general reader. Just enough technical mumbo-jumbo to be authoritative, but not overly long. Pithy, in fact." He raises his glass in a salute. "Well done, Manning." He drinks.

Smith gives Manning an elbow nudge, all smiles. "See there, Marko? *I said* you nailed it—and you had doubts!"

Manning tells him, "One of these days, Gordon, I'll learn to take you at your word." Then he says to Cain, "Thank you, sir. I appreciate your vote of confidence, but in truth, that story was not my best work. There were some loose ends—factually—that I wasn't able to bring together before deadline."

Cain asks, "The funding angle?"

"Right. And the computer power—I wanted to be quantitative, but Zarnik was either unable or unwilling to supply me with facts. What's more, he seemed totally thrown by my questions regarding his scientific method."

"So you ran with what you had," says Cain, indifferent. "That's the nature of this business, Manning—I needn't explain that to *you.*" He snorts his terse little laugh. "The main thing is, Zarnik's on the level." There's a pause. "About his discovery." Pause. "Right?"

Manning chooses his words with care. "His video demonstration was . . . compelling. He's presented us, in effect, with a redrawn map of the solar system. If it's inaccurate, intentionally or otherwise, the truth will eventually win out. It's *possible*, of course, that the video demonstration itself is some sort of fabrication, but I can't imagine any reasonable motive for deception. Why would Zarnik lie?"

"Why, indeed," echoes Cain. He warps his brows in thought. Then he leans forward, elbows on knees, coddling the snifter with both hands. "Let me be frank about this. My contacts in

Washington now seem satisfied that Zarnik isn't playing games, and that's really all that they've asked us to help them to determine—so we've done our job, and a favor has been repaid. But I have to tell you, Manning, that some of the issues you've raised have roused my own reporter's instincts. Would you like to keep digging on this a while longer?"

Manning tries not to appear too eager. "That might be a good idea, Mr. Cain. A fine suggestion. Thank you, sir."

"See if you can get him to come up with those missing numbers."

"That's a start," says Manning. "I'd also like to learn more about Zarnik's personal background—since he's a foreigner, I haven't found much file material on him. Maybe some secondary interviews with other sources."

"Sounds good." Cain leans back in his seat, visibly more relaxed. "And this time, Manning, there's no pressure, no deadline. Spend the next week on this. If you come up with something, great—we'll run with it. If not, we'll chalk it off as an investment in responsible journalism. After the Fourth, when things have calmed down, let's meet again and assess where we're at. Needless to say, if anything big develops, let me know at once. Gordon can give you my beeper number. Sound reasonable?"

"Very," says Manning, thinking, Too good to be true. He arrived at this meeting prepared to squirm, anticipating Cain's displeasure with his recent work. Instead, he's been ordered to proceed exactly as he intended.

Smith jots a phone number on the back of a business card and hands it to Manning while asking Cain, "Can I assume Mark has carte blanche on this project?"

"Absolutely. Entertainment, research fees, travel—whatever it takes to get to the bottom of this."

Smith reminds Manning, "And you've still got David Bosch in your hip pocket."

Manning responds dryly, "That's one way of putting it."

Their conversation is interrupted by a rap on the door to the outer office. Heads turn as Lucille Haring trundles in backwards, towing a serving cart stocked with a huge silver coffee urn, carafes of various juices, cups, glassware, and ice. "Pardon the intrusion, Colonel," she says, "but the kitchen said you'd placed an order."

Before Cain has said, "Thank you, Miss Haring," she has positioned the cart near the bar, returned to the door, snapped to attention, bowed, and retreated.

Cain says, "As I've mentioned before, she's a model of efficiency." As he rises and moves toward the cart, the others do also. "Coffee, Gordon?"

"Sure, Nathan. Thanks."

Cain pours a cup for himself as well as for Smith. "Mr. Manning?"

"Some orange juice would be great."

"How about something *in* it, Manning? An accelerator. Champagne, perhaps?"

"No, thank you, sir."

"*Hngh.*" He hands the juice to Manning, coffee to Smith. They all sip. Cain's lips gnarl. He dumps the remainder of his cognac from the snifter into his coffee cup, tastes again, and exhales a grunt of satisfaction. Smiling, he tells them, "Ambrosia, gentlemen. Sheer, silken ambrosia." He gulps half the cup. Then he shifts gears, saying to Manning, "Now tell me about Clifford Nolan. What have you learned?"

"Well, sir"—Manning instinctively grabs for the notebook in his jacket, but withdraws his hand from it, deciding that his report to Cain will remain vague on crucial details—"I've identified several possible suspects at this point, none of them very firm. One is an eccentric neighbor whose motive may have been no stronger than her displeasure with Cliff's loud music. But others may have had stronger, darker reasons to kill Cliff."

Both Cain and Smith look up from the coffee they are drinking.

Manning continues, "Two possibilities have come to light. First, there may be some connection between Cliff's murder and Pavo Zarnik's discovery."

"Such as?" asks Cain. His tone is skeptical.

Manning is not yet prepared to reveal to his publisher that Zarnik is a fraud, so he simply tells him, "Cliff may have been writing about Zarnik at the time he was killed, and there's apparently some political interest in Zarnik's discovery, but at this point, I'm merely exploring a hunch."

Cain swirls the mix of coffee and cognac. "And the other possibility?"

Manning moves a step closer, between Cain and Smith, tightening their circle. "Yesterday, while cleaning out Cliff's desk, I came across something very disturbing." Responding to Smith's questioning look of surprise, he explains, "I intended to meet with you, Gordon, first thing this morning, to tell you what I found, but, well . . . here we are. I regret to inform both of you that Clifford Nolan was involved in an activity that should be a profound embarrassment to the *Journal*. He had compiled dossiers, handwritten files of 'dirt' on numerous friends, colleagues, and public figures. He was running a profitable little sideline of extortion."

"Christ," says Smith, sitting on the arm of the nearest sofa. "I wondered how he managed that art collection on a reporter's salary—I should have suspected something." Smith is clearly crushed by this news, which reveals an entirely different facet of the science editor who had brought such esteem to the paper.

Nathan Cain may be similarly disheartened, but he does not show his emotions. All business, he says to Manning, "You mentioned 'colleagues.' Do Clifford's files point to suspicion of anyone here at the *Journal?*"

"Yes." Manning thinks of Lucille Haring, hoping Cain won't press further.

Cain asks, "Do the files point to suspicion of anyone in this room?"

"No, sir."

Cain and Smith share a sigh of relief. Cain tells Manning, "Well done. By all means, proceed with your investigation. It sounds as if you're on the right track."

Manning assures his publisher, "I'll do my best to sort this out. I'm wondering, though—What should I do with Cliff's files, turn them over to the police?"

Cain nods. "I suppose you'll have to." Then he reconsiders. "No, wait. I'm loath to sound calculating, but the *Journal* has to guard its own interests in this matter. We've been riding a wave of sympathy in the wake of Clifford's murder, but if those files become public, we'll be the goat of Chicago journalism. Just proceed with your own investigation, Mr. Manning, and let the police proceed with theirs. If the files are useful to you in naming Clifford's killer, use them. Ultimately, we should destroy what's not needed."

Manning concurs, "This is a gray area, I know, but it's important not to let these files get into the wrong hands. They would simply cause a lot of needless emotional pain. I have a call in to a detective friend at police headquarters, but I won't mention this to him, at least not yet. I'm hoping he can tell me what was the last piece of music played on Cliff's CD player. Also, the ballistics tests should be complete by now. Maybe he'll be willing to share some hard evidence. I'll phone him again as soon as I get back to my desk."

"You needn't bother." Cain dismisses the idea with a flick of his hand. "The report came over the city newswire last night. There were four bullets in Clifford's body, but the ballistics tests were 'inconclusive,' with no clues regarding the gun that killed him. The police are officially 'frustrated.' " He snorts his derision, presuming they have bungled. He turns, and his gaze travels to the showcase that displays his collection of rare firearms.

Noticing this, Smith walks over to the glass-doored cabinet. Tapping the window with a fingernail, he tells Cain, "I wish you'd let us run a feature on the collection. There's at least a dozen great stories in there. It's a natural for the Sunday magazine."

"I'm flattered," Cain replies, "but I don't care to draw attention to it. Other collectors would get interested; there would be requests for visits from curators and academics. I don't care to be bothered by all that. The collection is private."

Crossing to the display, Manning says, "Last time we were here, sir, you said you might share the history of the Nambu pistol." He peers through the glass at the gun in question, which rests on a small silk cushion, centered among the other weapons, gleaming in the beam of a miniature spotlight. The pistol itself is unremarkable, but its distinctive handle is inlaid with intricately carved jade. An easel near the cushion holds a gold-edged card that traces the gun's pedigree. Manning squints to read it.

"Very well, gentlemen." Cain snorts, moving toward them. "The story. That's a Nambu Type Two, a Japanese model that was rare to begin with, but this particular weapon is unique, as you might guess from the jade handle. It belonged to Field Marshal General Sugiyama, the Japanese minister of war. His wife nagged him into using it on himself in September of 'forty-five, to avoid being placed on trial for war crimes. After he did it"—Cain slurps from his cup—"she poisoned herself."

Smith chokes on his own coffee. "Whew!" he says. "They are a *strange* race. Clever, but strange."

With no humor, Cain tells Smith, "They are a people of high principles."

Manning asks, "How did you acquire the general's gun, Mr. Cain?"

"Our occupation forces were already in place in Tokyo, so it must have been picked up by one of the MPs investigating Sugiyama's death. The pistol found its way back to the States and many years later was presented to me as a gift from an old army friend—a buddy, you might say—who's now at the Pentagon. The Nambu has been the centerpiece of my collection ever since."

"Very impressive, sir." Manning sips his juice.

Their small talk moves on to politics, new restaurants, the approach of Celebration Two Thousand. At the mention of the festival, Cain waves an arm toward one of the huge Gothic arched windows that look out across the city. Even through the summer haze, the new stadium is visible a mile to the west. "That tranquil view will change before our very eyes, gentlemen. The fete, I fear, will transform this fair city into a veritable zoo. Oh I know, 'the people' will love it, and it'll be a boon for our circulation, but it'll bring with it that element of—what?—a certain *madness*. I, for one, plan to be out of town next weekend."

Smith is jovial. "Not me, Nathan. Wouldn't think of missing the opening spectacle, and *I've* got a press pass." He pats his breast pocket, where he keeps the credentials, which truly are coveted—anyone would be foolish to leave such a pass lying on a desk, or even in an unlocked drawer. He adds, "As for the congestion of the city, well, I guess that's inevitable. But it shouldn't be all *that* disruptive."

Even as he speaks, workers on a scaffold winch their way up the outside of the tower, rising just above the stone gargoyles, stopping smack in the middle of the window, blocking the view. Cain watches them for a moment, then turns to Smith with a look that says, I told you so. "That's been going on for a couple of weeks now."

The workmen are conversing in shouts with unseen brethren, some on top of the tower, others apparently on another scaffold hanging below. Inside, the particulars of this communication cannot be understood, reduced to muffled noise by the thick glass of the windows. There are repeated references to "fucking," however, that are transmitted loud and clear.

Manning stifles a laugh as he sips his orange juice. He asks his publisher, "What are they doing out there?"

Cain breathes an exasperated sigh. "Preparing for the great civic clambake, naturally. There's all manner of equipment to be installed atop the Journal Building as part of a laser show. We're to be one point of a triangle, I'm told."

"A pink triangle, in fact," Manning adds.

"You've heard about it, then?" says Cain.

Smith interjects, "*I* haven't. What laser show?"

"I guess the plans haven't been made public yet," says Manning, "but Neil told me about them. As a surprise finish to the opening ceremonies and human-rights rally, a giant pink triangle will appear over the stadium. There's some new laser technology involved, and the image will be simultaneously projected from the masts of three tall buildings, including this tower."

Smith looks confused. "What am I missing here? Why a pink triangle?"

"For Christ's sake," snaps Cain, "you're better-read than that, Gordon. It's the symbol of gay liberation . . . or pride or whatever."

Manning steps closer to Cain to tell him, "And I must say,

sir, that it's unexpectedly progressive and 'inclusive' of the *Journal* to take part in it."

"Don't be condescending, Manning. You're starting to sound like our bleeding-heart archbishop. The fact is, the *Journal* would appear unenlightened and prejudiced if we refused. I don't see that we had a choice—and I won't pretend to like it."

Manning smiles. "Regardless of the circumstances, sir, I think the company is doing the right thing. Thank you."

"Don't mention it." Cain does not return the smile.

Their conversation has grown louder to compete with the noise from outside the window, where winches now whine and scaffolding creaks as a huge, menacing contraption is hoisted into view.

"Holy shit," says Smith. "It looks like something out of *Flash Gordon.*"

"Jesus," echoes Manning, "It looks like a ... like a *gun.*"

With no discernible emotion, Cain tells them, "I believe it is a gun—of sorts. Probably part of the laser apparatus. One of the three projectors for the spectacle."

"Ohhh," says Smith. He should have guessed. He finishes his coffee and sets the cup on the cart.

"Beastly-looking thing, though," says Manning with a short, hesitant laugh. He can't take his eyes off the device. It has coils and armatures, an array of controls positioned in front of something like a tractor seat, and a long, tapered snout, like the barrel of some high-tech weapon. The casing is painted a drab gray-green.

"Well," says Cain with a tone of finality, "enough of this commotion." He steps to the window and turns a knob mounted in the trim. Heavy velvet blackout curtains emerge from pockets in the side walls and draw together over the glass. The workers' noise is reduced to a distant hubbub as the light in the room fades. Cain asks, "More juice, Mr. Manning?"

The offer, Manning knows, is not meant to be accepted. "Thank you, sir, but no." He sets his glass on the cart next to Smith's cup. "I think we're all set."

"Excellent." Cain begins crossing the room in the direction

of the door—clearly, Smith and Manning are being escorted out, and they walk along with him, one on each side. Cain tells them, "I'm glad we were able to have this little 'breakfast' together." He eyes Smith with a facial tic that's not quite a wink, then swallows the last of his fortified coffee. He turns to Manning, "Keep up the good work, and do keep me posted." He gives the reporter a pat on the back. The gesture is unnatural to him, and he delivers it stiffly.

When they pass through the door into the outer office, the pace of activity has picked up since their early arrival. Lucille Haring taps commands into a computer's keyboard, while an assistant stands nearby, waiting for the diskette that Haring hands over without looking at him. Other minions scamper about the room, breaking stride just long enough to deliver a curt "Good morning, Colonel." One of them takes the publisher's empty cup and whisks it away. No one seems fazed by the fact that he's standing there in his sleepwear.

When Lucille Haring notices Cain in their midst, she quits her keyboard and stands facing him, as if at attention. He tells her, "Mr. Manning is embroiled in some very important work and may be accruing some atypical expenses—travel and such— during the next week or so. Anything he sends through is author-ized and approved."

"Very good, Colonel."

Cain thinks of something. He tells Manning, "You might find a laptop useful. A modem too. Miss Haring can set you up."

"I'm already fully equipped," Manning assures him.

"Pager?"

"I have one, sir."

"These days, who doesn't?" Smith interjects.

Cain suggests, "Maybe a memory upgrade?"

"I'm fine," says Manning. "Thank you, though."

Cain thinks of something else. "Miss Haring, regarding that upgrade of the network server for these offices, we need to be certain that the new configuration won't allow users to breach the corporate mainframe." On a lighter note, he adds, "Too many people online these days. No telling what mischief some hacker might wreak if he gets access."

Miss Haring nods vigorously, attuned to his concerns. "Security has been our top priority in every phase of the new design."

"*Hngh.*" He returns his attention to Smith and Manning. "Gentlemen, good day. *You've* got a newspaper to put out, and *I've* got to get dressed." He erupts into a hearty laugh, then smiles (it's a genuine smile for once, not the wooden expression he forces for banquet photos with the mayor or the archbishop), waves (it's a single whirl of his hand that could pass for a salute), and retreats into the inner sanctum. The sturdy timbered door closes behind him with a thud.

Two minutes later, the door of the private elevator slides shut, leaving Manning and Smith alone together as they begin their descent through the Journal Building. "Well?" says Smith, speaking under his breath.

Manning tells him, "Wait." The glass eye of a camera watches them, but he doesn't know whether anyone is listening.

The elevator delivers its two passengers to one of the ground-floor lobbies. They walk a few steps down the busy arcade, stopping to talk in front of the window of a tobacco shop.

"Well?" repeats Smith. "What do you think?"

"I think he let me off too easy concerning my Zarnik piece. That story was riddled with shortcomings."

"But," Smith reminds him, "Nathan's main interest in the story was to repay a favor to his Pentagon pals. *They* were satisfied, so *he* was satisfied."

Manning considers. "That's true," he admits. "And the important thing is, Cain wants to keep me on the story. If he had ulterior motives, however far-fetched, he wouldn't order me to dig deeper—he'd transfer me out to the suburbs, writing obits."

"There now," says Smith, putting an arm over the reporter's shoulder. "We've snatched victory from the jaws of disaster. You've got a few more days to get the poop on Zarnik and determine whether Cain is being set up for something."

Manning grins. "Does that mean you're taking me off the Nolan story so I can focus on Zarnik?"

"You *want* me to?"

"No, Gordon." Manning laughs. "These two mysteries were made for each other. As I've already told you, I think the answer to one is the answer to both." Exchanging a nod, they're about to step away from the tobacco shop and return to the newsroom when Manning halts, frowning. "Hold on," he says. "Something's bugging me. What about all that computer business?"

As he asks the question, he notices someone inside the shop—a tall man, vaguely familiar—who may have been watching them. Or was he merely skimming the magazine covers displayed inside, below the window?

"What *about* the computers?" asks Smith.

"When we met with Cain four days ago, he claimed total ignorance of computers. Today he was talking like a techie. I didn't know he could even type."

The man in the store is now at the tobacco counter, his back to the window. The clerk hands him a foiled pack of imported cigarettes. He glances about the room.

Smith says, "Wasn't Lucy supposed to be giving Nathan lessons? 'Remedial training,' I think he called it."

"She's damn good if she can bring him up to speed *that* fast."

The man in the store has lit one of the cigarettes, which he puffs from a six-inch holder. Even from behind, Manning can tell from the man's posture, from the way he holds the cigarette, that his mannerisms are decidedly effeminate. And his face, what Manning can see of it, is familiar.

"She may well be a computer wiz," says Smith, "but she's one weird woman. Lucille Haring gives me the chills. Your first hunch may have been right, Marko—maybe the Pentagon did plant her in Cain's office to facilitate some hidden agenda."

Manning's attention is diverted by the man with the cigarette holder, who leaves the shop and brushes past them, apparently miffed at something. He does not make eye contact with Manning, but Manning gets a good look at the man, who limps through the lobby toward the street door. It is Victor Uttley, Chicago's cultural liaison to the world.

He twirls through the revolving door and disappears into the crowds on Michigan Avenue.

Shortly after six that evening, Manning returns home to the loft. The sultry morning became a sweltering afternoon, and Manning was grateful for the air-conditioned privacy of his car during the short ride home—pity those crammed into buses or dashing through crowds to catch trains in this weather. Environmentalist dictums notwithstanding, public transportation is a bitch.

In the hallway outside the loft, he slides his key into the lock, turns it, and opens the front door. Cool, dry air greets him like a hug as the security system beeps its warning—he's first to arrive, Neil's not home yet. He taps in the code that disarms the alarm, closes the door behind him, and heads for the kitchen, tossing his briefcase on the counter.

Cocktail time. Manning doesn't make a habit of fixing a drink every time he walks through the door at night, but this was a tense day, a hot one too, so he feels no qualms about digging from the freezer the bottle of Japanese vodka that is always stored there. He fills a short glass with ice and has begun stripping a sliver of peel from an orange when he hears a key in the door.

"Honey, I'm home." It's Neil, of course. The running gag line acknowledges that their household is anything but conventional. At the same time, it attests to a mutual commitment far more genuine than the cardboard marriages that populated the sitcoms of their youth.

Manning rattles the glass of ice, calling, "Drink?"

Silly question. Neil heads straight for the kitchen, dropping his briefcase next to Manning's. Manning plops ice into a second glass as Neil grabs his waist and plants a kiss on his mouth. "Hi there."

"Hi there. How was your day?" Manning pours the Japanese

vodka and twists the orange peel. This has been "their" drink since Neil introduced him to it on the night they first met.

"Busy," answers Neil, "but productive. Come hell or high water, Celebration Two Thousand *will* be launched this weekend."

"Bravo," says Manning, handing him one of the glasses. Then he lifts his own. *"Compai."* They skoal, then drink.

"And how was *your* day?" Neil asks.

Manning suggests that they sit down. When they have gotten comfortable on the sofa, looking out over the lake, Manning recounts to Neil his early-morning visit to Nathan Cain's office. He concludes, "So even though I was dreading Cain's reaction to Sunday's story, the upshot of the meeting was better than I'd hoped—I'm still on the story, with Cain's unequivocal support and pontifical blessing."

"All's well that ends well." Neil sucks an ice cube into his mouth.

"It's hardly over," Manning reminds him. "I still need to do a lot of digging on the Cliff Nolan story, and my reputation is on the line with this Zarnik business. It's a challenge that's mandated not only by my own professional curiosity, but now by Cain's as well. He said there was no deadline—but the pressure is on."

Manning swirls the ice in his glass, then drinks a hefty slug of vodka. He continues. "My suspicions about Zarnik got some reinforcement today from a linguistics professor down in Urbana. He'd seen my weekend story and was intrigued by Zarnik's use of the word *pfroobst*, so he did a little research. Not only is the word unknown in Zarnik's native dialect—it's not in the lexicon of *any* known language. It's a total fabrication. I might have guessed."

"What's next, then?" Neil's tongue is numbed by the ice, so his words are barely intelligible, but Manning gets the drift.

"It's time to talk to Zarnik again. I'm not ready to confront him, but I want to see if he manages to come up with any of the missing facts he promised. I've tried reaching him all day, but he's been 'unavailable.' If I can't get through to him in the morning, David and I will just head over to the planetarium and camp out for him."

Neil rattles the remnants of chomped ice in his glass. He tells Manning, "You've turned Zarnik into such a celebrity, no wonder you can't reach him. His aides, 'his people' are probably screening calls."

Manning snickers at the irony of it. "Zarnik's not the only one who's hard to reach. You'll never guess who came to see me at the office today—Victor Uttley."

"Get out."

"No, really. We had the strangest encounter—or *non*-encounter. Gordon and I were in the lobby discussing the meeting we'd just had with Cain, which had put me in a suspicious mood that bordered on paranoia. As we talked, I realized that this peculiar man was watching us from inside the tobacco shop. At least it *seemed* he was. I couldn't get a good look at him till he left the shop and limped past us through the lobby. That's when I realized it was Uttley. When I returned to the newsroom, there was a message that he'd come to see me." Manning laughs. "So I guess he wasn't there on a spy mission, but I don't have a clue as to what he did want. I phoned several times. He was 'out.' "

Neil has listened with interest. "That's not surprising. Victor's never in his office—he's out pestering other people, like me. But I am surprised that he came to see you. Could it have something to do with that ad he ran in today's *Journal?*"

"I doubt it." Manning finishes the last of his own drink. "I have nothing to do with advertising at the paper—he surely knows that. And besides, the ad ran in the *Post* as well."

Neil takes Manning's glass. His expression asks, Another? Manning nods. Sure. Rising with both glasses and crossing to the kitchen, Neil tells him, "I wouldn't lose sleep over it. Victor's something of a flake, and that's putting it charitably. Even when you do reach him, I bet he won't remember what he wanted. He's up to his ears working out logistics for the opening ceremony—the laser show and all."

"That reminds me," says Manning, rising and following Neil, "I saw the damnedest thing from Cain's office this morning.

There were workers outside the building hoisting one of the projectors up to the tower's mast platform. Have you ever seen one of those things?"

"Nope." Neil twists orange peel over the vodka he has just poured.

"It looked downright diabolical," says Manning, still confounded by the machine's appearance. He tries to be more precise: "It looked like some exotic piece of military hardware—it was even painted olive drab."

Handing Manning his drink, Neil shrugs. "It is, after all, some sort of laser gun. What's it *supposed* to look like?"

Manning sips from his glass, thinking. Then he tells Neil, "That's a good question: What's it *supposed* to look like?" He seems suddenly, calmly enlightened.

"You've lost me," says Neil.

Manning continues, *"You're* involved with all this. Is there any way you could arrange for me to get a look at a laser projector on one of the other towers?"

"What for?" Neil drinks.

"Just curiosity." Manning also drinks. He sits on a stool at the kitchen's center island. "You know—nosy me."

Neil is still confused. From the opposite side of the island, he asks, "What do the projectors have to do with Zarnik?"

"Nothing whatever. Let's just say that the Zarnik affair has piqued my interest in scientific reporting. Once the public sees the laser show, there's bound to be widespread interest in the technology behind it. It'll make a good story, and I'd like to get a jump on it."

Neil rarely has the opportunity to assist Manning on a story, and he's glad to have the chance. "I'm in no position to arrange it directly, but I know someone who could pull a few strings— Victor Uttley."

"Oh?" With heightened interest, Manning leans forward with his arms on the countertop.

Neil places his palms on the counter to lean closer to Manning, explaining, "Victor's got 'access.' Granted, he's just an overpaid bureaucrat in some dreamed-up job, but he *can* open doors."

"If he wants to," says Manning.

"Exactly. So find out why he wanted to see you today, help him out with it if you can, then ask him to return the favor. He might play along."

"I like the way you think," says Manning, stretching to lean farther over the counter till he's nose-to-nose with Neil. With an exaggerated pucker, Manning gives him a kiss, then relaxes again on the stool. "I've already left a stack of message slips for Uttley, so it's his turn to respond."

"Speaking of messages," says Neil, glancing at an answering machine that sits on the counter near the kitchen phone, "it looks like we've had a pile of calls." A little red light blinks drowsily.

Manning sighs. "We need a secretary." He pulls a notepad from the briefcase he dropped there when he got home.

Neil corrects him, "We need a vacation."

"Good idea. Let's talk about that   next week." He unscrews the cap of his pen and begins jotting some notes, plans for the investigation he will pursue during the next few days.

While Manning concentrates on the details of his schedule, Neil tidies up the minor mess of their drink-fixing and taps the button to play their phone messages. There are six or seven.

Several are from people who serve on Neil's festival committees. He nods while listening to the litany of ongoing projects and crises, reminding himself that a week from now, it will all be over—he will indeed get his life back. There are a couple of calls from friends thanking Manning and Neil for Saturday's party, suggesting future social engagements to repay the evening. There's a message for Mr. Manning from someone at Visa who wants him to return the call to Michelle at an 800 number. She has an exciting offer regarding a "buying club" that he'll surely want to join! Mr. Manning snorts with contempt—these people just won't give up. And there's a message from Roxanne in Door County. It's a long one, and Manning's attention drifts back to his notes—he'll deal with her vacation-and-romance gossip later. Neil listens while polishing the stainless-steel sink with a dish towel. Then he stops and turns to Manning with his mouth agape.

At that point, Manning realizes that Roxanne's tone has shifted from chatty to urgent, and she's not finished—her message has been left in installments. He tells Neil, "Better play that over."

Neil presses the "repeat" button. The machine beeps. They hear Roxanne's voice.

"Hi, guys. It's me, Roxanne. We made it up to Baileys Harbor safe and sound. The resort is a hoot—sort of a throwback to the fifties—but it's really quite lovely. And the weather's much cooler up here. Sweaters at night.

"I tried calling you at work, Mark, but you were out, and I didn't want to leave this message on your voice mail there. It's afternoon now, and I assume you won't hear this till tonight, at home. Obviously. That's where I'm calling.

"Something, well, *strange* happened this morning that you need to know about, Mark. Carl and I got up early today (we haven't quite programmed ourselves to relax yet), took a long walk, then went to breakfast. The dining room is in this separate building, sort of lodgelike, and breakfast is a big deal. The eggs Benedict, by the way, are fabulous."

The machine cuts her off. A moment later, there's another beep.

"Me again. Part two. Anyway, when we returned to our cabin at about nine, the message light on the phone was flashing, so Carl called the desk. He picked up a pencil and was ready to take notes, but he just nodded while he listened, thanked the desk clerk, and hung up. It was clearly business, and I frankly didn't care who it was, so I didn't ask. But here's where it starts to get weird.

"Carl went out to the *car* to return the call. I mean, Carl Creighton and I *work* together, I'm a partner in his firm, I'm privy to all of our clients' business. When he came back inside, he said, 'No point in squandering money on hotel long distance'— as if cellular rates are a bargain. At that point, of course, I was *plenty* curious as to what the call was about, but my instincts told me not to ask. I'd wait.

"Later, we went out for a nice lunch, and near the end, there was an awkward lull. He took my hand across the table and, apologizing profusely, told me that he had to drive back into the

city tomorrow—Tuesday—for an important conference, returning to Door County on Wednesday. He offered no explanation,
while sweetly insisting that I remain up here to 'enjoy' myself."

The machine cuts her off again. Manning and Neil exchange
a quizzical shrug that asks, So what? Big deal. A moment later,
there's another beep.

"Part three. I've got to wrap this up. This'll sound nuts, Mark,
but I've done a little sleuthing, and I need to see you—up here,
tomorrow, while he's gone. I know this is short notice, and I
know it's a long haul, but I'm telling you, it's important. I've
reserved a cabin in your name. I'll check with the desk later to
see if you've confirmed the reservation. Don't phone me
tonight—Carl will still be here. Now *I'm* on the car phone, so
anyone could be listening, and I can't go into more detail.

"But I will say this: It involves the Z-person. And I'm scared.
So get your ass up here. *Ciao.*" There's a click, then a dial tone.
The machine shuts off, signaling with a series of beeps that there
are no more messages.

Manning and Neil stare at each other in silence for a few
seconds. Neil asks, "What do you make of that?"

"For starters," says Manning, "the Z-person is obviously
Zarnik."

"Obviously."

"As for the rest, it all sounds pretty goofy."

"Sure does," says Neil, "but she was clearly upset, and Rox
is as levelheaded as they come."

"Now that she's sober." Manning adds, "Just kidding." He
pauses in thought for a moment. When he speaks, his tone has
turned serious. "There's something I haven't told you about the
files I found in Cliff Nolan's desk yesterday."

Neil draws his brows together. "What? You told me he was
keeping embarrassing dossiers on people. Cliff was a cad. So?"

Manning looks Neil in the eye. "One of those files pertained
to Carl Creighton."

Neil's astonished look asks for details.

"The file indicated that Cliff had recently met with Carl, and
there were notes containing cryptic references to dates thirty years

ago when they were both apparently students at the University of Chicago. My *impression* was that there may have been a cheating scandal."

"Uh-oh."

"Uh-oh is right. Carl's file was only one among dozens that Cliff kept, so I convinced myself that I needn't be concerned about it. But now these developments with Roxanne. . . ."

Neil sits on the stool next to Manning's and spreads his towel on the counter, folding it into progressively smaller rectangles. "So," he asks, "are you going?"

Manning exhales a noisy, frustrated sigh. He taps a finger on the schedule he's been drafting. "This is exactly the time when I can't afford to drop everything and spend a day or two at a resort just because a friend wants to 'talk.' Then, too, she raised some enticing possibilities, and she's not willing to elaborate on the phone, so I guess I'd better go. Funny," he says, laughing more at the irony than at the humor of the situation, "Nathan Cain all but ordered me to do some traveling this week."

"What's left to decide?" Neil asks, unfolding the towel and smoothing its creases with his palms. "Looks like you're getting a little vacation sooner than you thought."

"Hey." Manning's eyes widen. "Come with me. You could use a little time off."

"Not now I couldn't," Neil dismisses the suggestion. "These days, I barely have time to eat, let alone travel. Don't get me wrong—I'd love to tag along, and I certainly don't care for the notion of you and Roxanne spending a night alone together."

Manning chortles. "Come on. You know she's safe with *me.*"

"Most likely," Neil admits, "but I'm not at all convinced you're safe with *her.*"

"Oh . . ." says Manning. Neil has a point. It was Roxanne who first brought Manning and Neil together, a social courtesy never meant to lead to romance. To the contrary, she had for some time entertained the notion of her own carnal involvement with both men. Her fantasies had been doomed from the start, but the hopelessness of her plan was not fully evident till she witnessed firsthand a budding friendship, the seeds of which she herself had planted.

She did not deal well with what she'd wrought, so she attempted, only two weeks after bringing them together, to drive them apart. The same morning that Neil returned home to Phoenix from Chicago (his visit cut short by a drunken fight that Roxanne picked with him), she seduced Manning. His sexual history to that point, though sporadic and unsatisfying, had been strictly straight. When Roxanne lured him to her bed that morning, she assumed she had triumphed. Manning willingly capitulated, but their sex was cold and loveless, motivated by frustration. As Manning fucked her, he fantasized about Neil, and he then knew that his life would change. It would be months before he would summon the courage to act upon his desires with Neil, but ironically, it was that last intimacy with Roxanne—plotted to confirm his heterosexuality—that sent him down a different path, one that would change the very core of his self-identity.

It was a change that he had feared. He sensed that it might be coming, and he spoke of it openly with Neil one night when they first had the opportunity to stop flirting and get physical. Instead, they talked. Manning was faced with a "label crisis," as he called it. He was terrified by the names that have been used to label people like Neil, and he couldn't fathom taking actions that would attach those labels to himself. Ultimately, though, his own sense of honesty and self-worth won out, and he answered the calling that spoke from within him to love another man—a particular man—Neil. The labels didn't kill him. In fact, he has been enriched beyond measure by the new identity he feared.

Now, this evening, he wonders how Neil can possibly worry that Roxanne might come between them. He rises from the stool where he has been sitting and steps behind Neil, wrapping both arms around him. He says into Neil's ear, "Do you seriously think that I could ever stop loving you?"

"No." Neil lolls his head back, tucking it next to Manning's neck. "But I've known Rox a lot longer than you have. She likes to get what she wants. And she's always wanted you."

"We can't always have what we want," Manning reminds him.

Neil swivels the stool to face Manning, laughing. "She's a strong-willed woman," he says. Then he adds, "Look, it's not that I think you would ever succumb to her charms, and I doubt if she'd even try it, but I know she'd be *thinking* it, so why create a situation that invites that kind of friction?"

"Because," says Manning, "it's important that I go up there. I've asked you along—you're welcome to chaperon—but you're busy. What am I supposed to do?"

Neil stands. "Take David."

"That's not a good idea," Manning responds flatly, without thinking twice.

"Why not? He's your 'assistant.' Cain's told you to follow every lead. Take him along—he'd enjoy it."

"I'm sure," says Manning, more to himself. Then, incredulous, he asks Neil, "You mean to tell me that you're reluctant to have me spend a night in Door County with Roxanne, but you're willing to send me up there with *David?*"

Neil answers nonchalantly, "Rox'll keep an eye on you. If anything happens, I'll hear about it." He laughs. "Seriously, though. We both find David attractive—who wouldn't?—but we know he's off-limits. It's not as if you're *interested* in him. Are you?"

"Of course not," Manning tries to answer honestly. "Well . . . in the abstract, I suppose."

"Then what's the problem?"

Manning turns and ambles toward the central space of the loft, straining to mask the wariness of his reply. "There's no problem. No, I guess not."

Tuesday, June 29

At five-thirty Tuesday morning, the sun has risen, but the city sleeps. Manning's brain is off somewhere on planet Zarnik, where he runs, spinning the orb beneath his feet in hopeless pursuit of the horizon, like a schizoid rodent on a treadmill. Overhead, pink clouds alternately glow and dim with the ceaseless rise and set of a faraway starlike sun. His mind is addled. He thinks of nothing. And then a bitsy beeping noise begins to penetrate his ears, needling his consciousness. What is that?

The clock at his bedside, a travel alarm, was set the night before to rouse him at this early hour. He didn't want to fuss with the clock radio, leaving it programmed to wake Neil later at their usual time, to the classical music of their usual station. Manning is not quite awake yet, but he knows he should silence the alarm before it gets louder and disturbs Neil. He reaches for the clock, but can't remember how to turn it off. Fumbling with it, he knocks it off the table. It lands on the carpet with a thump, and the beeping stops. The bed shakes gently as Neil suppresses a laugh.

"Sorry, kiddo," Manning whispers to him.

"That's okay," Neil whispers back. "I was awake. Lots on my mind." He rolls over, resting the length of his body against Manning's, then kisses him. He whispers, "Good morning."

"Good morning," Manning replies, full-voice.

"Shhh." Neil's fingers cover Manning's mouth. "You'll wake the baby."

They look at each other with a mischievous grin. Like kids on Christmas morning, they scramble out of bed and pad over to the edge of the balcony, peering down into the main space of the loft. There, sprawled atop a sofa, side-lit by the eastern windows, sleeps the buffed young body of David Bosch. He has kicked away makeshift bedding during the night and scrunches a pillow, rump in the air. He wears boxers, a tank top, and white socks.

Hubba-hubba. Neil turns to Manning. "If we hadn't cranked the air-conditioning, we'd be ogling more flesh and less fiber right now. If you manage to get a look at that body, I want every detail."

Manning gives him a thumbs-up.

The cub reporter landed on their couch as the result of last night's phone calls, planning the quick trip to Door County. Manning first phoned the resort to confirm his reservation and to secure lodging for two—no problem, their deluxe cabin would have two bedrooms. He also received the desk clerk's message from Roxanne, suggesting he arrive before noon, stay Tuesday night, and leave early Wednesday. The drive takes about five hours, so he would need to get an early start.

Then he phoned David. As Neil predicted, he was thrilled to be included, but lamented the need to rise so early. His apartment's air-conditioning has been ineffective against the recent heat ("It needs a fresh shot of Freon or whatever"), so he hasn't been sleeping well ("I'll be a zombie in the morning"). Neil proposed the obvious solution. If David spent the night at the loft, he'd sleep more comfortably, and he and Manning could get an earlier start together.

So later that evening, duffle in hand, David Bosch arrived. The three talked awhile, then Neil offered drinks. To Manning's relief—he didn't want a replay of David's party behavior—their houseguest responded, "Maybe just a nightcap. I want to be fresh tomorrow." And everyone was tucked in by eleven.

Now Neil tells Manning, "I'll get the coffee going." He throws on a bathrobe and heads down the stairs, then turns back, adding, "You can get started in the bathroom. I'll wake the child."

"Be nice." Manning wags a finger. "I have to work with that 'child.' " And he snatches his own robe, heading for the shower.

Downstairs, Neil circles the sofa, drinking in different perspectives of David's repose. Even flumped there in his underwear, face smooshed, limbs flailed, the kid personifies beauty. And he's no kid—he's twenty-four, he's played the field. Neil leans over the back of the sofa. "David?" he says gently.

But David doesn't stir.

Neil moves to the front of the sofa and squats there, almost stepping on David's glasses, which were set on the floor. Neil picks them up and examines them. Armani—nice, very nice. David's face is inches from Neil's. "David?" Still no response. So Neil shakes his shoulder. *"David."*

"Huh?" David wakes with a start, bleary-eyed. Disoriented by the surroundings, he struggles to focus on the man at his side who is backlit by the big windows.

Neil slips the glasses onto David's head, hooking them behind his ears. Neil's fingers stall long enough to fluff the hair on David's temples. "Good morning."

As the whole room snaps into focus, David rolls onto his back. There's evidence of a morning erection in his boxers. "Oh. Hi there, Neil."

"Hi there yourself. Time to get moving. Mark's in the shower already." Neil stands. "Coffee?"

"Sure." David sits up. He flexes his shoulders.

Neil steps toward the kitchen, turning back to ask, "Cereal?"

"Sure." David stands, stretching.

God, what a sight. There's a bounce to Neil's step as he retreats to fix breakfast, a chore that he's wont to perform groggily at best.

By six-thirty, everyone is fed, dressed, and ready to go. Neil sits on a stool at the counter with a last cup of coffee, leafing through the *Journal*. It's too early for him to leave for the office— he probably couldn't get into the building yet. But Manning and David are set to hit the road, their overnight baggage readied near the door.

Manning carefully uncaps his Montblanc and writes a note for Neil. "Here's the phone number at the lodge," he tells him. "Car phone, cell phone, and pager too, so you won't need to look them up. Give me a call if there's anything I need to know— you may hear from Victor Uttley. Anyway, I'll check in with you later tonight."

Neil looks up from the paper with a get-serious smirk. "You think I'll be *here*, holed up alone?" His tone is playful.

With a menacing tone, Manning tells him, "You'd better be." He smiles. "No, have some fun. It's important to claim your own space now and then."

"You're right. I'll pee on all the furniture, like a dog marking its turf."

Manning musses Neil's hair. "You know what I mean."

"I know what you mean. You're a wise man, Mr. Manning." Neil rises, caps Manning's pen for him, and slips it into his pocket. Then he wraps his arms around Manning's waist, preparing for a proper good-bye. He tells David, who is standing by the door, "You can watch, but don't blush."

David covers his eyes with one hand, feigning exaggerated discretion while sneaking an obvious peek from the crack between his fingers. He witnesses a kiss that is a routine, daily gesture, not passionate but clearly loving. He has seen men kiss before— he's kissed a few himself—but never in a context of such domesticated happiness. This is a *home*, he tells himself. He has slept under their roof.

For the very reasons that the kiss is unremarkable, it is remarkable to David. His self-outing (that is, his recognition and ultimate acceptance of his own gayness) has not yet progressed to the stage of openness with others (unless, of course, the vino has worked its veritas). His gayness, then, is still an exclusively *sexual* identity, and he can not yet imagine a life—a normal, nonsecretive, loving, workaday life—with another man. And in witnessing this kiss, which is evidence that such relationships can and do exist, he learns in a flash that men need not always love with their dicks. He is stunned by this revelation. But then, he's only twenty-four.

"So," says Neil, returning to the newspaper, flipping a page, "you guys drive safely, comfort Roxanne—and stay out of trouble." He notices a new ad, another full-pager placed by Victor Uttley, heralding Professor Zarnik's momentous discovery.

"Don't worry," David tells Neil, hefting both his own bag and Manning's. "I'll take good care of Mark."

Grinning out of control, Manning wags his fingers at Neil, a wordless parting gesture. Then he opens the door for David, following him into the hallway and down an elevator to the garage.

Within minutes, the car with the two reporters swoops up the ramp to the expressway that will take them out of the city, heading north. Manning assumed they would have the road to themselves this early, so he's surprised to discover that the traffic is heavy.

It's another muggy day, and even at this hour, heat rises in waves from the pavement. David has dressed for the weather, wearing baggy black pleated shorts and a blue polo shirt. Manning also wears a polo shirt (his is yellow) with a comfortable old pair of chinos. They look like they might be on their way to a golf game.

With windows shut tight, the inside of the car is quiet and comfortable, easily cooled by the powerful engine, without the droning racket of gushing air that is typical of smaller cars. As the vehicle merges into the fast lane, quickly achieving highway speed, Manning and David sink deeper into their seats, responding to the force of acceleration. The unexpected journey, planned less than twelve hours ago, has truly begun. It feels good to get away. Manning's grip on the wheel relaxes.

David tells him, "It's going to be a long drive, Mark. Any time you want me to take the controls, just say the word."

"I'll let you know," says Manning, though he has no intention of turning over the wheel.

There's a pause. "So," David says, "what's all this about Roxanne?"

"All I know is what I told you on the phone last night. She's up there on vacation with her boss, Carl Creighton, who happens to be her current love interest, and he's been called away overnight. She's got the idea that this has something to do with Zarnik. I assume she has no idea that I found a dossier on Carl among Cliff Nolan's dirt files. In any event, she said she was scared, and she insisted on talking to me—*up there*—so off we go. You're my chaperon, by the way."

David is skeptical. "I thought I was your assistant."

"Never mind." Manning laughs. "It's a long story, a family matter." Which reminds Manning—"Is your uncle enjoying his visit?"

"Hector mostly enjoys grousing, but I know he's having a great time. I'm glad Claire is here with him. She's the one person who refuses to take him seriously."

"Good for her. Has she found the city to her liking?"

David turns in his seat to face Manning. "Where there's theater, Claire is happy. She's wasted no time checking out the local scene, dropping in on rehearsals as well as attending performances. She likes what she's found here."

Manning looks over at David. "Miracles never cease—a New Yorker discovers the heartland."

They ride in silence for a while. David stifles a yawn.

Manning asks him, "Didn't sleep well last night?"

"I did, actually—thanks for putting me up. I'm just off-schedule, not much of a morning person. Way too much clubbing lately."

"Feel free to snooze."

"Thanks." David experiments with the controls on the side of his seat, adjusting it till he is almost fully reclined. He sighs contentedly, spreading his legs—an enticing sight that momentarily diverts Manning's eyes from the road.

Several minutes pass, and Manning realizes that he too feels drowsy. The car is too quiet. He asks David, "Mind if I play something?"

"Sweet."

There are CDs loaded in the trunk, but Manning is tired of them—somehow they never get changed. So he switches on the radio. His favorite station is stored on button number one. The car fills with the sprightly strains of an early Beethoven piece. Name that tune, Manning tells himself—a challenge he's imposed upon himself since high school. It's the first piano concerto. Last movement. Piece of cake. He asks David, "Too loud?"

The kid laughs. "That'll put me to *sleep*."

A clock radio clicks on, blaring the final cadence of the Beethoven. "Good morning, friends." The radio's volume has been set far too high. An announcer shouts from the bedside table, "It's seven o'clock in Chicago. Sorry to report, we're in for another hot day, but cooler weather is due before the opening of this weekend's festivities. . . ."

Beneath a heap of disheveled bedding, Victor Uttley groans. The sheets thrash. A leg appears. Then a lanky arm. Fingers grope for the radio. They find the dial.

". . . ALREADY EIGHTY-NINE DEGREES AT O'HARE . . ."

Wrong way. The fingers race to counterspin the dial.

". . . humidity's a sticky ninety-six percent . . ."

Uttley's head peers out from under a pillow, surveying the room, squinting at the window, confirming that Tuesday has dawned. He tosses back the covers, sits up in bed, swings his feet to the floor, plants his elbows on his knees, winces at the contact with his Rollerblading injury, and holds his head in his hands. His willowy naked body is hairless and smooth, devoid of muscle tone.

In an ashtray on the nightstand rests his silver cigarette holder. He stands, picks up the holder, loads it with one of the long imported cigarettes he bought yesterday, lights it, and inhales his first drag of the morning. With his free hand splayed on his hip, the other poised before his mouth, he savors the tobacco that has kept him so lean—that, and the fact that his dead-end career as an actor has until recently necessitated the lifestyle of a starving artist. That's all changed, though, since the mayoral appointment. He's now a cultural liaison, whatever that is, and he's begun to enjoy some of the rewards of patronage. His pale body has even begun to sprout the curve of a belly, as though he may one day, months later, give birth to a volleyball. Victor Uttley smiles. Blue smoke whorls from the cracks of his ecru teeth.

He limps from the bedroom into the living room, headed for the kitchen. He's lived in his new apartment for only a few weeks. Owing to his new position, it was time to move up, so he took the cue literally and signed a lease on these high-rise quarters. It's a decent address, and he's on the top floor, but the view isn't much, dominated by another building across the street. The decorating is still sparse, and what old furniture he has is strictly thrift-shop. Leaning against a wall, not yet hung, are framed mementos—playbills, clippings, reviews—of his few acting triumphs. There's a consensus that he's able and talented enough onstage, but his height works against him. He was jilted a dozen years ago by a high-school sweetheart for the same reason; her head barely reached his shoulders.

In the kitchen, he fusses with a new machine, unboxed only yesterday, determined to enjoy a cup of real cappuccino. But he hasn't read the instructions (badly translated from Italian into ten other languages, including Japanese), and the gizmo won't froth. Uttley is growing frustrated—and a tad fearful that the damn thing might explode. The hell with it. He slams the cast-metal filter full of grounds into the sink, flicks his ashes into the drain, and draws a pot of water for his trusty Mr. Coffee.

While it brews, he traipses to the front door and cracks it open. Yes, the newspapers have arrived. He looks into the hall in both directions, opens the door wider, squats, and reaches over the threshold, wagging his butt. Got 'em. He shuts the door.

He places both papers—the *Journal* and its competitor, the tabloid *Post*—squarely, side by side, on the kitchen table. The front pages are predictable: hot-weather photos (kids opening hydrants, flesh on the beach), festival planning, Christian fundamentalists cooking up another protest. Uttley farts. He's not interested in news. He's looking for ads. He reaches, ready to riffle for them, but stops. This is important, a moment to relish. He's being too hasty. He ought to at least put something *on*.

He hobbles into the bedroom and flounces back wearing a luxurious dressing gown—not a plain old bathrobe, but a full-length dressing gown with wide quilted lapels. It's frayed here and there, stained as well, but it's gorgeous, it's . . . him.

Uttley turns the first page of the *Journal*. Then the next, and the next. He keeps flipping pages till he sees it, the latest in his series of full-color tributes to Chicago's hero of the hour. He leans close to scrutinize the tiny line of type at the bottom of the ad, making sure everything is spelled right. With a satisfied smile, he sets the *Journal* aside and sets to work on the *Post*. It doesn't take him long to find the second Zarnik ad. God, they're good. These will be framed, he decides. They will join the other scraps of newsprint on his wall of fame.

It's all too exciting. Uttley is wired, and he hasn't even had his coffee yet. He grabs the phone—a vintage baby-blue Princess with lighted rotary dial. He checks the time—there's a Kit-Cat Klock, rhinestone-studded, basic black, swiping its tail against the kitchen wall. Barely a quarter past seven. Too early? Nah. He looks up a number, dials, then waits while the other phone rings. Twice. Three times. "Actors . . ." he mutters. An answering machine clicks in, and Victor hangs up.

He has another idea. Picking through a pile of office work he dumped on the counter last night, he plucks a message slip, returns to the table, snaps up the Princess, and dials. The other phone rings once. Someone answers, "City room."

"I was phoning Mark Manning." Uttley has no idea whether the reporter would be at his desk so early—journalists keep odd hours—but he thought he'd give it a shot.

"He hasn't arrived yet. Is there someone else who can help you, or would you like to have his voice mail?"

"Voice mail, please."

There's a click, then Manning's recorded message, then the beep.

Uttley says into the phone, "Good morning, Mr. Manning—*Mark*—this is Victor Uttley with the mayor's office, returning your call. First off, a big thank-you to you and Neil for Saturday's party—it was fabulous, and the digs are to-die. Second, I stopped by to see you yesterday because we really need to talk, relating to Zarnik. Seems we're doomed to play phone tag. What else, alas, can I say? Except, of course, you're 'it.' Ta, now."

In a roadside shop near the Wisconsin shore of Lake Michigan, a couple of hundred miles north of Chicago, Mark Manning and

David Bosch are taking a break from their long drive. Manning is surprised to see cherries displayed among the produce, since they're not usually ripe till mid-July. Tasting one, he confirms that they're still sour, but he takes a quart anyway—a trip to the peninsula would be incomplete without cherries. He sets the box on the checkout counter, where a grandfatherly clerk stands ready to compute the "damages."

With the approach of the holiday, many people have chosen to book their summer vacation this week, which will be extended by a day. So there's steady traffic on the highway in both directions, and the shop is busy this morning, swamped with motorists from Door County, the peninsula of touristy-but-still-quaint villages that juts northward like a craggy thumb between Green Bay and the lake.

David mingles easily with the younger clientele, engaged in an enthusiastic commentary on the variety of fudge. Saran-wrapped bricks of the homemade confection are piled in wooden barrels that bear hand-lettered labels: *Walnut, Macadamia, Chunky Cherry, Double Chocolate, White Chocolate,* and so on. David is torn, but opts for the plain variety, *Classic Country Kitchen,* choosing a one-pound block of it from the barrel. Manning extends a hand, telling David, "I'll get it."

David gives Manning the fudge. "Thanks, Mark."

Manning hefts it in his palm. With a skeptical expression, he looks first at the fudge, then at David, whose body he studies with a gaze that travels from head to toe, returning to make contact with David's eyes. Manning says, "Given your obvious investment in time at the gym, I'd think *this* stuff would be a no-no."

"Sugar won't kill me, or you," says David. "It's all the other crap—preservatives and additives—that can really screw you. An occasional calorie-bomb isn't lethal, as long as you sweat it off later. But hey," David aborts his nutrition lecture, clapping a hefty arm across Manning's shoulder, "I hardly need to preach to *you* about diet. You're as fit as they get."

"For a doddering geezer," Manning jokes, enjoying the flattery, fishing for more.

"Right," says David, holding Manning's shoulder at arm's length, returning his up-and-down body check. "Some geezer." Then he pulls Manning close for a side-to-side hug. It's the kind of public jock-gesture at which David excels, totally at ease with this display of affection, in touch with his own physical nature.

Manning recognizes that David's self-confidence, his gregarious manner, has been spawned by the attractiveness that was his luck of the draw from the gene pool. People want to be near him. Strangers readily offer a smile, hoping he will deign to return it. He has never had to think twice about approaching others with a question or a joke or a flirtation—they always respond, and he has never learned to fear rejection. Of *course* he exudes self-confidence, and that assurance has fed upon itself over the years, shaping a young man whose bodily charms have been honed by training and complemented by a quick intellect. He is truly a golden child, one in a million, whom the world will emulate, envy, and revere.

Why then, Manning wonders, has David been so reticent to deal more openly with his own sexuality? Can it be explained by a single factor so simple as a disapproving uncle? Surely not. Or is David now grappling with the same insecurities that Manning fought and conquered only two years ago? Manning has never know the open arms of the adoring world that David's out-and-out beauty is heir to, but Manning has feared the exact same labels that David cannot fathom applied to himself. For the first time in his life, David is dealing with the fear of rejection, and for someone who has never, *ever* known that fear, the stakes are high indeed.

In reaching this plausible understanding of the dilemma that David faces, Manning feels a rush of sympathy for the kid. He wishes he could help assuage the fears that tug at David's still-young psyche. He also recognizes the sublime irony of these emotions—that he should condescend to pity the golden child from his own enlightened middle-age perspective.

Without a qualm, he returns David's shoulder hug. In the milling activity of the shop this morning, no one notices the uncharacteristic ease with which Manning has indulged in this minor but public display of affection. No one cares that he has crossed another hurdle in a lifelong race for emotional maturity. No one—least of all David—can appreciate the significance of this exchange.

Waiting in line to pay, Manning says to David, "You were right. It's been a long drive. If you'd like to take over at the wheel, be my guest."

Does David want to drive? Needless question. He answers by slipping his fingers into Manning's pants pocket and extracting the keys. It isn't time to leave yet, but he wants to hold them in his hand—now. He wants to possess them.

He'll soon put the keys to use. The couple in front of them load a bag with cheese and trinkets for their trip. They're college kids, a guy and a girl. He wears an Illinois sweatshirt, knee-length jeans, and sandals with socks. A tattoo, a big one, wraps around his right calf. It looks like an eagle, or maybe an Indian war bonnet, but it's impossible to be sure, since the whole image cannot be seen from one angle.

David notices Manning eyeing the decorated leg. He turns his head to whisper in Manning's ear, "Gross, huh?" Manning laughs his agreement.

The man behind the counter finally sends the tattooed student and his companion on their way. Manning and David step forward with their fudge, and Manning reminds the proprietor of the cherries, already parked there. "No tax on the produce," says the old man, thinking aloud, "but the governor gets five percent on the fudge." He pulls a figure out of thin air, Manning pays him, and David picks up the brown paper bag, fondling the keys in his other hand.

Outdoors, walking to the car, Manning notes, "It's a lot cooler up here." Indeed, the jet stream that's working its way south toward Chicago has already dipped into Wisconsin, bringing with it drier air and a blue sky without haze. A breeze carries the scent of pine.

David eagerly opens the driver's door and sits behind the wheel, setting the brown bag in back, on the floor. By the time Manning opens the passenger door for himself, David is busy readjusting the seat, mirrors, and steering wheel. With both authority and childlike anticipation, he inserts the key and turns the ignition. With a whir of the engine and the chiming of various system checks, the car comes to life. David just sits there, both hands stuck to the wheel, savoring a moment he has longed for.

"Whenever you're ready. . . ." Manning tells him.

David needs no further prompting. He shifts into drive and steers Manning's black sedan out of the gravel parking lot and onto the highway. "Awesome," he says—there's no other word that suits the experience, and he offers no apology for it.

Any apprehensions Manning felt about letting David drive are soon overcome, and he gets comfortable—for the first time—as a passenger in his own car. He sees that David's manner behind the wheel is conscientious and mature, revealing a facet of the young man's personality that Manning might not otherwise have discovered. He glances at his watch. It's just past ten-thirty. They should arrive in Baileys Harbor within an hour or so. The time will pass agreeably, Manning decides, and he considers the possibility of napping during this last leg of the journey.

Oddly, though, Manning finds he is no longer tired. The cooler weather, the wooded scenery, the ability to relax and not concentrate on the road—all these factors have made him alert and conscious of his surroundings. What's more, there's something in the back of his mind that needs attention, some bit of unfinished business. Several miles pass in silence as he mulls the gnawing thought. Damn. He'd like to set it aside, forget it, but he just can't put a period on it.

"Ah!" he says.

David, startled, looks at Manning, breaking his steady gaze on the road. The car swerves, but its course is quickly righted.

"Sorry," Manning explains, "but I was trying to think of something. It just came to me."

"Care to share it?" asks David, eyes ahead.

"Yes, actually. It's about you. Back in the shop, seeing that guy's tattooed leg reminded me of a discussion you and I had at the party last Saturday."

"Oh?" David pretends not to recall it.

"Don't be coy now. You did your share of teasing that night. We were talking about the popularity of tattoos among young people, and you dismissed the fad as kids' stuff, informing me that you were 'into' something else entirely. If your intention was to tantalize me, you've succeeded. So 'fess up. What is it?"

David smiles. He turns just long enough to look Manning in the eye and tells him, "Body piercing."

"What?" Manning wasn't prepared for that, not by a long shot. He thought, more than likely, drugs. That's something David would be reluctant to discuss with an older coworker. If not drugs, then Manning might have guessed some playful but kinky fetish—ladies' underwear maybe. Well, maybe not. But body piercing? Manning stares at David. There's no apparent trace of this interest, not even a single dot in his earlobe.

"*Where?*"

David doesn't move his eyes from the road. The pause is not a reluctant one, but intended to deliver maximum impact. "Nipples."

Ouch. "Both?"

David nods. "I had the first one done, the left one, a few years ago, one summer during college. Some of the guys were doing it, and I thought, Why not? It took some getting used to, but I eventually came to like it. More important, *other* people seem to like it. And because they don't see it till . . . well, till clothes start coming off, it always brings an element of surprise to the situation."

"I'll bet," says Manning. "Your pierced nipple becomes a conversation piece—something to talk about, like the weather."

David laughs. "Yeah, you could say that. Anyway, I figured, if this doesn't work out, it's easily removed, and the hole eventually fills in again—I'd be done with it, no permanent scars. But I found that I really liked the look and the feel of it, plus it had that unexpected payoff with other friends at the right moment.

"There was one minor problem, though. I always felt sort of 'unbalanced' by it. I've worked hard on my body, and the symmetry was shot. This bothered me so much, I finally decided I'd have to either undo the left nipple or get the right one pierced too. So, a few weeks ago, nipple number two got the treatment. I feel much better about myself now."

This is all too bizarre. Manning still suspects it's a joke, but he hasn't heard the punch line yet. He says, "I'm not at all sure I believe you."

David says nothing. Instead, he removes his left hand from the wheel and places it over his right breast. He splays his index and middle fingers, stretching the piqué of his polo shirt over his nipple. Sure enough, there's a peculiar bulge beneath the fabric. It looks like something man-made, something like hardware.

Okay, Manning believes his own eyes. He's surprised to realize that he's highly intrigued—and a bit aroused—by this revelation. "Are they, uh, rings?"

"The new one is." David pats his right breast. "But the first one is something like a little barbell, which required a bigger hole. It hurt like hell and took forever to heal. I didn't want to go through *that* again, so I chose a simple ring the second time. It's already healed."

Manning is so amazed by this story—it's the last thing he expected to discuss this morning—all he can say is "This I've got to see."

Though Manning has spoken figuratively, David takes him at his word and, without hesitation, begins pulling his shirt out of his pants. The car swerves.

"Whoa"—Manning reaches to steady the wheel—"that can wait." Once David has control of the car again, Manning adds, "I do want you to show me. But later."

"Just say when." David is clearly pleased that he's sparked Manning's interest.

He's sparked more than that. David's story has affected his listener in many ways. Manning is surprised—he just wasn't prepared to hear these things. He's amused—it's all so goofy, a kid thing. He's intrigued—what would compel this levelheaded young man to willingly endure, twice, the pain of self-mutilation? And Manning is, by now, the more he ponders these things, highly aroused.

Needing to sort this out, he says to David, "I'm curious. You've had some body piercing done because, at least partly, it's a fad, pure and simple. And you've said you like the way it looks, so there's an element of . . . let's say, 'aesthetics.' But you could have pierced your ears, or your nose, or any number of places, but you opted for the nipples, and you said that you also like the way it *feels*. It sounds as if this goes way beyond fad or fashion. It sounds as if you get an erotic charge out of it."

David's grin confirms that Manning has nailed the issue. He admits, "There's definitely that edge, yes."

Manning turns to peer vacantly through the side window. He puckers his lips, exhaling a silent whistle. Giant pines, responding to his call, march from the cool shadows to the edge of the roadway like a wall of quiet sentries. Their frilly-skirted greatcoats rush past the car in a bluish blur.

Professor Zarnik checks his watch. It's eleven o'clock, and he quickens his pace. Even though he keeps his own schedule at the planetarium, he knows that he slept too late and dawdled too long at home this morning. Traversing the long hallway, he stops just long enough to drop some change into a gaudy vending machine. With a *ka-chunk*, a can of Diet Rite lands in the black plastic trough near his knees. Already burdened with two tote bags and a smaller sack containing his lunch, he struggles to consolidate the load in one arm. While he stoops to pluck the can with his free hand, his chrome whistle swings on its chain, clattering against the fluorescent-lit front panel of the machine. Wet with condensation, the chilled can slips from his fingers. Skittering to pick it up, he kicks it, sending it rolling down the hall in the direction of his laboratory door.

"Let me help you with that, Professor," says a young lady, stifling a laugh as she approaches from the opposite direction. They meet in front of the lab door, where she crouches to retrieve the cola. In her other hand, she carries a sheaf of pink message slips. "I heard you were in the building," she tells him, "and wanted to make sure you got these. Some of them look important." She wags the chits. "They really piled up yesterday. I'd have put them on your desk, but you've got the only key."

"Thank you, Miss Jenner, most kind." His funny little accent delights the woman. He puts his key in the lock and opens the door a crack. "I regret to become such a nuisance, but could I ask you to screen my calls again today? I have entered a critical phase of my research, and it is important that I not be disturbed."

"Certainly, Professor." She giggles.

"Good of you to look after me." He takes the messages from her, slips into his lab, and tries nudging the door closed.

"Wait, Professor"—Miss Jenner thrusts a hand through the narrowing crack—"your soda!"

"Ah, clumsy me." He takes the can, nods a smile, and pushes the door shut.

Inside, the room is lit by a dim security light. The rows of computers, the multitude of monitors, and the various other electronics scattered about the lab are all still—no humming, whirring, winks, or flashes. Zarnik flips a bank of switches adjacent to the door, near the fire cabinet. Overhead lighting flickers on, filling the room with its cold, sterile energy. The equipment remains dark.

He crosses to the desk and sets down his things, putting his lunch bag with the cola off to one side, the messages near the phone. Propping his tote bags on the chair, he removes paperwork from the first—a stack of computer printout, various magazines that include *People* and *Buzz*, and the morning editions of both the *Journal* and the *Post*. From the second, he removes half a dozen Blockbuster videotape cases. These he stacks atop the VCR that he has used to demonstrate his "graphic realization."

Zarnik tosses the totes onto the floor and plops into the chair, sliding the phone and the pink slips in front of him. He puts on his reading glasses, looks at the top message, and heaves a weary sigh. Pausing a moment, he reaches to open the desk's file drawer. Inside is a two-liter bottle of Jack Daniel's. He lifts it from the drawer, removes the cap, and downs an eye-opening swig. Shaking his head and flapping his lips, horselike, he recaps the Jack and plunks it on the desk next to his bagged peanut butter sandwich.

Sorting through the message slips, he arranges two piles. The shorter stack, only three, are calls he must return. The deeper pile consists of messages from the press—local television, national newsmagazines, and scientific journals worldwide. One by one, he crumples the press queries and lobs them blindly, backwards, over his head. There's a wastebasket against the far wall, but the little pink projectiles don't even come near it, falling randomly, ticking upon impact with the cement floor.

The reason there are so many messages is that Zarnik didn't come in at all yesterday. He had thoroughly enjoyed Saturday night's party, and Sunday's hangover was, in the imaginary parlance of his assumed homeland, a *drechtzyl*. He awoke dry-mouthed around noon with a headache that left him longing for death. Searching his apartment for aspirin, finding none, he asked himself, What would Dr. Zarnik do? Certain that the ancient bromide regarding "the hair of the dog" must trace its roots to Eastern Europe ("the hair of the *gmuut*"), the course to his cure was clear. Jack and Coke to the rescue. But he had not done his weekly shopping on Saturday—the breaking news of his discovery had kept him busy at the planetarium all day—so there was no cola, diet or otherwise, among the sparse supplies in his pantry. No problem. It wasn't the pop that bit him. Jack did it. And Zarnik was always careful to keep plenty of Jack on hand.

By Sunday evening, though, Jack was long gone, and Zarnik awoke sometime Monday with the mother of all *drechtzyls*. Fruitlessly searching his apartment again for aspirin, he asked himself, What would Dr. Kevorkian do? While clever enough to pose the question, he hadn't the courage to answer it, so he unplugged his phone and took to his bed.

Now, Tuesday morning, the crisis has largely passed, and Zarnik feels a sense of accomplishment in being up, dressed, and seated at his desk before noon. To his credit, he hides the residual hangover well, due largely to the fact that the astronomer *always* looks as if he slept in his clothes. He's also pleased at the efficiency with which he has dispatched so many inconsequential messages that accumulated yesterday. But the time has arrived to deal with those remaining calls, the three important ones that must be answered.

The first is from the mayor's office, asking Zarnik to return the call. There's no message, only a phone number, but he assumes they simply want to make sure he has seen the new ad campaign. Indeed he has—those ads provided the only bright spot in his dismal Monday, and the new ones that appeared this morning helped to get him out of bed and send him on his way. He opens both newspapers on his desk to peruse them again. He slips off his glasses and stands, stepping back a foot to enjoy their impact. Marvelous!

He sits again, reaches for the phone, and dials the number on the slip, eager to express his gratitude.

The other phone rings. A man answers, "Cultural liaison's office."

"Yes, hello. Dr. Pavo Zarnik here, returning your call. Might this pertain to the beautiful advertisements that grace my desk this morning?"

"Indeed it does ... *Professor.*" The response has a twisted, cynical inflection.

Undaunted, Zarnik continues. "I'm flattered beyond measure, of course, and wish to thank whoever is responsible."

There's a pause. *"I'm* responsible, Arlen. Can't you read?"

Zarnik yelps, dropping the receiver as if it had bitten him. It lands near the bottom of the *Journal's* open page, emitting bitsy bursts of laughter. Zarnik fumbles with his glasses and leans close to read the tiny type of the ad's credit line. Victor Uttley's cackling pours from the phone. Horrified, Zarnik watches the laughter spill like mire upon the page, despoiling the tribute with its mockery. The crowing breaks off long enough for a little voice to call from the receiver, "Arlen! Still there?"

With a gingerly touch, Zarnik picks up the phone. It's worth a try. *"Pfroobst!"* he says, feigning anger, laying on the accent. "I have never heard such rudeness. You surely mistake me for another party."

"Cut the crap." Uttley's voice is calm and emotionless. "It's been quite a performance, Arlen Farber, but the curtain is about to fall. Unless . . ."

One more try. "I do not know what you talk about."

"Then let me spell it out. You have been posing for some weeks now as Pavo Zarnik, an astrophysicist, and you have made recent claims of a discovery that has generated widespread interest among the press, the public, and even the military. But in fact, you are not Zarnik. You are Arlen Farber, an actor who's enjoyed reasonably steady work over the years, but who still awaits his 'big break.' I, Victor Uttley, know you well. About five years ago, we were cast together in a couple of summer-stock productions in New England—Are the pieces falling in place now, Arlen? After that run, I returned home to Chicago, and you, as I recall, got into the dinner-theater circuit down in Florida. We didn't cross paths again till that party on Saturday night. I don't think you saw me—if you did, you didn't recognize me—but I saw you. *Everyone* had their eyes on you, Mr. Instant Celebrity. I intended to approach you, to tell you about the ad series I was planning, so I waited while you hobnobbed with Claire Gray, whom I was *dying* to spend some more time with—but you hogged her most of the evening. As I waited, watching, I kept thinking that I already knew you, but that was impossible, since we had presumably never met. And I found it strange that you had taken such an interest in Claire Gray, her theatrical background being so removed from the career of a foreign astronomer. And then, well, it clicked. So tell me, Arlen—how'd you fall into *this* gig?"

The man posing as Zarnik drops his accent and says into the phone, "I admit nothing. Tell me what you want."

Victor Uttley overplays a chummy tone. "I want to know how you've *been*, Arlen. I want to know how you managed to parlay a third-rate acting career into a stint as director of Civic Planetarium. I'd also like to know how you think you can possibly get away with this. And naturally, I'm curious about the whereabouts of the *real* Dr. Zarnik. But most important, I'm wondering what it's worth to you if I keep all these questions to myself."

Arlen Farber repeats, "Tell me what you want, Victor."

"Ten."

"Ten what?"

"Grand."

Now it's Arlen Farber's turn to laugh. "For Christ's sake, Victor, you sound like a small-time hood. 'Ten grand,' indeed. What have *you* been up to—rehearsing a two-bit role in some off-Loop mob-land melodrama?"

"Really, Arlen." Uttley is getting testy. "Ten thousand dollars—is that better? Precise and proper? However you say it, it's still the price. Or else."

Farber laughs louder than before. "There you go again, Victor. 'Or else.' Big man. Big threat. Or else what?"

"Or else I'll tell Mark Manning everything I know."

That catches Farber's attention. He doesn't respond.

"I called him at the newsroom ten minutes ago. Turns out, he's not in town today, but he knows I need to talk to him. I'm sure he'll see me. Soon."

Farber needs to explore his options, to weigh Uttley's leverage. "I'm not sure I can do what you're asking. If I can't, and if you talk to Manning, then it's over—and there's nothing in it for you."

Uttley has planned this conversation carefully, and his tone conveys confidence. "If I tip Manning off, there'll be a big, splashy exposé, and I'm the source, the hero. It'll look great for the mayor's office, and I'll be sitting pretty for the next thirty years or so. If, on the other hand, you 'collaborate' with me, I'll simply tell Manning what a splendid job he's done of reporting your discovery, how it's a boon to the city, how the mayor's pleased as punch—the usual crap. The ads I'm running will reinforce all this, and the mayor already *is* pleased as punch. Plus, I can turn a little profit on the side. *Comprenez?* Either way, I win."

Farber has little room to wriggle. "I'll have to make a few phone calls."

"I bet you will. So get cracking."

"Hold on, Victor. Some details: When do you need it?"

"No rush. End of the week. Let's say Friday—payday."

"Cash, check, or credit card?"

"Don't be funny."

"How do we get it to you?"

Uttley hasn't considered the logistics. "Uh . . ."

"Shame on you, Victor. The serious extortionist is always prepared for—how do you quaintly phrase it?—'the drop.' "

"First things first. You let me know when, and I'll tell you where."

Farber tells him, "I can't make any promises, but I'll do my best."

"You'd better," Uttley growls (with attempted menace but lacking impact—he was never much at Method acting), and he slams down the phone.

"Grrr . . . !" Arlen Farber mocks Uttley's bravado, slamming his own phone. The slimy dweeb, the very idea! He rips the Zarnik ads from both papers and crumples them into a single wad, which he serves like a volleyball, hurtling it to the ceiling. The mashed newsprint glances off a light fixture and plummets behind a stack of electronic equipment.

That was an unexpected crimp in Farber's morning. He uncaps the Jack Daniel's and takes a swig, then turns his attention to the two remaining messages. One is from Manning, but Uttley just said the reporter is out of town today, so there's no point in calling him. The other slip contains only a phone number, no name, no message. Farber recognizes the number—it's a pager— and yes, they need to talk. He picks up the phone, punches in the number. He hears three short beeps, then punches in his own number and hangs up.

He waits, checks his watch. It's not yet noon, but he decides to get his lunch ready. Opening the brown paper bag, he removes the sandwich, unfolds the waxed paper, and smooths it before him on the desk. He picks up half of the sandwich, sliced neatly on the diagonal, and swipes the cut edge beneath his nose, as if sniffing a wine cork or a fine cigar. His eyelids flutter as he inhales the musky rush of peanut butter. Then he lifts the Diet Rite from the pool of its own sweat—the can isn't cold anymore, barely cool—and pops it open, swallowing three big gulps. Farber isn't thirsty; he's making room in the can. He steadies the jug of Jack

Daniel's over the can and drizzles booze through the hole. He reminds himself that he really ought to bring a glass from home.

The phone rings. Farber spatters whiskey on his sandwich. He answers the phone. "Yes?"

The other voice echoes, "Yes?"

"Zarnik here."

"Where the hell have you been, Farber? I tried reaching you all day yesterday."

He hesitates. "Something came up—at home. I didn't get your message till now."

"Not a minute too soon," the other voice tells him. "You've been booked for a special performance this afternoon, a 'matinee,' so to speak—"

"Listen," Farber interrupts, "we've got a problem. A big one."

An impatient sigh. "And what might that be?"

"Someone in the mayor's office recognized me. We once worked together." Farber recounts the call from Victor Uttley, concluding, "He wants ten thousand dollars, or he's taking the whole story to Mark Manning."

"Ten? He's undersold himself. Pity he doesn't know who he's dealing with."

Farber swirls the cola can, mixing his cocktail. "This is only the beginning, I'm sure. He'll be back for more."

"That's what you think." The voice snorts. "That's what *he* thinks. When does he want it?"

"Friday."

"Perfect. A cheap price for a bit of time, which is all we need, really. A week from now, this character's threats will be decidedly irrelevant."

Farber drinks from the can. "I don't know what you mean."

"You're not supposed to, remember? Just keep up the act—you're being well paid for this role. As I said before, you've got a command performance this afternoon."

"I do, huh?" He covers the phone, aiming his mouth sideways to belch.

"Be at the new Gethsemane Arms Hotel at three. You'll be

expected at the penthouse suite, the temporary encampment of the CFC."

"*What?* The Christian Family Crusade? What in hell do *they* want?"

"As you probably know, they've set up temporary headquarters in Chicago to mount their protest of that gay-rights rally at Celebration Two Thousand. As long as their board is in town, they're screening some political candidates—local would-bes and other hopefuls—for recommendation to their membership."

"What's that got to do with me?"

"Very little, actually. But all the recent publicity has raised concerns about the anti-fundamentalist implications of Zarnik's 'discovery.' They want to question you."

"Now look"—another slurp—"I'm getting a little tired of all these extra demands. Playing the role is one thing, but there's been way too much dirty work, *serious* dirty work, that we never agreed to."

The other voice commiserates, "I know, I know. Just play along with the CFC. Be respectful. Try not to rile them. We don't need to incite a religious war over this. Let's just buy a little time."

Farber sets his can down. He asks point-blank, "What are we buying time *for?* What exactly is this all about?"

"Tut-tut. That's off-limits. All you need to know is that, for now, you *are* Pavo Zarnik. And Zarnik's mandate is to convince the world, through Mark Manning, that he has discovered a tenth planet. Understood?"

"Yeah yeah yeah." Farber thinks of something. "Manning has been trying to reach me. I'm sure he wants to follow up on those technical points I couldn't provide last week. I need some help here."

The other voice is assuring. "Say no more. We'll get you the information. And we'll get you some cash, the 'loot' for Uttley. Now remember, Gethsemane Arms at three." And the other voice clicks off.

Farber sets the receiver back on the phone. It's almost noon. He has nearly three hours to kill before leaving for his meeting—

and he knows exactly how to spend it. Plucking a cassette from the pile of videos, he switches on the VCR and removes the tape that was in it, labeled *planet demo*, tossing it to the far side of the desk. He loads the new tape.

Then he scurries behind the desk to turn on the television monitor and position its wheeled cart so the screen aims squarely at his chair. When the picture tube warms up, those white crosshairs still run through its center. He's dealt with this before, without success. Once again he twiddles a few knobs on the back of the set, pounds the cabinet, but it's no use—the crosshairs remain. He'll have to live with them for the next two hours and twenty minutes, but it's a small annoyance that he will gladly endure.

Seating himself, Farber leans forward to tap the "play" button. A few seconds later, he hears the fanfare and sees the spotlights on the Twentieth Century-Fox logo. It's an old one. It's black-and-white. It's . . . *All About Eve*. God, what a magnificent film, even on its umpteenth viewing. It'll be fifty years old next year, made shortly after Farber was born—he wishes *he'd* aged so well.

He pushes his chair back, plops his feet on the desk, and watches the opening scene, the awards ceremony, narrated by George Sanders as that sleazebag critic Addison DeWitt. He loves the way the movie freeze-frames on Anne Baxter, Eve, just as she reaches for the award. Then begins the flashback that tells the whole story.

From one hand, Arlen Farber munches the peanut butter sandwich. From the other, he sips Jack and Diet Rite. Celeste Holm, wearing a big mink, has just bumped into Baxter—dear, sweet, innocent, unspoiled, youthful, star-struck Eve—skulking around like a drowned rat in the drizzle outside the theater, hoping to get a glimpse of Bette Davis. It doesn't get much better than this.

Ah, the rigors of astrophysical research.

Manning and David are running a few minutes late. They had no difficulty finding their way to Baileys Harbor, a little town on the lake side, the quiet east side, of the Door County peninsula, but they took a wrong turn in search of the road that leads them miles beyond town to the secluded resort. They think they've got their bearings now, but it's difficult to be sure—the winding road provides no sense of direction, and there's nothing in sight but pine trees. "There's a sign," says David, leaning forward to peer over the wheel. "We made it."

As they turn onto the property, the dashboard clock flashes noon. The long, narrow driveway, deeply shaded by the towering pines, leads at last to a clearing. There are tennis courts to one side, the lodge ahead, water beyond. Everything has a rather dated/modern look—its heyday must have been in the fifties—but the grounds and buildings have been meticulously maintained. And the place seems to draw a well-heeled clientele, judging by the caliber of cars parked here and there. Not among those cars, however, is Carl Creighton's new roadster, so Roxanne predicted correctly—he's gone.

The main lodge is situated on a point of land that juts into the water. Lake Michigan laps against the outer shore, while a smaller inlet, a bay, forms the inner shore. Cabins are tucked among the trees along both shores. At a glance, they appear comfortable, slightly rustic, and totally private.

While checking in at the main desk in the lodge, Manning asks David, "Should we phone Roxanne here and now, or do you want to get settled first?"

"Excuse me," says the clerk, "but Miss Exner isn't in her cabin at the moment. She asked me to tell you that she's arranged for lunch. She'll stop by for you."

David shrugs. "That answers that. Let's check out the cabin and put away our stuff."

The clerk points the way—they'll be on the bay side—and within a few minutes, Manning's car pulls into a shady clearing just a few feet from the cabin's door. David bounds from the car, his steps cushioned by a mat of fallen pine needles, and unlocks the door with a key that's attached to a well-worn plastic hotel fob. There are none of those newfangled magnetic-strip key cards with blinking doorknobs up here. Security just isn't much of an issue.

"Hey," David calls from inside as Manning grabs their duffles and a garment bag from the trunk, "you've gotta see this." David returns to the door and takes the baggage from Manning, who then enters the cabin.

Stepping into the first bedroom is like stepping into a time warp, replete with knotty-pine paneling, white chenille bedspreads, and woven rag rugs. David has rushed ahead to the living room. "Too cool!"

Joining him there, Manning silently shares David's reaction. There's a stone fireplace in the corner, its grate freshly heaped with logs, kindling, and newspaper, ready for the match. There's comfortable stuffed furniture, all vaguely "colonial," and the obligatory television, fly swatter, bar setup, and a clunky beige phone with a domed red light for messages. But the focal point of the room is its oversized picture window, which looks onto the water, only a few yards away. The uninterrupted curve of forest around the bay, the overhead sweep of cloudless sapphire sky, the balsams framing the view just outside the window—it's almost absurdly cliché and postcard-perfect, but there it is. Right on cue, a family of ducks paddles past. "God," Manning muses, "now I understand why people are willing to make the drive."

David is near the bar, squinting at a framed map of the area. "That water out there—guess what they call it." He laughs. "Moonlight Bay."

Manning turns to him. "Not terribly original."

"No," David agrees, "but very romantic."

"So," says Manning, ignoring David's comments, "let's see the rest."

There's another bedroom, identical to the first but on the opposite end of the cabin, which they arbitrarily decide will be David's. In a center hall there's a closet and a door that leads to the bathroom, which is bigger and more modern (there's a whirlpool) than Manning would have expected, surely a recent upgrade intended to lure jaded city folk.

Someone raps at the screen door. "Hey, guys. Anybody home?"

"Back here, Roxanne," Manning calls to her. "Come on in."

Roxanne waltzes into the cabin, meeting Manning and David in the living room. "Welcome to Wisconsin," she singsongs, kissing Manning's cheek. She turns to David. "David Bosch, correct?" He looks surprised. She explains, "I remember you from the party Saturday."

Chagrined, David tells her, "I'm afraid I don't remember much of that party, but I hear it was a blast." He shakes her hand. "Miss Exner, I presume?"

"Roxanne," she insists. Her demure tone, Manning notes with wry amusement, reveals that her thoughts of the young reporter have already turned torrid.

"You're certainly in a chipper mood," Manning tells her. "After that message you left, I was braced for the worst."

"I apologize for all the theatrics, but I do have some serious concerns. I'm anxious to share them—you'll understand why I was so rattled."

"But you said you were *afraid.*"

"Oh, that." She tosses her hands in the air, dismissing some imagined bugaboo. "I had a rather sudden, severe reaction to all the pollen or sap or whatever up here. Luckily, I brought my antihistamines, and they've got me back in shape, but I guess I overdid it. They can really wack you out—I got paranoid."

"Then you're not in danger?" David asks.

"No." She pauses in thought. "I don't think so. Certainly not at the moment."

"I'm relieved to hear that," Manning tells her, "but we've traveled a long way. So: What's the story? And it better be juicy."

"I can't tell you *here,*" she says, as if he should know better.

"We've already driven two hundred miles." He sounds testy. "Where, then?"

She jerks her head toward the window. "Out there."

In unison, the guys turn their heads, looking out over the bay. They exchange a quizzical glance.

"On the *water,*" she amplifies. "I've arranged for a charming little lunch on this adorable little boat—I think it's a punt or something. It'll be totally private, and we can talk dirt in detail."

David breaks into a broad smile and wraps an arm around her

shoulder. He tells Manning, "Story or no story, I like the way this woman thinks."

Manning allows a smile as well. It's been a long morning, and he's hungry. "Were you able to arrange for a decent bottle of wine?" he asks her.

"Of course," she snorts, nettled that he would even ask. "I'll stick to iced tea, but you boys can lap it up."

Manning tells David, "Hope you brought your sea legs, matey." And the three head out the door, not bothering to lock up. As they walk past the car, Manning remembers, "Dessert." He opens the back door and retrieves the fudge and cherries.

The resort dock isn't far. Strolling toward the main lodge, they pass the dining building. Across from it, on the upper floor of a boathouse, there's a cocktail lounge called the Top Deck. "It draws a pretty old crowd," laments Roxanne, "more like the Poop Deck." They walk past a swimming pool and a shuffleboard area, toward the water. Even though it's the height of vacation season, there aren't many people around—during the day, guests of the lodge usually drive over to the more active villages on the Green Bay side of the peninsula or perhaps drive up to the tip and ferry out to Washington Island.

Ahead, moored along a cement pier, the rented boat bobs on the placid surface of Moonlight Bay. It's not a punt, but a lavishly appointed pontoon boat, sporting a circus-striped canopy. Roxanne's arrangements have been carried out to the letter, and an attendant fusses with something on board. "Ahoy!" she calls to him.

"All set, Miss Exner," he tells her as the threesome steps aboard. "Who wants to play captain?"

David readily volunteers, ever-eager to drive—and in fact, the controls resemble those of a car. The boatman explains their operation, which seems simple enough, and cautions them to stay inside the bay, avoiding the choppier waters of Lake Michigan itself. He reviews with Roxanne details of their catered lunch, which is stored in several Styrofoam chests. "Have fun," he tells them. "Stay out as long as you like. I'll be back to help you dock when I see you heading in." And he saunters off down the pier toward the lodge.

Donning a pair of big white-framed sunglasses, Roxanne asks the guys, "Am I good, or what?"

"Damn," Manning concedes, "you *are* good."

As Roxanne strikes a self-satisfied pose, reclining on a canvas-upholstered chaise longue, David gets the feel of the controls, and they shove off, headed straight for the center of the bay.

It's a perfect summer day with a brilliant noontide sun. Deep waters surrounding the peninsula cool the breeze that waggles the fringe of the boat's canopy. The drone of the engine seems restful and comforting, adding to the scene's pervasive, almost palpable serenity—a stunning contrast to the heat, grime, and tensions of the city they have left behind. Manning wishes that Neil could have made the trip with him, that they could share this sublime experience. For the moment, Manning couldn't care less about Nolan's murder, Zarnik's ruse, or Roxanne's mysterious discovery.

As the boat reaches the middle of the bay, David cuts the engine, and they begin drifting in a silence broken only by the distant call of a loon. Water plays beneath the two long, sausage-shaped pontoons—the boat lifts and falls, lifts and falls, rocked like a cradle at sea. They are perhaps a half mile from land, with the mouth of the bay and the grounds of the lodge behind them. The shore is otherwise undeveloped. Nothing stirs in the woods that surround them. The sweep of trees is interrupted only by the occasional protrusion of rickety fishing piers, probably abandoned.

Manning tells Roxanne, "If your idea was to provide absolute seclusion for the telling of your tale, you've succeeded. No 'ears to the keyhole' out here."

She feigns a serious tone. "One can't be too cautious." Then she laughs. "I just thought this would be . . . *nice.*"

"That it is," David assures her, moving from the captain's chair and sitting next to Manning at a low table across from Roxanne's chaise. He's within reach of one of the coolers, so he asks, "Shall I serve?"

Roxanne suggests, "Let's just relax over a drink first, and I'll tell you why I dragged you up here." She turns to Manning. "It's all rather troubling. I hate to spoil such a pleasant afternoon, but you do need to know about this."

"That's what we're here for," Manning tells her. David sets glasses on the table, pours iced tea for Roxanne, and hands Manning the bottle of wine—Far Niente, a first-rate chardonnay. Manning is impressed. He sets to work with the corkscrew, saying to Roxanne, "Let's hear your story."

She sits up on the chaise and leans toward them, as if to tighten their circle of conversation. She tastes the tea, swallows, pauses. Then she begins: "Carl Creighton and I have know each other for five or six years, since I entered the law firm. He had some say in hiring me, and it was on the basis of his recommendation three years ago that I got an early promotion to partner—the first woman to hold that rank in an esteemed (and I daresay crusty) old firm. I've always had profound respect for his skills and intelligence, his ethics and good nature. It's safe to say that the admiration was mutual."

She pauses. Manning has the wine open, and he pours a glass for David and himself. The three exchange a silent toast.

Roxanne continues, "From the start, then, our relationship had always been friendly, but it was strictly professional—till last year, when his marriage broke up. Shortly after the divorce, he asked me to dinner one night. His manner was bashful and self-conscious that evening, which is totally out of character for him, so I knew something was up, something personal. And it was. He asked if we might begin to 'see each other socially.' If that worked out, we might 'move on to the next phase.'

"I was floored. Carl had been something of a father figure to me. The notion of 'dating Dad' had never crossed my mind, but it had a certain appeal. After all, we already *liked* each other, and we had everything in common professionally. We were—what?— *simpatico*. And if I had any reservations about his being twelve years older, that was more than compensated for by his middle-age charm, his good looks, and—I confess it—his wealth."

Manning sips his wine, saying, "Calculating broad." He smiles.

She throws a napkin at him. "And it *did* work out. We're great together. The office doesn't seem to mind; neither do the clients. We're practically living together now, which brings us to the next phase. . . ."

"The *m*-word," Manning volunteers.

"We're openly discussing it, yes. Carl's ready. I need some time to get more comfortable with the idea, but it's clear enough where we're headed—unless, of course, something throws a wrench in the works."

Manning sets down his glass, leaning forward. "Your phone message sounded as though you may have found that wrench."

David also leans forward, closing their circle. "How does this relate to Zarnik?"

She tells him, "Patience, my young friend. We're getting there. The point, so far, is that I have come to know this man intimately, not only in the carnal sense, but in every facet of his life—his work, his past, his views, his politics, you name it. I know Carl Creighton inside out. Or at least I *thought* I did, till yesterday."

"After breakfast," recalls Manning, "when he got that phone message."

"Right. That, I'm afraid, was the turning point. Whoever it was, Carl returned the call from the car so I wouldn't hear it, then at lunch, he announced that he had to run back to the city today—with overblown apologies, but without a word of explanation."

Manning absentmindedly rubs the tip of his middle finger around the rim of his wineglass. "That's when I would have asked what was going on."

"Well, I didn't. Naturally, I expected him to offer some sort of reason, however lame, but his manner was so baldly evasive, it was clear that I was supposed to play along and not ask questions. As it turns out, I didn't need to. Soon enough, I made a startling discovery."

"What?" asks David. He, too, rubs the rim of his glass, more earnestly than Manning, and manages to make it chime—an eerie sound that rings out over the hushed bay. Manning gives him a look that tells him to stop horsing around.

Roxanne continues her story: "After lunch, we spent some quiet time in the cabin. I lay down, resting, though of course my brain was in a spin, wondering what the hell was happening. Carl unpacked his laptop and booted it up on a desk there in the bedroom. It was only a few feet from the bed, but he was sitting at an angle that made it impossible for me to see the computer screen.

"He seemed engrossed in what he was doing and worked at it for nearly an hour, typing away at the keyboard. I was lying still, and he may have thought I was asleep. Eventually, he got up and went to the bathroom. There's a turn in the hall, and you can't see the bedroom from there."

Manning grins. "Your big break."

"Yup. I tiptoed over to the desk to get a look at his screen, and guess what I found." She pauses for effect. "Solitaire."

"Huh?" David flops back in his seat.

"There was a *card game* on the screen. That struck me as fishy—he'd been typing too much. So I moused up to the button that minimizes the solitaire program, wondering if something else was open in the window underneath. And sure enough, there was a page of a document in WordPerfect."

"Aha!" David leans forward again.

"But it was just a memo updating a personnel issue at the office—a tedious matter, but by no means clandestine, involving nothing that Carl would bother to conceal from me. I heard the toilet flush, and assuming I'd struck out, was about to call up the solitaire window. But I knew I had a few more seconds—Carl *always* washes his hands—so I decided to check beneath the Word-Perfect window to see if anything else was open. And there it was, his day planner: Tuesday, June twenty-ninth."

She sits back, looks at her watch, then asks, "Do you know where Carl will *be* this afternoon at three o'clock?"

"Where?" the guys ask together.

"To quote Carl's own notation: 'Gethsemane—CFC Board—Zarnik.'"

"*What?*" Manning's mouth gapes.

"You heard it." Roxanne crosses her arms.

"Sorry," says David, "I don't understand."

Manning tells him, "The Gethsemane Arms is that new hotel built to profit the work of the Christian Family Crusade. It's their temporary headquarters while they try to save Chicago—and the nation—from the forces of perversion."

Roxanne adds, "Carl Creighton, the man whom I've recently decided I love, is obviously a legal advisor to their board, or maybe he's even *on* their board. And the whole movement is somehow tied to Zarnik, whom you've determined to be a fraud."

Manning sounds a cautionary note. "There are a couple of leaps in your logic, Roxanne, but I admit that you've drawn some compelling assumptions."

"It's the best theory we've heard yet," David says. "In fact, it's the *only* theory."

David has a point, Manning knows. So far, his investigation of Zarnik has only raised questions. Roxanne has at least pieced together the beginnings of a plausible answer. "Has Carl ever mentioned contacts within the CFC?"

"Never," Roxanne answers.

Their discussion of the CFC reminds Manning of Cliff Nolan's neighbor, Dora Lee Fields, who watches the Christian Family Network day and night. Manning asks Roxanne, "Can you recall if Carl has ever spoken of the CFC, even in passing?"

"No, I can't recall. I'd surely remember if he ever indicated that he was a sympathizer. I mean, he's a conservative guy fiscally, but I've always found him surprisingly open-minded on social issues—he readily accepted you and Neil as friends, for instance. Or so I presumed."

All along, Manning has suspected some connection between Zarnik's ruse and Nolan's murder; then on Sunday afternoon, he discovered a dossier linking Nolan and Carl Creighton; and now Roxanne has revealed some apparent connection between Creighton, the CFC, and Zarnik. It suddenly seems that the common thread in this mystery may be none other than Carl Creighton.

Out of the blue, Manning asks Roxanne, "Do you happen to know if Carl was ever a student at the University of Chicago?"

Though puzzled by the question, she answers, "Yes, as a matter of fact, he was an undergrad there. It's the 'Harvard of the Midwest,' you know—nothing but the best for Carl." With her empty glass, she toasts Carl's alma mater.

As Manning ponders all this, the conversation lapses. The boat has been drifting for some time now, and they are closer to the far shore than to the lodge, though still well out of earshot. Thinking, peering vacantly over the water, Manning notices a glint of chrome through the woods. He hadn't realized there's a back road that circles the bay, veering toward the shore here and there. Near one of the old piers, there's a van parked among the trees. Its driver, a fisherman, has hauled his gear onto the pier, where he sits lazily in the early-afternoon sun, rod and reel in hand, line dangling in the water. Arrayed around him on the pier are a couple of tackle boxes, maybe a lunch basket, and an open umbrella.

David breaks the lull. He asks whoever will answer, "Let's suppose, for the sake of discussion, that Carl does play ball with the Crusade. I can understand how that might alarm Roxanne— they're so totally bogus—but how does that involve Zarnik?"

Roxanne tells him, "I never claimed to have any answers, but I'm certain that something weird is in the works, and I thought that Mark would appreciate the tip."

"Indeed I do," Manning assures her, mustering a smile to mask his deeper concerns, one of which is his growing hunger. "Before taking on the mysteries of the cosmos, why don't we have lunch?"

Roxanne and David need no convincing. It's nearly one-thirty, not only time to eat, but time to lighten their discussion and enjoy each other's company. As they set about unpacking their meal and arranging it on the center table, they exchange idle pleasantries about the food, the boat, their plans for the holiday weekend. Roxanne must have truly charmed the caterer—the table is crowded with salads, pastas, huge chilled shrimp, a platter of sliced chicken breasts. They pick and scoop from the serving dishes at will, assembling plates to their own liking, drizzling them with an assortment of sauces.

Roxanne refills her glass of iced tea from a carafe within reach of her chaise. The bottle of Far Niente is chilling in an ice bucket at Manning's side, where David cannot reach it. As a not-so-subtle hint that the wineglasses are empty, David wets his fingertip and rubs it around the rim of his glass, causing it to chime again, far more loudly than before—he's perfected his technique. So reverberant is the piercing, harmonic sound, Roxanne quits her fork and applauds with shouts of "Bravo!" Laughing, Manning turns to reach for the wine, and as he does so, his peripheral vision detects movement on the shore. He glimpses sideways just in time to see the fisherman drop his rod into the bay, grabbing at his ears with both hands.

Manning leans over the table, signaling with a wag of his fingers that Roxanne and David should do likewise. With their faces only inches apart, he says to them in a voice that is barely a whisper, "You see that fisherman over there with the umbrella? He's no fisherman, and that's no umbrella—it's some sort of listening device. He's heard every word we've said."

Sweating and panting, jacket draped over his arm, Arlen Farber ducks into the shade of the canopy stretching taut from the polished new facade of the Gethsemane Arms Hotel. A glance at his watch tells him that it's not quite three—thank God, he has a couple of minutes to put himself together.

Shrugging into his jacket, he passes between two doormen who stand at attention with tacky foil-tipped spears. They wear centurion guard outfits, complete with sandals, skirts, breastplates, and brushy-topped helmets. One of the guys is really buffed and fits the role to a tee (he looks like Ben-Hur), but the other guard, who's short and black with skinny legs, doesn't quite fill the bill (in fact, he's a dead ringer for Marvin the Martian in those Bugs Bunny cartoons). They're both ridiculous, of course, but Arlen Farber has neither the time to notice nor the inclination to sneer. They're actors doing a job, drawing a check, just as he is.

Inside the doors, a cavernous lobby yawns before him, with huge tiers of marble stairs descending from the street level to the main reception room. The new air-conditioning system is not yet fully tweaked, and Farber is momentarily stunned by a chill that convulses his body. Strains of harp music waft through the space and echo from the stone walls. He needs to find a men's room.

Walking through a door marked *Bethren* (he didn't see the ladies' room and can't imagine what they'd call it), he's relieved that there's no attendant. He's never liked the idea of having someone wait for you, running water while you pee. Besides, he needs to be alone for a minute. He stands before the urinal, urinating, studying his face in the gold-framed mirror that hangs there. His eyes don't look so great—he should have gone a tad easier on the Jack Daniel's, but it's easy to get carried away with Bette Davis. Zipping up, he crosses to the sink, splashes water on his face, and studies his face again. He musses his hair, looking instantly more absentminded. He chortles at the transformation, then calms himself, breathing deeply, and closes his eyes. Focusing inward, he thinks the thoughts of an Eastern European astrophysicist, entering the mind of a fusty genius. Arlen Farber opens his eyes. The man staring back from the mirror *is* Pavo Zarnik.

Leaving the men's room, Professor Zarnik crosses the lobby toward a bank of elevators, where there's an enshrined reproduction of a Raphael painting in which a spaced-out John the Baptist (he looks like he's high on something other than religion) points up. Zarnik gets into the first elevator, marked *Chariot One*, and presses the top button, marked *Golgotha Suite*. When his chariot arrives at Golgotha, the doors open, not with the expected *ding*, but with a tinny, digitized harp flourish. All this hokum would be laughable if Zarnik were to ponder it, but his mind is occupied instead with the uncertainties of the meeting to which he has been summoned.

A nicely dressed young lady awaits him in the hall. "Good afternoon, Professor Zarnik." She has a charming southern twang. "So nice of you to come see us on such a dreadful hot day. Can I getcha lemonade to take into your meetin' with the board?"

He'd prefer a julep. "Thank you, my dear. So kind of you to offer."

She fetches the lemonade, then leads him into the conference room, which is actually the dining room of the hotel's finest suite. Around a big oval mahogany table sit perhaps a dozen men, no women. This is the governing board of the Christian Family Crusade, the organization's Council of Elders. They stand as Zarnik enters, and one of the board members, a portly man in a slick black suit, introduces himself as Elder Burlington Buchman (though he's not very old—fifty, tops), instructing Zarnik to be seated in the empty chair at one end of the table. His tone is humorless. His manner and accent lack the charm of the lady with the lemonade, whom he dismisses as soon as Zarnik sits.

Buchman seems to be in charge of the meeting. He brusquely introduces the others at the table, who nod and grunt as their names are called. Most have titles of "Elder" or "Deacon." There's an archdeacon in the bunch, and Zarnik thinks he caught a subdeacon. But one of the men, sitting across from Zarnik at the opposite end of the oval, has no title; he is simply Mr. Creighton.

Zarnik doesn't know that the man is a lawyer, aged forty-nine. He doesn't know that Carl Creighton has an aggressive edge that he often vents on racquetball courts as well as in courtrooms— today Carl Creighton gives no hint of that vitality and drive, watching the proceedings with a fixed, empty expression. Though seated, he is obviously an inch or two taller than six feet. His body looks ten years younger than his years, but his hair has the opposite effect. Prematurely gray even in college, it is now pure white, and Zarnik wonders if it has been bleached.

"Well," Buchman drawls, "enough of the niceties. Do y'understand why we've had to call you here, Professor?"

"Actually, no," Zarnik answers. He removes his fingers from the glass of lemonade and dabs the cold condensation on his cheeks. "I would be grateful for some explanation."

Buchman defers to another board member, Elder Phipps, a shrunken old figure in a bad suit. Phipps doesn't mince words.

"You've been dabblin' in some queer science, Professor. You've been preachin' heresy. You've been raisin' hackles."

"I beg your pardon."

"Don't play dumb with me, Dr. Smarty-Pants. God created the universe in six days. On the seventh day, He rested. And now *you* come alone preachin' this poo about a so-called 'tenth planet.' What the hell is *that*, Professor?"

Zarnik is stunned. The man questioning him is such a ludicrous caricature, he wants to laugh. He wants to ask, Is this a joke or what? But he remembers his instruction—Play along and don't rile them. He explains, "The tenets of modern astronomy were established by Copernicus nearly five hundred years ago. The theory of a solar system was convincingly argued—"

Elder Phipps interrupts. "Can you show me any of that hooey in the Bah-ble?"

"Of course not," Zarnik tells him. "The Bible is an ancient book. Even the New Testament is two thousand years old."

"I rest my case," Phipps says smugly, crossing his arms.

"Do you suggest that the Bible was written as the culmination, the end-all, of human discovery and learning?"

"I don't 'suggest' anything, sir—I *know* it."

A murmur rises from around the table. Phrases like "You tell'm" and "Praise Jesus" and "Amen, brother" pop like balloons over the heads of the faithful.

Zarnik says, "Clearly, then, we disagree. What do you expect me to tell you? One cannot contradict *fact*, can one?"

"What arrogance!" says Phipps, puffing up his chest. "Facts be damned. 'I am the way,' our Lord Himself told us. 'I am the way, the truth, and the light.' " Phipps grabs a pile of newspapers from the center of the table, poking with an arthritic finger at Zarnik's front-page stories, at the congratulatory ads from the mayor's office. "We have no need for your heathen, foreign science, riling up good, wholesome Americans with your blasphemous tales of godless worlds." Seething, he flings the papers in disgust. They glide across the waxed mahogany table, coming to rest in a disarrayed heap in front of Elder Buchman.

Sensing that Elder Phipps has perhaps overplayed the CFC

position, Buchman adopts a conciliatory tone and, shoving the sleeves of his jacket halfway up his stocky forearms, leans forward on his elbows to tell Zarnik, "I hope you'll forgive my esteemed colleague's testy manner, but y'see, these are issues that cut to the very core of our Bah-ble-based beliefs. It don't help none, either, that you've posed this challenge so quickly after arrivin' here in our country." Buchman cocks his head and smiles. It's a false smile, toothy and menacing.

Zarnik isn't cowed, now that he sees so clearly what he's dealing with. He sips his lemonade (daintily, hoping it will further annoy the elders) and tells Buchman, "I was always taught in my homeland that America prides herself as—how do you say?—the great melting pot. And yet, there are those who now espouse the concept of 'America for Americans.' It strikes me that such an isolationist attitude contradicts this great nation's heritage. In the final analysis, are we not all, every one of us at this table, an immigrant people?" The elders visibly bristle at such a suggestion. Zarnik adds, "Then again, I am a foreigner, so I may be a smidge fuzzy on this issue."

Buchman condescends to explain, "The immigration policies of the past, though noble in theory, simply don't apply to these present times, Professor. When our country was founded, it was a vast, untamed wilderness, in need of manpower from whatever corners of the earth to settle its new frontiers, to conquer its savage natives, and to spread the word of Jesus. With God's blessin', those goals have long been met, and our nation now faces a moral obligation to be a little more—shall we say?—*selective* in its policy toward outsiders. F'rinstance, I'm sure y'understand that it's simply not in our interest to admit fast-breedin' Hispanics, Muslims of any stripe, or the AIDS-infested. What's more—"

"Mr. Buchman," Zarnik interrupts him, standing, "mind your words, lest you be branded a hypocrite." The Council of Elders gasps as one. "Surely I need not preach to an assembly so devout as yours, but this discussion reminds me of a fable that is the heritage of my own homeland. It is a scrap of our history, far older than yours, that teaches a lesson in tolerance. May I share it with you?" Zarnik smiles.

Clearly, Elder Buchman wasn't expecting such a question. Hesitating, he looks to the other elders, who in turn exchange uncertain glances—but it's Buchman's call. Slowly, he leans toward Zarnik, the bare skin of his forearms squeaking on the polished table. Something in his steely stare tells Zarnik there is no interest in his parable of tolerance. Buchman's mouth opens to comment. "When hell freezes ovah."

Angry voices swell around the table as the elders and deacons add their own invective to Buchman's ruling—Zarnik's matinee has bombed in the Golgotha Suite. Everyone is talking, everyone is laughing, except Zarnik, of course, and the man at the opposite end of the table. Carl Creighton looks down at a folder spread open before him, in which he calmly jots a few notes.

After dinner, Manning, Roxanne, and David stroll outdoors from the dining room, bracing themselves against a lake breeze. Roxanne says, "I told you the evenings were chilly." She snuggles inside a fuzzy knee-length sweater styled like a topcoat with giant buttons and a shawl collar. The guys wear lightweight blazers—Manning's is linen, David's is silk—over knit shirts buttoned to the neck.

The sun has not yet set. These are the longest days of the year, and they stretch even longer this far north. But the sky's western glow ends abruptly at the massed pines, which appear black and solid, like a craggy-topped wall constructed to keep out the light. Crickets choir antiphonally from their hidden cricket lofts. Locusts whir. David yawns.

Manning says, "I know it's been a long day, and we were all a bit rattled by Maxwell Smart this afternoon. But it's too early for bed—there's still light in the sky—so why don't we check out the Poop Deck?"

David's not so tired after all. Gesturing toward the front door of the boathouse, he suggests, "Cocktails, anyone?" The three switch directions and head for the lounge, where lights beckon and music thumps.

Opening the door, entering, Manning sees in a flash that Roxanne wasn't joking earlier when she said that the place caters to an older crowd. David is now easily the youngest person in the room—Roxanne and Manning are next. The other patrons stop gabbing for a moment to inspect the new arrivals, raise a few eyebrows, and drift back to their drinks. " 'I just called *[cha cha cha]* to say *[cha cha cha]* I luuuv you,' " croons a one-man act in a burgundy jacket. He has a rhythm machine cranked so loud the windows throb, a keyboard with more controls than a Univac, and hair dyed so black it's blue. Manning and David stifle a laugh while Roxanne grins, I told you so. They cross the nautical-themed room and settle at a table alongside one of the windows overlooking the bay. Near their table, a ship's wheel is mounted to the floor. David can't resist—it's too loud to talk anyway—and he excuses himself from the table to take command of the wheel.

At last the rhythm machine seems to run out of steam. *Cha cha chunk.* There's a smatter of applause. The musician acknowledges the crowd, shuffles his sheet music, and . . . thank God, it's time for his break. Heading for the bar, he grabs a few bills from his tip jar, a snifter the size of a muskmelon.

Now that conversation is possible, David scoots back to the table, asking, "What can I get you from the bar?"

Manning tells him, "Straight vodka on the rocks with a twist of orange peel—Japanese vodka if they have it."

Roxanne is tempted, but no. "Perrier's fine, or whatever."

As David turns to go to the bar, Manning asks him, "Got your wallet?"

"Sure."

"Just charge the drinks to the cabin," Manning tells him, "but they'll probably card you—in *this* crowd."

David and Roxanne laugh. Yes, David is young, but his blazer, glasses, and mature bearing give him the air of a gentleman. Roxanne tells him in a coddling tone, "If the man gives you any grief about the booze, sweetheart, have him talk to Mommy." As David traipses off to the bar, Roxanne's lips ripple with a smile.

Noting the direction of Roxanne's gaze, Manning tells her, "He's a great kid."

"*I'll* say."

"No, seriously. He's a hard worker, smart, well mannered. . . ."

"Don't tell me—he cooks too."

Manning laughs. "I wouldn't know. My point is: when my editor first assigned him as my 'assistant' last week, I thought he'd just get in the way. But I was wrong. He's been a great help, and I enjoy his company."

Roxanne leans close over the table. Her tone is confidential. "I'll bet you do."

"I mean, he's . . . *interesting.* I haven't really known anyone of his generation. They've got some different ideas."

Roxanne leans back in her chair. Examining her nails at arm's length, she ponders aloud, "I wonder if he likes older women."

Now it's Manning's turn to be coy. He leans toward her. "Don't bank on it."

"What do you mean?"

With a know-nothing shrug, he again tells her, "You'll have to ask David."

David reappears with their drinks. "Ask me what?"

Roxanne eyes Manning wryly, then says to David, "I'm supposed to ask you about your taste in women."

Unprepared for the topic, David stammers.

Changing the subject, Manning pulls out a chair for David and tells him, "Join the party. Did he card you?"

"Nope," says David, distributing the drinks, "he was so stooped-over, he never even looked me in the eye. Hey, time for a toast."

They all raise their glasses. Roxanne says, "For starters: To the successful completion of your big story. May a Partridge Prize await you."

Manning returns the courtesy. "To the successful resolution of this crink in your relationship with Carl. May your worst suspicions prove unfounded."

"And to Neil," says David. "I wish he could be here with us."

"Here here," says Roxanne.

"To Neil," says Manning.

And they all drink.

Just as they are about to settle into some frivolous conversation, having exhaustively discussed plots and counterplots all afternoon, Manning feels the tingle of the pager on his belt. He unclips it and reads the number. "Speaking of Neil," he tells the others, "a summons from the home front. It might be important, and besides, I'd like to talk to him." He rises. "Do you mind?"

"No," they assure him. "Not at all."

He picks up the glass that he has barely sipped, to take it with him to the cabin. "I don't know how long this'll take, so don't wait around for me. If I don't see you later, Roxanne, sleep tight." He steps to her side of the table and leans to kiss her cheek. "Behave yourself," he says into her ear.

"*I'm* not the one who's drinking," she reminds him, tapping her water glass.

He squeezes her shoulder, tells David to have fun, and leaves the lounge.

It's noticeably darker outdoors now, cooler too, and Manning paces briskly toward the cabin, only a few hundred yards away, carrying his icy drink. Underfoot, the asphalt paving changes to gravel driveway. His shoes crunch the stones as he approaches the cabin, guided by the glow of a yellow bug-light near the door. Arriving on the stoop, he fishes for his key and turns the lock. (After that incident on the bay, he decided he'd been too lax and trusting. It was stupid to leave the cabin unlocked earlier. To everyone's relief, there were no signs of intrusion during their afternoon absence. There was little worth stealing anyway—Manning's computer, files, and notes were all safe in the trunk of his car.)

Entering, he switches on lights, crosses to the bedroom desk, and sets down his glass. Through the picture window in the living room, he sees the evening's last glint of orange on the water. Even the indoor air is chilly now, so he leaves his jacket on, but doesn't take time to fuss with the heat—he wants to return Neil's call. The message light on the phone is blinking—but Neil comes first. Manning sits at the desk, unbuttoning the top of his shirt. He flips open his reporter's notebook and sets his capped pen next to it, in case Neil has business. He sips his vodka, then dials.

The other phone rings four times, then the answering machine starts its spiel. Manning glances at his watch. Damn. Then Neil picks up the phone, interrupting the machine. "Hello?" He sounds winded.

"Hi there. Did you just walk through the door?"

"I just jumped out of the shower," Neil tells him.

"Going out?" asks Manning, trying not to sound as if he's prying. "You usually shower in the morning."

"Rest easy, Mark. It's been another hellacious day, and I had a few errands to run this evening. Just trying to cool off. They say better weather's on the way."

"It's already here." Manning huddles into his jacket. "It's cold tonight."

"Then you'd better build a fire."

Manning relaxes in the chair, stretching his legs. "Matter of fact, there's one ready to go. There's a wonderful stone fireplace—none of that gas-log nonsense."

Neil is impressed. "Sounds great."

"Everything's lovely, kiddo. I wish you were here to share it."

"Me too. Here in the loft, I enjoyed having some 'personal space' for a change—for an hour or two—but the flush of independence faded fast. I want you back here."

Manning sips his drink. "Come morning, David and I will be on our way."

"How *is* the lad?"

"Fine. He's over at the cocktail lounge with Roxanne."

"And what about Rox—what was so urgent that you had to hightail it up there?"

Manning leans forward on the desk, as if inching closer to Neil. "Get this: Carl was called into town for a board meeting of the Christian Family Crusade."

"*What?*"

Manning cups the receiver to his mouth, as if speaking into

Neil's ear. "It gets even screwier. Zarnik himself was apparently at the same meeting. Roxanne suspects the worst: Carl is involved with the CFC, and they're all knee-deep in the Zarnik scam. Plus, I can't help wondering about Cliff Nolan's dossier on Carl."

"There's got to be some other explanation," says Neil, his voice laced with doubt. "This is starting to sound way too sinister."

Manning is tempted to tell Neil about the eavesdropper on the pier, but that would only worry him, and right now he has pressures of his own to fret over. Manning says, "You're probably right. Even if Roxanne has correctly concluded that Carl Creighton is somehow associated with the CFC—he is, after all, a lawyer, and I'm sure the Crusade pays plenty of them—I can't think of any plausible connection between a bunch of irrational fundamentalists and Zarnik, a man of science. Granted, he's just putting on an *act*, but why?"

"Oh!"—Neil remembers—"The reason I called. Did Victor Uttley phone you?"

Manning looks at the winking red light. "I'm not sure. There's a message."

"Victor phoned you here at home tonight, and I gave him your number up there. You guys have been missing each other's calls, right? He wouldn't tell me exactly what he wanted, but he did say to let you know that he needs to talk to you about something important. In turn, I told him that you, too, have something to discuss with him—access to the laser projectors. He seemed to think he could pull some strings; he wants you to call him about it. Then, after we hung up, it occurred to me that he has theatrical connections all over the city."

Manning swirls the ice in his glass. "So?"

"What did Claire Gray tell you? The man posing as Zarnik must be a professional *actor*, right? Maybe Victor could help put the finger on him."

Manning has begun taking notes. He stares at them in silence for a moment. "Thanks, Neil. That's an interesting angle. Remember, though, that Uttley ran those ads, so he already has something of a professional investment in Zarnik. He may not enjoy hearing that he's involved the mayor's office in perpetrating a hoax."

"That's a valid concern," admits Neil. "But knowing Victor, I'd characterize him as a publicity hound. He'd *love* making headlines, even if they proved he was injudicious in running those ads. He could claim he was 'victimized.' "

Manning laughs. "You've got this all figured out, haven't you?"

"No one to talk to but myself tonight—I've been giving it a lot of thought."

Manning hears the key in the door, then David enters, along with a rush of cold air. He carries a fresh cocktail with a lime in it, probably gin and tonic. David tells Manning, "Our lounge lizard started in again on Stevie Wonder's greatest hits. Roxanne and I couldn't take it, so we called it a night."

"Shrewd move." Through the phone, Manning tells Neil, "David's back."

"So I hear." Then Neil shouts, his voice buzzing through the earpiece, *"Hello, David!"*

David laughs, having heard it clearly. *"Hey there, pal! Wish you were here."*

Manning holds the phone at arm's length, avoiding the crossfire. With his other hand, he lifts the glass and finishes his vodka.

Neil shouts, *"Be sure to tuck Mark in for me tonight."*

"You got it." Crossing past the desk, David picks up Manning's empty glass and heads into the living room, where he switches on a lamp and closes the blinds at the big window.

Manning tells Neil, "He's left the room. You can scream yourself hoarse, but it'll be for naught."

Neil laughs. "Thanks for the tip. By the way . . ." He cuts himself short, then asks in a secretive tone, "Can David hear you?"

"I think so, yes."

"Then just answer yes or no. Have you gotten a look yet at the whole 'package'?"

Manning smiles. "No." David has moved from the living room farther into the cabin, to the bathroom or his bedroom.

Neil says, "You're on a mission, remember. And I expect a full report."

"Yes, sir," Manning answers dryly. "I'll do my best."

There's a pause. Neil says, "I love you. And I miss you. So hurry home."

"I love you too, Neil. We're heading home first thing in the morning. And thanks for the information—sorry to force you into secretarial duty. 'Night, kiddo."

They hang up, and Manning sits for a moment, simply savoring their contact, counting himself a lucky man. The message light continues its persistent winking. As he reaches for the phone and dials the front desk, David returns from the other end of the cabin wearing workout shorts, bulky sweat socks, and an old Northwestern sweatshirt with its arms cut off. It's an athletic, grungy frat-house look that contrasts sharply with the refined design of his eyeglasses.

He steps in from the living room and tells Manning, "I didn't feel like bed yet," referring to his change of clothes. "Can I get you another drink?"

"Sure," says Manning. Why not?

As David returns to the bar in the living room, the desk clerk answers Manning's call.

With pen poised over his notebook, Manning asks if he has a message. There was a call from Victor Uttley. He makes note of the number and hangs up, checking his watch. Nine-thirty. It is indeed too early for bed, but probably too late to be phoning people on business. Besides, Neil has already delivered the gist of the message. He'll return the call tomorrow.

David reappears in the doorway, carrying two glasses. Setting one on the desk in front of Manning, he tells him, "As I suspected, they don't have your Japanese brand in the minibar. And I had to recycle your old orange peel."

"This is fine," Manning assures him, raising his glass. They exchange a casual toast. As they drink, Manning eyes David's bare legs and arms. "Aren't you cold?"

"Actually, yes." David laughs. "I thought I'd start the fire. Do you mind?"

"Not at all. Good idea." Manning rises. "Need some help?"

"I think I can handle it—it's all set to go." He retreats into the living room.

Manning follows, watching as David squats before the hearth, strikes a long match, and sets it to the newspapers crumpled beneath the grate. The room instantly fills with the glow and warmth of burning paper and kindling. As Manning removes his jacket and drapes it over the back of a chair, he asks, "Are you sure the flue is open?" The room already smells smoky.

"Oh, Christ," David mutters, scampering to turn the mechanism in the chimney. "Better open the door awhile."

There's a door from the living room that leads out to a small terrace overlooking the water at the back of the cabin. Manning unlocks it and fans it back and forth, drawing in fresh air. After a minute or two, the smoke has cleared, but the room is colder than it was before they lit the fire.

"Sorry," says David, turning to Manning from where he still hunkers by the hearth. "I'm starting to get the hang of reporting, but I'd make a terrible pioneer." He rises, smiling. Reflected flames cavort in the lenses of his glasses.

Manning closes and locks the door, reminding him, "Pioneers didn't have chambermaids, either. All *you* have to do is strike a match. *Those* guys had to rub sticks together." He returns to the center of the room carrying his drink, which he sips. Noticing David's glass on the coffee table, he picks it up and offers, "Here."

David crosses to Manning. "Thanks," he says, taking the glass, which looks suddenly small in his beefy hand. The room is warming up again, but the glass is icy, and as David drinks from it, Manning sees the little hairs on David's upper arms standing erect in their follicles—he has goose bumps on his biceps.

"You're cold," Manning tells him.

"I'm fine."

"I'd suggest you bundle up, but . . ." Manning hesitates. Dare he broach this? He doesn't want to send the wrong signal, but he's curious. It has gnawed at him since their conversation in the car. "There's something you haven't shown me yet."

David stands no more than a foot from Manning and can easily read the confusion in his hero's eyes. "I'm not shy," David tells him. "Just say when."

So it's come to this—it's Manning's decision. It could stop right here, and it probably should. Or, Manning could ask the kid to take off his shirt. Big deal. David regularly shows more of himself when he goes to the gym, thinking nothing of it. It doesn't *mean* anything. This isn't an *overture*. It's not as if Manning is *interested*. Just curious. He needn't feel accountable, let alone guilty, for an inquisitive foray into the cultural identity of a younger generation. That's all it is, really. And besides, only two minutes ago, Neil actually encouraged him to get a look. Neil couldn't possibly object to this, could he?

Manning hesitates, then whisks his eyes from David's waist to his face, commanding quietly, "Show me."

David's lips curl. It's not exactly a smile, not exactly smug. It's a grin, expressing not victory, but relief. He hasn't tried to conquer Manning—he's simply been eager to display what he's done to his body. Of *course* he finds the situation erotically charged. So what? There's nothing dirty, nothing seedy, nothing underhanded about this. He's twenty-four and built. He's *always* horny. So David gives his drink to Manning (who now holds one in each hand) and removes his Armani glasses, which he sets with care on the coffee table. Then he lifts the remnants of the sweatshirt over his head, shakes his hair, and tosses the shirt to the floor.

There, precisely as he described them, are the pierced nipples, a ring through the right, a little barbell through the left. Both bits of jewelry are made of silver, flashing with the fire mirrored by their curved surfaces. The nipples themselves are cold and hard, like the metal running through them. David stands proud, gently flexing his biceps, pectorals, abs—or is that merely the play of firelight on his skin? His eyes ask, Well, what do you think?

But Manning isn't looking at David's eyes. He stares, transfixed, at the bizarre body ornaments. Though David had described them in detail, Manning was utterly unprepared for the sight of them, for the visions they conjure of David willingly enduring the pain of their installation. The intensity of Manning's stare is dreamlike, unreal, out-of-body. He tries to analyze the situation, to weigh what might, could, should, or shouldn't happen next. He tries to ask himself what Neil would advise at this point, but his brain is now focused solely on David's nipples. In his mind's eye he watches himself—from high in a corner of the cabin's ceiling—watching David.

David again asks the question, this time verbally, "Well, what do you think?"

There's no answer. What could Manning possibly say? He cannot even *think* about what he is seeing. He can only react. Even Neil would surely understand—wouldn't he?—that this situation allows for, indeed demands, but one response.

Manning watches from the ceiling as he himself steps toward David, lowers his head, and drags his tongue across the barbell. David stands perfectly still, except to drop his head back on his shoulders and gasp. From on high, Manning watches David's eyelids flutter. Then the man on the floor puts his mouth over the barbell, closes his lips, and draws it into his mouth. He tastes the metal, discerns its shape with his tongue, hears it click against his teeth, feels signals from deep within his jaw, like some inbred alarm—caution! don't swallow! there's a bolt in your mouth! But it's not a bolt, and there's no danger of swallowing it because it's attached to David's nipple. Manning tongues the fleshy knob that stretches around the barbell's shaft. David pants. A tremor, a shudder, ripples through his chest. But he remains standing still, taking it.

Manning sees his tongue glide to David's right breast, the one with the ring. It seems intended for one purpose. Manning takes it into his mouth, grabs it with his teeth, and gives a tug. David yelps, placing his hands on Manning's head. But it's a restrained protest, and as soon as Manning releases the ring, David guides Manning back to it. While Manning explores it with his tongue, David kneads Manning's hair.

From the ceiling, Manning watches, dazed, as the man on the floor takes the two icy cocktails, one in each hand, and touches them to David's nipples. As David laughs, his jewelry clacks against the glassware. With his hands still in Manning's hair, he pulls his hero's face to his own. He gets the glasses out of Manning's hands, sets them nearby on the mantel, then returns his attention to Manning's face, blindly rubbing his open mouth around the other man's features until their tongues meet.

As they kiss, Manning tweaks David's nipples, fingering the silver ornaments that hang there, inserting the tip of his pinkie into the ring, pulling. When David opens his mouth wider to emit a deep, guttural groan, Manning forces his own tongue farther into his assistant's throat.

In David's mind, this is mere foreplay. He's heating up for some serious sex, the most energetic orgasm of his young life, the fulfillment of a fantasy he's harbored for over two years.

Manning's mind, however, is blank. If he could rationally classify what he's doing, he'd know that it is not foreplay, not sex. And even though he likes the kid, it is certainly not love. No, it is simply a form of passion—instinctive and unwilled, a response to an overpowering stimulus, utterly beyond his control. He is no more able to back off right now and hand David his shirt than he is able to doubt for an instant his love for Neil. They are equally impossible.

So the scenario is set. Though David and Manning lead separate lives, each its own story, tonight's chapter is a shared one, and it draws steadily toward a mutual climax that neither can now edit or revise. Though their motives and instincts may differ, they both respond to the same cues. This scene can end only one way.

Manning's hands are still busy on David's chest. David's hands have been working the lump in his own shorts. Now he slips the waistband below his hips, lets the shorts drop to his feet, and kicks free of them. With one hand, David masturbates against the khaki of Manning's slacks. With the other, he grapples to unfasten Manning's buckle.

From his voyeur's perch overhead, Manning watches the two men's bodies tangle before the fire. Finally, he averts his eyes— knowing, even with the limited cogency of this moment, that such scenes are more vigorously enjoyed from the perspective of the imagination.

Wednesday, June 30

David awakes early the next morning, well before six. He didn't
think to close the blinds in his room when he finally went to bed
last night, and the eastern sun now skims across the water and
through the window, reflected in the dresser mirror, targeting
his bed. It hurts to open his eyes.

His nipples are sore. His face is sore, abraded by the night-
stubble of another man's beard. And his penis is sore. But these
are minor agonies, the price of an evening's pleasure, a bargain
by any measure.

He lies in the bedroom at the far end of the cabin, alone. He
and Manning shared every known intimacy (and invented a few
new ones) in front of the fire last night. With their repertoire
exhausted, it was finally time to sleep, and each took to his own
bed. Half awake now, blinded by daylight, he kicks the covers
off the bed and feels his genitals. His morning erection invites
attention, and the escapades of a few hours ago are still fresh
enough in his mind to fuel some steamy jack-off fantasies. So he
gives it a shot—but quickly concludes that his efforts will get him
nowhere. There's simply nothing left for now.

Lacking sufficient energy to get out of bed and close the blinds,
he rolls over, shading his face with an arm. There's time for more
sleep, but it's so *quiet* up here—no traffic, no car alarms, no
garbage trucks, nothing. Well, birds, sure. A hungry duck. God,
that's annoying. And what's that other sound? Movement in the
cabin, beyond the living room. Mark. Was that the door? Someone is being careful to be quiet, but David has definitely heard
the sound of the screen door.

He puts on his glasses, gets out of bed, finds his workout shorts, steps into them, and pads out of the bedroom to explore. There's a light on in the bathroom, as if Manning was in there earlier, while it was still dark. The living room is much as they left it last night—no particular disarray, just a couple of empty glasses. The spent embers of the fire smolder like a tired cliché, a tangible metaphor, there in the grate.

David pokes his head through the doorway into Manning's bedroom and finds that he's already up and packed, bed made— what a neatnik. But Manning isn't in the room. The outside door is open, so David crosses to it, folding his arms over his chest to shield his cold-sensitive nipples from the damp morning air. Through the screen, he sees Manning with a terry cloth towel, wiping one of the car windows, wet with dew. He's scrubbing intently, frowning. "Hey there," says David, speaking in a stage whisper that seems appropriate to the early hour.

Manning looks up. "Hey there, yourself." He smiles. "Sorry if I woke you."

"No, of course not." Awkward pause. David asks, "Why the big rush?"

"No rush." Towel in hand, Manning comes to the door and steps inside. "I had trouble sleeping. Thought I'd better make myself useful." He sets the towel on a dresser and unzips his jacket. Seeing that David is shivering, he closes the door. "By the way"—he gives David a hug, not a kiss, nothing intimate—"good morning."

David holds on to Manning a moment longer than Manning intended. "Yeah. Good morning." He pecks the side of Manning's face.

"Let's talk, David."

"Sure." David sits on the edge of the bed, hands folded in his lap.

Manning paces once in front of him, turns to address him, but does not look him in the eye. Predictably but uncertainly, Manning begins, "About last night . . ."

"Mark," David interrupts, "let me make this easier for you. I know you're committed to Neil. I don't want to wreck what you've got, and even if I did want to, I doubt if I could. I understand that you have qualms about what happened, and because you do, I do. But I've got to tell you—it was prime." He grins up at Manning, his boyish features flushed with the morning-after glow of a sated libido. He really is a sight, sitting there on the bed, twiddling his toes. It's enough to lure anyone into a quick romp.

Manning isn't blind, and he's only human. His knees go weak at the very thought of what he could have—right now, again— if he gave the slightest hint of interest. His guilt, after all, is already complete. They have plenty of time. Another hour's ecstasy may prove anticlimactic, but it won't make his soul any blacker, and he'll get no gold stars for refraining. He need only extend a finger to touch that little silver barbell, and David will be ready for action. They may never have this opportunity again.

But even as Manning weighs these possibilities, he knows there's a flaw to his premise. The cold truth—the summation of the issue that robbed his sleep—is that he feels little if any guilt about last night. What troubles him most this morning is the feeling that he *should* feel guilty, plus the knowledge that Neil will never be able to appreciate the incident so analytically, *if* he finds out about it, and Manning is further vexed by the question of how much, if anything, he should tell Neil.

He knows, as surely as he breathes, that he was powerless to ignore the unexpected stimulus that confronted him last night. He was sapped of his will. Not that he was morally weak or lacked integrity, but rather, he simply *could not* fail to react as he did. Any jury of twelve reasonable peers would surely conclude that he must be held blameless, not guilty.

This morning's situation, though, is another matter. By virtue of last night's experience, he now knows exactly what erotic power David holds over him. Last night was something like temporary insanity, but that's a defense that cannot be invoked twice. Opening himself to future sex with the kid would brand Manning with the blackest, lowest stripe of guilt. Even so . . .

He tells David, "You're right. Last night was indeed 'prime'— I'd be a liar to tell you otherwise. But it can never happen again, David. It *will* never happen again. Do you understand that?"

"I understand." He sighs. "I don't like it, but I understand."

Confident that they're in sync, Manning sits next to David on the bed, telling him, "I hope this won't affect our relationship— at work, I mean. You've been doing a great job for the *Journal*, and during the past week, I've truly grown fond of you, getting to know each other as we have."

David's grin almost erupts into laughter.

"I *mean*," Manning clarifies, "I've grown fond of you as a friend. Neil has, too. I hope we can continue to see each other socially, the three of us."

"I wish Neil had been here last night," says David.

"So do I. Then nothing would have happened, and we wouldn't be in the midst of an awkward conversation this morning."

"Like hell." David is wide-eyed. He rests his arm across Manning's shoulder. "Neil could have *joined* us. Talk about rad!" He isn't joking.

Manning offers no comment.

"Hey," David continues, dropping his arm, drawing one knee onto the bed so he can face Manning, "why not? I don't want to come between you guys, but in the *literal* sense . . ." He trails off suggestively.

David has painted a vivid picture, and Manning's mind sketches at least a dozen variations of the contorted scene. Might David's suggestion be something that Neil would actually buy into? Manning knows that it would signal a subtle but deep shift in their relationship. What would it mean? As a couple, would they be stronger or weaker as the result of it? He tells David, "It's an intriguing notion, but not yet. I don't know if I'm ready for that, or ever will be."

"Squaresville."

Rising from the bed, Manning shrugs with a smile. "I'm *old*."

"Sure, Gramps." David also rises, plants his hands on his hips, and eyes Manning up and down. "All I know is, this kid got the workout of his life last night."

Really? Well. Manning decides that if he doesn't switch topics, this conversation will get him into trouble. He suggests, "Why don't you start putting yourself together? I've got some fussing to do with the car, then we can tackle a major breakfast before we leave."

That sounds just fine to David. Nodding, he starts to leave the room, but stops in the doorway to the living room, facing Manning. He leans against the jamb, nipple ornaments glistening. Big smile. "Seriously, Mark. It was incredible last night." And he turns, leaving the room.

Manning stands there mulling all that has happened, uncertain how or when to broach it with Neil, then he shakes his head, dismissing these thoughts for now. He grabs the damp towel that he dropped onto the dresser and picks up another, a dry one. Zipping up his jacket, he opens the door and steps outside.

Though it did not rain overnight, everything is wet with dew, including the car. Parked beneath the drooping branches of pines, its black paint appears beaded and frosty, littered with needles and flecks of stuff dropped from the trees. After yesterday's long drive, Manning wanted to get the car washed, but he and David haven't left the resort since their arrival, and now it's almost time to return. Since the car is normally garaged overnight, Manning was unprepared for the sight that awaited him this morning. At first disheartened (he can't stand the idea of setting out for a long drive in a dirty car), he then resolved to take advantage of the situation. Since the car is thoroughly wet, he can at least wipe it down, hoping to swab away yesterday's road film as well as the overnight detritus from the trees—sort of a sponge bath. It's worth a try, Manning tells himself, making a mental note that he should always store paper towels and some glass cleaner in the trunk.

He starts with the hood, the most crucial target of his efforts. He picks away needles one by one, then sets to work with the bathroom towels, the damp one followed by the dry one. Swirling the second towel, hoping to buff up a shine, Manning soon learns that while he can dry the car, he cannot clean it. It was peppered with droplets of sap, invisible beneath the dew, but now smeared by the towel, causing a random pattern of ugly swipes to appear on the paint. He cannot simply whisk away the grime—hot water, sudsy with detergent, is needed to cleanse it.

Giving up on the hood, he works his way to the side panels. And then he notices it. A stone, possibly an errant chunk of gravel that had spilled from a driveway to the road, has dinged the front passenger's door. There's a dimple in the metal and, at its center, the period-size crater of a missing chip of paint.

The sturdy sedan, which was perfect, in which Manning had invested his pride as well as his cash, has been tainted. Though the damage is slight—indeed, this loss of automotive innocence was inevitable—it must be patched, quickly and thoroughly, lest it spread, corroding the car to its very frame.

Manning rubs the pitted, exposed metal with his fingertip, nursing the wound with a dab of spit.

O nly a few minutes later, on the top floor of the Journal Building, Lucille Haring boots up her computer terminal in Nathan Cain's unlit outer offices.

When she arrived, she caught the security guard dozing at his post and told him she'd seen men shot for less. She was joking, but never cracked a smile, and the guard fumbled with his key to admit her. While passing through the door, she asked, "Did the Colonel spend the night in his quarters?"

"No, ma'am. He left the tower before midnight."

Good. She gave the guard a curt nod, shut the door behind her, and marched straight through the labyrinth of quiet rooms to her desk.

It will still be nearly two hours before the rest of the staff arrives, but she needs all the time she can get—there's work to be done.

Her computer clicks and whirs, displaying cryptic start-up messages on its monitor. It pauses now and then for passwords, like a dog begging for scraps of breakfast. When she enters the codes, the machine churns onward, gobbling the information from her fingertips. While waiting for this electronic feeding-frenzy to digest itself, she sits erect in her chair, drumming the desk. Shafts of orange morning light angle in through the room's windows, partly obscured by the hulking cabinetry that houses yet another phase of the office's newly installed computer power.

At last the desired prompt appears on the screen. What is her command? Though she knows she is alone, she instinctively checks over both shoulders before proceeding. She unbuttons the breast pocket of her pleated jacket and fishes out a little key, which she uses to unlock the file drawer of her desk. From the drawer she removes an unlabeled folder and spreads it open on the desk. Inside is a stiff cardboard envelope. And inside that is an unlabeled diskette. She slides the disk into her A-drive, types a command, and hits the "enter" key.

As the computer begins to churn, Lucille Haring holds her breath. Outside the window, an unmanned scaffold winches into view, hauling more equipment roofward. Then a message appears on the computer screen: "Welcome, Mr. Cain."

Lucille Haring smiles—she's in.

By midafternoon, Manning is seated back at his desk in the *Journal*'s city room. He's been away only a day and a half, but there's a pile of pink slips by his phone and enough voice mail to crash the system. He's barely made a dent in all this when Daryl waltzes into the cubicle with another fistful of messages. "My my, gorgeous," he coos, "aren't we casual today? Tennis, anyone?"

Manning didn't think to pack his office "uniform" for the trip to Door County, and he didn't want to take time to stop at home and change while driving back into the city. He wears a white camp shirt, chinos, and topsiders. He tells Daryl, "Not that it's any of your business, but I was on an overnight assignment."

"Where?"

Manning grabs the sheaf of pink slips. "Wisconsin." He tries to organize the mess of notes, diskettes, files, and morgue folders that clutter his desk.

"Huh?"

"For Christ's sake, Daryl, it's a state. North of here." He looks up from the rubble. "They make cheese."

"Oops." Daryl flashes the whites of his eyes. "Sounds like bwana got up on wrong side of the bed this morning."

Manning exhales. He swivels his chair to face the copyboy. "Sorry, Daryl. As a matter of fact, I *didn't* sleep well. The Nolan and Zarnik stories are getting more convoluted, raising lots of new questions, but no answers. What's more . . ." He hesitates, then stops. He was going to mention his car's door-ding, but that would sound absurdly trivial. "Never mind. This hasn't been my best day."

Daryl knows that Manning is investigating Zarnik's identity; the reporter confided that much of the mystery to him on Monday and asked him to do some research in the *Journal's* morgue. Responding now to Manning's despondency, Daryl moves behind the chair and places both hands on Manning's shoulders. His tone is instantly soothing. "There there, sugar. You just keep digging. Keep your eye on the coveted Brass Bird."

"Thanks." Manning reaches up to pat one of Daryl's hands. "Sorry to say, the Partridge committee would be singularly unimpressed with *this* investigation."

Daryl steps in front of Manning and parks on the edge of the desk. "What have you got so far?"

Manning has other things to do right now, but a summary might help focus his thoughts. He tells Daryl, "Zarnik is a fraud, but who *is* he, and *why?* I've learned that he's probably a professional actor and that he may have some connection with the Christian Family Crusade, but there's nothing to suggest a motive for his claimed astronomical discovery, which is bunk. The Pentagon has expressed interest in his research methods, which are nonexistent, fearing that the time lag between his announced discovery and its independent verification may open a 'window of opportunity' for something menacing, but what?"

"I see what you mean, love—plenty of questions, damn few answers."

"Not yet, at least. What really intrigues me, though, is the possible link between Zarnik's ruse and Cliff Nolan's murder. I couldn't help sensing a connection from the very moment when I discovered Cliff's body. His laptop computer was missing, and it has never been found. He was working on a story when he was shot, and I have every reason to believe that it would have exposed Zarnik as a fraud. The woman next-door to Cliff said that he was playing loud music on the night he was killed, and in fact, when I found his body two nights later, the stereo system was still humming loudly, cranked to the max. I wondered what music was playing when Cliff was killed, and I just got an answer." Manning plucks one of the message slips from his desk.

Daryl leans forward, but can't read it.

Manning tells him, "Jim, my detective friend at headquarters, left word that the last CD played on Cliff's stereo had no fingerprints on it. It was a recording of the Verdi *Requiem*. I should have guessed."

Daryl's mouth hangs agape as he ponders this revelation. "Sorry," he says after a moment, "I don't follow you at all. *What was playing?*"

Manning repeats, "The Verdi *Requiem*—the traditional Catholic Mass for the Dead, as set to music by Giuseppe Verdi. He was a nineteenth-century composer of grand opera and other large-scale works. The *Requiem* is one of his most enduring and 'popular' pieces, probably the most bombastic. It's a very long setting of the Mass, requiring a huge orchestra and chorus. The point is, I don't know anyone who sits down and actually listens to the whole thing. The part that everyone *likes* is the "Dies Irae" section, near the beginning. It opens with four explosive bursts of sound, depicting the wrath of doomsday. Played loudly enough, those blasts could easily mask four gunshots. Cliff had four bullets in his back."

"Okay . . ." says Daryl. Having never heard the music, he'll have to take Manning at his word. "But there were no fingerprints on the disc."

"Exactly. CDs are fingerprint *magnets*. That disc should have been covered with prints—Cliff's prints. The fact that there were none at all means that the disc was almost certainly handled, cleaned, and played by the killer, not by Cliff."

Daryl nods. "And that brings us back to the central question: Who killed Cliff Nolan?"

Manning inches his chair closer to Daryl, who leans forward to listen. With lowered voice, Manning tells him, "I now have five possible suspects. First, there's the actor who is posing as Zarnik. His obvious motive for murder would be to avoid exposure as a fraud by Cliff, but why the whole ruse in the first place?

"Second, there's Lucille Haring, who works up in Nathan Cain's office, on loan from the Pentagon. She's a computer wiz, with access to drafts of reporters' stories, even as they're being written. The Pentagon may have some involvement in the Zarnik scam, and Haring would have known that Cliff was ready to blow the whistle. What's more, she's a lesbian, and Cliff had threatened to expose her to the military brass, which would be the end of her career—so she was *plenty* motivated."

Daryl asks the obvious question: "Have you *talked* to her?"

"I've been trying," Manning assures him, "but we can't seem to connect. I got another voice-mail message from her today— she can't meet tonight or tomorrow night because she's 'terribly busy with an important project.' It sounds like a runaround, and I should probably just confront her upstairs in her office during the day, but I don't want Nathan Cain to get wind of this till I have some firm evidence."

"A wise precaution," Daryl agrees. "Who else?"

"Third on my list is Carl Creighton, a prominent local attorney who was possibly being extorted by Cliff. He apparently has some connection with both Zarnik and the Christian Family Crusade— but what's *their* role in all this?

"Fourth is Dora Lee Fields, Cliff's next-door neighbor, a real character. She's an Elvis impersonator, a CFC member, and a pistol-packing redneck who threatened to kill Cliff for some peace and quiet—she couldn't stand his loud music, and it was loudest on the night he died. She may be trying to divert suspicion from herself, but she told me that Cliff had a visitor that night, a tall man with a limp.

"And that brings us to suspect number five, Victor Uttley, Chicago's cultural liaison to the world. He was at Saturday's party—that tall, effeminate number with a limp from a recent Rollerblading mishap. He's the one responsible for all those expensive ads that have been running this week, congratulating Zarnik. So he has an interest in Zarnik's discovery, which we know to be a sham. What's more, he's well connected in the theater world, and we're reasonably sure that 'Zarnik' is an actor. That might be an important connection, which is why I asked you to do some research on Victor Uttley."

Manning glides his chair back a few inches, dropping his arms to his sides. "And that, I'm afraid, is all I've got."

Daryl taps one of the manila folders on Manning's desk. "You've got a morgue file on Uttley. I dug out everything I could, but there wasn't much—a couple of tepid acting reviews, a metro story about his appointment to the mayor's office, a few mug shots from his agency."

As Manning thumbs through the folder, Daryl adds, "You've also got a shitload of messages from him. He's antsy to talk to you. In fact"—Daryl plucks one of the slips and dangles it in front of Manning's face—"he'll be stopping by the office this afternoon, right about now, hoping to catch you."

Daryl has barely finished his sentence when David Bosch pops into the cubicle. "Hey, Mark." He's winded and grinning. "Guess who's out front."

Daryl picks lint from his sleeve, showing no interest in David's news. At the same time, he notes with great interest that David's casual attire is virtually identical to Manning's.

"Okay," Manning tells David, "I'll bite. Who's out front?"

"Victor Uttley! I happened to hear him tell the receptionist that you were expecting him, so I said I'd run back to get you."

"Damn, what a coincidence," says Manning, straight-faced.

This prompts a chortle from Daryl, who's busy admiring the contour of David's firm buttocks. When David notices the direction of Daryl's gaze, Daryl looks up to tell him, "Nice pants."

"Oh. Thanks." Then David tells Manning, "So . . . grab your notebook."

Obediently Manning rises, picking up his notes, his calendar, and his Montblanc. Noticing that Daryl's gaze has returned to David's pants, he says without inflection, "Stop that."

Oblivious to the subtopic, David asks Manning, "Mind if I tag along?"

"I insist," Manning tells him, clapping an arm over his shoulder. "After all, you're part of the team." And they start off down the aisle together, affording Daryl a nice view of both backsides.

Daryl calls after them, "Oh, David?"

He turns. "Yeah?"

"How was Wisconsin?"

"Sweet, man."

Uh-huh. Daryl smiles, rises, and strolls off in the opposite direction toward the heart of the newsroom, where he's late for switchboard duty.

Manning and David escort Victor Uttley into one of the little conference rooms that surround the reception area outside the editorial offices. It's a stark closet of a room with white, undecorated walls, badly scuffed by chairs on casters, clumped around a center table.

"Have a seat and get comfortable," Manning tells Uttley, adding, "or at least try to." Manning shrugs an apology for the tight quarters, shuts the door, then joins David and their guest around the table.

Uttley winces as he sits, trying to find a comfortable space for his lame leg. "Thank you, Mark," he says, "for seeing me without an appointment." His lanky frame and long features appear drawn and emaciated in this sterile environment, which is too brightly lit, seemingly from nowhere.

Manning replies, "Sorry I've been so hard to reach. David and I have been working on a story that took us out of town. Have you met, by the way?"

They mention having seen each other at Saturday's party, shaking hands to make it official. As they reach across the table, their chairs shift position, banging the walls.

"So, Victor," Manning continues, flipping open his pad, "what is it that you've needed to see me about?"

Uttley hesitates. Through a skittish laugh, he says, "Actually,

I understand from Neil that you've been wanting to see *me*." He pulls one of his skinny cigarettes from an inside jacket pocket and lights it, not bothering with the holder, not bothering to ask if anyone minds.

"Come on, Victor. You're first. What's this about? I spotted you downstairs in the lobby Monday morning."

He sucks his first drag, then blows the smoke sideways, over a shoulder. "I wondered if you'd seen the ads we ran—from the mayor's office—congratulating Professor Zarnik."

Manning snorts. "They were hard to miss. And while the *Journal* appreciates the revenue, I must admit that the ads baffled me. From the mayor's perspective, what's the point—to pump up the prestige of the city?"

"Precisely!" says Uttley, suddenly energized, fluttering both hands. "A city's self-perception is a tenuous, gossamer thing." The orange dot of his cigarette traces circles in the air. "We owe it to the citizens of Chicago to seize any opportunity to remind them that they inhabit a miraculous urban playground of culture and science."

David stifles a laugh. Catching a glance from Uttley, he pretends to cough, shooing smoke with his hands.

Uttley looks about for an ashtray, but there is none, only a lipstick-stained Styrofoam cup left on the table from a previous meeting. There's an inch of coffee in it, to which Uttley adds his cigarette, extinguishing it with a hiss.

"Thank you," David mumbles through another feigned cough.

"*Anyway*," Uttley continues, "I just wanted to make sure you had seen the ads. Plus, the mayor asked me to convey his personal thanks to you for breaking the story and helping to spread the city's good name." He smiles.

"Do express my gratitude to the mayor," says Manning, aping the smile. This doesn't make sense, though. Uttley could have simply phoned the message, or sent a card, maybe a plant. Why all this skulking-about, this urgent face-to-face meeting? Uttley's behavior has been more typical of an informant's, a "source" who's about to impart a hot tip. But this is *nothing*. Manning tells him, "I was only doing my job."

"Your humility," says Uttley, "is a credit to your profession."

Oh brother. "I was wondering, Victor, if perhaps the mayor's office could be of assistance in facilitating some background research for another story I have planned—it has nothing to do with Zarnik."

"We'll be happy to try. Is this the matter that Neil mentioned on the phone yesterday, the laser show?"

David looks to Manning with a quizzical blink, having never heard of this story.

"That's right," Manning tells Uttley. Then he explains to David, "At the end of Saturday night's human-rights rally, some new laser technology will be used to display a huge pink triangle over the stadium; special projectors are being installed on top of the Journal Building and two other towers. The sky show will continue every night for a year, throughout the run of Celebration Two Thousand. Nothing has been published yet about Saturday's finale—it's being kept as a surprise. But once people get a look at it, there's bound to be widespread interest in how it works. So . . ." Manning turns to Uttley. "I'd like to arrange access to one or more of the projection sites to get a firsthand look at the equipment." He opens his datebook. It is Wednesday—the week is half gone already. "I'd like to do some snooping by Friday. Any later, it's anyone's story."

Uttley tells Manning, "One of the projectors is on top of this building. Why don't you just hop on an elevator and take a look?"

David looks from Uttley to Manning—it's a logical suggestion.

Manning tells them, "Let's just say I have my reasons. Can you help me?"

"Probably. I'll let you know by tomorrow. We'll shoot for Friday."

"I appreciate it, Victor." Manning makes a note in his calendar and closes it. While capping his pen, he thinks of something. Uncapping the pen again, he flips open his steno pad. Adopting a chatty, conversational tone, he says to Uttley, "Even without the laser spectacle, it sounds as if the opening ceremonies on Saturday should be sensational. Neil tells me you've had a hand in the planning, Victor."

He puffs with pride. *"That's* putting it mildly. The mayor's office is keenly aware that Saturday's program will affect the world's perception of this city for years to come. Planning is crucial, of course, and I've tried to keep an eye on the committees."

"I've always been something of a music buff, so I'm especially interested in that aspect of the festival. I understand there's a possible glitch in lining up the Three Tenors." He pauses, deciding to gamble, then asks, "Is it true that Paganini may cancel?"— naming not a reigning tenor, but a long-dead violinist.

"That's just a rumor," Uttley assures him. "All systems are go—he'll be here."

"Oh, good," says Manning, adding with wry understatement, "I wouldn't want to miss *that.*" He jots a brief note, telling himself, This guy wouldn't know Bach from Bruckner. If he could mistake Paganini for Pavarotti, he surely lacks sufficient musical knowledge to synchronize four gunshots to the "Dies Irae" of Verdi's *Requiem.* Victor Uttley did not kill Cliff Nolan. As suspected, Dora Lee Fields may have invented the man with a limp.

Manning closes his notes and pockets his pen. The meeting, it seems, is finished.

Victor rises from his seat, extending his hand. "I'm glad we finally connected. If there's anything else—"

"Actually," Manning interrupts, "there is one other bit of unrelated business I wanted to discuss with you."

"Oh?" Victor settles into his chair again, scraping the wall.

"You're an actor," says Manning. "Correct?"

"I was, yes, but my new position leaves no time for such pursuits."

"Of course," Manning tells him, "but I understand that prior to your cultural-liaison days, you were building a promising career within the professional theater here." That's a stretch, Manning knows, but he's trying to ingratiate himself.

And it works. "The critics seemed impressed," says Uttley. "I was starting to get consistently favorable press. But . . . civic duty called."

"Might one say, then, that given your background, coupled

with your new position, you're thoroughly 'connected' to the theater scene in Chicago?"

"Oh my, yes." Victor squares his shoulders. "And beyond."

Manning again flips open his notes. "Excellent. The reason I ask is that I may have use for a contact within the theater world. I'm sniffing out a future story that could turn into something of an exposé. It involves a prominent figure—a local woman who's been getting some publicity recently—who I have reason to believe may be an impostor, a professional actress. If that's the case, do you think you'd be able to help me identify her?"

Uttley leans forward on his elbows, beads Manning with a stare, and lowers his voice. "If she's ever worked in the Midwest, I probably know her."

"When I'm ready to get the investigation rolling, can I enlist your help?"

Uttley leans closer. "My hard-earned background deserves compensation."

Manning leans back easily in his chair. He doesn't bother to hush his words. This is business. "I can't authorize that, but my editor can. I'll speak to him. This could be an important story, and we need a source." Manning closes his notebook.

"**H**e wanted *money?*" asks Neil that evening, seated at the center island of the kitchen. He and Manning have arrived home within minutes of each other.

"Most informants do," says Manning, pouring vodka over ice. "The difference is, most aren't so brazen."

"Why did you tell him the impostor is a woman?"

"Uttley's weird. Something told me not to tip him that I suspect Zarnik. It's a detail he doesn't need to know yet. Even though I no longer suspect him of Cliff Nolan's murder, I haven't ruled out the possibility that Uttley could be involved in the Zarnik ruse. He's demonstrated a conspicuous self-interest in Zarnik's discovery, fake or genuine, by running those ads."

"Tantalizing idea," says Neil. "But frankly, I don't think Victor's that clever."

Manning laughs. "Neither do I." Garnishing the two glasses with orange peel, he hands one to Neil.

Rising for a toast, Neil tells him, "Welcome home, Mr. Manning. It's been a long thirty-six hours—and yes, I counted every one of them."

Before drinking, they take a moment for a leisurely kiss. Their embrace is made clumsy by the cocktails in their hands, but it's good to be back in each other's arms, and neither one flinches at the few drops of alcohol spattered down their backs.

Holding tight, Manning is secure in the innocence of his attraction to David—it could never possibly threaten his bond with Neil. Their identity as a couple is rooted far below the fertile topsoil of sex, deep in the spiritual substrata where their intellects, their shared past, and their planned future are nurtured. By any reasonable measure of commitment, they are "married." And yet, Manning knows that he cannot simply dismiss last night's transgression as an inconsequential slip. The marriage—Manning's *sense* of their marriage—has been damaged. It's up to me, Manning tells himself, to focus and to fix it. And Neil doesn't even have a clue.

"What's wrong?" says Neil, sensing an unexpected intensity, something almost desperate, in Manning's hug.

Manning holds him at arm's length. "I missed you. Being apart isn't good for us."

"I'll drink to that." And Neil does so.

Manning also drinks. "How's everything shaping up for this weekend?"

Neil considers before responding. He strolls to the main space of the loft, toward the sofa that looks out through the windows. Manning follows. Neil sits, telling him, "Now that you ask, I realize that the whole project is finally winding down for me. Sure, the next couple of days will be hectic, but come Saturday, my committee days will be over. I look forward to getting my life back—getting *our* life back."

"You have no idea how good that sounds," says Manning as he sits next to Neil, close, thigh to thigh, wrapping an arm around him. "I'm sorry things have been so . . . uncertain lately. I haven't had much time for 'us.' "

"No need to apologize," Neil assures him, dropping a hand between Manning's legs to squeeze his inner thigh. "We've both been busy. That's life."

Manning's been busy, all right. "I've got an idea," he says. "It's Wednesday, 'date night.' May I have the pleasure of your company at dinner, Mr. Waite? How about that trendy new bistro everyone's yapping about—what's it called?"

"Bistro Zaza. But we'd never get in."

Manning won't be deterred. "I'll call the office and have someone in Features phone for us. Ten-to-one they'll think we're food critics. You watch: We'll get the best table in the house, and they *won't* keep us waiting at the bar. But"—Manning raises a cautionary finger—"we'll come home for 'dessert.' "

"A thoroughly intriguing proposition," says Neil, sliding his hand from Manning's thigh to the crotch of his chinos. "But I've always been sort of a pig about dessert. Let's have it *now*—and I'm not talkin' tiramisu."

Yow. "Should I call the office first?"

"Later, big boy." In one deft move, Neil has set their drinks on the coffee table, knelt on the floor, and unbuckled Manning's belt.

Manning laughs, getting into the spirit of Neil's spontaneous foreplay, when the phone rings. "I don't believe it," he says. "Not again."

Neil looks up with a good-natured frown, wondering aloud, "Is nothing sacred?" They stare at each other through another ring or two. Then Neil says, "It might be important."

"That's what has me worried." But Manning can't let it ring. There's a phone on the console table behind the sofa—he lifts the receiver. "Yes?"

"Hello, Mark? It's Roxanne." By the sound of all the background noise, she must be calling from the convertible.

"Hi, Roxanne. What's up?"

Neil, hearing this, gets playful again, unzipping Manning's pants.

Roxanne asks, "What's up, yourself?" Her manner is breezy, almost giddy. "You sound . . . funny."

Dryly, Manning tells her, "Let's just say you caught me at an awkward time."

"Oh." She is momentarily subdued. Then she hollers, "*Hello, Neil!*"

"*Hi, Rox,*" he shouts back, giving up on the project at hand.

Manning asks them both, "Shall I pass the phone?"

"No," says Roxanne through a laugh, "I was calling *you*, Mark. About Carl."

"How . . . is he?" asks Manning.

"Never better. In fact, he's right here. We're driving home. We'd like to take you two to dinner tomorrow night—it was his idea."

Manning chooses his words carefully, thinking that Carl may be able to hear their conversation over the car's speaker phone. "Is everything all right regarding yesterday's meeting? You're sounding rather lighthearted this evening."

"Couldn't be better. I was *way* off base, Mark. We can't wait to tell you the news."

"I'm listening," Manning reminds her. "So tell me."

"Unh-unh. Too important. Only at dinner."

Manning covers the mouthpiece to ask Neil, "Dinner tomorrow okay? I need to have a talk with Carl anyway." Neil nods. Manning says into the phone, "Fine, Roxanne. Where and when?"

"We were thinking, there's this marvelous little bistro we haven't tried. . . ."

"Zaza's," says Manning, "but you'll never get in."

"Nonsense," she snorts. "The office can reserve for us—plenty of pull. How's eight o'clock?"

"Sounds great. We'll be there."

"With bells on. 'Bye, kids." And she's gone.

Neil gets up from the floor and perches next to Manning, retrieving their drinks from the coffee table. "What was that all about?"

Manning zips his pants, takes his glass from Neil. "We're

double-dating at Zaza's. Roxanne and Carl can't wait to tell us 'the news.' "

Neil nearly chokes, spitting an ice cube back into his glass. "*What?* Did she mention the *m*-word?"

"No"—Manning sips—"but she was ditzy as a schoolgirl."

Neil flumps back into the sofa. "It just can't be—Roxanne married?" He blinks. "Besides, I thought Carl skulked off to a meeting with the Christian Family Crusade. How would *that* lead to *this?*"

Manning swirls his ice. "Maybe they gave him a sermon on family values."

"Smart-ass." Neil leans forward, sets down his glass, and starts to unbutton Manning's shirt. "Gee," he says wistfully, not watching what he's doing, "do you suppose they want us to stand up for them?"

"I doubt it." Manning sets down his drink, watching Neil's fingers work their way down his chest. "They probably want us for ring boy and flower girl."

"If they do," says Neil, pulling Manning's shirttail free of his pants, "I get dibs on the ring."

"Like hell you do." Manning lunges at Neil, and they roll from the sofa to the floor, Neil on top. If they were really wrestling, Manning could doubtless pin Neil, but he doesn't even try, submitting to Neil's mastery, arms outstretched in defeat.

On his knees, Neil straddles Manning's hips and fully parts the shirt, baring Manning's chest, which heaves from the exertion of their brief struggle. Neil leans forward to kiss Manning's chin, then trails his tongue down Manning's neck to his chest, where Neil notices the nipples, hardened like purple pebbles. He sucks one of them into his mouth, clamping it with his teeth. Manning gasps, but doesn't move, eyes closed to heighten a fantasy. Then Neil bolts upright, back on his knees.

"Hey," he says, "I forgot. Did you ever get a look at David with his clothes off?"

Manning's eyes are open now, and his panting stops abruptly. "Yeah," he answers. "As a matter of fact, I did."

"Well . . . ?" says Neil, eager for details. "Is he really built?"

"Yes, he is," Manning answers dryly, tempted but not daring to give a few more details. Overcoming a momentary pang of guilt, he nudges the memory of Door County from his head, telling Neil, "I thought you were ready for 'dessert.' "

Neil pauses, grins. "I'll get the whipped cream."

Thursday, July 1

The powdery surface of planet Zarnik retreats behind the sprint-paced beat of Manning's shoes. Clouds of unknown gases whorl overhead, pink beneath the cold and distant sun. As Manning speeds toward the curved horizon, the clouds' hue grows ruddy, then bloody, then black, invisible against the night sky. Naked except for his white leather running shoes, Manning trundles onward blind, spinning the globe under his feet in the darkness. His erect penis slices a path through the thin, pristine atmosphere, creating a wake of inertia that fans out behind him. Just as the sky begins to glow with yet another morning, Zarnik's tiny yellow moon, Eros—the wad of nylon once launched by Manning himself—rises, darts through the clouds, and sets behind him.

Glancing down, Manning notices that he runs along a path of footprints in the dust. With surreal clarity, he sees that the prints are in fact those of his own shoes—he has circled the miniature planet countless times, never veering from the equator he has traced around its featureless terrain. With the discovery that his run has been futile as well as infinite, Manning feels his body drain of the energy that has propelled him. His penis sags. His pace slows. His feet tread heavily across the chalky sands, churning cumulous puffs of grit that trail from his shoes like dwarfed thunderheads of roiling talc.

Can he stray from the trail that his shoes have imprinted on this faraway world? Or is he forced—by the intangible but powerful momentum of repetition—to run faithfully, exclusively, forever in this rut of his own making? He can't even remember how long it has been since he first trod this path that now seems so restrictive. Has it been an eternity, or merely a moment? Or something in between, about two years?

He knows, however, that the trail itself, while straight and narrow, is not an active force. It emits no magnetic field, no insidious cosmic rays that he is powerless to resist. Rather, he has grown so accustomed to his perpetual path that he fears his own ability to swerve from it. He left a former life billions of miles behind, but he's forged a new routine out here in the wilds of the universe, running a familiar path that offers all the comforts of home. Why would he even flirt with the temptation to sidle into unknown territory?

Because he's human, of course. He's a man, with all his instincts intact—passion, curiosity, and a deep-rooted drive to fight confinement and convention. Dare he try, just once? Dare he even think of it?

The thought of transgression, while frightening, excites him. His hard-again penis pulls him like a leash, tugging him to the edge of the path, toward unexplored desert, challenging him to soil those immaculate white shoes. His sluggish pace halts. He stands at the brink, mulling an option he has never before considered. He knows, though, that a decision has already been made for him, as if fated. Both the mental enticement and the physical pull are so strong that he has no will to resist them.

So he sets one foot across the line. The other follows. He stands in the hinterland, within stepping distance of his equatorial path, under the rosy haze of Zarnikal noon. Newly energized, Manning sets off at a run, at first alongside the rut in the sand, but gradually skewing farther and farther from it, till it disappears beyond the horizon. Wispy tendrils droop from the clouds to slip past Manning's limbs and tease him to higher euphoria.

Winded from his run, aroused to the point of pain, Manning slows his pace and stops. He lies on the ground, face to the sky, his body encircled by a pinpoint beam from the daystar sun. Closing his eyes, he reaches to his groin and coddles his genitals with both hands. Flopping his knees wider, he digs the heels of his shoes into the sand, piercing the planet's surface. He strokes himself at a comfortable rate, not ready for an orgasm, prolonging his stay at this erotic plateau, riding it out. The sun glows red through the veins of his eyelids.

But then his vision blackens. Something has passed over him, perhaps the shadow of Zarnik's nylon moon. Or perhaps it is *someone*, a visitor who has come to share his launch to ecstasy— Neil or David. Or *both*. They both arrived here once before to goad and witness his climax. He hopes they have returned, the best of both worlds. Manning resists the temptation to open his eyes, preferring to revel in the possibilities, exhilarated by the uncertainty, like a kid waiting to open a present. He breathes more deeply now, inhaling the heady atmosphere in uneven jerks.

Manning gasps, once, when he feels another man's testicles lowered onto his forehead, dragging to his chin. He gropes in the sand around him, feeling for the other man's feet, which he locates on each side of his chest. With eyes still closed, he fingers the visitor's shoes, and he can tell, he *knows*, that they are white leather, identical to his own. He feels the edge of the treaded soles, the crossweave of the laces, a few inches of socks, and the fuzz of hair sprouting from the shins. Manning moans, lifting his head to nuzzle the other man's groin. Then the visitor shifts his weight and bends over Manning, lips to cock.

My God. Manning's eyelids flutter open. His eyes turn in their sockets to view the form of the man above him, a shadow rocking against the drifting clouds. Glancing to his side, Manning laughs, confirming that he knew the color of his visitor's shoes. Manning watches the flexing of the muscles in the other man's thighs. From this curious perspective, he examines details of the physique that are rarely seen. The view is enjoyable, indeed spectacular, but reveals no features that might hint at the visitor's identity. Manning considers stopping him for a moment. He could tap the guy's ass and ask, Excuse me, sir, but who exactly *are* you? But that would be rude. If this guy is so eager to slake the libido, Manning shouldn't pester him with trivial questions.

But it's *not* trivial—it matters. Who *is* he? Manning flops his head from side to side, brushing his temples against the other man's calves, trying to get a better look at his face—but the guy's busy down there. Manning can't tell if he wears Armani glasses; from this angle, he can't even get a look at his nipples, wondering if they're ornamented with bits of silver jewelry. It might be David. It might be Neil. Or it could be anyone else, anyone at all. The uncertainty, at first so stimulating, is now vexing. Gripped by the onset of panic, Manning feels his penis shrivel in the other man's mouth. Gobbling deeper, the faceless visitor literally has Manning by the balls.

This never would have happened if Manning hadn't wavered from the path. It was a rut, yes, but one of his own making, the product of countless hours' effort, ongoing work, predictable but reassuring. Now he's trapped—splayed on the sands of a never-never land. Even if he could escape this lusty aggressor-thought-friend, he couldn't find his way back. He is lost.

"Good morning." What? "It's six o'clock in Chicago, and cooler weather has at last arrived, pushing in from Wisconsin through the night."

Manning sighs, relieved but still shaken. He opens his eyes and feels the tension start to drain from his body, which is curled into a tight fetal knot.

"It's the first of July, which means that the opening of Celebration Two Thousand, our long-awaited civic festival of culture and science, is now only two days away. It's the buzz of the town, and indeed, the nation. The White House has announced that the president will definitely attend Saturday's ceremony. . . ."

Neil groans from his side of the bed. "I wish I could enjoy five waking minutes without hearing about that damned festival."

Manning laughs, relaxes his body, and rolls over on the bed to gaze squarely into Neil's eyes. "Good morning, kiddo. I've missed you."

"Oh yeah? Where have you been?"

"Goofy dream. Guess I've been struggling with something."

Neil smooths Manning's hair, mussed from a restless sleep. "Anything you want to share with me?"

Manning flops onto his back, staring at the ceiling. "Yes, as a matter of fact. Only not right now."

"Sounds a trifle heavy."

The radio continues. "The human-rights rally, which will be the central event of Saturday night's celebration, will be dressed up with a little extra dazzle. A press release issued from the mayor's office by fax overnight . . ."

Manning and Neil turn their heads to eye each other with a deadpan stare.

". . . announced that preparations are now complete for a surprise spectacle that will be staged as a finale to the evening. Details are sketchy, but the city's cultural liaison revealed that the spectacle involves cutting-edge laser technology. The display will be repeated nightly throughout the yearlong festival. . . ."

Manning asks, "*Now* what's Victor up to?"

"Beats me," says Neil.

"Turning now to our musical programming, let's enjoy a portion of the oratorio *The Raft of the Medusa*. Today we celebrate the birthday of its composer, Hans Werner Henze."

Manning and Neil ask in unison, "Who?"

Around eleven o'clock, Manning is working at his desk in the city room of the *Journal* when he senses that there is someone behind him. He looks over his shoulder to find Gordon Smith standing there, arms crossed, watching, grinning. The managing editor says, "Knee-deep in it, eh, Marko?"

Manning swivels to face him. "No, Gordon, I'm *neck*-deep in it, but so far it's only questions and loose ends. Clearly, something very strange is going on, but nothing fits. I can't make sense of it."

Smith plants a palm on the desk and leans to ask Manning quietly, "Is there any reason to think Nathan Cain is endangered by all this?"

Inching closer, Manning responds, "Nothing I've learned points to that, but still, I've uncovered nothing that explains the military's interest in Zarnik. If my suspicion is correct—that they're using Cain for something clandestine—we could *all* be in danger. Cliff Nolan didn't fit into the plan, and look what happened to him."

"Then maybe it's time to confide your suspicions to Nathan."

"Not yet. Give me another day or two. I've been trying to unravel this from too many angles, and I've gotten nowhere. So now I'll concentrate on a single issue—Zarnik's true identity. If we can lay bare the Zarnik scam, I'm reasonably certain we'll hold the key to Cliff's murder. I've got a lead, a slim one, on Zarnik now. And by the way, I may need to come up with an 'honorarium' for my source."

Smith reminds him, "Cain gave you carte blanche. Go for it. I'll sign."

"Thanks, Gordon. I don't like bribing people for clues, but so far, my 'free' information hasn't been worth much. I wasted a day and a half up in Door County."

"I know. Nathan mentioned it to me."

Manning blinks. "Really?"

Shrugging, Smith says, "He must have seen some expenses come through."

Possibly, thinks Manning, but not likely—he returned only yesterday. He asks, "Has Cain shown much interest in my progress with the story?"

"He's asked me about it a couple of times, but only in passing, while discussing other business. Of course, Nathan's a hard guy to read. Why do you ask?"

Manning rises, stretching his shoulders, working out a crick that developed from his morning at the keyboard. "No reason, just natural curiosity. It's always worth knowing when the boss is breathing down your neck."

Smith laughs. "Don't I know it! So keep me posted, okay, Marko? I'd sure like to report *something* to Nathan."

Sitting again, Manning assures him, "You'll be the first to know, Gordon."

Smith pats him on the shoulder, turns, and saunters off through the newsroom toward his office.

Manning slides his keyboard aside (he's not on deadline—he was typing his notes to help focus his thoughts) and pulls Victor Uttley's morgue file from the stack on his desk. There's a phone number on a Post-it note stuck to the front of the folder. Manning checks his watch. He's getting anxious, so he reaches for the phone and punches in the number. He flips open the folder while the other phone rings.

A man answers, "Cultural liaison's office."

"Hello. This is Mark Manning from the *Journal*. Is Victor Uttley available?"

"Speaking," he says. "I may have a title, Mark, but I don't have a secretary. I'll try to remedy that during the mayor's next budget review. What can I do for you?" Then he adds with a chortle, "As if I couldn't guess."

Manning stares at Uttley's photo while speaking to him. "Just wondering if you've had any luck securing access to one of the laser sites. Tomorrow would be great if you could swing it."

"Consider it done." Uttley's voice rings with the pride of accomplishment. "I had to pull a few strings, but that's what I'm here for."

"A true public servant," Manning says dryly.

"That's right," says Uttley, attuned to Manning's cynicism, which, perversely, he seems to enjoy. "Let's see now. . . ." The sound of shuffling papers carries over the phone. "Here we are. The other two projector sites, in addition to the Journal Building, are Sears Tower and the MidAmerica Building. Sears won't work for you—too many tourists—I don't even know how they managed to get all that equipment up there without drawing a lot of attention. Which leaves us with MidAmerica Oil. You're in luck, Mark. The mayor's pretty thick with their chairman, Bradley McCracken. I know from the mayor's calendar that he often has lunch with Brad at the Central States Club—*very* exclusive, you know, top floor of the MidAmerica Building. Anyway, a favor was called in, and you're welcome to explore the tower platform tomorrow evening at five-thirty."

"Nice job, Victor," Manning tells him, surprised that he was able to arrange it. "Where do I go? Who do I see?" Manning uncaps his pen and makes detailed notes of the logistics that Uttley recites to him. Manning asks, "This is all hush-hush, right? It's just a feature story, not hard news, but I want to be the first to break it."

"It's all yours, Mr. Manning, compliments of Chicago's cultural liaison to the world. I hope that you'll consider these arrangements a favor from a friend."

Manning rolls his eyes. "Indeed I shall. Tell me, Victor, why the overnight press release hinting about the spectacle?"

"No harm in drumming up a little extra interest—and it certainly won't tarnish the luster of my own office. What's more, tantalizing the public early will only heighten the impact of your story later."

"I suppose you're right," Manning tells him. "Most of the stories I work on don't involve hype—they're just news."

"Bullshit. Journalism *is* hype."

"No," Manning insists, "I can't agree with that. I admit that journalism can sometimes stray into sensationalism, and television does it all too often, but *real* journalism—reporting, pure and simple—is not entertainment. It's an essential component of a truly free society."

"Yeah, whatever." Uttley doesn't care enough to argue. Changing topics, he asks, "Any progress with that story on the mystery woman, the actress?"

Manning's tone is cautious. "It's coming along. As we discussed yesterday, I may need some help."

Uttley reminds him, "As we discussed yesterday, *I* may need some help. Have you spoken to your editor about the, uh . . ."

"Honorarium," Manning supplies the missing word. "Yes, we had a chat about it this morning. He's looking into it for me. As soon as I get the go-ahead, *if* I get the go-ahead, we can talk terms." Manning poises his pen above the note with the phone number. "How much did you have in mind?"

"That depends on how valuable the information is."

Manning retorts, "*That* depends on what you're able to tell me."

"If I draw a blank, you owe me nothing. But if I finger the gal, I want ten."

Manning is silent.

Uttley amplifies, "Ten grand."

"Jesus, Victor, who writes your material? Ten *grand?*"

"All *right* already. Ten thousand—or would twenty make you happier?"

"Let me work on ten first." Manning discreetly jots the figure on the yellow note. While capping his pen, he notices David Bosch approaching his cubicle. He tells Uttley, "I have to go now; I'll let you know about the money. Whatever the outcome, I really do appreciate your help with the laser business."

"I'll bet you do," says Uttley. "And I hope we'll be talking again real soon."

"Soon enough," Manning tells him. "Good-bye, Victor." And he hangs up.

Grinning, David sits on the corner of the desk. It's not just Manning's imagination—David *has* been emulating his dress lately. He wears a pinstripe oxford shirt, a preppy knit tie, and a pair of dressy khaki slacks that Manning hasn't seen before. David looks even hotter than usual in them, and Manning would surely remember them.

"A call from our neighborhood extortionist?" David asks.

Manning leans back in his chair, getting a full view of David. "No, actually, I phoned *him*. It turns out, he was able to arrange for me to examine the laser projector at the MidAmerica Building. Tomorrow at five-thirty."

David's brow wrinkles. "I've been meaning to ask you—what's that all about? You don't write 'soft news.' We've got a whole separate staff for features."

Manning recounts to David the incident in Cain's office on Monday when he saw the menacing device being hoisted to the *Journal's* tower platform. "It just didn't look like the type of apparatus that might be used for a light show, so I want to get a look at one of the other projectors to see if it's the same. More than likely, I'm acting on an empty hunch, but even at that, it *will* make a damned good feature piece."

"Want me along?" asks David.

"Maybe," says Manning. "Let's see how tomorrow shapes up. Besides, five-thirty on Friday, you've probably got a big weekend planned."

David shakes his head. "I'm all yours." He grins slyly.

Oops. Manning does in fact want to talk about "that," but not here. He tells David, "Our friend Victor named his price, by the way."

"To identify your 'mystery woman'? How much?"

"Ten thousand dollars—pricey for a local tip, but both Cain and Smith have authorized whatever it takes, so Victor may be in for some easy money."

David flips open Uttley's folder. Victor's publicity photo smiles at the ceiling from the top of the pile. "When do you go to work with him?"

"Not yet." Manning lifts the photo from the file and stares back at Uttley's crooked smirk. "I just don't know if I can trust this guy. Let's see if he can actually deliver on his promised access to the laser projector before I reveal to him that it's Professor Zarnik, not some woman, whose true identity I need to establish. In order to stall, I said that the money wasn't approved yet." He tosses Uttley's photo back into the file and closes the folder.

David stands, and their conversation lapses. Shoving his hands in his pockets, he seems reticent to say what's on his mind. When he does speak, his usual breeziness is tempered by a hint of bashfulness. "I was wondering, Mark, if I might take you and Neil to dinner sometime."

"Of course," says Manning, amused that David would be apprehensive to ask such a question. "That would be great. But we wouldn't expect you to host."

"No, I want to," David continues. "You guys have been really good to me, and it's the least I can do." He gives a furtive glance over both shoulders, then leans toward Manning with a conspiratorial grin. "How about tonight? Afterwards, maybe the three of us could . . . *you* know."

Whoa. Manning should have seen that coming, but he wasn't ready for it. Awkwardly, he reaches for his calendar, already knowing what's on it, needing a moment to think. "Sorry, David, but we have plans with Roxanne and Carl tonight—presumably the mystery of his Tuesday excursion will be explained." Manning stops. The previous engagement is not the point, not by a long shot. He rises and rests a hand on David's shoulder, telling him, "Let's talk. Out front."

"Sure, Mark." And he walks off with Manning toward the reception area outside the newsroom.

The door to one of the little conference rooms is open, the same room in which they met with Uttley yesterday. Manning leads David inside, switches on the light, and closes the door. With a banging of chrome legs, they settle into chairs next to each other, ready to talk at close range. The room is eerily quiet, with no ambient noise other than the hum of fluorescent lights in the tiled ceiling. Compared to the charged atmosphere of the newsroom, with its two-story ceiling and muffled but constant din, this cramped, silent space evokes the feeling of a confessional.

With elbows on the table, Manning leans near the young reporter. "David," he begins, "I just can't forget what happened Tuesday night."

"Me neither," says David, beaming.

"I mean I can't *dismiss* it," Manning clarifies. "I want to, and I thought I could, but I can't. Believe me, I'm overwhelmingly flattered that you've taken such an interest in me, and I'd be a liar if I tried to deny that I find you attractive—hell, you're one of the most beautiful young men on the planet—but I'm committed to Neil. He's the man I love. And there's just no room in that relationship for fooling around. Yes, I've wondered if there *might* be, but I've come to the conclusion that it's just too risky, especially with you. It's not only risky, but dishonest— primarily to Neil, but to you and to myself as well. Do you understand why I'm telling you that sex can't be a part of our future friendship?"

David eyes him with a wan smile. "I don't like it, but yes, I understand it."

Manning laughs softly. "It's ironic. Last week this issue crept into my dreams, a full-blown fantasy of what might develop between you and me. Last night I had a similar dream, but it concerned the aftermath of what I'd done, and now I can't shake the . . . *guilt*. Oh sure, on a purely intellectual level I can rationalize that what happened between us was merely a no-fault extension of natural, physical drives that led to a situation we were powerless to resist. I never intended to cheat on Neil or to harm our marriage—but that's precisely what I've done."

David rests his fingers on Manning's forearm. "Mark, aren't you being a little hard on yourself?"

Manning rests his own fingertips atop David's. "Yes, I am. But it's the only way I can face the reality of what needs to be done."

Warily, David leans back in his chair, withdrawing his fingers from Manning's arm. "What do you mean?"

Manning exhales, pauses. "I mean that I'll have to tell Neil what happened."

"Don't be nuts, Mark. That'll serve no purpose whatever."

"It'll clear the air," Manning insists.

"For you, maybe. But what about Neil?"

"He's rational and mature. He'll understand why I need to level with him. He'll doubtless be pissed, but I'm confident we'll be stronger for it in the end."

"Possibly," says David, "but he'll come after *me* with an ax."

Manning forces an uneasy laugh. "Neil isn't that sort of person."

David dismisses the thought with a wave of his hand. "Oh, I know he won't lash out physically, but he'll *hate* me. I'll be the villain, the homewrecker."

"Not if the home isn't wrecked, and I won't let that happen. Besides, I'll be careful not to cast you in that light. I'll be baring *my* soul, not yours. I also happen to know that Neil has harbored a few fantasies of his own about you. If he suffers a bout of jealousy over this, it won't be because you and I had sex—it'll be because I got you before he did."

David wags his head. "Totally bizarre."

Manning leans back in his chair to tell him, "Yes, my young friend, the complexities of human relations present a mystery that only deepens with years. Just when you grow confident that you've at last got it all figured out, you learn that you don't know squat."

"That's encouraging." They both laugh before David continues. "I'd like to talk you out of this, but it sounds as if you've made up your mind."

"I have, David. I don't want you to fret over it, but I thought you deserved to know my intentions."

Resigned to the inevitable, David asks, "When will you tell him?"

"Soon. Maybe tonight."

David puckers, exhaling a silent whistle. After a long pause, he nods—once, decisively—as if he's reached a conclusion of his own. "Let me know how it goes, okay?"

Manning smiles. "Sure, David. Thanks for being so mature about this." Glad to be through with this conversation, but still dreading the one yet to come, he checks his watch. "Let's get back to work."

They squeeze out of their chairs, trying not to scuff the walls, but their good intentions are for naught. As Manning opens the door for them to leave, he notices the back of a familiar figure standing at the receptionist's desk. The man's frumpy frame and frizzy hair can belong to no one else. "Christ," says Manning, stopping David in the doorway, "it's Zarnik. What's he doing here?"

David states the obvious. "I assume he wants to see *you.*"

Manning strides forward, calling, "Good morning, Professor. What an unexpected pleasure."

Zarnik spins on his heel. "Ah, Mr. Manning, hello! And Mr. Bosch." He trundles toward them, and they all shake hands, David engaging him in the pinkie-shake. "I was running an errand along Michigan Avenue when I realized that your offices are here in the tower. I had planned to phone you this afternoon, so I decided to pop in for a visit. Big-city newspaper—how exciting!"

"Would you care to see the newsroom?" Manning offers.

"Ah, pfroobst. I would like that very much, but remorsefully I am running very late." He shakes his watch free of his cuff and squints at it. "Perhaps you could extend the courtesy of a tour some other day. I shall take—how do you call it?—a rain note."

"Rain check," David corrects him, playing along with the actor's faulty command of idiom.

"Whatever," says Zarnik to David, lapsing out of his accent for a moment. Recovering, he tells Manning, "I simply wanted to inform you that I have compiled the data with which I was unable to supply you last week. I am sorry that it has taken this long, but I had to be certain the numbers were correct."

"I appreciate that," says Manning. "I need to flesh out my next story with more hard facts. Have you brought notes that you can leave with me?"

Zarnik crosses his hands over his chest. "I am desolate, Mr. Manning. Since I did not intend to come here this morning, I did not bring my notes. I wonder if you might pick them up at my lab tomorrow."

"You could just fax them," David suggests.

Zarnik wags a finger. "No, my friend, that is not possible. You see, the data are supported by background information that is highly confidential. I must deliver it into the hands of Mr. Manning."

"Fine," says Manning, aware that Zarnik is blowing smoke, but happy to play along and let him take the lead. "What time would you like to see me?"

"Five o'clock."

Friday at five is an odd time for a business appointment. Besides, Manning is due at the MidAmerica Building at five-thirty. He says to Zarnik, "Could we make it earlier in the day? That's not a very good time for me."

Zarnik hesitates. Then he steps close to Manning and looks him straight in the eye. With no inflection and barely a trace of his usual accent, he says, "Please come at five. It's very important. You'll understand."

Manning looks to David for a moment, then back to Zarnik. "Five o'clock."

"Excellent," says Zarnik, clapping his hands, fully in character again. "I am so delighted that we had the opportunity to have this little chat." He skitters away from Manning and David toward the bank of elevators, where one of the cars has just arrived with a *ding*, ready to go down. He taps his watch and tells them, "I truly must dash now." He waves his fingers and hops into the elevator. Its doors slide shut, and he is gone.

David turns to Manning. "What was *that* all about?"

Manning shrugs. "We'll find out tomorrow." Still staring at the closed elevator door, he asks, "David? That goofy walk of Zarnik's, that skitter—do you suppose that someone might describe it as a 'limp'?"

Bistro Zaza is mayhem. Trendy restaurants come and go, first blessed by the adulation of a jaded, fickle public, then doomed by the ennui that sends patrons packing for the next garage gone gourmet. Indeed, it seems the brighter the initial flame burns, the quicker it is snuffed. Judging by the chaos and noise here tonight, Zaza's won't make it till Christmas.

At ten minutes past eight, Manning and Neil squeeze through the mob at the door, having waited at the curb for an overworked valet to roar away with Manning's car. "Jesus," says Neil, reacting to the confusion at the host's podium, "it'll be a miracle if Rox and Carl actually got a table." Would-be diners clump about as if they've been waiting for hours. Some bitch, most drink, all are loud.

Manning elbows his way to the podium, fetching perturbed glances from others standing nearby. The host is model-perfect with sunken cheeks, wearing expensive casual clothes, all black. He looks up from his clipboard with a may-I-help-you expression. Manning says, "We're meeting another party. I don't suppose Carl Creighton has arrived."

The man in black smiles, utterly unfazed by the commotion that surrounds him. "Why yes, Mr. Manning, they're here. Your table is waiting." He parts the crowd. "This way, please." The others' perturbed glances turn indignant as Manning and Neil whisk past, traversing the cavernous dining room beneath its raw I-beam rafters, finally arriving at a prime booth in the far corner, raised a couple of steps on a platform, like a throne from whence to survey the underlings.

Carl rises, reaching his long arm to shake hands with the guys. Roxanne just lolls there against the tufted velvet cushion, asking, "See? I *told* you we'd get in."

"I should never have doubted," says Manning. He leans over the table to kiss her, then sits next to Carl.

Neil scoots into the booth next to Roxanne, telling her, "I've always said you were ballsy."

She admonishes him with a rap on the hand, then smiles and kisses him. "I know a compliment when I hear one, and I'll take all I can get."

Neil and Manning are seated at the ends of the booth, forming a semicircle with Roxanne and Carl in the middle. They look like characters in a play, with half the table open to the proscenium. In front of the table (downstage, as it were), a bottle of champagne chills in a bucket on a silver stand. Though only the neck of the bottle can be seen, there's no mistaking the clear glass and gold foil—it's Roederer Cristal, the best.

A waiter steps forward and distributes four frosty champagne flutes, placing them on the white kraft paper that covers the top of the tablecloth. The word *Zaza* is rubber-stamped randomly on the paper in acid green.

"It seems we've stumbled into a special occasion," Manning says.

Carl laughs, raking his fingers through a shock of that distinctly white hair. "Well, Mark, it *is* special. And we wanted you guys to be the first to know." The waiter pops the cork.

Neil eyes Roxanne's glass. "You're *drinking* tonight?"

She assures everyone, "Just a taste," signaling the waiter to pour only an inch for herself. "We don't get to share this sort of news with our friends very often, and I want to take an active part in our toast to the future."

With the champagne poured, they finger the stems of their glasses, then raise them together. "So," says Manning, "to the future." They all taste the Cristal, savoring the delicate bubbles on their tongues before swallowing. There's a round of approving coos.

Roxanne dabs her lips with a napkin. "Well, gentlemen, I suppose it would be cruel to keep you in suspense any longer. Our lives are about to change dramatically. You'll never guess how."

"Oh, I think we've got an inkling," Neil says.

Roxanne tweaks his cheek, "I don't think so," she singsongs.

Neil tweaks and singsongs back, "Yes we *do-oo.*"

"No, seriously," says Roxanne, straight-faced, "you'll never guess. Carl, this is your big moment. Tell them."

Carl Creighton pauses. He beams. Then he blurts, "I've just been appointed deputy attorney general for the state of Illinois!"

"My God," says Manning, "congratulations, Carl." He shakes Carl's hand.

Roxanne is effusive. "Isn't it marvelous?"

Neil doesn't get it. "But Carl, you've already got a great job. You're a senior partner in one of the city's top law firms."

Carl and Manning chuckle. Roxanne explains, "Neil, a DAG appointment is about as good as it gets for a lawyer. It brings tremendous prestige to the firm, it brokers both power and influence, and it puts Carl in a position to contemplate a future run for *significant* political office. This could be the start of something very big." Noticing that Neil has reacted to this information with a disappointed scowl, she adds, "You're supposed to be impressed."

"Sorry, Rox. Sorry, Carl. That's wonderful news, really. It's just that . . . well, Mark and I were expecting something else."

With innocent expressions, Roxanne and Carl ask in unison, "Like what?"

Neil and Manning look at each other. Neither wants to say it. Neil finally tells them, "Well, the *m*-word."

Roxanne and Carl appear momentarily stunned, then break into laughter. "Heavens," says Roxanne, "I guess I was sending the wrong signals."

Carl adds, "As a matter of fact, that topic *has* been discussed lately, but Roxanne and I need to concentrate on one midlife upheaval at a time."

She pats Carl's hand. "Fair enough." She tells the guys, "You'll be the first to know if and when there's news on that front." Then she hails the waiter and orders mineral water for herself.

Manning drinks more of his champagne. At a lull in the conversation, he tells Carl, "You certainly had Roxanne in a dither over your meeting in Chicago on Tuesday. She was under the impression you'd gotten involved with the Christian Family Crusade."

Carl signals the waiter to pour more champagne. "Roxanne told me about that, and I'm sorry, Mark, that as a result of my secretiveness, she dragged you up to Door County. No—God no—I've never had any connection with the CFC. Frankly, I detest all they stand for. Somehow they learned of my impending appointment, and they wanted to grill me about my background— you *know* how politically active they've become. My position is appointed, but the attorney general is elected, and they could make things really tough for him in the next election if I didn't pass inspection. I resent being put through that, of course, but those damned hicks have become a political reality that's hard to ignore."

Manning grins. "How did you make out with them?"

"Fine, I guess. I tried to wow them with my credentials while evading the stuff they'd find sticky. They know I'm no Bible-thumper, so I took care not to come across like a flaming libertine, and apparently they bought it. I got word from the attorney general's office yesterday that the appointment is a done deal— it hits the news tomorrow."

Neil has listened while idly stroking the stem of his glass. He looks up to ask Carl, "When did you first get wind of the appointment?"

"A few weeks ago. But it wasn't till last Friday that I learned it was looking like a sure thing. Great timing, I thought—I wanted to surprise Roxanne with the announcement at your party on Saturday. Then there was that union snafu at JournalCorp, and Nathan Cain called an emergency meeting Saturday night. Since I had to miss the party, I decided to wait and pop the news to Roxanne while we were on our trip—*then* I got called back by the attorney general's office to attend the CFC's inquisition. So Roxanne didn't hear my news till yesterday."

Roxanne leans forward over her water glass. "What still has us stumped, though, is how the CFC found out about the appointment so quickly. Carl learned about it Friday and didn't say boo to anyone at the office. Saturday was, well ... *Saturday*, and the only people he talked to were the *Journal* bigwigs at that strikebreaking session. Sunday we drove north; Monday he was called back."

"It must have been a leak within the attorney general's office," Carl suggests.

"I suppose," says Roxanne.

Manning has pulled the Montblanc from his breast pocket and started scratching notes on the white paper that covers their tablecloth.

Neil snaps his fingers. "I *knew* there was something else, Carl. Rox said Pavo Zarnik was involved with your CFC meeting. What was that about?"

Carl laughs. "I wish I knew. Yes, he was there, and he gave quite a performance, attempting to defend tolerance and diversity. The elders didn't buy it, to say the least. Neither did I, for that matter, since Roxanne had already clued me that Mark suspects Zarnik to be a fraud."

"What actually happened?" Manning asks.

"The board grilled Zarnik first, then me. I got the impression that the point of the whole show was to impress upon me their ability to summon someone of Zarnik's celebrity stature. Maybe the guy was just acting, but it seemed they genuinely made him squirm."

Manning has ripped bigger and bigger pieces from the paper on the table, stuffing ragged notes—written around the bright green *Zaza* logo—into the pockets of his jacket. "Carl," he says tentatively, "I hate to dampen this evening's celebration, but there's something I have to ask you about."

"Yes, Mark?" he responds, surprised by Manning's change of tone, but sounding unconcerned by it.

"As you're probably aware from Roxanne, I've been assigned by the *Journal* to investigate last week's murder of our science editor, Clifford Nolan."

"Such a brutal tragedy," says Carl, looking directly into Manning's eyes. "Any progress?"

"Yes, actually," Manning answers. Roxanne leans forward with interest. Neil leans back, aware of what's coming. "I made the startling discovery last Sunday that Cliff was keeping dozens of 'dirt' files, extorting hush money from a number of victims. I'm sure it won't come as news to you, Carl, that Cliff kept a dossier"—pause—"on you."

Roxanne's mouth drops in astonishment. Neil closes his eyes. Carl responds dryly, "Indeed he did." His tone is forthright and unemotional. "Clifford was a grad student at the University of Chicago while I was still an undergrad. I hope you'll respect that I'm telling you this off the record, Mark."

Manning nods, capping his pen.

"I admit that I was involved in a minor academic infraction at that time, but my involvement was tangential, and indeed, the facts of the incident were open to dispute. The school never took disciplinary action against me, and ultimately, I graduated summa cum laude. That was thirty years ago, and I rarely gave the matter a second thought. At the time, though, it was reported in the school paper. Clifford was an editor, and he must have begun keeping his files way back then."

Carl downs a mouthful of champagne, swallowing hard. He continues, "I don't know if his timing was sheer coincidence, or if he had somehow gotten wind of the attorney-general business, but he phoned me out of the blue a few weeks ago and said we needed to talk. I couldn't imagine what he wanted." Carl shrugs. "You can surely figure out the rest. He had the information, and he wanted money. I put him off for a while, but I knew that if he ever went public with his file, my chances for the DAG appointment would be shot to hell—there would be zero tolerance for even a *hint* of scandal. Then, at the height of my quandary, I learned that Clifford was dead. Murdered. Was I relieved? You betcha. Was I in any way involved? *No.*"

Roxanne takes his hands. "My God, Carl, I wish you'd shared this with me. What a terrible dilemma to deal with alone."

Carl wags his head, talking to both Roxanne and Manning. "I've been wracking my brain, and I *think* I can establish an alibi for that Monday night—if I ever have to—but I must admit, I can't account for those crucial late-evening hours. I was alone, working, without witnesses."

"Whoa, Carl," says Manning, assuring him, "no one is accusing you of anything—no one even knows that your file exists, just us at this table."

Relieved, Carl asks, "Just out of curiosity, what *happened* to Clifford's files?"

"I found them. I kept them. They're safe at home. Conferring with Nathan Cain, we agreed not to turn them over to the police. The less they're handled, the better. When all this is over, I'll destroy them."

"Thank you, Mark." Carl touches Manning's sleeve. "Since coming to know you and Neil through Roxanne, I've learned to think of you as friends. Now, I'm truly indebted to you."

"Nonsense," Manning tells him. "At this point, you're merely the victim of suspicious circumstances, and those circumstances are known only to us. I hardly think you're the sort who'd put three bullets in a man's back."

"Let alone *four*," Carl corrects him with a laugh. He adds, "I believe that's what the news accounts said."

The waiter returns with menus and pours the last of the Cristal from the bottle. Carl orders another. Before long, the foursome is involved with dinner, switching topics with the progression of courses, frequently interrupting the festivities with further toasts to Carl's success in public life. Everyone is pleasantly surprised to discover that Zaza's has not been overrated—in spite of the noise and the frenetic atmosphere, it's a top-notch meal.

By the time dessert arrives, all four feel overfed and sated, cowed by the platefuls of rich, fanciful creations that bristle with chocolate twigs, wallowing in pools of exotic fruit purees. "I'll never eat again," moans Roxanne.

Neil tells her, "You say that now, Rox, but come noon tomorrow, you'll be chowing down with the best of them."

Carl snorts. "I don't know what plans Miss Exner may have for tomorrow, but as for me, I *will* be lunching with the best of them—MidAmerica Oil chairman Brad McCracken and *Journal* publisher Nathan Cain."

"Oh, really?" says Manning, forking a gob of something crusted with a crackly substance that looks like electrified shredded wheat. "You seem to see quite a bit of Mr. Cain. Are you . . . friendly?"

Carl swirls his spoon in a puddle of something purple. "Interesting question. Nathan's a hard guy to get to know—stiff, opinionated, strictly old-school. But I *have* come to like him. He brings a unique perspective to any discussion, and of course he's brilliant as well as powerful. I've done business with him for years, and with time, he's become something of a confidant, sort of a father figure."

"Same with Bradley McCracken?" Manning asks.

"Lord no. Brad is Nathan's friend. The two of them, along with the mayor and the archbishop, constitute a rarefied social circle all their own—way too rich for this humble lawyer's blood."

"Oh *please*, Carl." Roxanne licks a smear of chocolate from her thumb.

"It's true," he insists. "With that kind of wealth, commanding their individual empires, they're in a class uniquely theirs. I'm honored to rub elbows with them. It's not *every* day I'm invited to lunch in a private dining room at the Central States Club— high atop the MidAmerica Building."

"Hey," says Manning, "I'll be up there myself tomorrow— not as a lunch guest at noon, but to research a story at five-thirty. The mayor's office got me clearance to inspect a laser projector up on the tower platform."

Neil explains to Carl and Roxanne, "It's part of a surprise finale to Saturday night's human-rights rally at the stadium. There was talk of it in the news today."

"I heard about that," says Roxanne. "Sounds exciting. Carl and I can't wait."

The evening has grown late—it's after eleven—and all four will have a busy Friday. They agree to skip coffee, and after some initial check-tugging, Carl prevails as host. A few minutes later, they are on the street exchanging good-byes.

Manning gives the valet his stub for the car while Roxanne and Carl get into a cab. They wave and yoo-hoo through an open window as the cab pulls away from the curb, disappearing into traffic.

Neil turns to Manning. "Do you suppose they're sleeping together?"

Manning shrugs. "They're adults."

"I know, but I do feel sort of protective of Rox—even though she'd scoff at the idea. We've known each other so long. I mean, I used to *live* at her place whenever I was in the city. I still have her key somewhere."

"She's been a good friend to both of us," says Manning. "And I like Carl too, in spite of this stickiness about Cliff Nolan. All said, it's been a nice night out. A perfectly good time."

Then, from around the corner, appears a sight that brings their perfect evening to an abrupt end. The valet pulls Manning's big Bavarian V-8 to the curb—there's a deep scrape running the entire length of its passenger side. The sheet metal is dented badly, the mirror is missing, and the door doesn't quite close. Manning gapes at it, dumbstruck.

The valet hops out and holds the driver's door open for Manning as though nothing had happened. Upon questioning, he mumbles something about a tight squeeze, a cement guardrail, an insurance form.

Manning just wants to go home. He needs to pop a Xanax, crawl into bed, and put this behind him—he can't possibly deal with it now. In a daze, he pulls the car away from the curb and manages to wing the back of the car parked in front of him, smashing a headlight and crimping his hood.

Manning and Neil arrive home before midnight. It was a quiet ride, Manning driving in glassy-eyed silence, Neil trying to assure him, "They'll fix it good as new." Neil didn't realize, though, that Manning was preoccupied not only with the car, but with a difficult conversation he was saving till their return.

"Nightcap?" Neil asks him as they walk through the door, switch on the lights, and lock up behind them.

"A very short one," Manning tells him. "We had quite a bit of champagne, and I plan to take a pill tonight."

Neil pours shots of vodka over ice and garnishes them with orange peel. Manning removes his jacket and shoes, drops onto a sofa, and puts his feet on the coffee table. Then he broods. Neil joins him on the sofa, putting an arm around his shoulder, handing him one of the glasses. They don't bother with a toast. Neil sips his vodka; Manning just holds the glass in his lap.

"Neil," says Manning, looking straight ahead, through the dark window, "there's something I need to talk to you about. This isn't easy. It's about David."

Neil looks up from his glass and turns to Manning. "Yes?"

"Something 'happened' in Door County."

There's a long pause. Manning doesn't seem ready to volunteer more information, so Neil gives a nervous laugh, telling him, "If you're trying to make me jealous, Mark . . ."

Manning turns and interrupts him, "No, that's the last thing I'm *trying* to do. But I need to be honest with you—because I love you so much—even though I wouldn't blame you if you didn't believe me."

"What happened?" Neil asks flatly.

Manning can't face Neil as he tells him, "David and I had sex."

Neil strains for patience as he asks, "What did you do—exactly?"

"Everything."

"Was it safe?"

"Yes. I may have lost control, but at least I held on to *that* shred of sanity."

"Thank God." Neil falls silent. Then he rises from the sofa and paces the room. When he turns back to Manning, there are tears in his eyes. He shouts through a sob, *"Why would you tell me such a thing?"*

Manning didn't know what reaction to expect, but this wasn't it. Rising, he sets his drink on the table and takes a single step toward Neil. Astonished, Manning tells him, "I violated your trust, but I didn't intend to deceive you. I thought you'd prefer to know about this."

"Well I don't!" He takes a single step toward Manning. "All right, you made a slip. All right, you've got a guilty conscience. But then you dump it on *me?* You decide to feel better by making it *my* problem?" Neil throws his glass on the floor—"You son of a bitch!"

Uh-oh. That unassuming little rocks glass was Baccarat crystal. Fifty dollars' worth of shattered glass attests to Neil's anger more eloquently than any soap-opera clichés he might hurl. Manning tells him, "What I did was inexcusable, but there *were* extenuating circumstances."

"I'm sure. You were alone in the woods with a twenty-four-year-old. Now *that's* extenuating."

"Seriously, Neil, listen: It was your idea to send him up there with me—"

"I don't recall telling you to fuck him."

"But you did tell me to get a look at his body. You're never going to believe this, but the kid's got *pierced nipples*, and when I—"

Spinning his back toward Manning, Neil tells him, "*Spare* me the sordid details. I already have a perfectly vivid picture of what went on."

"I don't think you do, though," says Manning, stepping up behind Neil.

"Stop *talking*," says Neil, turning to face Manning again. "You're only making this worse. Can't you understand that it's pointless to discuss what happened that night? Right now, I'm considerably more worried about the future—our future. And this is the worst possible time to clutter our lives with emotional uncertainties. Christ, *I'm* up to my ass in this damned festival, *you're* at loose ends over your murder mystery, and now we're *both* stressed to the max because you can't keep your dick in your pants. There's really not much else to say, is there?"

Manning puts both hands on Neil's shoulders. "I can ask you to forgive me."

Neil brushes his hands away. "That's easier said than done, so don't count on it. We've both got a lot of thinking to do."

Friday, July 2

Pink clouds drift through Manning's brain as his feet trod the barren surface of a faraway planet. Mechanically, without thought or will, one clean white shoe springs ahead of the other, tramping in the dust a path that meanders across a patchwork of his footprints shooting toward the horizon in all directions. There is no order to this run. He circumscribes no Zarnikal equator. The remote daystar scribbles random patterns in the black sky.

Pink clouds hang low to blur Manning's vision, stinging his eyes with their glowing cosmic gases. This isn't pretty. It isn't fun. It's a frustrating excursion through a bland, passive world made hostile by its sheer desolation. The dream ensnares Manning with its pointless drudgery, goading him onward to a new morning in the real world that never dawns.

Pink clouds swipe past his naked body, whirling round his legs, slipping past his genitals, keeping him constantly aroused. But it doesn't feel good. His erect penis slaps from side to side in rhythm with his gait. It hurts.

Exhausted by his nightlong run—he can't even remember when it began—Manning finally slows his pace and stops. His chest heaves as he gulps the clouds into his lungs, not knowing whether they will nourish or poison. He must lie down.

Supine on the desert floor, he feels its powdery grit against his calves, buttocks, and shoulder blades. He wags his head, grinding his hair in it. His mind becomes focused on the starry noonday sky, lost in the levels of infinity that separate innumerable layers of lustrous pinpricks. One of those dots, the one shining brighter than all others, is the sun, seven billion miles away, commanding the movement of the planet beneath Manning's body. Somewhere near the sun, but hidden in darkness, is planet Earth.

There, people go about their lives, waking, breathing, talking, eating, working, fighting, loving, sexing, lying, sleeping, dreaming. Still dreaming.

But here, all is silence—except for the tick of the tips of the laces against the leather of his white running shoes. Here, nothing moves—except the jerking of his hand between his legs and the drifting of the lifeless clouds above him. He shuts his eyes, concentrating on the tension that builds in his groin.

Stroking himself, Manning waits to feel the presence of those muscular visitors who always seem to join him at this stage, bringing him to the brink of orgasm. There were two of them. Lately, only one. Where is he? *Who* is he? Where are they? They should be here. He needs them.

Manning opens his eyes, hearing music (that's odd) but seeing no one. He is totally alone in the sands and the clouds— there is no faithful lover, no secret trick—but there is music all around him now, lovely and familiar. What is that? Name that tune. Mozart, surely. A later symphony, maybe the fortieth, or is it the forty-first? They're easily confused, those middle movements. Yes, the forty-first, the "Jupiter." Strange venue, Jupiter on Zarnik. . . .

Manning opens his eyes, hearing the radio at his bedside. He has overslept. He normally awakes the second it switches on, during the early-morning newscast, but that's long finished, and the Mozart grinds toward its finale. He took a Xanax before bed and still feels groggy. The memory of the fight, the car, rushes back to him and knots his stomach. At least he slept.

He squints at the clock. It's nearly seven. Why didn't Neil wake him when the radio switched on—didn't he hear it either? Manning rolls over to nudge Neil on the other side of the bed. But Neil isn't there. And the knot in Manning's stomach tightens, secreting something acidic.

Not the least groggy now, Manning sits upright in bed, peering about the balcony. Then he switches off the radio, holding his breath to listen for any evidence of activity. There's an unremarkable background noise from downstairs—something mechanical, probably the refrigerator—but otherwise the loft is dead quiet. When at last he exhales, the sound of air rushing up his throat and past his teeth seems magnified in the silence, like a metal rake dragged across concrete.

He swings his legs to the floor and stands. Grabbing a seersucker bathrobe, he slips it on and flaps it around him, padding to the bathroom for a look inside. The lights are on. All is in order. But then he notices that the toiletries near Neil's sink seem different. Neil normally groups them precisely and aesthetically, composing something of a miniature skyline against the backsplash, but some of the items are now missing, and the ones that remain are askew—not a promising sign. Although last night ended on a terrible note, Manning fears that this morning is beginning on a worse one.

So he heads downstairs, determined to learn what has happened, but dreading what he may find. It doesn't take long.

First he notices that the broken glass has been cleaned up. Crossing to the kitchen, he sees that there is still coffee warm for him in the pot. And then he spots it—a folded sheet of paper propped on the counter next to his usual coffee mug—a very bad sign indeed. Stepping closer, he reads the word *Mark* written in Neil's distinctive hand on the letter's outer flap.

On the one hand, he wants to grab it at once and read what's inside. On the other, he wants to postpone it as long as possible. He at least needs to pour a cup of coffee first, which he does. He lifts the paper, still folded, and carries it with his cup to the center island. Plopping himself on a stool, he takes a first sip of coffee. Then, bracing himself, he opens the letter.

Dear Mark,

Last night really threw me. I need some time to think about what's happened. Suddenly I don't know where we're headed. It's ironic that I should feel this way just as we've finally gotten settled into the loft. Maybe I was naive in equating the completion of our home—its physical structure—with the stability of a relationship that I assumed was unshakable. But I'm an architect. It's a mind-set.

You may have noticed that I packed a few things and took them to the office. I'll go to Roxanne's tonight and stay there awhile. It'll be better for us.

(Actually, I have no idea what's better for us, but I just don't care to face you right now. You've hurt me terribly, I feel nothing but anger at the moment, and I don't know if I can forgive you. If I can, I don't know how long it will take. Like I said, I need some time to think.)

You're sleeping soundly as I write this. I don't know whether that's the result of your cleansed conscience or simply the benign effect of champagne and Xanax. In either case, I resent it. You did what you had to do, then drifted off to dreamland—while *my* night was sleepless because my life had been turned upside down.

Because of the festival, the weekend that lies ahead would be, even under ideal circumstances, the most anxiety-ridden of my life. And now the whole situation has become infinitely more complicated. Though many things confuse me right now, I can say this with absolute objectivity: Your sense of timing is atrocious.

So, where are we? You act as though nothing has happened, yet the fact that you felt the need to "confess" your dalliance shows that you understand the gravity of what's happened to us. I do believe you when you say you're sorry. I'm also willing to believe that you truly want to put the incident behind us. In other words, I think your head is in the right place. Even so, I feel as if *my* brain has been fucked and fried. Sorry, but that's where I'm at.

Please do not phone me. We've both got plenty else on our plates right now. Let's just get through the weekend. Maybe next week we can talk. Let's hope that the love we've found and the "home" we've built (the life we share, not the loft) will be sufficient to see us through.

But I have to tell you, Mark—I'm just not sure.

Neil

Manning hasn't touched the coffee. He stares at the letter as if it's not real. Surely he is dreaming now—this is one of those dreams that haunt the predawn hours with specters of death or missed exams or bowel movements in public places. He shakes his head, hoping to wake to a bright, normal morning of his everyday life. But no—this morning, this letter, this cup of cold coffee are real.

Neil may have packed little more than a toothbrush and razor, but that could signal the beginning of the end. Toiletries today, but what about tomorrow? There could be a U-Haul sputtering at their loading dock.

Neil has packed very little, but he's gone. It may not be forever—Manning can't even fathom such a possibility—but the cold, hard fact remains that Neil has left him.

Activity in the *Journal*'s newsroom is more hectic than usual as the city gears up for the festival's opening, the visiting pantheon of cultural and political celebrities, the presidential address, the human-rights rally, and the counterdemonstration by the CFC. With the approach of the late-morning deadline for the afternoon edition, the commotion intensifies with ringing phones, scurrying copy kids, and conversations shouted over the partitions of reporters' cubicles.

Manning, however, is assignment-free this morning. Nathan Cain had made it clear that his time should be dedicated to the Nolan and Zarnik investigations. When Manning arrived today, he talked to his editor, Gordon Smith, volunteering to help with one of the festival stories, but Smith only reiterated Cain's orders. Since there's nothing Manning can do with his assignment until his five-o'clock meeting with Zarnik at the planetarium, he's been spending his time on the phone arranging for estimates to get his car repaired. As he feared, the procedure is shaping into a bureaucratic hassle, but at least it keeps his mind occupied with something other than his situation with Neil.

In spite of Neil's request that Manning not phone him, Manning has called Neil's office several times already. There's always some excuse—he's out, he's in a meeting, he's on the other line. While Manning can assume that Neil is truly swamped today, he suspects that the receptionist at the architectural firm has been instructed by Neil to screen Manning's calls.

While scribbling another note to clip to his insurance policy, Manning hears something that catches his attention through the hubbub of the newsroom. Daryl's voice lilts above the others, saying, "What's the big rush, David?"

But David doesn't answer. Instead, it's the unmistakable voice of his uncle, Hector Bosch. "Get out of my *way*," he snarls, and there are sounds of a struggle with something that clatters against the wall—possibly Daryl's mail cart.

Manning rises from his chair to see what's going on. He hears David say, "Wait, Uncle Hector—don't!"

Manning has barely stuck his head from around the partition to look into the corridor when Hector rushes into the cubicle, slamming Manning back into his chair. With fire in his eyes, he yells, *"You reprehensible scapegrace!"*

Stunned, Manning watches David and Daryl rush up behind Hector. David claps an arm over Hector's shoulder; Daryl keeps his distance, gaping from the hall. Heads bob up from behind the partitions, wondering what the uproar is about. At a loss for words, Manning says lamely, "Good morning, Hector."

"Don't 'good morning' me, Mr. Manning. There are times when civility is but a mockery of decency."

"Hector . . ." says Manning with a calming gesture of his hands, trying to rise from his chair.

But with a jab of his fingertips, Hector forces Manning down again, telling him, "Quiet! You've said enough—God knows you've *done* enough."

People are gathering in the corridor, straining for a look inside the cubicle. David leans over his uncle's shoulder. "Please, Hector. Not here, not now."

Brushing his nephew's hand away, Hector turns his head to tell him, "When I want your advice, I'll ask for it. You certainly didn't heed *my* counsel, and now it's led to this."

Hector returns his attention to Manning, but now David is angry. He tells Hector, "It's only 'led to this' because *you've* chosen to have a cow over it. I'm an adult. Mind your own damn business."

Hector spins to face him. "You *made* it my business by baring your soul to me this morning."

"You can bet I won't make that mistake again."

"Your only mistake, young man, was sleeping with *him!*" Hector whips an accusing index finger toward Manning. There's a collective gasp from the growing pack of onlookers. Manning's jaw drops. Hector turns to tell him, "My God, just look at the two of you. Now you're even dressing alike. But you, Manning, you're a seducer, a predator"—he lunges to grab Manning by the shirt—"a disgrace to the profession of journalism."

Both David and Daryl rush to pull Hector back.

"Watch it," Manning warns Hector, rising. Facing him nose-to-nose, Manning controls his anger but tells him firmly, "If there's something that needs to be discussed, we can go to a conference room. You've already strayed into slanderous territory, so I'd recommend that you zip it."

Hector puffs his chest and smooths the jacket of his natty black suit, ruffled during the brief skirmish. "If that remark was meant as a threat, Mr. Manning, you're wasting your breath." He strokes the bristles of his trim little moustache, first the right side, then the left. "If there are any threats to be made, they'll be coming from me, and they won't be nearly so veiled. Are you aware that I'm on a first-name basis with virtually every publisher in New York?"

Manning is tempted to ask him, So the hell what?

Hector continues, "Though this whole sordid episode is profoundly embarrassing to me, you can rest assured that I shan't hesitate to share it with my publisher, who happens to be not only a colleague but a friend of your own publisher, Nathan Cain. They share many of the same values—values that are affronted by your reprobate actions. Your harassment and seduction of a much younger *male* coworker will surely shock the refined sensibilities of these upstanding gentlemen. I would be very surprised indeed if Nathan Cain concluded that your presence in this office is still an asset to the *Journal.*"

There's a moment of silence. Hector notes with satisfaction that the impact of his words is now reflected in the pallor of Manning's face. Hector smiles. He touches up the knot of Manning's necktie. With a curt bow of his head, Hector tells him, "Good day, Mr. Manning." Then he turns on his heel and struts down the corridor, parting the gaping crowd of onlookers.

David is about to take off after him when he turns back to Manning. "Sorry Mark. He's drawn the wrong conclusions about this. I'll try to set him straight." He reaches to give Manning's shoulder a squeeze, then scurries after Hector.

Daryl hasn't said a word, but has witnessed the entire confrontation, absorbing every delicious detail. With a broad Cheshire grin, he sidles into the cubicle and opens his mouth to speak.

"Don't," says Manning, fumbling to sit in his chair. "Just don't."

The rest of the day doesn't improve much. Though there are no subsequent shouting matches volleyed over Manning's desk, news of the one that did occur has spread throughout the paper. While he expected to become the butt of relentless taunting because of the incident, he was wrong. Far worse, he has been shunned. Coworkers won't look him in the eye. Many actually shift directions in the hall in order not to encounter him. It's as if . . . as if they actually *believed* Hector's exaggerated, misinformed accusations.

Shortly after four-thirty, Manning decides it's time to head out. He needs to meet Zarnik at the planetarium by five and work out the logistics of getting to the MidAmerica Building by five-thirty—it's going to be a tight squeeze. He switches off his desk lamp, then lifts the phone and dials an extension. "David? Let's get going. It might be better if you just met me in the parking lot."

Outside, behind the Journal Building, a bright afternoon is cooled by a brisk wind off the lake. Manning normally anticipates the first sight of his car after work as one of the little highlights of his day, but today he dreads seeing it. He walks out of his way in order to approach it from the driver's side, avoiding the view of last night's damage. Unlocking the car with the fob button, he tosses his laptop carryall and his blazer onto the backseat, then gets it. The black car is hot inside, so he starts the engine, running the air-conditioning while waiting for David.

Not more than a minute later, David trots out of the building and zigzags between the other cars toward Manning. Then he sees the damage, which stops him in his tracks. He approaches with caution, mouthing through the closed windows, "What happened?"

Manning waves him in.

David tosses his own blazer, which matches Manning's, onto the backseat. Sitting in front, he repeats the question.

"Let's just say I had a bad night," Manning answers, and pulls out of the lot.

David tries to assure him, "They'll be able to fix it." After a pause, he says, "I'm afraid to ask, but did you tell Neil?" Manning nods. Almost inaudibly, David asks, "And how'd it go?"

Eyes on the road, Manning answers without inflection, "Not well at all. He packed a few things and went to stay with Roxanne for a while."

Subdued and thoughtful, David tells him, "I'm sorry, Mark. I've done a lot of thinking since yesterday, and I've come to understand that this is all my fault."

Manning turns his head to voice a feeble protest, but David continues, "Don't tell me—I know—it takes two to tango. But the truth is, I started it. I pursued you, I tantalized you, I lured you into a situation that all your instincts told you to avoid. I thought it was just harmless fun, but it's made a mess, and I'm sorry. I'm stupid."

"No," Manning tells him, "you're young, that's all. And I think you've just gained a little wisdom."

The Friday-afternoon traffic is heavy, with many city people getting out of town to avoid the weekend crowds. Many others pour into town to take part in the festivities. Everyone, though, seems headed for the new stadium, eager to circle the just-finished structure and glimpse its avant-garde architecture, its grand entryway, its flowering boulevards. A battalion of specially recruited white-gloved traffic cops practices guiding the torrent of cars with civility and humor, a dress rehearsal for tomorrow's big opening.

David has been peering at the distant stadium through the side window when Manning takes a turn that will lead them away, toward the planetarium. Manning asks him, "Why did you decide to talk to your uncle about this?"

"Like I said: I'm stupid."

"No, David, not at all. I know that your uncle means a lot to you, and I know he's had a big influence on your upbringing. I heard that you came out to him during college and that he didn't react well. Still, it was a brave move on your part—it showed a lot of integrity. My guess is that you confided in him again today in order to give him a second chance to put this issue at rest between you."

With a lame laugh, David tells Manning, "You're more analytical about it than I was—I just wanted to level with him. Trouble is, he was in no mood for honesty, and as you heard only too well, he got the situation backwards."

Manning turns to face David with a smile. "It doesn't help that we've started dressing like the Bobbsey Twins."

"You've noticed," says David, embarrassed. They *are* dressed like twins today—khaki slacks, white shirts, striped silk ties, navy blazers. "I wasn't even conscious that I was doing it till Hector pointed it out. Sorry."

"Stop apologizing. You look great. And I'm flattered."

"I've arranged to have a talk with Hector later tonight. I'll make sure he understands what happened. Maybe, when he calms down, he'll make an apology in the newsroom. I'll try to work it out."

Manning sighs. "Any effort in that direction would be greatly appreciated." The planetarium is now visible beyond the next turn of the road. "Meanwhile," says Manning, "we've got some reporting to do. Unfortunately, I didn't expect traffic to be this heavy, and we can't be in two places at once."

"Can you postpone your appointment at the MidAmerica laser site?"

"No," says Manning, "it's nearly five already, and Uttley had to pull strings to book the five-thirty inspection. I can't fiddle with it now. But here's another idea: *I'll* meet Zarnik here at the planetarium while *you* turn around in the car and go to the MidAmerica Building for me."

"Sounds like a plan."

Pulling into the parking lot at the planetarium, Manning asks, "Do you have your press pass and cell phone?" David nods. Manning tells him, "Drive to the east parking entrance of the building—it's not very well marked because it leads to the private parking ramp for the Central States Club. They're expecting my car at the gate, and the guard will direct you. Use your pass if you have to, explain that I sent you, and hope they play along. When you've made it up to the laser platform at the top of the tower, call me."

"Sure," says David. "I think I can handle that."

Manning stops at the curb in front of the steps to the planetarium, and they both get out of the car. They grab their jackets from the backseat, making sure each has the right one. Manning takes his computer case, then David gets in behind the wheel. Before closing the door, he reaches to shake Manning's hand. "Good luck in there, Mark. And thanks for everything. In spite of the glitches, these have been the best two weeks of my life."

Manning musses David's hair. "Call me from the tower."

Just inside the main door of the planetarium, Manning is surprised to find Pavo Zarnik waiting for him, chewing one of his fingernails. When Zarnik sees Manning, he glances at his watch and says, with no trace of an accent, "Thank God, you're about two minutes early. Come on, hurry." And he leads Manning toward the back stairs that lead up to his laboratory.

Over the clatter of their feet on the metal stairs, Manning asks, "Why the big rush, Professor? What could be so time-sensitive about the technical notes you've prepared for me?"

At the top of the stairs, Zarnik stops, facing Manning. With a featureless expression, he says flatly, "There are no notes. Did you really expect any?"

Manning senses that at last this charade may unravel. He does not answer Zarnik's question, but merely jerks his head in the direction of the door to the laboratory. "I'm at your disposal, Professor."

Zarnik nods, leading the reporter down the hall. He walks with quick, sure strides, not the skittering shuffle that has previously characterized his gait. Arriving at the door with the red plastic sign, he unlocks it with a key that hangs with the whistle around his neck. He pushes the door open for Manning, who steps inside. The lights are already on, but the banks of computers are dark and silent. Zarnik closes the door behind them.

Manning stands in the clearing near the center of the room. Zarnik says nothing, but crosses to his desk, checks a page of the calendar, checks his watch, checks for something in a drawer, chews a hangnail. Manning asks, "Is there something you wanted to tell me?"

"Not yet," says Zarnik. "Things will soon begin to explain themselves. Come here, please." And he walks beyond the desk, behind a row of metal cabinets.

Manning follows. There are a few square yards of clear floor space behind the bank of electronic hardware, where a pair of sturdy wooden chairs flank a small table. There's nothing on the table till Manning sets his computer there—it seems that the furniture has been hastily arranged.

Zarnik gestures that Manning should sit, telling him, "You'll be able to hear everything from here. Have your notebook ready, and for God's sake, be quiet."

At several minutes past five, all is quiet in Nathan Cain's outer offices. There are often projects that keep people working late in the publisher's suite, but with the approach of the long holiday weekend, everyone has managed to be out the door on time—except Lucille Haring, who sits at her desk staring at the clock.

She tidies some clutter on her desk, then rearranges files in a drawer, stalling. Having not yet logged off her computer, she poises her fingers over the keyboard, hesitates, then stands up. She paces once, smartly, toward the window, turns, and marches back to her desk. Biting her lip, she drums her fingers on the plastic shell of the computer monitor; the clacking of her nails resounds in the quiet office.

But that noise is overpowered by the clank of heavy brass hardware—Lucille Haring jumps—as the timbered door to Nathan Cain's inner office opens. Cain steps through, closing the door behind him and locking it with a key that Lucille Haring has never seen him use. He also carries a briefcase, which is not his habit.

"Good evening, Colonel," she says, stepping forward. "I was wondering whether you'd left yet. I thought you might be in residence here this weekend."

He grunts vacantly. "No. The holiday and all. With all the hoopla, I've decided to go north for a few days."

"Ah," she says, nodding, "that's probably a good idea, sir. We could all use a bit of R and R. But it looks as if you're taking some work along with you."

He glances down at the briefcase, then up at her. "No, Miss Haring." He steps closer and lowers his voice. "I've been a little nervous about our security of late. This is material I'd rather have with me while I'm gone. Just a precaution."

"Oh, really?" She steps to her computer terminal and calls something up on the screen. "I assure you, Colonel, there's been no evidence of a breach—your offices are tight as a drum."

"Well," he bounces the key in his palm, "they are now." He pockets the key. "Enjoy the Fourth, Miss Haring. And don't forget to turn out the lights."

As he walks down the corridor toward the outer door, Lucille Haring calls after him, "Thank you, Colonel. Have a happy Independence Day."

When the door closes after him, she pauses, listening to the pervasive silence of the office. Then she sits down at her desk, back straight as a board, and begins typing codes into the computer. Now and then, the machine asks for more, which she feeds it. Finally, she relaxes in her chair and waits. Then she smiles.

The message on the screen says, "Welcome, Mr. Cain."

Manning checks his watch—it's nearly five-fifteen. He's had a few minutes to settle into his hiding space, wondering what, if anything, is about to transpire. He's discovered a crack between two of the cabinets through which he can see Zarnik's desk, the door, and not much else. Sitting in the shadow of the cabinets, there's sufficient light for him to take notes, but since the rest of the room is relatively bright, he's confident that he won't be seen peeking.

There's a rap at the door. Zarnik turns in his chair at the desk and asks, "Yes, who is it?" Manning notices that the accent has resurfaced.

A woman's voice says from the corridor, "It's me, Professor. Miss Jenner. Your guest from the mayor's office is here." Manning's brows arch with interest.

Rising, Zarnik tells her, "Coming, Miss Jenner. Thank you." He skitters across the room, completely in character, then turns the lock and opens the door. Miss Jenner, who's a perky little thing, stands outside with the visitor. As Manning has already deduced, it is Victor Uttley. His lanky frame stretches more than a foot above the woman's. He wears dark sunglasses, a fifties-vintage pair of classic Ray-Bans, conspicuously inappropriate inside the building—a lame attempt at disguise, no doubt.

Zarnik extends his hand. "Mr. Uttley, I presume?"

"It's an honor, Professor," Uttley responds dryly, shaking Zarnik's hand.

Zarnik tells the woman, "Thank you, Miss Jenner. You may run along now. And please—do enjoy your holiday."

She titters, excusing herself with a clumsy gesture that resembles a curtsy, and disappears down the hall.

Zarnik waves Uttley into the lab, closing the door behind them. Dropping the accent, he says, "Well, Victor, it's been a while. It seems that both of our careers have finally taken off, though in divergent and unexpected directions."

"Spare me the rhetoric, Arlen." Uttley looks around the room. "Impressive. Do you have any idea how to work this stuff?"

"Not a clue."

Uttley lights one of his imported cigarettes. "Next question, the more important one: Do you *have* it?"

The actor who has pretended to be Zarnik asks, "What?" With feigned naiveté, he adds, "The payoff money? The loot?"

"Now now, Arlen," Uttley scolds him, "you know better than that. Let's just call it the price of silence, or better yet, a token of past friendship."

"Yeah, right. Ten thousand bucks is a heap of friendship."

Manning rolls his eyes, stifling a laugh. Ten here, ten there—it adds up.

The actor named Arlen leads Uttley to the desk. He opens the top drawer, takes out a standard letter-size envelope, about an inch thick, and hands it to Uttley, who hefts it, looking disappointed. The actor asks him, "What's the matter, Victor? Were you expecting an attaché case? It's a hundred bills, a hundred each. Count them—ten thousand even."

Uttley peeks inside, then closes the flap of the envelope, satisfied. The cigarette bobs in his mouth as he asks, "Where'd you get it? Who supplied it?"

"That, I'm afraid, is none of your business. You've gotten what you wanted—now go away and keep your mouth shut."

"I'll be quiet," Uttley assures him, then he adds, "for now."

"Victor, so help me . . ."

Manning's got the idea. They're going to bicker for a while. He wishes Uttley *would* leave so that he could question Zarnik— or Arlen or whoever he is—at length. The man is obviously ready to confide in Manning, but for some reason, he wants Uttley kept in the dark.

What time is it? Almost twenty-five past five. Then Manning remembers with a start that he instructed David Bosch to phone him when he arrives at the top of the MidAmerica Building. The cell phone in Manning's breast pocket could ring at any moment. If Manning switches off the phone, he could miss David's call and blow a promising story. If he leaves it switched on, he could blow his cover behind the cabinet. He wants Uttley to leave. Now.

David spots the garage ramp on the east side of the MidAmerica Building. Manning was right—it could easily be missed, marked only with a discreet plaque that says *Central States Club*. He pulls up to the gate and lowers his window, prepared to talk his way past the guard. But the guard has seen the car coming, checked his clipboard, and now leans to tell David, "Good evening, Mr. Manning. We've been expecting you. Please park at the top level of the ramp. The host at the elevator will direct you."

That was easy. David thanks him, raises his window, and drives the big black car up four or five levels. When he can go no farther, he sees the private elevator lobby. Gold lettering on the glass door reads *Central States Club*. An attendant stands there at a podium. There's a red carpet leading from the spartan concrete environs of the garage to the lavishly decorated interior.

David gets out of the car and puts on his blazer, checking pockets for press pass, phone, and notebook. He locks the car and walks the red carpet, removing the pass from his jacket, ready to do some explaining to the attendant. The man at the podium has watched his arrival, and when David steps up to talk to him, he says, "Welcome, Mr. Manning. They phoned up to say you were here. I understand the mayor's office has arranged for you to visit the tower platform."

"That's right." David is enjoying this—he'll fill in for Manning anytime.

"Simply take this elevator to the top floor, eighty-nine. You'll arrive in the lobby of the club, with the bar entrance straight ahead. Before you get to the bar, though, along the right-hand wall, you'll find an unmarked door to a stairwell. Since it's still too early for the club's dinner crowd, there will be no one on duty in the lobby, so the door has been left unlocked for you. Take the stairs three flights up to the tower platform. If there are still workers up there, they will know to expect you, but they may have left already. I'm sure I needn't caution you, but it's open air up there, so do be careful."

"Thank you," David tells the man. "You've been very helpful." Then he gets into the elevator, presses the top button, and begins his rapid nonstop ascent. During the course of the trip, which seems to take well over a minute, he swallows several times to clear his ears. When the doors slide open, he finds himself in the club lobby, just as it was described. The bar is ahead, backlit by a spectacular view. There is an inconspicuous door along the right wall, partially hidden by a potted plant. There is no one else around, so he crosses the deep carpeting to the door and tries it—sure enough, it's not locked.

On the other side of the door, the walls are bare cement block, with metal stairs leading up. David climbs several turns of the stairway, and on the sixth landing, the stairs end at a door. He opens it, finding himself in a short hall, no more than six feet long, which leads to another door. Hearing the howl of wind beyond the second door, he concludes that the double-doored hall was designed as a buffer—it might otherwise be impossible to close the outside door against the wind.

Even with the inside door closed securely behind him, David has a struggle with the outer one, but he manages to step through and get it closed. Then, turning, he finds himself standing atop one of the city's tallest buildings. Earth itself seems to spread out before him, radiant in the late-afternoon sun, teeming with anonymous millions who scurry to launch their weekend. He views the lower half of Lake Michigan as though on a map. Indiana, he knows, is below it, Michigan across it, Wisconsin just up the shore from where he stands. And nothing can be heard but the sound of the wind.

While Manning holds the cellular phone in his hand, deciding whether to switch it off, it rings.

"... trying to make ends meet ..." Uttley lops his harangue midsentence, choking on the words. "What the hell?"

The phone rings again. Manning steps out from behind the cabinet, answering, "Yes?" Uttley removes his sunglasses to gape at Manning with bulging, unbelieving eyes. The tension of his stance suggests he's ready to bolt from the room. But Manning is careful to keep his own body language relaxed and unthreatening. He says into the phone, "Hello, David. No hassles? Great."

Uttley turns to face the other actor, seething. "Traitor!" He throws his cigarette on the floor and stamps it out as a child might, verging on a tantrum.

"For heaven's sake, Victor. Can the melodrama." The actor named Arlen plops himself into the chair at the desk. "You're an extortionist. Do you really think you deserve the loyalty of friends—particularly friends you've *blackmailed?*"

Manning plugs a finger in his ear so he can hear the phone better. "You caught me at an awkward moment here, David. Listen, you try to locate the equipment, look it over, and I'll call you back in a few minutes." He folds the phone shut, slips it into his jacket, and tells the others, "Sorry for the interruption, gentlemen. Nice to see you again, Victor." He extends his hand, but Uttley stands there ramrod stiff, fuming. Then Manning turns, extending his hand to the other man. "I don't believe we've met, actually."

Zarnik's impostor rises from his chair, reluctantly steps toward Manning, and shakes his hand. "My name is Arlen Farber. I'm an actor, and I've been hired to play a role. It sounded like a fun gig, and the money's really good. But something's up, Mr.

Manning—something sinister, I'm afraid. So I decided it was time to, uh . . . blow the proverbial whistle." With a humorless expression, he gives his chrome police whistle a feeble toot.

Manning has his notebook ready. "Who's paying you, Arlen?"

"As I told you before—truthfully, in fact—I get checks from the planetarium. But where does the money *really* come from? I have no idea."

"And Victor's hush money?"

Arlen Farber shrugs. "It's a mystery. The envelope was couriered to my secretary, but I don't know the source. I have a contact, of course. It's a man. But I know him only by his phone number."

"That's a start," says Manning. "Phones are easily traced. May I have it?"

Uttley steps between them, interrupting, "You two are too much." His tone is pissed. "Arlen Farber, two-bit actor, running to the press with some half-baked conspiracy theory, hoping to grab more headlines. What'sa matter, Arlen? Haven't you gotten enough ink in the past two weeks?" He doesn't wait for an answer, but spins his attention to Manning. "And you, Mr. Hotshot Reporter—is this any way to treat a contact from the mayor's office? Don't forget, I pulled some strings to arrange for your access to the MidAmerica laser site." Uttley remembers something, checks his watch. "Why aren't you *there*, instead of *here*, entrapping *me?*"

"David, my assistant, went in my place—that's who called." Arlen Farber looks confused by this exchange, so Manning explains to him, "I'm working on another story, unrelated to all this, about a sky show promoting gay rights to be staged as part of tomorrow's ceremonies at the new stadium. It involves some laser equipment that's been installed on top of three tall buildings, including the *Journal*'s tower. I saw something while visiting my publisher's office earlier this week that made me want to examine the equipment at one of the other buildings."

Uttley butts into the conversation again. "I *still* don't understand why you just don't examine the projector at the *Journal*."

"Simple," says Manning. "It might irk the man who signs my

check. If this story pans out, Nathan Cain will be pleased, naturally. But it might turn out to be a non-story altogether, and if that's the case, he won't appreciate any attention I draw to the sky show, let alone the company's time I'd spend pursuing it."

"Why not?" asks Uttley. "The whole thing was his idea."

"Hardly," Manning tells him. "Cain's support of the project is grudging at best. He's a traditional-values sort of guy, certainly no advocate of gay rights. The only reason he agreed to allow one of the projectors to be installed at the *Journal* is that the paper might be perceived as 'unenlightened' if he didn't play along. But he resents it—he told me so."

"Ha!" Uttley laughs, limping to the door, envelope of cash in one hand, sunglasses in the other. He turns to tell Manning, "Nathan Cain himself came to the mayor *months* ago to propose the sky show. He volunteered technical assistance with the hardware as well as use of the *Journal*'s tower platform. He felt strongly that the whole spectacle should be kept as a surprise finale for the opening ceremony, and the mayor agreed. I sat in on the meeting and heard every word."

Manning has taken a few notes, but stopped, truly confused by Uttley's claim.

Satisfied that his words have produced the intended effect, Uttley puts on his Ray-Bans again, opens the door, and steps into the hallway. Before closing the door behind him, he tells Manning, "You really ought to get your facts straight, Mark. And hey, we're friends—no charge."

As soon as Uttley is gone, Manning retrieves his carryall from the hiding space behind the cabinets and moves it to the desk, where he unpacks his laptop and modem, as well as several manila folders containing handwritten notes, morgue photos, and clippings. Adding to the clutter, he unloads his pockets—steno pad, phone, datebook, fountain pen, and wallet. There's no longer room on the desk for Arlen Farber's things, so Manning hands him a brown paper bag that holds an extra peanut butter sandwich. As if ravenous, Farber unwraps the sandwich and begins to gobble it, pacing the room.

Manning thinks of something. Riffling through the wallet, he finds the business card that Gordon Smith gave him in Nathan Cain's office on Monday. He flips it over and finds Cain's pager number, written there by Smith as instructed. Manning really ought to beep Cain and discuss Victor Uttley's claims about the laser show. And he owes David a call, too. What's more, he now knows the identity of Zarnik's impostor, which deserves page-one treatment in the next edition—as does the extortionist he's discovered in the mayor's office. But where to begin with all this?

He opens a computer file and scrolls through his notes while Arlen Farber wolfs his sandwich. Manning tells him, "Let's start with the big question: Why have you pretended to be Pavo Zarnik?"

Through a mouthful of mush, Farber answers, "They *told* me to."

"Who did? And why?"

Farber swallows. "I don't know."

"Do you know where the real Pavo Zarnik is?"

"You're asking the wrong guy—that's what I wanted to know. They told me he was away somewhere, 'on vacation,' they said."

Manning scrolls through more notes. "You were insistent that I alone would report Zarnik's story. You said that you chose me because I had a reputation for being scrupulous, insightful, and fair—and I was flattered enough, *dumb* enough, to buy it. Okay, Arlen, what was the *real* reason for my exclusive?"

Farber tosses his hands in exasperation. "I don't *know*." The last remaining wad of his sandwich hurtles through the air and lands in the guts of a rack of electronics. "I did what I was told, but they never told me why."

Manning looks up from his computer. "Then why in hell did you drag me down here today? All you've told me is your name."

Farber approaches him at the desk. He speaks calmly, but there's an intensity to his stare that reveals desperation. "I'm telling you, Mr. Manning, that I'm scared. I don't know who's behind this or why, but there's obviously big money at stake, or power, or *something*. I didn't know what I was getting into, and I still don't know what it's about, but I'm growing more and more convinced that I won't get out of it *alive*. Please, Mark. Help me!"

Manning wasn't expecting that. He has thought of the actor as part of a plot, but now he understands that Farber is more a pawn than a perpetrator. Manning also realizes, with sudden clarity, that he, too, has been made an unwitting participant in a sinister scheme that he cannot yet fathom. He, too, is in danger.

"I'll do my best, Arlen. Let me call David first. I've got him on another story, but let's concentrate on this one. I'll get him back here, he'll bring the car, and we can all go somewhere and try to sort this out—we may not be safe here."

"Oh, Lord." Farber resumes pacing as Manning picks up his cell phone and punches in David's number.

David scratches his head. Clearly, he's located the laser projector—the equipment looks brand-new, and the immediate area is littered with debris from its installation—knocked-down crates, scraps of cable, bolts and other hardware. What's more, it's at the corner of the roof that points toward the new stadium, which makes sense. Otherwise, what he sees doesn't tell him much. It's just this . . . *device*. He can't imagine why Manning was so interested in it.

Then he notices a panel on the side of the housing, attached with thumbscrews. It should be easy enough to remove the panel and expose the innards, which may be of use to Manning. He squats in front of it, working on the first of the screws, when his phone rings. He answers, "Hi, Mark. I found it."

"David," Manning's voice buzzes through the phone, "I don't have time to explain, but it's important that you leave there now and drive back here to the planetarium. 'Zarnik' and I will meet you in the parking lot. We all need to get out of here and hole up somewhere."

David laughs. "You're suddenly sounding very mysterious. What's up?"

"Let's just say I've got a lot on my mind today."

"Don't worry about that scene with Uncle Hector," David

assures Manning. "I'll iron things out with him when we meet later tonight."

"I'll appreciate that," says Manning, "but that's not the issue right now. Just get yourself back to the planetarium."

"Aren't you even curious about what I've found up here?"

Manning hesitates. "Actually, I am. Describe the projector for me. For starters, is the housing a drab olive color?"

"No," says David, "it's black. Flat black."

"What about its shape? Is there a long snout in front and a tractor seat in back with lots of mean-looking controls?"

David double-checks. "None of the above. It's just a big black box. There's a slit on the outer side—I assume that's where the beam comes out. Otherwise, it looks something like a big transformer. There's a panel here with thumbscrews."

"See if you can get it off and have a look inside."

"I've been trying to do exactly that," David says with a laugh, "but it's slow going with the phone in one hand."

"Good work," Manning tells him. "There may be more to this than I thought. Listen, David. Just put the phone down—that should speed things up for you—then tell me when you can see inside. I'll stand by."

"Okay, Mark." David sets the phone aside, just around the corner of the projector housing, where it won't be damaged if the panel should fall when he removes it. Then he sets to work on the rest of the thumbscrews, about a dozen.

One by one, he removes them, setting them in a neat pile in front of him. That's five, six, halfway there. The wind howls around him, flapping his jacket, tousling his hair. Far overhead, pink-edged clouds drift over the lake in a perfect azure evening sky. David whistles a tuneless ditty, content to perform this menial task, learning the ropes of a profession he loves, determined more than ever to master his craft. Ten down, all but the top two corners.

In that instant, everything changes. "That's far enough!" screams the voice of an assailant from behind. "You're dead, Manning!" And the shot is fired.

David's body is thrown forward. He sees the metal surface of the laser housing approach his eye, but he does not feel it smash against his face. As his head hits the tar-covered surface of the tower platform, he hears the rasp of Manning's voice screaming his name from the phone—once, twice, but no more. In a flash, the blue sky blackens. The clouds are sucked away into oblivion.

Seated at the desk in Zarnik's lab, stunned and panicky, Manning now whispers, "No, David, no . . ." Tears slide down his face as he tells the phone, "I'm so sorry, David. . . ."

Arlen Farber shakes Manning by the shoulders. "What's wrong, Mark? What happened?"

Manning turns to look at him, but doesn't take the phone from his ear. He tells Farber, "David's been shot."

"Oh my God!"

Manning frantically waves for Farber to shut up—he hears something—the footsteps of the assailant approaching the phone. He hears the man's voice again. "David? *Hngh*. My apologies for so untimely a death, but rest assured, Mr. Bosch, it must have been God's will."

The murderer is apparently unaware of the phone. Manning listens to an odd little noise, the sound of some prolonged activity at the scene. He concludes that the murderer is methodically reinstalling the thumbscrews.

Then it all clicks, and Manning feels his heart stop. *He has recognized the voice of the killer.* It sounded like none other than . . . *Nathan Cain*. But it couldn't be—could it?—even in light of Victor Uttley's unlikely revelation that Cain was the planner of tomorrow's laser spectacle.

Suddenly, the pieces start falling together. With his mind in a spin, Manning realizes that Cain's own computer savvy gave him direct access to reporters' drafts. It was he, not Lucille Haring, who discovered that Cliff Nolan was preparing to expose Zarnik. David Bosch was caught in the act of discovering something that warranted his murder as well. The Zarnik plot is therefore directly related to the laser spectacle, and David's murder was an extension of Nolan's.

What's more, the Verdi *Requiem* was played to mask the gunfire that killed Cliff Nolan. Shortly after the murder, but before Manning had learned what music was played, the words of the "Dies Irae," the medieval dirge, were on Cain's lips. He said in English, " 'Day of wrath and day of mourning,' " speaking of the obituary he planned to write for Nolan.

Most obvious of all—and Manning berates himself for not picking up on this—Cain's war injury left him with a stiff walk that could easily be described as a "limp." A tall man, always impeccably dressed, he fits Dora Lee's description to the letter.

Manning now *knows* who killed Cliff Nolan and David Bosch, but there's no way to prove that Cain is the person up on that rooftop right now with David's body.

Ah, but there is! With sudden inspiration, Manning sifts through the things on Zarnik's desk, plucks up a business card, and hands it to Farber. He covers the mouthpiece of his cellular phone and tells Farber, "There's a number on the back. Call it on your phone. It's a pager. You'll get a signal, then—"

"I know how they work," Farber tells him as he starts dialing.

"Don't use your own number. After the signal, punch in the weather lady."

Farber nods. He gets the signal, dials, then hangs up.

Manning raises a finger, commanding silence, pressing the cell phone to his ear. A moment later he hears it—the beeping of Nathan Cain's pager on the roof of the MidAmerica Building. Then he presses the "end" button on his phone, sets it down, and exhales a sigh of disbelief.

"Hey," says Farber, "wait a minute." He thrusts the card under Manning's nose. "This pager number—this is *my* contact, the guy behind the whole Zarnik scam."

"*What?*" Manning rises, studying the card. "Are you certain?" But he doesn't need an answer. He himself now recognizes the number, the one with all the sevens. He saw it on the blackboard the day of his first visit to Zarnik's lab; next time, it was partially erased to make room for a grocery list.

The conclusion is inescapable: Nathan Cain, publisher of the *Chicago Journal,* one of the city's most prominent, wealthy, and powerful citizens, has masterminded a complex plot with many seemingly unrelated threads. And although there is no apparent motive for the Zarnik ruse or for the secrecy surrounding the laser spectacle, something highly sinister must underlie his actions, for the man is guilty of cold, passionless murder.

Manning sits at the desk again, telling Farber, "You were right, Arlen. You're danger, and so am I. The bullet that killed David was meant for me." Manning connects a gadget between his laptop and his phone—it's the modem.

Farber leans over the desk. "Then we'd better get moving—we're not safe here." But Manning doesn't budge. He's busy with the computer. With mounting panic, Farber asks, "What are you *doing?*"

"I need a few minutes here, then we'll run. I have no idea what's behind all this, but the time for circumspection is past. I'm going to blow this story wide open in the next edition. There." Something appears on Manning's computer screen. "I'm online with the *Journal*'s newsroom." He types in a code, assigning his story top priority. "This'll end up on page one first thing in the morning."

Then, with hands trembling over the keyboard, Manning assigns his article the brief title, or slug, "hijinx." Stories like this don't come along often in a reporter's career, and he wants the opening to be a grabber. He writes:

"Recent claims of a newly discovered tenth planet, coupled with secret plans to surprise the city with a laser spectacle Saturday night, are mysterious elements in a complex conspiracy master-minded by *Chicago Journal* publisher Nathan Cain. The scheme turned murderous when Cain shot and killed two of his own reporters, Clifford Nolan and David Bosch. . . ."

PART THREE

CATACLYSM

HIGH-TECH HIJINKS
Stunning developments leave unanswered question: Why?

by Mark Manning
Journal Investigative Reporter

July 3, 1999, Chicago, IL— Recent claims of a newly discovered tenth planet, coupled with secret plans to surprise the city with a laser spectacle Saturday night, are but a few of the elements in a complex plan to dazzle the world with a yearlong display of Chicago's scientific, cultural, and architectural achievements.

The festivities get under way this afternoon with the opening ceremonies of Celebration 2000, which will also serve as the inaugural event of the city's new stadium, itself an eloquent testament to Chicago's progressive architectural legacy.

Today's program includes brief performances by many of the most esteemed artists in all genres of music, from opera to pop. This evening's human-rights rally will feature a long roster of political and cultural figures speaking on behalf of gay rights, culminating in the presidential address. At the program's end, the crowds at the stadium, and indeed throughout the city, will be wowed by a high-tech laser show. Details of the spectacle are still incomplete, as the surprise event was announced just this Thursday by the mayor's office.

A comprehensive schedule of the first week's festivities can be found on page 1 of the Life Section of today's *Journal*.

COUNTERDEMONSTRATION PLANNED BY CFC

In response to the human-rights rally being staged at the stadium, the Christian Family Crusade will mount a demonstration of its own, opposing the expansion of gay rights and calling for a constitutional amendment that would allow states free reign in legislating protection of family values.

Elder Burlington Buchman, CFC board chairman, has confirmed that the march will take place on the grounds of the Gethsemane Arms, a new North Side hotel built and managed by the CFC, some five miles removed from the rally at the stadium. ❏

Saturday, July 3

Manning hurls the paper onto the bed. It's noon already, it took all morning for an inept room-service staff to get a paper up to him, and when it arrived, he found his story buried on page five, altered beyond recognition.

He looks around him. The hotel room is cramped and sparsely furnished, but it's clean and new—in fact, he's probably the first guest to stay here. It was an expensive night, three hundred dollars for himself, another three hundred for Arlen Farber—the desk clerk refused to allow two men to share one room. Since Manning registered under a false name, he couldn't use a credit card, so his wallet is running on empty—he doesn't normally carry so much cash, but he was prepared for a weekend that would be filled with uncertainties.

Last evening at the planetarium, after Manning filed his story attempting to expose Nathan Cain as a murderer, he and Farber decided that neither of them would be safe at home that night. Manning could at least find scant consolation in the fact that Neil was staying with Roxanne—he was out of harm's way. Nonetheless, Manning phoned Roxanne's apartment from the planetarium and left a cryptic message for Neil, cautioning him to stay away from the loft.

Manning and Farber decided they should find a hotel, no easy feat with the world converging on the city for the festival. But Manning had a hunch, which turned out to be correct. The Gethsemane Arms Hotel was already surrounded with controversy—because of its owners, because of the protest march to be staged there, because of its exorbitant rates—so there were plenty of vacant rooms. The Gethsemane also struck Manning as the perfect hideaway, as no one would think to look for him there, of all places.

So Manning counted out six hundred dollars to the desk clerk—brotherhood and trust are one thing, but hotel policy is another, requiring payment in advance. The he retired to his room, needing sleep. Before parting ways with Farber in the hall, he asked the other man to come to his room around noon.

Manning slept, but he's not feeling rested. Yesterday was easily the worst day of his life. Neil walked out on him; Hector Bosch publicly humiliated him and threatened his career; his friend and coworker David Bosch was murdered by their boss, who had already killed another reporter; and the victim of this latest treachery was meant to be Manning himself. What's more, he learned that Nathan Cain is the guiding force behind a complicated scheme with enormously high stakes that Manning cannot begin to fathom. All these disjointed, deadly details are pointing toward a foreboding climax—but what, when, and where?

The "tenth planet" scam is somehow related to the secretly planned sky show, and both seem related, by virtue of their timing, to the opening of the festival. So: Manning has three pieces to the puzzle (the planet scam, the sky show, the festival), but a fourth piece is missing. He knows from experience that it's out there—it's been there all along, close enough to bite him—but he needs a clue, just one more clue, to complete the picture and reveal the hidden motive behind Cain's machinations.

These are the questions, the circular thoughts, that bubbled through Manning's subconscious as he slept, preyed on him the moment he awoke, and now obsess him as he paces the confines of the hotel room. He has switched on the television, hoping for distraction, wondering whether the story of David's murder has broken yet, but the hotel's cable system delivers only good, decent, sanitized Christian programming, fifty-some channels of it. Manning's search for news of current events is reduced to a frustrating bout of zapper surfing.

Dismayed by the fact that his story in the *Journal* was spiked (he might have guessed it would happen, and he's not sure who did it, or how, but he's got a theory), Manning decides that he'd better tell the police what he knows. If his story, as written, had made headlines, an arrest would already have been made, or at least a manhunt would be under way. But his tampered-with story was drivel, so he needs to inform the police directly.

Manning is dressed, ready as can be for the unpredictable events that will shape this day. He removes his cell phone from the inside pocket of his blazer, which hangs from the back of a desk chair. Sitting, he punches the same programmed number that he called on the night when he discovered Nolan's body. His detective friend will listen, will believe Manning, will know how to handle the situation. The other phone rings too long. When someone finally answers, Manning says, "Jim?"

But it's someone else. It's Saturday. The president's plane is due to land, there are dignitaries all over the city, throngs are already converging on the stadium, and a major demonstration is about to be staged by a bunch of religious wackos. In a word, the police are busy. Jim's not in. No one knows when to expect him.

"But this is important," Manning insists. "Can I leave him a message?" And Manning finds himself instantly connected to Jim's voice mail. He tries to keep it brief, giving all the details he can before he's cut off by a beep. Rattled, Manning hangs up the phone, not knowing if or when Jim will get his message.

Returning his attention to the television, he zaps an old rerun of a Billy Graham crusade and lands, to his amazement, in the middle of a local newscast. Manning turns up the sound on a cap-toothed talking head with big hair.

". . . racing to put finishing touches on the stadium grounds, in preparation for the president's visit." Then the head frowns. "On a tragic note, the lifeless body of a young man was discovered this morning atop the MidAmerica Building, near one of the three projectors that will be used to create tonight's sky spectacle. The victim's identity has not been released, pending notification of his family. He suffered a single bullet wound to his back; routine ballistics tests will be conducted. There was no apparent motive for the murder." The head smiles again. "Don't even *ask* about tickets for this afternoon's opening ceremonies. There are none to be had, and the mayor's office warns the public to beware of scalpers. Widespread reports of counterfeit passes . . ."

There's a knock at the door. Manning mutes the sound of the newscast, rises from his chair at the desk, and crosses the few steps to the door. Swinging it open, he says, "Good morning, Professor." As Arlen Farber slips inside, Manning corrects himself, "Or rather, good afternoon."

"Sorry I'm late. I couldn't sleep." Farber looks terrible—unshaven, unkempt, same ratty tweed jacket. He wears the chain around his neck with the keys and whistle.

"Still in costume?" Manning asks him. "The act is over."

Farber glances at the stuff hanging on his chest. He forces a smile. "Just a habit, I guess. Besides, I don't have a key ring—some of these are real, not props." He rattles the chain, then sits heavily on the bed, crumpling the newspaper.

Manning thinks of something. "On the topic of props," he says, "I'm curious. That whole setup in your lab at the planetarium, the computers and all the electronics—that's just set-dressing, right?"

"Hardly," Farber tells him. "Sure, the equipment I used for the 'graphic realization' was pure theater—a VCR, a monitor, and a few cabinets rigged up with blinking lights and fake dials. But to the best of my knowledge, which is admittedly limited, all the rest of that stuff is genuine. It's strictly off-limits. I was instructed never to touch it."

Manning's brow furrows. "What's it used for?"

Farber shrugs. "Ask Nathan Cain. I was there every day for a month, basically locked in the lab twiddling my thumbs and watching movies, and I never once saw anyone go near all that equipment. But it does get used somehow. Now and then it fires up on its own, grinds away for a while, then shuts down again. There's no rhyme or reason. Let me tell you, it still makes me jump, and it's annoying as hell in the middle of a good flick."

"Hmm." Manning sits at the desk, drumming his fingers in thought. "Let's go back and have a look. By now, anyone who'd try to find us there knows that we're somewhere else. Once the ceremony is under way, we'll be as safe at the lab as anywhere."

Farber is wary. "Can we eat first? Actually, I could use a drink."

Manning laughs, rising from his chair. "Let's pop downstairs. It ought to be quiet in the lobby—the crazed masses are outside on the street, gathering with their torches in defense of marriage, the family, and hetero sex. Finding some lunch should be no problem, but you're out of luck with the booze. Christ may have turned water into wine, but the Gethsemane Arms is dry as a bone."

"Shit." Farber heaves a sigh. "What's *with* these people?"

"Good question." Manning slips his jacket on. "After we eat, let's come back upstairs to freshen up before we check out. Ready?"

"Sure." Farber stands. Then he sees something on television. "Hey, look," he says, pointing. "I know that guy. It's Elder Buchman. He's the chief goon at this joint. He and some of his boys 'interviewed' me on Tuesday. What a prick."

"I heard about that," says Manning. "I know someone else who was there." He turns up the sound.

Buchman is talking to a reporter, live, outside the hotel. "So the purpose of our gatherin' today is to express, in the strongest terms possible, our revulsion with all this special treatment bein' accorded to homosexuals. We're especially distraught that the president of the United States has added his own voice to these perverted pleas for 'tolerance.' With the good Lord marchin' at our side, we're determined to stop all such politicians in their tracks."

The reporter asks, "Wouldn't your march have greater impact if you staged it near the stadium? The mayor's office has cordoned off a special area for such protests."

"We're safer here on our own turf," Buchman tells him. "There's no tellin' what *those* people are capable of."

"Come now, Elder Buchman, security has never been tighter. . . ."

Manning tells Farber, "I've heard enough. Let's eat." He walks to the door and opens it. Farber follows, stepping into the hall.

Manning says, "Now tell me about that meeting you had with Buchman." And he closes the door behind them.

Inside the room, Elder Burlington Buchman still blusters on the television, having grabbed the microphone from the reporter's hand. He leans toward the lens, spouting through an evangelical drawl, ". . . and the work of the Crusade, the work of Jesus, has flourished here in Chicago thanks to the selfless efforts of so many fine local citizens. Our legions of contributors are too vast to name, but there is one man who must be mentioned with a note of special recognition. Without his guidance, influence, and yes, his extraordinary financial assistance, the Christian Family Crusade could not have won this beachhead in the North. We thank you, Nathan Cain. And may God bless you."

Lucille Haring's stomach growls. It's past twelve-thirty, and she didn't bother with breakfast this morning. Arriving early at her desk in the top-floor offices of the *Journal*, she resumed her hacking, digging into Nathan Cain's files, consumed by her growing suspicion that the publisher has been hiding something monumentally evil.

It began as a groundless hunch—the man's arrogant manner and pampered lifestyle have long inspired wild, far-fetched gossip—but her subjective hunch turned to hard, objective suspicion as she worked with him on a daily basis. Her purpose at the *Journal*, from the beginning, was to assist Cain's office in its efforts with the Pentagon to establish a next-generation communications network. Her expertise in computers, however, was put to use solely in tutoring Cain, who pleaded utter ignorance of anything more advanced than a typewriter. Then, every day, he proved that he knew far more than he claimed. His questions, his demands, the speed with which he assimilated even the most arcane theories of applied electronics—all of this convinced Lucille Haring that Cain has lied and that he's up to something.

Whatever it is, she has deduced, is going to happen soon. So she's become a hacker. She hates that word—it stands for everything she's worked against during the course of her career.

What she's doing is illegal, and she knows that she will throw away her life's work (to say nothing of her freedom and her security clearance) if she's unable to confirm her suspicion of Cain's treachery. But that's a risk she must take. It's simply the right thing, the moral thing, to do.

She started to make some headway last night, plumbing deeper through the security levels of Cain's directories. By that late hour, though, she was exhausted and no longer trusted her judgment. So she went home, slept, and returned early today, Saturday, knowing the executive offices would be vacated. She asked the guard by the elevator, "Has the Colonel come in this morning?"

"No, ma'am," he replied. "He's left town for the weekend."

"Of course," she mumbled. She hadn't forgotten Cain's plans; she just wasn't sure if she believed them.

Back at her desk, clacking away at the keyboard, she quickly retraced her way to Cain's most sensitive directories, having already discovered the path. The morning has been spent sifting through file after file, mounds of data, corporate financials— nothing that would suggest a hint of impropriety. She's been getting frustrated, and now she's getting hungry.

She sits back in her chair, stares at the screen, pushes her fingertips through her cropped red hair. Too many details, too much minutiae. Let's start over. Let's close down these files, get out of these directories, go back to "file manager," and look at the big picture. One by one, she scrolls through Cain's directories, studying the lists on her screen, hoping something may pop out at her. But there is nothing abnormal, just the slugs (newspaper parlance for file names), their lengths, and the date and time they were last opened.

Then she finds a path to a subdirectory she had not previously noticed, "editorial." She figures it's worth a check. It's a huge directory, containing every story currently in the *Journal*'s editorial pipeline. However, only the ones that Cain has tapped into have a date and time notation, and there aren't many of them. While she glances through this much shorter list, one of the stories grabs her attention. The file is slugged "hijinx," and it was opened by Cain last night at eight o'clock. That can't be right, she tells herself. She was here all evening—Cain left around five and never returned. She calls up the file.

Manning's bylined story appears on her screen, exactly as it appeared on page five of this morning's paper. She had rushed through the *Journal* before leaving the house this morning, but Manning's story caught her eye because of its headline about "stunning developments." Intrigued, she read it, disappointed that the story never delivered on the headline—almost as if it were a mistake, the product of sloppy editing. She wonders . . .

If the story has been edited, its previous version is still lurking somewhere in an electronic limbo. Most people wouldn't have a clue as to how to undo a file's revisions, but it's child play to Lucille Haring. After a few keystrokes, her screen blinks, then an earlier story appears. Same headline. Same opening. . . .

What? She can't believe what she's reading. "The scheme turned murderous when Cain shot and killed two of his own reporters, Clifford Nolan and David Bosch." With mouth agape, Lucille Haring reads through the rest of the story, learning the details of David's death as he investigated the laser projector at the MidAmerica Building. Mesmerized, she reads that Cain was also responsible for promoting the hoax of planet Zarnik. Manning's article concludes, "Many questions still surround this tragic charade, but recent developments have propelled this story beyond the realm of mere journalism. As mastermind of a baffling but deadly subterfuge, Nathan Cain has betrayed the *Journal* and the public. He now must answer to society and to the law."

Just as Lucille Haring reads the last line, she hears voices down the hall, out by the elevator. She hears a key in the door as the guard swings it open, saying, "Sorry about your trip, Colonel. Let me know if you need anything."

Christ. Does he know I'm here? wonders Lucille Haring. There wasn't much conversation with the guard. She decides that Cain does not know she's in the office. She wants to keep it that way. She'll hide.

She gets up from her chair, swiftly steps to the back side of her desk, and crouches on the floor. While listening to the approach of his footsteps through the outer offices, she realizes that Manning's story—his original story—is still brightly displayed on her screen. If Cain sees it, she assumes that he will not hesitate to kill again. She pops up for a moment, taps a few quick keystrokes that blacken the screen, then hunkers down again behind the desk. Holding her breath, she watches Cain's legs scissor past; he carries the same briefcase he had yesterday. She hears him stop at his door, fishing for the key.

Her stomach growls—a long, rubbery rumble. Cain silences his keys, listening. Her heart pounds in her ears. She's not sure, but she thinks she's peed her pants. Then she hears Cain slip his key into the lock. The door opens. He steps into the inner sanctum and thuds the door behind him, locking it again.

She breathes, gasping for air. She feels her crotch, sniffs her fingers—no, thank God. Then she sits at her desk again, stretching her fingers like a concert pianist preparing to tackle Schoenberg. Calling up a new directory, she smirks, thinking aloud, "Now then, Colonel, let's see what else you've been up to."

Neil unlocks the front door to the loft and pokes his head inside, expecting to hear the warning alarm of the security system, but it is silent. "Anybody here?" he calls. Hearing no response, he turns behind him to say, "Come on in, ladies." Then he ushers Roxanne Exner and Claire Gray into the loft.

The space seems eerily quiet—not only has the alarm not been set, but there is no sound from the refrigerator, from the air-conditioning, from any of the sources of house-noise that contribute to the usual background murmur. It's as if the electricity has been shut off, but Neil notices the microwave clock running, the light on the answering machine. He steps to the kitchen's center island and plops a pile of mail on the counter, yesterday's and today's, collected from the lobby—Manning has not been home since Friday morning, after Neil wrote his note and walked out.

That's why the place seems so quiet, he realizes. Mark is gone. It was one thing for Neil himself, the wronged lover ("loftmate," that is), to walk out in a display of pique, but it's another matter entirely for Mark to abandon the place. Did their home together mean that little to him? Or can't he face the empty space? Either way, where *did* he spend the night? Has Neil sent him scampering back to David? That would be a monumental backfire; perhaps Neil should have listened more and reacted less. He makes a mental note that he still needs to replace that broken glass. While mulling all this, he sorts through the mail, making four stacks—two bulky piles of junk mail, his and Manning's, and two smaller stacks of first-class, one for each of them.

"What's wrong?" asks Roxanne, studying Neil's scowl as he stands there in the kitchen, lost in thought.

Neil snaps out of it. "Sorry. It's just that I expected the security alarm to be set, and it wasn't. Also, I get the feeling that Mark didn't sleep here last night."

"You mentioned that he left a message at Roxanne's. What was it?" Claire asks.

Neil strolls toward the big east window. "He sounded really strange, but maybe he just felt awkward leaving the message, knowing I didn't want to talk to him. He said that something big had developed on his story, that he wouldn't be able to make it to the stadium today, and that he was glad I was staying with Roxanne for a while. I could tell by his tone that he wasn't being snide. The implication, which makes no sense at all, was a concern for my safety, as if there might be some danger lurking here." He glances around the loft, then shrugs his shoulders. "Everything seems okay, though."

"Of *course* everything's okay," Roxanne assures him with a hug. "You need to work this out with Mark. Concentrate on what's been right between you. And for God's sake, dismiss any notions of boogeymen under the bed." She pecks his cheek, reminding him, "You're not the paranoid type, Neil."

Claire snorts. "I wish I could say as much about Hector. He's still in a snit over all this, and yes, he is most definitely paranoiac. I was with him at the hotel yesterday morning when David dropped over to have his talk. Hector turned irrational and put his own spin on everything David told him. Then he stormed off to the *Journal* to confront Mark, and I understand he put on quite a performance. Hector and I argued about it into the afternoon, only to be interrupted by David on the phone. David was calm, and he tried to get Hector calmed down, insisting that we all meet again later. Then, of course, Hector's suspicions were fed all the further when David, offering no explanation, never showed up last night. It sent Hector right off the edge."

David didn't show up? That's news to Neil, firing a suspicion of his own.

Claire continues, "The bottom line is that I didn't stand a chance of getting Hector to the festival today. The *last* thing he's in the mood for right now is the gay-rights agenda. He'd rather sulk in his room." She laughs, but it's bitter. "I told him he should join the march at that Christian hotel. To my amazement, he said he had a mind to. Anyway," she steps to Neil and Roxanne, grasping their hands, "thanks for letting me tag along today. Sorry to be the third wheel."

Roxanne pats her hand. "We're all in the same boat today, just three singles looking for fun. It's ironic. Carl has been trying to wheedle out of this for weeks—he truly doesn't like crowds, not even football games—but I finally had him convinced that this will be the event of the decade, something he'd hate to miss. Then what happens? Nathan Cain phones him at home this morning, Saturday, with another corporate crisis that no one else seems capable of handling. So at this very moment, Carl is strapped into a puddle-jumper, winging his way over Lake Michigan to Grand Rapids. He'll be back tomorrow morning, but he'll have missed the big spectacle."

"Well," says Neil, "buck up, sob sisters. We'll make the best of this outing, in spite of our missing menfolk. I just need to change clothes, so you gals make yourselves comfortable, then let's discuss lunch. We've got plenty of time before the stadium gates open." He heads toward the stairs that lead up to the balcony.

"There's not much to discuss," Roxanne calls after him. "I've got a table booked at Zaza's in fifteen minutes, so shake it." Neil bounds up the stairs, leaving the ladies to settle themselves on the sofa while gabbing an appreciative commentary on the view of the lake—it is indeed a perfect day for the open-air festivities that will launch Celebration Two Thousand.

Neil's need to change clothes is the purpose of this midday visit to the loft. When he wrote the note to Manning and left early yesterday morning, he took a few basic toiletries, but no extra clothes. He was so angry he couldn't think straight, and he had no idea how long he'd be away, but his principle reason for not packing was that he didn't want to wake Manning and explain what he was doing. He just wanted out. If tensions didn't ease, he might have to *buy* clothes as he needed them—he really couldn't predict how the near future would shape up between Manning and him. Fortunately, their day apart has lent an uneasy calm to the whole situation. This morning, Neil decided he'd risk a run to the loft to get a few things. Manning probably wouldn't be there, but just in case he was, Neil brought the ladies along so that he wouldn't be stuck alone with him—Manning would surely want to talk things out then and there, he'd want to reconcile, but Neil isn't ready yet.

One step at a time. For now, he'll be happy enough to get into some fresh clothes. He reminds himself that even though it's the middle of summer, they'll be at the stadium till after dark, and the night could turn chilly. Planning his outfit, he decides he should carry a sweater.

These thoughts end abruptly, though, as he walks into their dressing room and gasps. The place is a shambles, with clothes thrown everywhere, drawers emptied . . . Then he hears a scream. It's Claire.

"What's wrong?" yells Neil, rushing to the edge of the balcony, looking down at the sofa. Both women are convulsing with laughter.

"Sorry, Neil," Claire calls up to him, "but your friend just told me the most deliciously lewd story."

"Oh." Neil cautiously returns to the dressing room, grasping the doorjamb as he looks within. What the hell? His first theory is that Manning did this—a declaration of war—but Neil quickly dismisses the notion, ashamed, for Manning's things have been trashed too. Did Manning's obscure message attempt to forewarn

Neil of this? Neil can't be sure, but it doesn't seem that anything has been stolen. Downstairs there are all kinds of expensive things that might have been taken but weren't even touched. So this wasn't a robbery. And the motive couldn't have been vandalism, or there'd be damage throughout the loft. No, it appears as if someone was searching for something. Then Neil thinks of Cliff Nolan's dossiers. Of course. Carl Creighton asked about them Thursday night at dinner, and Manning told the table that he was keeping them at home. Now Carl has been called away (supposedly) on urgent legal work in Grand Rapids (of all places). Was he *that* threatened by Nolan's files?

Neil gingerly picks through a few things on the floor, assembling a fresh outfit as best he can, then changes clothes fast and traipses back downstairs, anxious to leave.

"All set?" he asks, striding toward the sofa. He's decided not to mention what happened—there's no point in burdening the ladies with his own fretful thoughts.

They rise. "Raring to go," Roxanne tells him.

Neil leads them without comment to the door, then, as he opens it, he turns back to ask, "Rox, could you grab that last stack of envelopes, please? There, in the kitchen—the smallest pile. I'll deal with it later, mostly bills."

Roxanne picks up the mail, drops it in her purse, and joins the others at the door. Neil takes a furtive look back into the loft, setting the alarm as they pass into the hall. Biting his lip, he makes a point of double-locking the door behind them.

Manning checks his watch. It's three-thirty already—he's wasted the middle of the day. Standing on the curb outside police headquarters, he asks Arlen Farber, "Hold this, will you?"

Farber takes the handle of the zippered nylon carrying case and is surprised by its weight. Packed inside is Manning's computer, charger, modem, disks, and an assortment of file folders. Farber says, "You don't exactly travel light, do you?"

"That's just the half of it," says Manning, patting his jacket. "I've still got my phone, pager, and pocketfuls of notes that I ought to get organized—but there's been no time." He doesn't need to mention that he carries his pet fountain pen, the antique Montblanc, clipped to the inside breast pocket of his blazer.

"Where to now?" asks Farber, positioning the strap of the case over his shoulder.

"If we can get a cab—and that's a big 'if'—I'd like to head over to the stadium and cruise around a bit. I want to see firsthand what's happening there, and there's a long shot I might spot Jim. Then we'll drive back to the planetarium."

He steps off the curb into the street and tries hailing a cab that's working its way through the traffic. This may take a while. The streets seem crowded all over the city—everyone's outdoors today, and many need cabs to the stadium. Manning has mixed feelings about his own car, which he didn't even try to retrieve from the MidAmerica Building, assuming he should steer clear of the place after what happened to David. If he had the car now, he and Farber would be on their way, but there would be nowhere to park it when they arrived at the stadium. It's much too far to walk, so the only solution is a taxi, and one of them just cruised by, packed shoulder-to-shoulder with passengers. Manning's only option is to venture farther into the street and keep waving.

It was bad enough getting here from the Gethsemane Arms. Throngs of the righteous were gathering noisily, the voice of intolerance preparing to march, raising a war cry against the forces of Sodom. Some of the marchers had stayed at the hotel, but most were converging from elsewhere in the city, so there were plenty of cabs available as they arrived to disgorge the placard-hoisting moralists.

Funny, Manning thought, watching them step from their taxis—most of them look like ordinary folk, people with whom he might have grown up. What happened to them, though? Where did they get their goofy ideas, their irrational sense of certitude? What kind of brainwashing has transformed these probably decent people into a mob of narrow-minded zealots? These questions, Manning knows, are purely rhetorical. He knows exactly what force has robbed these people of their innate ability to think straight. He knows exactly what force has clouded their reasoning and stolen a slice of their very humanity. They have been infected by the force of religion.

To their credit, though, they delivered an abundance of empty cabs, so Manning hopped into one with Farber, telling the driver to take them down to police headquarters. The ride, which should have taken about twenty minutes, took more than an hour and cost Manning the remaining bills in his wallet. So he replenished his funds with a stop at a cash machine before ducking inside headquarters with Farber, hoping to catch his detective friend on the run.

It wasn't meant to be, though. Jim wasn't there—he hadn't returned since Manning called around noon. With everyone so busy with the president's visit, the offices were in the grip of bureaucratic deadlock, manned by assistants and other underlings who seemed confused at best. The urgent pleas of a reporter to tell a tale of murder were met with a stack of forms to fill out and an endless wait on a bench in a hall.

Disgusted, Manning decided his time would be better spent doing some sleuthing of his own. So he nudged Farber, who dozed next to him on the bench, telling him, "Let's get out of here."

Standing in the street now, he waves at a cab in the distance, and this one, at last, switches lanes to pull over and pick him up. Moments later, he and Farber jump into the backseat. Manning tells the driver, "Stadium, please." The cabbie nods, saying nothing—he could easily guess their destination.

As the cab nudges its way into the congested traffic, Manning turns in his seat to zip open the computer case and dig out a folder. As he glances out the rear window, something catches his eye. A familiar figure, lanky and catlike in his Ray-Bans, has just rushed out of the building and limped to the curb, frantically hailing a cab several car-lengths behind them. Under his breath, Manning asks, "Huh?"

Farber turns to him. "Huh, what?"

"Take a look," says Manning, jerking his head over his shoulder. "It's our pal Victor Uttley. He just flounced out of the cop shop. Do you suppose he was there on business of his own? Or was he following us?"

"**W**ay down there?" asks Roxanne. "I'm impressed, Neil."

Roxanne, Neil, and Claire have arrived at the stadium, worked their way through the main entrance, passed through the metal detectors, and followed directions to the gate that takes them inside the arena itself. They stand at the top of a steep aisle that leads down past many rows of seats—hundreds, it seems—to a special seating area on the field. Neil has secured passes for an enviable block of seats only eight rows from the stage.

"You may wield clout at Zaza's, Rox, but this is my domain, at least for today. I deserve some special treatment—I've worked my butt off for over a year on this project."

Roxanne glances behind him, eyeing his derrière. "It's still there," she assures him, "and it's fetching as ever."

"Thank you," he says dryly. "Shall we descend through the masses, ladies?"

They begin the long trek toward the field, stepping past row after row of spectators, who form giant concentric rings of fluttering color. The rings grow tighter with each step downward, until at last the threesome has arrived on the ground. From that perspective, the sky has been reduced to a luminous blue circular ceiling, as if painted there in the manner of an old movie palace. Wisps of a few unthreatening clouds drift silently eastward. From huge stainless-steel poles topping the aisles, flags of every nation snap in the warm July breeze.

"Here we are," says Neil, finding their row. "Those must be ours." He points to a section of six empty seats, conspicuous among the crowd, which by now is packed tight, numbering nearly a hundred thousand.

As they excuse themselves and sidestep past other seated spectators, Claire comments, "What a pity that the others will miss this."

Sitting, Neil sighs. "Who knows?—maybe they'll see it on TV." He can't shake the uneasiness of finding the loft trashed.

And he's still plenty angry about Manning's episode with David. He knows, though, that Manning would have enjoyed today's ceremonies, and he's proud to have helped make this happen. He's proud to have secured this seating—they wouldn't have gotten nearly so close if they'd relied on Manning's press connections. This is Neil's day to shine, and Manning's not here to share it. Yes, Manning is involved with an important story, but Neil knows only too well, in the final analysis, that Manning isn't here today because Neil walked out on him, Neil made a show of smashing a crystal glass on the floor, Neil called him a son of a bitch. Neil tells the others, "At least we have the luxury of a little elbow room."

They arrange themselves with Neil in the middle. There are two empty seats next to Claire, one next to Roxanne. Claire tells the others, "There's plenty of room here for our sweaters, if you'd care to pass them over," which they do. Then Roxanne offers, "I can keep an eye on the purses over here." Claire passes her purse to Roxanne, thanking her, but Neil tells her, "I forgot mine." Roxanne jabs his ribs with her elbow.

Claire squints at her watch. The sun glares on its too tiny face. She asks, "What time do you have, Neil?"

He checks. "Four-forty. Only twenty minutes to go. Having been involved with much of the planning, I'm sure the program will begin at the stroke of five precisely. It's funny: I've spent a heap of time on all this, but it's out of my hands now. Even so, I'm a nervous wreck." Discovering the intrusion of his home hasn't helped either.

Claire laughs. "That will pass, dear, as soon as things get under way. I've sat through enough opening nights to know exactly what you're feeling." She pats his arm. "And believe me, I sympathize. It's a long show, isn't it?"

"Right," Neil tells her. "It's a four-hour program, so it has to move like clockwork. The president doesn't finish till nine, then the sky show begins. We're not certain how long that will last—it's all been so hush-hush—but by then it won't matter. It'll all be over."

"God, Neil," says Roxanne through a chortle, "you make it

sound like doomsday." She snaps open her purse and puts on a big pair of rose-tinted sunglasses.

Outside the stadium, Manning and Farber scan the crowds from the backseat of their cab, which moves at a crawl. The driver asks, "Want me to drop you here?—we're not gonna get much closer, and the meter's pushin' fifty bucks."

They've wasted another hour in traffic, and Manning checks his wallet before answering. "No," he says, confident he won't need to visit another cash machine, "just keep going. We won't be getting off here anyway."

The driver looks over his shoulder as if Manning must be nuts.

Manning fans the cash from his wallet, jerking his head onward toward the stadium. The cabbie shrugs, returns his eyes to the road, and drives forward, deeper into the crowd.

Farber is half asleep, but tries to appear alert, assisting Manning in his search, although he wouldn't recognize Jim, Manning's detective friend, even if he saw him. Manning's gaze darts through the crowd from face to face, but he knows, of course, that the odds of actually finding Jim are infinitesimal. Jim could be anywhere in the city at this moment, and even if he happened to be out here, working the throng, Manning could not reasonably hope to find him.

What Manning hopes, in fact, is to spot Neil. Even if only in passing, only through a glimpse, Manning wants to see with his own eyes that Neil is safe, that he's made it here to this event, the opening of a festival that he's worked so hard to create. He knows that Neil will be with Roxanne and Claire—with Carl and Hector, too, he presumes—so Manning is searching for any of those five faces. But it's Neil's face he wants to see, and he wonders what that face will tell him. Will Neil be giddy with the excitement of the day (he certainly deserves to be), or will his happiness be overruled by the tyranny of emotions that forced him away from the loft to stay with Roxanne? And what if Manning were to beat the odds and actually *see* him here? What would he do—stop the cab, elbow through the crowd, drop to his knees, and make a scene that would only humiliate Neil, dashing any possibility of reconciliation?

This is absurd, Manning tells himself. Yes, he has hurt Neil. Yes, he wants him back. He wants things the way they were. But he's not going to achieve that here, not now. He has already said that he's sorry, and he has tried to explain that his slip with David was partly—largely, though not altogether—beyond his control. Neil's reaction has also been partly, though not altogether, beyond his own control. Neil will have to work this out in his own mind, and that's going to take some time. Whether or not they resume a life together, the decision is now Neil's. There's nothing else Manning can do to persuade him.

Manning's mind feels numbed by all this, and he realizes that his emotional state has not yet allowed him to deal with the tragedy of David's sudden death. Manning has tried for nearly a week to forget what he and David did that night, to put the experience firmly behind him. But it did happen, and it surely meant *something*. It was more than just a dirty little episode to be swept away and tactfully forgotten. David was a friend, a young colleague, and that night he became something *else* to Manning, though Manning's vocabulary is not equipped with a word to define that expanded relationship. Certainly, they became more than friends. Just as certainly, they were much less than lovers. With time, Manning may have been able to analyze it, to define it, to reconcile it with the bedrock relationship he has worked to build with Neil. But now, of course, those issues are moot. David is gone. And for all Manning knows, Neil may be gone as well.

The crowds outside the cab are starting to thin in the minutes that precede the opening of Celebration Two Thousand. Arlen Farber has nodded off to sleep, chin to chest. Manning can afford to agonize over his emotions no longer. He tells the driver, "You can turn around now. Civic Planetarium, please."

At the stroke of five precisely, a clock radio clicks on just as an announcer says, "Ladies and gentlemen, our national anthem."

Nathan Cain's eyes blink open. He has napped all afternoon in the dark-curtained bedroom of his office suite, exhausted from the ordeal of yesterday evening and the hectic night that followed. He needed to catch up on lost sleep, rejuvenating himself for the evening that will follow, an evening that has been planned to the minute for nearly a year.

Through a thick Italian accent, a vigorous tenor (certainly not Paganini) wails, "And the rockets' red glare, the bombs bursting in air . . ." That soaring verse never fails to stir Nathan Cain's patriotism. He can't just sit there, let alone lie there, while a hundred thousand people at the stadium have risen to their feet. So he hops out of bed, stepping into his ostrich slippers, cinching the blue silk dressing gown around him, but he feels momentarily dizzy, and his injured hip aches—he ought to know better than to get up so fast. "O'er the laa-aand of the freeee, and the home of the braaaave." Tumultuous whoops and applause crackle through the radio. Cain switches it off. Silence.

He sits on the edge of the bed, kneading the torn and never-healed musculature of his leg. Its throbbing creates an eerie sensation that reminds him of a field hospital in Korea where overhead lights throbbed to the beat of a faulty generator. He grimaced as an exhausted surgeon drew the shard of metal from his thigh. Under those makeshift circumstances, anesthesia was crude at best, and that night Cain was certain that it wasn't working at all. But he grit his teeth, he didn't yell, he didn't faint. Buddy, the young man who saved him—not the doctor, but the fellow soldier who dragged him from the fray and carried him to safety—sat at his side through the surgery and gripped his hand, letting Cain siphon strength from their friendship. When the wound was at last cleaned and sutured, Cain slept.

It was a restless sleep, interrupted by the delirium of drugs and the racket of war. But then arrived that lucid moment, a brief stillness in the night when his mind cleared and guns stopped and others slept. He turned his head on the cot and saw Buddy sitting there, alert and smiling, still holding his hand. Cain smiled back at him. "I owe you for this one," he said quietly. "You could have gotten yourself killed. What's the matter with you, Buddy? Are you nuts?"

"No, Nathan," Buddy told him, leaning close to his ear. Then, in a moment of supreme weakness Buddy added, "I'm your friend. I love you." He gently pressed his lips to Cain's temple and kissed the salt of dried sweat from his sideburns.

Cain stopped breathing, but his mind spun. Under the life-or-death circumstances of battlefield heroics, Buddy's display of affection was acceptable, even appropriate, wasn't it? But Cain knew that Buddy's words were a testament to more than friend-ship. Cain also knew, deep between the crags of his drugged consciousness, that Buddy had tapped into something mutual that had never been spoken. Those unspoken words—I love you too, Buddy—stuck in Cain's throat, and he knew that now, if ever, was the time to speak them. Dare he?

He breathed again. "Are you nuts?" he asked. Sliding his hand from Buddy's grasp, Cain rolled onto his shoulder, turning his back to his friend.

Now he stands, bends over, reaches under the bed, and pulls out his briefcase, stowed there for safekeeping while he rested. Tossing it on the bed, he covers it with a fold of the comforter, leaving a telltale lump in the bedding. Then he crosses the room and opens the door to his bath.

Inside, he removes his robe, slippers, and silk undershorts. He reaches through the doorway to a huge tiled shower room and turns the faucets. When the water running on his forearm meets his satisfaction, he steps inside and ducks under the hot spray. Without closing his eyes, he lets the drops hit him squarely in the face, remembering the next chapter in the history he has shared with Buddy.

Both men rose quickly in the military ranks, with Buddy enjoying an extra boost from the valor he exhibited in saving Cain. Cain would retire with the rank of colonel, then focus his energies on building a communications empire, while Buddy remained in the military and eventually found himself at the Pentagon, where he now answers to only a handful of others. Cain still calls him Buddy, though he is known by his given name, of course, to the press, the public, and the presidents he has served. These two powerful men have remained close friends for nearly fifty years since that night in Korea. And they have never discussed that incident on the cot—except once, earlier this year.

Standing in the shower now, purging his nap-grogginess, Cain goads his brain back to full alert. This accomplished, he soaps his body, washing efficiently. The finishing touch, as always, is to lather up a finger and scrub the crack between his buttocks. Then he rinses, turns off the water, and dries himself with a blanket-size Turkish towel.

He grooms himself quickly, combing his thinning hair with a sharp, precise part that runs from the left temple to the center of his scalp. Then he slips on a clean pair of underwear and pads out of the bathroom, leaving the robe behind.

In his bedroom, he opens several closet doors, revealing a complete wardrobe that allows him to dash from the office perfectly attired for any event, be it golf-casual or white-tie. This evening, though, he needn't impress anyone (God knows, he won't be *seen*), so he settles on basic black—turtleneck, tropical wool slacks, and plain-toed oxfords. Checking himself in a mirror, he gives a grunt of approval, then closes the closets.

Cain crosses to the bed, uncovers the briefcase, and carries it to the door, which he opens. Walking into the vaulted space of his main office, he switches on a few lights (the blackout curtains on the west wall have been closed to the afternoon sun) and steps to the case that houses his collection of firearms. He opens the glass-paneled doors of the cabinet. Then he sets down the briefcase and opens it as well.

Inside, there are no papers, no sensitive files, only the Nambu pistol with its unique jade handle. Maybe that's what got him to thinking about Buddy this evening—the gun was a gift from him years ago, from his own collection, marking his rise to power at the Pentagon, an odd token of friendship, a perverse expression of love, but one that Cain understood completely and implicitly. The gun was once used by a Japanese general who took his own life as a matter of principle. More than fifty years later, it is still in perfect working order. It has been used again recently, twice, again as a matter of principle.

Lifting the pistol, he cradles it in his hands with a reverence befitting the Eucharist, then returns it to its little silk cushion, plumping the edges, realigning the gilt-edged display card on its miniature silver easel. Perfect. Cain closes the glass doors and, noticing a smudge, buffs it clean with the fabric of his sleeve.

Picking up the empty briefcase, he crosses the length of his vast office, arriving at the spiral stairs that lead up to his library loft. The winding stairway is a whimsical structure that anyone would find awkward to climb—even a man younger and more agile than Cain would mount these stairs with a measure of trepidation. When this is over, Cain tells himself, he really must have an elevator installed. The project would entail a mess, however, a lengthy disarray of his quarters, so he dismisses the notion.

Clunking upward, tread by tread, he arrives at last on the balcony among the library stacks. The bookshelves are arranged tighter than they used to be in order to accommodate the metal cabinets that have recently been installed. They house electronics that are part of the *Journal*'s massive computer upgrade. Even now, on a quiet Saturday evening, they hum a low-frequency drone, emitting heat—the loft space is much warmer than the office below.

Cain retreats into one of the aisles of books, arriving behind a metal cabinet. Instead of vents, this one has doors, which he opens. There are no electronics inside, just some shelving and a few hooks, like a locker. Cain tosses the briefcase inside. It thuds against the back wall of the cabinet. From one of the hooks, he removes a hooded nylon windbreaker, black, draping it over his arm. From the top shelf, he takes a pair of dark sunglasses, a ring of keys, and a sizable black book—there's going to be time to kill, and he might as well not waste it.

Equipped with these provisions, he closes the cabinet and turns to the back wall of the loft. There, hidden from the view below, is a door. Cain unlocks it with one of the keys, steps through, and closes it behind him. Beyond the door is a tiny room—it may have been a broom closet—just big enough to contain a second spiral stairway, leading up. He breathes a sigh of determination, then starts his climb. His bad leg darts with pain, just as it did yesterday when he trudged those last few flights to the top of the MidAmerica Building. He knew then that he could not be encumbered by something so trivial as physical discomfort, and he knows it again now. Yesterday's mission was a diversion, a tactical necessity, a preemptive strike, but today's is the real thing—everything, absolutely everything, is at stake.

Arriving at the top of the spiral, Cain rests, breathing, gripping the tendons deep within his injured thigh, waiting for the throbbing to subside. Fully a minute passes before he can move on. Then he chooses another key from the ring in his hand, opens another door, and steps out onto the tower platform of the Journal Building.

Blinded by the slant of the early-evening sun, he dons the dark glasses and surveys the rooftop. The Journal Building is only half the height of MidAmerica, and its tower platform is much smaller, only a few yards square atop the peaking Gothic limestone structure. While David had difficulty yesterday locating the laser projector amid the clutter on the MidAmerica Building's spacious roof, Cain has no difficulty whatever finding the projector's counterpart up here—there is room, in fact, for nothing else. Years ago, there were radio transmitters up here, broadcasting from a single mast, but as the city grew, the transmitters moved to taller buildings, leaving the defunct antenna as a decorative finial.

There are any number of taller buildings, better situated, that might have served as the third point of the triangle for tonight's spectacle. But the whole plan was developed by Nathan Cain, presented to the mayor by Nathan Cain, funded largely by Nathan Cain, with no one else involved in the project who would dare suggest overruling Cain in his insistence that the Journal Building be used as a projection site. He argued that there would be a promotional advantage for those companies taking part, and it was unthinkable to deny him JournalCorp's participation.

Cain takes a slow walk around the apparatus. Though by no means a timid man, he is prudent enough not to let his steps veer far from the device, which is mounted only a few feet from the building's edge. A low parapet surrounds the platform, but it was built there more for aesthetics than for function, offering little protection from the wind or from the hazards of a fall. Peeking over it, Cain recoils in response to the sweeping sense of vertigo as he glimpses past the gargoyles' heads to the ant-stream of cars moving on the boulevard below.

He steadies himself with a hand on the projector, dragging his fingers across the machine's drab-painted surface as he moves around it, examining it in detail—its menacing snout, its ungainly shape, its coils and meters and dials. No, this instrument bears no resemblance to the one David Bosch examined yesterday. They look different because they *are* different. This one has a special, unique function. And in spite of its profusion of cryptic controls, only two must be manually operated, both simple switches, one green, one pink.

Nathan Cain assumes his post, sitting on a folding camp stool, waiting to pull these switches. He knows when to do it, and he knows what will happen when he does. He looks at his watch; there's still plenty of time till he must act. He's glad he brought the book.

It is the Bible. He rests it on his knees and opens it from the back, finding the first chapter of John. He's always loved the way the opening verses of that book mimic those of Genesis, a sort of theological loop, a circular, perpetual, self-conscious evangelistic hiccup that spans the millennia. "In the beginning . . ." Cain sees the words, but his mind does not absorb them. He mulls instead the events that brought him here, the conversations and cajolery that allowed him to solidify a daring plan.

Project Zarnik is the work of many dedicated men, but he knows he can justly take pride as its creator. The idea was so simple—it sprang to mind so naturally and will achieve its goal so cleanly. Execution of Project Zarnik, however, has been unforeseeably complex, requiring the assistance and cooperation of men less purely committed than himself—men like Buddy.

His friend at the Pentagon was speechless when Cain first told him what he wanted, what he expected. When Buddy could at last muster words, he said, "Nathan, you're mad." Anticipating such a reaction, Cain was ready with his response. "Buddy," he said, "you're queer. Men of your rank have shot themselves for less grievous infractions. Project Zarnik needs you. I need you. If you're not willing to sign on, I'll understand. But I'll also return something to you—General Sugiyama's jade-handled pistol. You may have use for it." So Buddy reconsidered and proved his friendship, as Cain knew he must.

Cain sits calmly in the shadow of the apparatus, Bible open in his lap. He checks his watch again. At six o'clock precisely, he will flip the green switch. At nine o'clock precisely, he will flip the pink switch.

Cain peers at his watch. He closes his Bible.

Downstairs in Cain's outer offices, Lucille Haring pecks away at her keyboard. Hours have passed since she discovered that Cain had altered Manning's story exposing the publisher as a murderer, and she has no way of knowing when Cain might reappear from his office. So the pressure is on, and she's been digging feverishly in Cain's directories, but she has yet to discover anything that might shed light on his motive to kill.

After her near-encounter with Cain when he returned to his *Journal* offices around one o'clock, Lucille Haring felt faint and sickly—not only because she narrowly escaped discovery of her hacking, which might have led to fatal consequences, but also because she was so hungry. As soon as she caught her breath, she got busy at the keyboard again, but decided she'd better eat. So she hurried down to the building's main lobby, telling the guard at the elevator that she'd soon return, and grabbed a ham sandwich and a candy bar from vending machines. Arriving upstairs again, she asked the guard if the Colonel was still in his office. "Affirmative," the guard answered, then admitted her with his key.

She rushed back to her desk, peeled the plastic wrap from the sandwich, and wolfed a couple of bites, hardly taking time to taste it. Then she realized that the sandwich felt funny in her mouth, not quite right. Lifting the bread, she saw swirls of the slightest gold-green iridescence tinging the surface of the ham—probably a day or two older than it should be. She smelled it, finding it impossible to detect anything beyond the mustard. She decided to risk it, eating the rest of the sandwich quickly, without thinking about it. Having refueled, she set the candy bar aside and tapped a few keys on her computer, calling up Cain's "editorial" directory again.

Then she noticed a blank spot in the same list where she'd found Manning's "hijinx" story. Digging deeper, she determined that the blank represented a story that had been deleted altogether. No problem—she could easily track it down in the electronic recesses of the mainframe and "undelete" it. A few more key-strokes, and the missing story popped onto her screen. Above the byline of Clifford Nolan, Science Editor, appeared the headline "Requiem for a Small Planet."

Eyes widening with interest, she leaned closer to read Nolan's lengthy article, which presented a detailed analysis of why Zarnik's claimed discovery was surely fallacious. But during its concluding paragraphs, the story cut off abruptly, midsentence, without finish. Reading that dangling phrase, she knew that it was typed at the moment of Nolan's death.

Manning was right. He conjectured in his own story, later altered by Nathan Cain, that it was Cain himself who tapped into Nolan's exposé, visited Nolan as he continued to write it, then murdered him, absconding with Nolan's laptop after deleting the story from the *Journal*'s editorial files.

Lucille Haring can't shake the uneasy grief she now feels, having learned the circumstances of Cliff Nolan's demise. She detested the man—indeed, she hated him—for his unwelcome advances and his spiteful threats of recrimination, but she under-stands that his death was a noble one. He fell, as it were, in the line of duty, attempting to share the truth of his knowledge with the public. In his last act, he became an unwitting martyr to journalistic integrity.

She knows, as Manning does, that Cain has murdered two of his own reporters, but she can't fathom why. What could possibly warrant such treachery? All she can do is to keep on hacking, hoping that something will catch her attention and provide her with a hint, a tip, some mere suggestion of a motive.

It's nearly six o'clock. She's getting frustrated, tired—and hungry again. Glad to have that candy bar in reserve, she rips the wrapper from it and chomps a mouthful of nuts and chocolate. With her free hand, she scrolls through a list of Cain's recent correspondence, finding nothing of note. Then she cursors along an obscure path and spots a subdirectory that has till now escaped her attention: "E-mail."

She smiles, swallowing the lump of candy, tossing the rest into a wastebasket. Typing, she says aloud, "I wonder what dirty little notes you've been swapping with unseen partners in seedy, far-flung chat rooms."

She frowns. She can tell from the slugs that most of Cain's E-mail is just interoffice memos. But then she scrolls past a long sequence of files titled "Buchman01" through "Buchman88." They were all written within the last few months, the most recent ones only hours apart. Interesting.

She opens the last of these, sent yesterday afternoon, Friday, at four. It begins without salutation, "Urgent errand at Mid-America site later today, serendipitous clue at lunch with Brad and Carl. Will detail at our nightly meeting, may be late. Schedule is firm for tomorrow. Green switch at eighteen hundred, pink at twenty-one. God bless America."

Lucille Haring stares at the words, perplexed. She knows from Manning's original story, filed by modem last night, that Cain's reference to an urgent errand must refer to the killing of David Bosch, mistaken for Manning. But what does Cain mean by "Green switch at eighteen hundred, pink at twenty-one"? Surely, he's referring to six and nine o'clock tonight, but what's with the colored switches? And to whom was this E-mail sent? Who's Buchman?

She glances at her watch—it's a few minutes before six. *Something's* going to happen, and she really ought to tell Manning about it. Maybe if they put their heads together, they could figure this out. And what, if anything, should she do about Cain? He's still in his suite, somewhere in the inner sanctum, and he ought to be arrested. She needs to talk to Manning, but how is she to reach him? He's undoubtedly in hiding, hardly likely to be sitting home by the phone.

She remembers that he carries a cell phone and a pager, but doesn't know how to get those numbers. Maybe a little more surfing of the *Journal*'s mainframe will provide that information. It's worth a try. She checks over her shoulder, confirms that Cain's office door is still closed tight, then sets to work at her keyboard.

A few minutes before six, Manning gets out of the cab with Arlen Farber at the steps to the planetarium. The parking lot is deserted, the building dark. Manning bounds up the stairs and rattles the main doors. He asks Farber, "Can you get in?"

Farber trudges up the stairs behind him, lugging the computer case. He rattles his neck chain and says with his Zarnik accent, "A man of my esteemed position is accorded total access." Arriving on the top step, he sets down the case and slips a key into the lock, opening the door. Once inside, he taps a security code into a touchpad, then locks the main door behind Manning.

Without its usual queues of gabbing tourists, the vaulted lobby seems unnaturally quiet, like a sanctuary they have invaded. The terrazzo floor, freshly waxed, lends to the place the smell of an empty school. As Manning and Farber cross the lobby toward the back-hall stairway, their footfalls reverberate between the hard floor and the high ceiling.

Rushing up the back stairs, Manning says, "This place is dead—there doesn't even seem to be a janitor on duty. Everyone must be down at the stadium."

"Or watching the ceremony on TV," adds Farber, "sipping a stiff one." He hasn't had a drink all day.

In the upstairs hall, on the way to Zarnik's lab, Farber breaks stride long enough to drop some coins into the vending machine and pluck up a can of Diet Rite. He scurries to catch up to Manning, arriving at the red-signed door that has a lock but no knob. Manning takes the computer case, allowing Farber to juggle the cold soda can with his keys. A moment later, they step inside the lab.

All is still, absolutely quiet. Farber switches on some lights, and their fluorescent hum seems amplified in the silence of the room. As Farber closes the door, Manning crosses to the desk and sets his case on it. Then they both meander cautiously about the lab, taking care not to trip over the thick black bundle of cables that snakes across the floor, making sure they are alone. Manning says, "We'll be just fine here for a while. Can you tell if there have been any 'visitors' since last night?"

"Looks the way we left it," Farber answers, visibly relieved. Then a sparkle lights his eye, the first such expression Manning has seen from him since the events of last night. Farber suggests, "How about a drink, Mark? There's some Jack in the desk."

Manning is tempted. "No thanks, Arlen." Manning smiles. "I've got work to do, but you go ahead. Rough day, huh?"

Farber just shakes his head. There's no need to answer. He crosses to the desk, sets his soda on it, and opens the big bottom drawer, pulling out a glass (a used jelly jar that he finally remembered to bring from home) and a two-liter jug of Jack Daniel's. He pops open the can—a piercing sound in the quiet, hard-surfaced room—and pours his cocktail, half booze, half soda. Bitsy bubbles of carbon dioxide rise through the glass, hissing from the surface.

Then a much louder noise makes both men jump. At six o'clock precisely—Manning checks his watch—the banks of computers stacked throughout the room power up in unison with a clicking, a whirring, a flashing of tiny lights.

"I *hate* it when that happens," says Farber, who has spilled some of the whiskey he was pouring. He dabs it up with the grimy handkerchief he carries.

"Jeez," says Manning, "is this what you were describing back at the hotel?"

"Right. That's how it always kicks in—when you least expect it. But it won't stay that loud. In fact, you can hear it settling down already. It'll just drone on like that till it shuts itself off. Sometimes it lasts a few minutes. Other times, hours." Farber picks up his glass, wipes its bottom, then drinks a long slug. He sighs, contented at last.

Perplexed, Manning walks around the various stacks of equipment, all of it churning busily, thinking electronic thoughts, performing intricate calculations for unknown purposes. What's it *doing?* Clearly, all these computers are linked and working as one—the foot-thick bundle of cables is evidence of that. Also, it's safe to assume that the computers in Zarnik's lab are somehow related to the sky show—Nathan Cain was behind the setup of both. But the last piece of the puzzle is still missing. Manning needs one more clue in order to fathom Cain's motive. He needs to think, really think. And the way he thinks best is through the process of writing.

"Excuse me," he tells Farber, returning to the desk. "Do you mind if I sit here? I need to work on another story. With any luck, this one may get through without being intercepted." He mumbles, "It's worth a try," already unzipping the case, setting up his computer, modem, and cellular phone.

"Be my guest," says Farber, moving away from the desk with his drink. "Okay if I watch the tube while you work?"

"If you keep it quiet," replies Manning, opening folders, spreading material on the desk, digging crumpled notes from the pockets of his blazer.

Farber wheels the large television monitor, the one on which he displayed the "graphic realization," to the far side of the desk and switches it on. He also turns on the VCR, using it to tune various stations, which flicker in sequence on the screen. Most of the channels carry coverage of the event at the stadium. Regardless of the channel, though, the picture is quartered by the thin white lines of the crosshairs—Farber still hasn't figured out how to get rid of them.

Manning glances at the screen and notices the crosshairs. He laughs. "I can't believe I almost fell for that."

"Live and learn," Farber tells him, swigging his Jack–and–Diet Rite, settling on a station that shows dancers at the stadium performing a surrealistic, pagan-looking tribute to the dawn of a new millennium.

As the camera pans away from the stage, it shows the faces of people in the audience. Most of the crowd in the stadium can be seen only as a blur of humanity, but the rows nearest the stage are clearly visible, and there sits Neil with Roxanne and Claire, intently watching the dance. Manning's eye was first drawn to them because of the empty seats around them, conspicuous in the tightly packed arena. But then he saw Neil's face, and Manning choked on his own breath. He longs to earn back Neil's affections and can't fathom the pain of a prolonged separation, let alone a permanent one. When this is all over . . .

As the camera swings to the stage again, Farber pulls up a chair, plops into it, and sets his drink on the edge of the desk.

Manning's attention is now focused on the screen of his laptop, where a message confirms that he is online with the *Journal's* newsroom—at least that's what it *says*, but he has no way of knowing whether this story, like the last one, will be waylaid. He slugs his new story "hijinx2" and assigns it highest priority. He pauses before he begins writing, wondering what tone to take with the story. Since he doesn't know the outcome of the mystery he will write about, but can only expose those facts that have become known to him, he hopes to involve his readers in the active process of working out the puzzle. This will not be, he recognizes, a conventional piece of journalism, so he decides to write the story in the first person, as if "thinking aloud" in a diary. He positions his hands over the keyboard and begins:

> I am Mark Manning, a reporter for the *Chicago Journal.*
> Ten days ago, I began investigating the claims of Dr.
> Pavo Zarnik, who announced his discovery of a tenth planet in the Earth's solar system. As this story unfolded, I learned not only that there is no such planet, but also that the man claiming the discovery is an actor. Even more disturbing, I learned that the instigator of this deception was Nathan Cain, publisher of the *Journal.*
>
> Last week, Cain murdered Clifford Nolan, the *Journal's* esteemed science editor, as he attempted to expose the Zarnik ruse. Last night, Cain murdered David Bosch,

another colleague and a friend of mine, mistaking the young reporter for me. The motive for Cain's treachery is still unclear, and I am frightened, not only for my own well-being, but for the safety of a city that has trusted and revered this man.

As I write these words, I am in hiding. While this great city revels in the opening ceremonies of Celebration 2000, I have taken temporary refuge within the laboratory of Dr. Pavo Zarnik at Civic Planetarium. Here with me is Arlen Farber, the actor recruited by Cain to impersonate the famed astronomer. Mr. Farber, fearing that his involvement in this scheme has placed his own life in danger, is now attempting to assist me in unraveling the conspiracy. . . .

Manning continues to write, detailing the events that have brought him to this moment, pleading with the public to come forth with clues to help solve the puzzle, when Zarnik's desk phone rings.

Manning and Farber freeze, staring at each other. Manning motions for Farber to turn down the sound of the television, then he reaches for the phone and lifts the receiver to his ear. "Yes?" he answers.

"Mr. Manning?" asks a woman's breathless voice. "Is that you? This is Lucille Haring."

"Miss Haring . . ." he stammers, stunned that she has reached him, still wondering if she has played a role in the conspiracy. "How did you . . . ?"

"I'm at my desk in the Colonel's outer office," she tells Manning, all business. "I've been here since morning, digging through his computer files, fearing he's been up to no good. Then I found your story, the original version, confirming my worst suspicions. The altered version was Cain's doing, of course. He's been intercepting all your work. As you suspected, he also intercepted Cliff Nolan's exposé."

"How?"

"You both filed those stories by phone; he must have picked

them up by phone. He could have done it from anywhere. But he wasn't here last night—I was."

Manning asks, "Where is Cain now?" At the mention of Cain's name, Farber reaches for his drink, needing renewed fortitude.

Lucille Haring replies over the phone, "He's somewhere in his suite of offices. He's been there for hours, but he hasn't logged on to his computer—I'd know if he had. I've found something that might be important, Mr. Manning, but I didn't know how to reach you. I was scrolling through Cain's editorial directory a few minutes ago, when I saw a new entry, 'hijinx2,' pop up on the list. I opened your story, reading as you wrote. When you mentioned being in Zarnik's office, I had no trouble locating the number in the crisscross," she explains, referring to a directory used by police, reporters, and other investigators.

"Most resourceful, Miss Haring," says Manning. "What have you found?"

"Some peculiar E-mail," she tells him, "tons of it, in fact, sent to someone named Buchman."

"Who's Buchman?" says Manning, thinking that the name sounds familiar.

"Buchman?" echoes Arlen Farber. "He's that fat-ass zealot with the CFC."

Manning grabs his steno pad, uncaps his pen, and clears some space on the desk so he can take notes. Brushing aside the scraps of paper that he earlier removed from his pockets, he says into the phone, "Let me get this straight, Miss Haring. Are you telling me that Nathan Cain has been in contact with Elder Burlington Buchman, board chairman of the Christian Family Crusade? That doesn't make sense—Cain has always been palsy with the archbishop. He and Buchman move in two different worlds." Manning absentmindedly picks at one of the crumpled notes, flattening it on the desk.

Lucille Haring's voice says over the phone, "I don't know *who* Buchman is, but Cain has been sending him weird E-mail. Listen to this one, sent yesterday: 'Urgent errand at MidAmerica site later today, serendipitous clue at lunch with Brad and Carl. Will detail at our nightly meeting, may be late. Schedule is firm for tomorrow. Green switch at eighteen hundred, pink at twenty-one. God bless America.' "

Huh? As Manning ponders the improbability of such an alliance, he glances down at the note he has unfolded, recognizing a corner of the acid-green *Zaza* logo. On the night he and Neil had dinner with Carl Creighton and Roxanne, Manning wrote notes on these scraps, torn from the paper tablecloth. He opens and flattens more of them. Of course—there are repeated references, in Manning's own handwriting, to Carl's inquisition by the CFC. Carl was mystified as to how the CFC got wind of his impending appointment as deputy attorney general; he had confided the news only to Cain. And yesterday, Carl lunched with Cain and the MidAmerica Oil chairman at the Central States Club. Manning mentioned his planned inspection of the laser projector to Carl, and Carl must have mentioned it to Cain.

"Good God," says Manning, talking both to Farber at his side and Lucille Haring on the phone, "Nathan Cain has been conspiring with the Christian Family Crusade. I'd never have believed it, but they're working together toward some common goal. Miss Haring, what do you make of that 'green switch' business?"

"It sounds as if there were plans to pull two coded switches, one at six tonight, the other at nine. It's well past six now, nearly seven. I wonder if anything happened."

Manning leans back in his chair, exhaling. "Something did happen," he tells her. "At six precisely, a shitload of computers went into action over here, and they're still humming away. They seem to be related to tonight's sky show at the stadium, which was also Cain's brainchild."

"Isn't the laser show scheduled for around nine?" Lucille Haring asks.

"You're right," Manning tells her. "The pink triangle, the pink switch. Conceivably, the pink switch might simply turn the whole display *on*. But if the plan was that innocuous, there'd be no reason to murder Cliff and David."

At the mention of murder, Arlen Farber is again on full alert. Manning motions for him to turn up the television sound—there may be clues to glean from the stadium event. Manning says into the phone, "We have a couple of hours before this all comes to a head, Miss Haring. We'll do what we can at this end. Could you continue to dig through Cain's computer files, please? And see if there's some way to get my stories—uncensored—down to the newsroom."

"Even as we speak," she tells him, "that's exactly what I'm doing." The sound of her keyboard rattles clearly over the phone.

Manning grins. "Lucy," he says, "you're wonderful." Then he asks, "Do you mind, Miss Haring, if I call you Lucy?"

"Not at all—Mark."

Seated at the stadium, Neil, Roxanne, and Claire listen as one of the speakers tries to rally the crowd for broader support of gay marriage. The entertainment portion of the program has concluded—the opera singers, rock stars, dance troupes, and orchestras have all strutted their most polished performances— and now the evening's political agenda rushes forward full tilt.

Local and state politicos are all here, as well as national candidates of every stripe, posturing and preening for the primaries that will lead to next summer's conventions. Tonight, everyone is backing gay rights, or at least mouthing support for the general concept of "equality for all." And so, even though Neil recognizes that this event is unprecedented, indeed historic, the message is getting a tad stale—there are only so many ways to say it, and it's been said.

Besides, the main event is drawing near. People have come to see and hear the president, not these legions of wanna-bes. His address is sure to set the stage for intense debate during the last year of his term and could well turn the tide of public opinion on issues that have been all too divisive.

Neil tries to remain attentive, but his mind wanders from the message and his gaze wanders from the podium. Security people are starting to line a pathway from a ground-level field entrance through which the president will doubtless be escorted. There's the distant sound of engines from helicopters hovering far overhead with television crews, Neil assumes, or security, or both. Neil concludes that the warm-up speeches are at last winding down, and he checks his watch. It's eight-fifteen; the president is scheduled for eight-thirty.

The sky still glows with daylight from the setting sun, but inside the stadium, most of the spectators now sit in full shadow, and the evening has gotten chilly. Neil says to Claire, "I think it's time for those sweaters."

"Good idea, darling." And she takes the sweaters from the empty seat next to her, keeping her own, passing the others to Neil.

"Bundle up, Rox," Neil says.

Roxanne takes the sweater, thanking Neil, then laughs. "I don't need *these* anymore," taking off her sunglasses and returning them to her purse in the vacant seat at her side. Looking inside her bag, she notices something. "I forgot, Neil—your mail." And she hands him a stack of envelopes.

The speeches are dragging on, and there are still a few minutes until the presidential address, so Neil decides this is a good time to review the mail. There are a couple of credit-card bills, a solicitation from a gay-rights group, another from the alumni association of the university he attended. These can all be dealt with later.

Then he glances at the one remaining envelope and notices the *Journal*'s logo with its return address. For a moment, he assumes that it contains something for Manning, that he sorted it incorrectly at the loft. But no, confirming that the envelope was in fact addressed to him, Neil works his index finger under the flap and tears it open. He extracts a letter from within and flips to the end of it to identify the sender. It was written by David Bosch.

Christ, Neil fumes, folding the letter. He didn't need this, not now. Here he sits, trying to enjoy himself, trying to put out of his mind, at least for a few hours, the emotional crisis that has tormented him for the past two days. And now *this*, a disembodied communiqué from that bastard, the rotten kid himself. He's tempted to rip the thing up and scatter its shreds on the ground,

to be trampled by the multitudes as they leave the stadium tonight.
And in fact his fingers pinch the folded sheets of paper and begin
to tear them, but then he stops, restrained by a sense of fairness,
or perhaps by sheer curiosity—he's not sure which.

Neil opens the letter, braces himself for its unknown contents,
then reads:

Thursday, July 1

Dear Neil,

Mark and I spoke at the office this morning, and he told
me of his intentions to talk to you tonight about what happened
in Door County. I tried to dissuade him from telling you about
this, but I have since realized that this decision to be truthful
with you is decent, well intentioned, and inevitable. That's
simply how Mark operates, as you surely know. That's what
makes Mark . . . well, *Mark*.

I'm ashamed of what happened, and I feel that I have
especially betrayed your friendship, which you offered so freely.
Because I have a hunch that Mark will not make this plain to
you, I must tell you point-blank that I seduced him. I still don't
understand my motivation for doing it—likely it was something
more akin to hero worship or gaming than to out-and-out
lust—but that doesn't excuse my actions. You can rest assured
that Mark wanted no part of the game I was playing. In the
end, he succumbed simply because I played the game too well.
I won, I got what I wanted, and I realize now that I've created
a horrible mess.

There can be no doubt that news of this incident has hurt
you greatly, and I'm sorry. I know that my apologies offer you
scant consolation, if any, so I will try to keep my distance for
now, while vowing never again to act in any manner that might
darken your relationship, your home, or your life.

You probably won't care (and I certainly wouldn't blame
you), but I want you to know that this experience has helped
me grow up a bit. I won't try to dismiss what happened as
simply a regrettable result of the raging hormones of youth,
though I think, in all honesty, that such an argument could be

made. The more important point, however, from my own perspective, is that I have learned how every action, each decision, produces a consequence. This should be self-evident, but a week ago I was still suffering from delusions of maturity, confident that my twenty-four years had taught me all I needed to know.

I was wrong, of course, and now at least I grasp the extent of those things that I have yet to learn. Whether you know it or not, people like you and Mark have had an immeasurable influence on my life. You are so self-confident with your love for each other—and so unremarkably open about it—that I am inspired to follow your course and claim my own self-worth. This is a tricky threshold for me to cross. Only once have I acknowledged my gayness to family or friends, but the time is now right to come clean, and I have you to thank for leading me to this peace.

First on my list is Uncle Hector. I tried once several years ago to discuss my budding homosexuality with him, expecting a sympathetic ear, but it was he, really, who slammed the closet door on me. I can't exactly *blame* him—he did what he thought was best for me—but I see plainly now that he was wrong. Very soon, I will reopen this discussion and hope for better results.

Meanwhile, Mark will have broached a tremendously difficult topic with you. In all likelihood, you now loathe me. You have every right to, Neil, but please, don't let that anger spill over and infect your love of Mark. What you have together is too special to be spoiled by the mindless actions of a dumb kid. That kid has learned a hard lesson. He's going to concentrate for now on building the skills of his career. He needs to bring some focus to his life.

That kid also wants to let you know that he loves you, both you and Mark. If you can ever forgive his unconscionable intrusion, he hopes once again to enjoy your friendship.

With profound apologies and heartfelt affection,

David Bosch

Neil has held the letter in his lap, staring at the words through the blur of moist eyes. He remembers that Manning had tried to invoke some "extenuating circumstances" when he related the incident Thursday night, but Neil wouldn't listen—he was too busy breaking glassware. He is still deeply hurt by what happened between Manning and David, but the letter has indeed lent a different cast to Manning's participation. He *knows*, after all, that Manning loves him. Neil also knows that Manning is the only one he has ever truly loved. He wishes that Manning were here right now, so they could try to talk this through again, with Neil in a more balanced state of mind.

His thoughts are interrupted by the uproar of the crowd as everyone in the stadium rises, cheering the entrance of the president. The combined symphony orchestras of Chicago, Milwaukee, and Minnesota thunder "Hail to the Chief."

Some fifteen minutes later, at a quarter to nine, Manning and Farber are still at the lab in the planetarium, watching the president's televised address. Manning is torn between the rousing speech, which is naturally of interest to him, and the story on his laptop computer, which he is trying to finish. After speaking to Lucille Haring earlier, he switched his modem over to the desk phone to conserve the battery in his portable, so he's had an open line to Lucy's computer terminal at the *Journal*.

Farber gets up from his chair and steps to the other side of the desk. Opening the bottom drawer, he pulls out the bottle of Jack Daniel's and pours a fresh drink. Referring to the president's speech, he says, "That guy's got guts. I don't agree with everything he's saying, but I have to hand it to him for going out on a limb."

"I feel as if *I'm* going out on a limb—with this story," Manning tells him. "There's a nine-o'clock deadline, but I don't know why. How does this all end?"

"Don't ask me," says Farber, sitting again to watch the speech. Over his shoulder, he reminds Manning, "You're the reporter."

"Thanks," Manning says dryly, returning to his typing. He pauses to gather his thoughts, and just as he's about to begin a new paragraph, his cellular phone warbles with an incoming call. He tries typing with one hand as he picks up the phone and punches the button. "Yes?" he answers.

"Hello, Mark? Jim here."

Manning stops typing. "Hey, Jim! I forgot about you. Busy day at headquarters?" He uncaps his pen, ready for note-taking.

"You might say that," the detective answers with heavy understatement. "Sorry to be so late getting back to you, but I just got your message."

Manning hesitates. Doodling on his pad, he asks into the phone, "Did it make any sense?"

"Sure did. You said that you knew details of David Bosch's murder at the MidAmerica Building. The victim's identity hasn't been made public yet—with the city in such flux today, we've had trouble reaching his parents—but *you* identified him, so I can draw one of two conclusions. Either you killed the kid, or you know who did. I figure you wouldn't be calling me if you'd pulled the trigger, so maybe you've got a useful tip."

Manning has to laugh at the soundness of Jim's reasoning, though of course he finds no humor in this. "I've got more than a tip, Jim. I can tell you the whole story—killer, conspiracy, and all." And he proceeds to do just that, relating how Nathan Cain murdered David and how Manning identified him by the sound of his beeper. "I'm reasonably sure that the bullet in David's back will match the ones that killed Cliff Nolan, linking Cain to both murders. Too bad Nolan's ballistics tests were inconclusive—they could have led you straight to the weapon."

Jim has listened without comment, probably taking notes. He says over the phone, "Our *press release* called the tests inconclusive because we didn't want to tip our hand. Actually, the ballistics were a no-brainer. The bullets that killed both victims had a caliber of eight millimeters. I don't need to tell you how unusual that is. In fact, it's virtually unknown. Then, at the Bosch kid's murder scene, our killer did us the favor of leaving behind a shell casing. He must have run out of time—or daylight—and couldn't find it in all the rubble on the roof. But *we* found the shell, and it was clearly of Japanese manufacture, pointing to a Nambu-model pistol. The last year those were made, in the early forties, only five hundred were produced. We've been trying to trace the few that are known to exist. They're collectors' items.''

Manning caps his pen. ''God,'' he says with a chortle of disbelief, ''I've actually seen the weapon. Cain has a gun collection, enshrined behind glass in his office. The Nambu was used by a Japanese general to kill himself after the war, so Cain must have attached some ritualistic significance to the murders he committed with it.''

''If we could locate it,'' says Jim, ''we'd have this whole thing sewn up, but Cain is surely smart enough to ditch it.''

Manning insists, ''He'd never ditch that piece. It's the pride of his collection, a gift from some bigwig at the Pentagon.'' Manning tells Jim exactly where to find it, adding, ''You can't miss it—it has a jade handle.''

''That wraps it up then. Any idea where we might find Cain?''

''I'm making this too easy for you. As far as I know, he's at his office right now. He often spends the night there. So get your warrants, then go get him *and* the gun. One-stop shopping, Jim.''

The detective laughs. ''We'll tidy this up as soon as the crowds at the stadium start to clear. And next time you call, I'll make a point of getting back to you sooner. In fact, here's my cell-phone number.''

Manning jots it down. ''Thanks, Jim. Now go fight some crimes.'' They say good-bye, and Manning hangs up the phone.

Arlen Farber has kept an eye on the television and an ear on the phone conversation. He tells Manning, ''That's a relief.''

''I guess so,'' says Manning, unsure. He scrolls through some of the story on his screen. ''But we still don't know what happens at nine o'clock, or why. So fasten your seat belt.''

Farber shrugs, downing more Jack and Diet Rite. He returns his attention to the television. The president is finishing his speech, and the crowd has risen to their feet, cheering. It's nearly nine o'clock.

Waiting atop the Journal Building for the second hand of his watch to point skyward, Nathan Cain rises from his stool and makes a final inspection of the laser apparatus, assuring himself that all is ready. Last Monday, downstairs in Cain's office, Manning saw this contraption through the window and commented that it looked like a gun. He was right, of course. And even though Cain drew the curtains to hide the view that morning, he was confident then, as he is now, that Manning couldn't begin to fathom the true nature and purpose of this device.

It is indeed a laser projector, as are the other units, to be used in creating the sky show that will spin a dazzling pink triangle in the heavens, a symbol of gay rights hovering over the new stadium as a finale to tonight's opening ceremonies. But this unit alone has special capabilities, developed with the reluctant assistance of Buddy, Cain's friend at the Pentagon. This unit alone employs a new laser technology born of devilish theories of electromagnetic physics understood by only a handful of military specialists. This unit alone is linked to an orbiting communications satellite. This unit alone is linked to vast banks of computer power that will enable it to perform dizzying calculations during the course of the spectacle, that will enable it to reprogram its linked satellite for a covert purpose. This unit alone has the power to kill.

Cain completes his walkabout of the device and laughs aloud at its fearsome, outlandish appearance. It looks like a prop out of some cheap sci-fi flick. In truth, it was cobbled together from various parts of existing hardware, a secret prototype of a sinister weapon that will be used only once. The tractor seat and its array of controls serve no purpose whatever, more easily left intact than removed for purity of function. No marksman, however accomplished, could operate this contraption with sufficient speed and precision; it must be guided by the simultaneous calculations of a hidden computer network, harnessing together innocuous banks of gigabytes and megahertz. Racks and cabinets bulge with electronics at three separate locales—in a basement in Washington, in Cain's suite of offices, and across town in the laboratory assigned to Dr. Pavo Zarnik at Civic Planetarium.

So the Zarnik ruse, the tenth planet, was merely a cover, a

diversion, to keep the press busy while the final phase of this project was readied for tonight. But the planet scam was nearly exposed, twice, and two of Cain's reporters had to die at his own hand. He is convinced that their deaths, though regrettable, will be far overshadowed and quickly forgotten in the wake of the climactic finale to tonight's spectacle.

It was ironic that Clifford Nolan titled his exposé "Requiem for a Small Planet." It was clever, succinct, and ever-so-slightly smug—qualities that Cain always admired in Nolan's writing. But when Cain saw that headline on his own computer screen while Nolan sat at home drafting the story, he knew that Nolan's phrase-turning days must end. Visiting Nolan at his apartment that night, Cain laughed with the writer as they discussed Zarnik's preposterous claim. While Nolan typed, he suggested to Cain, "Why don't you play something while I drive the final nails into Zarnik's coffin. A *Requiem* would be fitting. Take your pick— Mozart, Berlioz, Verdi."

Verdi, thought Cain. Perfect. He removed the CD from its case, scrupulously polished both sides of it with his black silk pocket handkerchief, and dropped it into the machine. Behind Nolan's back, he pressed the "play" button, his index finger covered by the handkerchief. The solemn opening measures of the music began to fill the room. "Scan to the good part," Nolan told Cain over his shoulder.

Cain knew what Nolan meant—he was asking for the "Dies Irae" section, the "Day of Wrath." With a silk-clad finger, Cain cued up the music, spun up the volume, and pressed "play" again. Then, timed to Verdi's four explosive blasts, the crack of doomsday, he fired four bullets into Clifford Nolan's back with the rarest of rare Nambu pistols, the one sent to him by a friend he called Buddy.

Again Cain recalls the hospital tent in Korea and Buddy's horrible admission of love. Cain remembers when Buddy sent him the pistol, a token of friendship that made it all too easy for Cain, years later, to threaten sending it back, to threaten he'd return it so that Buddy might fire it into his own temple. It never came to that, thank God. Buddy proved both his friendship to

Cain and his love of country. He knew how to accomplish tonight's spectacle. He was the builder, while Cain was the architect. And the "client," so to speak—the inspiration behind the whole project—was none other than the Christian Family Crusade and its guiding force, Elder Burlington Buchman. So, then, knowledge of tonight's plan is shared by only three people: Cain, Buddy, and Buchman.

Conspiracy is an ugly concept, Cain tells himself, but at times it is necessary—times like these. These are the times when the perversion of homosexuality has broken out of its closet and thrust itself upon society at large. The plague of AIDS might have stopped it, but failed. There's been talk of "gay rights" for over a generation, and by now it's crept into the national consciousness. It's gone so far, politicians routinely pay lip service to it and even the archbishop has begun blathering about "inclusion"—so much for *his* friendship. The agenda it clear enough: Homosexuality is to be placed on an equal moral footing with heterosexuality. That's just for starters. Then comes job protection, marriage, and finally, that last holdout of decency, the military itself. If the courts don't ram it down our throats, eventually the sway of public opinion will. It must be stopped. The CFC has waged a noble war, but now, just when their efforts have begun to reverse this hideous trend, the homosexual agenda is glorified by a festival that will be watched by the whole world. Politicians can't line up fast enough to add their voices to the din, hoping to curry favor with this powerful minority as the stakes are raised for the next election. They're all here tonight, down at the stadium, raising their voices in a sordid plea for "tolerance." My ass! And worst among them, a traitor to his nation who has betrayed every principle of traditional values, is a sitting president of the United States.

"With a single magnificent gesture," Cain told Buddy, "working with the CFC, we can rid our nation of this menace. The president himself and thousands of vocal sympathizers will all be silenced."

"Nathan, you're mad," replied Buddy, certain Cain was joking.

But Cain's threat to return the Nambu pistol proved he was in earnest, and Buddy, for the first time in his life both helpless and frightened, signed on. He committed untold resources, shrouded beneath the tightest levels of national security, to construct and install the laser hardware. In order to help prevent detection or tracing, however, he insisted that the final phase of Project Zarnik would have to be executed by hand. Nathan Cain was to pull the switch—two of them, in fact—an assignment he eagerly accepted.

According to plan, tonight at six o'clock precisely, he flipped the green switch, which fired up the intricate network of computer power, linking the three projectors and running them through a lengthy warm-up cycle of checks and counterchecks.

Now, at nine o'clock precisely, just as the president has finished his speech, Cain is ready to flip the pink switch, which will initiate the sky show while linking the whole system to laser weaponry that orbits silently overhead in the black void of space. As the spectacle of light progresses, it will gain power, climaxing in an "accident" of cataclysmic proportions. In a meeting late last night with Elder Buchman, Cain predicted, "When the firestorm explodes within the stadium, it will consume the president and everyone on the field." While those in the stands may escape instant annihilation, thousands more will surely perish, trampled in the pandemonium.

Now, at nine o'clock precisely, the words of the "Dies Irae" echo from Nathan Cain's childhood: "Day of wrath and day of mourning. See fulfilled the prophets' warning." The next line of the ancient dirge has taken on new meaning and immediacy: "Heav'n and earth in ashes burning . . ."

Now, at nine o'clock precisely, Nathan Cain knows that the moment has arrived to execute the final phase of a plan that has consumed him for nearly a year. Standing atop the Journal Building's tower platform with his thumb poised above a pink switch, he wonders what Buddy is doing right now. What's he thinking at this moment when his technical expertise is about to change the course of history? And Burlington Buchman—what's going through his mind in this instant when his great crusade will enter its finest hour?

Overhead, the sky glows purple with twilight. Below, the city glows orange with the light of countless sodium-vapor lamps.

But the brightest lights down there—Cain sees them clearly—emanate from the new stadium where a hundred thousand citizens cheer their president. Cain is sure he can hear them through the constant winds that blow past the peak of the tower.

These thoughts and perceptions, real and imagined, have coursed through Cain's mind in a mere millisecond. With a decisive snap, his thumb engages the simple mechanism of the switch.

With a jolt, the projector powers up and shoots dual beams from its long snout, aimed at the other two projection sites. Simultaneously, the other two projectors emit their own beams, forming a miles-wide triangle over the city. The perfectly straight beams of pink laser light look like giant tubes of neon in the sky, aglisten with the random passings of dust, insects, a bird here and there.

Nathan Cain is awed by its beauty, though he detests what it represents. Be patient, he tells himself. This spectacle is far from over.

At nine o'clock precisely, the banks of computers in Zarnik's lab suddenly shift to a more active mode. Their hum, which Manning and Farber have ceased to notice, rises in pitch and settles into a steady, irritating whine.

"Here we go," says Manning, bracing himself in his chair, not sure what may happen next, expecting the worst. But nothing does happen, and after a minute has passed, he relaxes his grip on the edge of the desk. Then—just in case—he rises from the chair, crosses to the fire cabinet mounted near the door, and opens it. He tells Farber, "I may not know a lick about computers, but this stuff sounds like it's working too hard. If something overheats, I want to be prepared." He removes the ax and sets it on the floor. The water hose would be of no use for an electrical fire, so he leaves it stowed. Then he lifts an extinguisher from its hook and carries it back to the desk.

"Hey," says Farber, pointing to the TV screen, "check it out."

The crowds at the stadium coo as one, looking skyward as the lines of the huge pink triangle sparkle in the heavens. A camera cuts to the presidential party, seated onstage. They clap and smile, pointing to the laser display. Then the camera pans a bit of the crowd nearby, and once again Manning spots Neil seated between Roxanne and Claire. Neil's head is thrown back to gaze at the light show; in his hand there's a sheaf of folded papers. A collective gasp rises from the spectators, and the camera again aims at the night sky, where the triangle, which at first consisted of lines that stretched all the way from projector to projector, has begun to condense itself. As the triangle shrinks to the size of the stadium itself, it no longer appears merely in outline, but hovers overhead as a solid plane of glimmering, undulating pink light.

The computers in the lab whine even louder now, and the clicking of relay switches intensifies to a racket. Farber's glance darts about the room as he reaches for his glass and downs the last of his drink. Manning sits at the desk again, watching the spectacle on television, drumming his fingers on top of the fire extinguisher.

At nine o'clock precisely, at her desk in Nathan Cain's outer offices, Lucille Haring is navigating the deepest recesses of Cain's personal directories when something happens to the computer— a network glitch perhaps, a momentary flash on the screen. Then she realizes that the computer is responding more slowly to her commands. It seems the whole system is bogged down.

That's strange. She wrings her brows. Backing out of Cain's directories, she takes a look at the *Journal*'s mainframe, wondering if anything might catch her eye. And it does. The data flashing on her screen reveal sudden, intense activity on many of the *Journal*'s phone lines, which are being used to both transmit and receive complex digital signals—there's a heap of numbers being crunched. Very strange.

She sits back in her chair, locks both hands behind her head, and stares at the screen, watching the activity of the mainframe as a whole, which is dominated by all this phone stuff. Then a little stream of data prances past, which she can identify as editorial matter, a story, being sent to the newsroom. What was that?

She hunkers over the keyboard again, intrigued, and tries to trace that errant bit of coding. It was sent to the editorial page, an opinion column, but who sent it? Manning? No, she sees his stories, queued up and blinking, right where she left them. So she traps the stream of data, stops it, and keyboards a code that will trace its source—and *bang*, she finds herself right back in Nathan Cain's directories. A hidden subdirectory, "editorial buffer," is now exposed. Cain had a story waiting there all along, coded to be sent to the newsroom at this hour. A few keystrokes later, the story, slugged "cataclysm," appears on her screen.

Lucille Haring reads the first couple of sentences, then stops with a loud gasp. She needs to catch her breath before she can read on.

With his fingers still drumming the top of the fire extinguisher, Manning watches the pink triangle as it floats above the stadium. He wonders, with the crowd he sees on television, whether the spectacle has climaxed or if there is more to come. Their question is soon answered as the triangle shrinks tighter and grows brighter, descending slowly through the sky till it rests not far from the top row of bleachers. The spectators roar their approval.

With the transition to this next phase of the laser show, the equipment in Zarnik's lab revs to an even higher pitch. "This is all very nice," Arlen Farber tells Manning, slurring, wagging his empty glass at the monitor, "but if someone isn't careful, they're going to blow a fuse."

Manning isn't sure how many drinks Farber has swilled this evening, but they've been sufficient to dull his concern for any impending danger. He actually seems to be enjoying himself now, getting into the spirit of the festival. Manning, however, feels nothing but dread—an uncertain but intense uneasiness. He wishes there were some way to communicate with Neil and tell him to get out of there.

The crowd whoops as the triangle, brighter still, levitates within the walls of the stadium and begins to rotate, majestically, like an alien mothership George Lucas might dream up. The flags around the perimeter of the stadium glow pink in the light of the spectacle. The banks of computers there in the lab churn all the louder. Farber applauds. The president watches with an awed smile.

Then the television coverage switches to the scene of the Christian Family Crusade's protest at their North Side hotel. They've been marching since early afternoon, and the troops are looking weary, though zealously determined. Elder Burlington Buchman has just stepped up to a microphone on a makeshift stage erected on the hotel grounds. His followers cheer wildly as his amplified words echo in the night. He speaks of abomination, of Sodom and Gomorrah, of fire and brimstone. He speaks of the dawning of a new age, a new millennium, freed from the forces of perversion and liberalism. He speaks of the will of Jesus. He speaks of God as a wrathful executioner.

Manning has heard enough. He needs to return to his story, writing his impressions of the spectacle as it unfolds. Mentally, he tunes out Buchman's ranting, tunes out Farber's laughter, and begins to type—but then his cellular phone warbles, breaking his thought midsentence. He answers, "Mark Manning."

"Thank God I reached you, Mark." It's Lucille Haring, and her voice wavers with panic. "I don't know where to begin . . ."

Reacting to her tone, he says, "Calm down, Lucy. I'm listening. What is it?"

"I've discovered that the *Journal*'s computer power is linked to other computers somewhere here in the city. . . ."

"They're here in this room, in Zarnik's lab," Manning explains to her. "It has something to do with the laser show, but I don't know how they're connected, and more important, I can't figure out why."

"That's what I'm about to tell you. They're connected by phone lines—simple phone lines, lots of them. Tons of data are being exchanged at this very moment. That's the 'how.' But it's the 'why' that's so stunningly evil."

Manning doesn't speak. He's not sure he's ready to ask the question or hear the answer. On television, the coverage has switched from Buchman, returning to the spectacle at the stadium, where the laser triangle now spins and undulates. The camera catches the moment when one of the points of the triangle veers off-course and shears through one of the huge steel flagpoles. With a spray of sparks, it drops outside the stadium and clangs loudly as it hits the cement of the parking lot. The crowd goes silent, then spontaneously yelps its approval. There's a close-up of the president, whose smile is now tainted with wariness. Manning views his face through the crosshairs on the screen, as if targeted in the sights of a weapon.

"Good God," Manning says into the phone. Ready to confirm his worst fears, he asks, "What did you find?"

"An editorial," Lucy tells him, "scheduled to run tomorrow morning." Her voice trembles with the gravity of the words she is about to read. "Cain's column is slugged 'cataclysm.' It begins: 'The nation mourns the death of a president this morning, who died here as a visitor, a leader, and a messenger. The special grief of our city is magnified, of course, because the accident that claimed his life has also silenced the still-uncounted thousands of our own friends, neighbors, and loved ones. When last night's laser spectacle went awry at twelve minutes past nine, precipitating this cataclysmic disaster, history was rewritten. . . .' "

Manning looks at his watch. It is eight minutes past nine—only four minutes remain until Nathan Cain's dream of a cleansed nation is made real. As Lucy continues to read the editorial, Manning's eyes are fixed on the television screen, where he sees the whirling triangle, no longer pink, but hottest red. Even Arlen Farber, who has been enjoying the show through an alcoholic haze, now looks concerned. The electronics in the lab click and whine even more frenetically.

Manning searches through the clutter on the desk and finds his note. "Hold on, Lucy," he says into his cell phone, "and stay on the line." He sets down the cell phone and unplugs the modem from the desk phone. Lifting the receiver, he dials the number Jim gave him a few minutes ago. Manning waits, heart pounding, as the detective's phone rings. At last he answers.

"Jim, this is Manning again. Listen. Alert the feds to get the president out of the stadium. I'll explain later, but it's urgent. Act now—or he'll be dead in three minutes." Manning hangs up the phone and glances around the lab, feeling he should *do* something.

Arlen Farber, who has heard Manning's message to Jim, now stands with mouth agape, backing toward the door, quaking at what he has learned. His foot bumps the fire-ax that Manning leaned against the wall.

"Arlen"—Manning thinks of something—"wait there!" He says to Lucy, still on the cell phone, "If we could shut down the computers here at the planetarium, we might hobble the whole system, right?"

"Very likely," she answers. "Give it a shot, and I'll monitor the results on the *Journal*'s mainframe."

Manning turns to Farber. "Arlen, help me. Help *them*"—he points to the television screen—"and grab that ax. Chop through the main bundle of cables there on the floor." Farber hesitates. Manning tells him, "The ax handle is wooden. You'll be fine. Please, Arlen, now!"

Farber bites his lip, nods, and grabs the ax. Positioning himself with a wide stance alongside the bundle of cables, he raises the ax over his head, jangling the keys and whistle that still hang from his neck. He flexes the muscles of both arms, then swings, hacking solidly into the cables. A few sparks spit from the heavy plastic tube, but there's no danger—these cables apparently carry information, not raw power.

Immediately, the computers in the room seem to belch, becoming much less active. They no longer churn in unison, but make random little noises, independent of each other. Farber beams with pride and continues to chop at the cable bundle till it is completely severed.

Lucy's voice says over the phone, "I don't know what you did, Mark, but all the telephone activity between here and there has ceased. Well done!"

And in fact, Manning notices on television that the sky show at the stadium appears to have powered-down—with two minutes to spare. The triangle is pink now, no longer red, and it rotates slowly above the crowd, much less menacingly. Farber tosses aside his ax and struts toward the desk, preparing to reward himself with another drink. As he lifts the jug of Jack Daniel's, his police whistle clangs against it.

"Uh-oh," Lucy's voice sounds a note of warning over the phone, "something's happening." Even as she speaks, Manning notices that the laser spectacle appears to have powered-up again—it's brighter, redder, moving faster. Lucy explains, "When the *Journal*'s mainframe lost communication with the planetarium, it began establishing phone connections elsewhere. There's now intense digital activity between the *Journal* and some other location that's not in Chicago. I think—yes, I see area codes—the *Journal*'s mainframe is now linked to Washington."

Manning watches on television as a security force scurries about the president and begins leading him off the field. A camera near the stage shows him leaving. Faces in the crowd look confused, wondering about the abrupt departure. There's Neil, turning quizzically from Claire to Roxanne.

Manning asks Lucy, "This whole system is linked by phone lines, right? Can you identify the trunk line between the *Journal* and Washington, then patch me into it? I want to hear what the transmission actually sounds like."

"Uh . . ." Lucy stammers over the phone, "I think so, Mark. Sure. Here we go—you'll lose my voice now."

Manning presses the phone closer to his ear and listens to the secret digital chatter of computers plotting a massacre. The bleeps and tones shoot back and forth with dizzying speed, exchanging technical commands that are executed with instantaneous precision. Manning checks the time. Eleven minutes past nine—there's less than one minute remaining.

At the stadium, cameras follow the laser display. Fully energized, it spins cyclonically above the top bleachers, roiling with internal heat. Then it tips, darting with its points to slice cleanly through two more of the flagpoles. One of them falls outside the stadium, but the other drops within, trailing a burning American flag. The white-hot steel mast slides down one of the long aisles, narrowly missing row after row of horrified onlookers.

Farber stands there fidgeting with his drink, trying to gulp from it, but unable to swallow. Manning watches the laser triangle condense itself further as it begins its descent to the field. He hears the electronic scenario of doom beeping in his ear. He sees Farber.

Then inspiration strikes. Manning shouts, "Give me that!"

Utterly dismayed, Farber tenders to Manning his cocktail.

"*No!*" Manning reaches toward Farber's chest, grabs the neck chain, and yanks it, sending keys clattering to the floor. But in Manning's hand remains the big chrome police whistle.

He jabs the whistle into his mouth, positions the phone in front of it, inhales so deep that his gut burns, then he blows.

Stunned by the pitch and the decibels, Farber claps his hands to his ears, dropping his jelly jar to the desk, where it crashes, sloshing Jack and Diet Rite squarely into Manning's lap.

But Manning doesn't care. He's listening to the phone again, and when the ringing in his own ears has cleared, he hears . . . absolutely nothing.

Seconds before twelve minutes past nine, the television pictures from the stadium are following the descent of the laser spectacle toward the field, when without warning, it suddenly . . . blinks out. The crowd is hushed as a few charred birds drop to the ground. Then a hundred thousand spectators burst into applause, roaring their approval of the big finish.

Seconds before twelve minutes past nine, something goes wrong —again—with the laser projector atop the Journal Building.

Two minutes ago, Nathan Cain was distraught to realize that the unit was losing power. Perhaps the computer link with the planetarium had been severed. He was confident there was still sufficient time for the system to establish communication with its backup link in Washington, but he figured he'd better take action, just in case things got out of control. So he managed with difficulty to hoist himself onto the weapon's seating fixture, taking hold of two armatures with which he might aim the device if the automatic controls should fail.

It turned out that this precaution was unnecessary—the backup link functioned flawlessly, and within moments, the laser gun was powered-up again, putting on quite a show at the stadium. Because the gun was now making jerky movements as part of its programmed routine, Cain decided to remain in the tractor seat—it might be dangerous to dismount. Besides, he discovered he had a much better view of the stadium from the seat up here, and he looked forward to witnessing the final moment of the spectacle, when his daring plan would be fulfilled.

With that moment at hand, Cain congratulated himself for masterminding a scheme that was, at the same time, both profoundly complex and devilishly simple. It was complex because of the conspiracy, the timing, and the computer technology behind it. The scheme was simple, though, in its brutally direct approach to curing a social ill and also in the rudimentary telephone technology used in patching together an invisible but powerful control system.

Telephones, he gloated. Just think—everyday household phone lines were made to serve as an indispensable component in a high-tech project that would, within moments, change the destiny of a nation.

But now, with only seconds remaining, something goes wrong again. Cain will never know it, but his foolproof, baby-simple telephone links have just been bested by a police whistle. A screech in the phone lines has just made mush of the network's electronics, bouncing a jumble of conflicting commands to Washington, then back to the top of the Journal Building.

The light show at the stadium is over, but the fireworks have only begun in Nathan Cain's laser cannon. Capacitors pop, relays fizzle, and circuit boards melt as the control systems of the device are shorted by a voltage surge that could blow fuses from Waukegan to Peoria. Nathan Cain's body is equipped with no such fuse, of course, so the metal tractor seat, quite literally, fries his sorry ass.

For decades, Nathan Cain has been revered as Chicago's living icon of journalism. In death, he is now but hissing meat.

EPILOGUE

THE CRITIC CRITIQUES HIMSELF

A new season's opening gives pause for reflection and reconciliation

by Hector Bosch
Senior Critic, New York Weekly Review

September 3, 1999, New York —Each year at this time, when the theatrical world prepares to lure, entertain, and enrich us with its latest wares, we inevitably look to the future with dewy-eyed optimism. This critic, however, before allowing himself to move forward, must first indulge in a painful bit of soul-baring to you, his gentle readers.

As most of you have already read elsewhere, I suffered a terrible loss two months ago when my nephew, David Bosch, 24, was murdered in Chicago by Nathan Cain, late publisher of the *Chicago Journal*, which employed David as a reporter.

The day he was killed, David, who was gay, approached me for advice on a personal matter. Instead of listening, instead of proffering the wisdom of my years, I rebuffed him—as I had done before when he first confided his sexuality to me—and I lashed out against his mentor at the *Journal*, Mark Manning, the heroic reporter whose name is now a household word.

David planned to talk to me again that same night, but then his life ended in pursuit of a career he loved, and I never had the opportunity to renounce the irrational prejudices that led to my thoughtless behavior.

I must now confess that those prejudices once led me to write a check to the Christian Family Crusade, the fundamentalist group that played a role in killing David. As all now know, they also conspired, in the name of righteousness, to slaughter our president and untold thousands of gay-rights sympathizers.

The check I wrote was not a large one, but it contributed to a cause that has now been thoroughly discredited, and I am remorsefully sorry.

David, I miss you and will always love you. Mr. Manning, I admire you and thank you for your investigative efforts, which both inspired my nephew and saved so many innocent lives.

Hector Bosch has spoken. ❏

Saturday, September 4

Manning steps up to the curb outside Bistro Zaza and turns back to look at his car. He tells the valet, "And for God's sake, be *careful* with it this time."

"Absolutely, Mr. Manning!" The car-parker gives an obsequious little bow, opens the door with a handkerchief so as not to smudge the handle, waits for a long, clear opening in traffic, then slowly pulls the black sedan into the street.

Standing on the curb with Manning, Neil says, "I told you they'd be able to fix it." Then he adds sheepishly, "I had no idea it would take this long, though. Pretty gutsy—bringing it back *here* the first week it's repaired."

As they step toward the door of the restaurant, Manning muses, "Now and then, one must simply confront one's fears." Dropping the rhetorical tone, he adds, "It's only a car. I had too much of an emotional investment in it. I've come to recognize the obvious: Other things are far more important." He puts his arm over Neil's shoulder as he opens the door and escorts him inside.

At eight o'clock on the Saturday evening of Labor Day weekend, Zaza's is booked to its I-beams. Clumps of patrons, who have been kept waiting more than an hour, drink and whine near the host's podium. The noise from the stark warehouse-style dining room is oppressively loud, with people shouting to be heard above the din, only adding to it. Stepping through the door, Manning winces at the aural assault.

The host—he looks like the same sunken-cheeked young man who seated them two months ago, but he may be a black-garbed clone—rushes toward them with his clipboard, effusing, "Good evening, Mr. Manning. What an honor! Two of your party have arrived already. This way, please." And he struts through the crowd with Manning and Neil in tow.

Traversing the dining room, they are stopped again and again as people recognize Manning, thank him, even ask for his autograph. As a prominent local journalist, his name has been widely known in Chicago for years, but now he is known on sight, especially since his visit to the Oval Office. He responds with good-natured indifference to his recent celebrity, assuring those who greet him that he did nothing extraordinary, that he was only doing his job. Extricating himself from a knot of admirers, he guides Neil by the elbow, leaning close to tell him, "Fame is fleeting. By Christmas, we'll have to *beg* for a table."

"For some reason," says Neil, "I doubt that."

Through the crowd on the main floor, they see Roxanne and Carl waiting for them, seated along the wall at the same prime, stepped-up booth they had occupied in July, when Manning and Neil learned the news of Carl's political appointment. The curved booth can seat four, and tonight there is also a chair at the table, a fifth place, with its back to the room. As before, there is an ice bucket, stocked with champagne. Manning can tell from the protruding neck that it's the good stuff again, a bottle of Cristal, which he ordered in advance. Roxanne waggles her fingers as they approach; Carl stands.

"Rox!" says Neil, leaning into the booth to kiss her. "You look great, as usual. Letting your hair grow back?"

She spruces. "The convertible season is waning, so I decided to get a jump on my winter look."

Manning greets Carl with a handshake, mocking the formality of strangers. "Congratulations, Deputy Attorney General Creighton. Neil and I were delighted to learn that your appointment was confirmed without incident." Then he drops the stiff manner. "Really, Carl—nice going."

"Thanks, Mark. We've wanted to get together, but I guess we've all been busy."

"That's one way of putting it," Manning says wryly. "I'm glad you suggested this, but I reiterate: Tonight I host."

Roxanne tells him, "I must admit, your pull has improved. Great table."

"You taught me everything I know, Miss Exner." He gestures that the others should sit. "Shall we? If you don't mind, I'll take the chair—we'll have too many interruptions if I'm facing the room."

They all get settled with Carl and Roxanne centered in the booth, Manning in the chair. Neil sits at the end of the booth, between Roxanne and Manning, leaving an empty spot at the end of the booth, next to Carl. A waiter appears, delivering mineral water to Roxanne, then uncorking the champagne and pouring, leaving an empty glass next to Carl. As they finger their stemware, preparing to toast, Roxanne says, "I hate to be blunt, but who's missing?"

Manning grins. "You'll see."

Roxanne snorts, "You coy thing." She hoists her glass. "Need we wait?"

"No," says Manning, "our fifth may be late. So . . ." He raises his glass and opens his mouth to propose a toast.

But Carl interrupts, "If you wouldn't mind, Mark, may I do the honors? You see, we have an announcement that we're eager to share with you guys."

"Not again," says Neil with a smirk. "Don't tell me this is 'it,' Rox."

" 'It'?" she asks. Neil flashes his ring finger. She aborts a laugh with a hand over her mouth, then gives his wrist a gentle slap, telling him, "*No*, Neil."

Carl says, "We're still toying with that, but tonight's news is career-related."

"Don't tell me," Manning says to Carl. "The governor died, and you're it."

"Hardly." Carl laughs. "This relates to Roxanne's career. Since I'm now effectively out of the picture at the law firm, there'll be a name change announced next week, as soon as the new stationery gets back from the printer. Kendall Creighton Yoshihara will soon be known as Kendall Yoshihara Exner."

"God, Rox," says Neil, "that's fabulous! Congratulations." He gives her a big kiss while raising his own glass. They all toast, then drink.

Manning tells her, "You'll be working even longer hours now."

"Yes," she admits, "but I'll also be billing even higher fees."

"That'a girl!" says Carl, beaming. He tells the guys, "She's a natural."

They share a round of good-natured jabs before settling in quietly for their evening together. Despite the surrounding noise of the restaurant, they have created their own space, a protective shell of friendship. Manning leans forward on his elbows to tell the others, "I'm glad we were able to get together tonight." His tone has turned pensive. "We haven't really 'talked' yet."

"I know," says Roxanne, "but we didn't want to push you, Mark. So much has happened, it's surely turned your life upside down. So we've been waiting to give you the opportunity to open up. No pressure, though."

"Hey, thanks." He sips his champagne. "So—the update. The main thing, of course, is that Neil and I are very much back together." He smiles.

Neil pats Manning's arm, telling the others, "I was ready to come back anyway. I'd overreacted to the David thing, and I knew it. Then I got David's letter, and *then* I learned David had been killed. . . ."

"In effect," says Manning, "David died for me. It's been awful sorting through this—"

"Shhh . . ." Neil grips Manning's hands.

Manning continues, "And in a more direct sense, I was responsible for Nathan Cain's death. I'm not used to killing people—I'm a *writer*. I've been thinking that a bit of therapy may be in order."

"You did the nation a service," Roxanne assures him. "And you've got the medal to prove it."

"However," Manning reminds her, "with Cain silenced, we'll probably never know the identity of his contact in the Pentagon. Whoever it was, he knew how to cover his tracks, and Burlington Buchman claims he never knew him. Buchman seems to think that Cain 'had something' on the military man, and now that

Project Zarnik has failed, the guy is no longer a danger—but who can trust Buchman?"

Carl says, "That sanctimonious bastard, the so-called 'Reverend Elder'—I'll never forgive him or his crew for the interrogation they put me through. Thanks for bringing him down, Mark."

Manning allows himself a smile. "That did feel good, I admit. By the time they finish with his 'trial of the century,' Buchman will be in prison for life, and his Christian Family Crusade has already collapsed. I dealt them a setback once before, but now they're through. Even the Gethsemane Arms was abandoned—within a week of its opening. Yes, I did enjoy squelching their fundamentalist diatribe, if only for a while. Unfortunately, there are plenty of other nut groups, even worse."

Neil pulls the champagne bottle from the ice and refills their glasses—they've all been sipping. He says to the group, "I never met Nathan Cain, but instinctively, I could never stand the guy."

"Not so fast now," says Carl, feigning a note of sympathy for Cain. "He had the decency to send me on that wild-goose chase to Grand Rapids. I'd like to believe he intended to spare me from the cataclysm. At least he had *that* much heart."

Roxanne says, "Try telling that to your friend Brad McCracken at MidAmerica Oil. He was duped to his eyeballs by Cain, who connived him into contributing *millions* to the CFC under highly specious pretexts. The litigation against Cain's estate, which is a mess, will spell some handsome bonuses at Kendall Yoshihara Exner." She grins, tracing her finger around the rim of her water glass.

"Cain was a piece of work, all right," says Manning. "He had us spied-on in Door County, he had the loft ransacked for Nolan's dossiers after he killed David, and of course he masterminded the whole Zarnik plot. It was supremely shrewd of him to keep me occupied with the 'tenth planet' scam, which diverted me from the true conspiracy and convinced me that *he* was being used by the Pentagon. As for his unholy alliance with the CFC, I didn't realize—no one did—that his rift with the archbishop was so fervid. In hindsight, Cain should have been my primary suspect from the start, but instead I got sidetracked by five others—Zarnik himself, Lucille Haring, Dora Lee Fields, Victor Uttley, and even you, Carl."

Roxanne leans to tell Carl, "Sorry about that, dear. It was all my doing. My imagination shifted into overdrive when you were called away from Door County." She asks Manning, "What became of the others?"

"It's no secret now that Lucy engaged in a bit of computer hacking that provided the key to foiling Cain, and she's been duly commended for it. She's still at the *Journal*, up in the executive suite. Now that Gordon Smith has been named acting publisher, he finds her indispensable. I think she'll be around for a while— so you should phone her for a lunch date, Roxanne."

Roxanne smirks. "I don't think she'll like me in longer hair."

"Dora Lee is happy as a clam. The new tenant in Cliff's old apartment is a disabilities consultant who happens to be deaf, so there's no music-playing at all anymore, and Dora Lee is enjoying the peace and quiet."

"What about her Elvis act?" Neil asks.

"With the demise of the CFC"—Manning sighs—"she abandoned the stage and packed her jumpsuit in mothballs."

The others laugh, then Manning continues, "As for Victor Uttley, no one was surprised when he got booted out of the mayor's office. Lucky for him, he'd had sense enough to return the money he extorted from Arlen Farber, so there were no charges against him. In fact, he took the loot directly to police headquarters the same afternoon I was there filling out forms. I spotted him outside the building and thought he was following Arlen and me. His record is clean now, but he's out of work again, just another unemployed actor."

"Just like Arlen Farber," Roxanne observes.

Neil jumps back into the conversation. "Not at all," he tells her. "You've had your nose buried in too many torts, Rox. Because of the publicity Arlen got for helping Mark crash the computers, he's become something of a media darling himself. Just last week, Arlen landed a new gig hosting a cable talk-show."

They all lean back to chuckle at fate's strange twists, at the series of events that brought them to this table. Neil puts a hand on Manning's shoulder. He tells the others, "Even Mark has been getting TV offers—very lucrative network stuff, at that."

"God, Mark, that's wonderful," Roxanne tells him. "Any interest?"

"Nope." He shrugs. "I'll leave television to the talking heads. I'm a journalist. I write. That has it's own rewards."

"And *awards*," she reminds him. "Your copyrighted Zarnik series ran for a week on every front page in the country. You missed the Partridge Prize once before—it was stolen from you— but this time, it's yours, I'm sure."

"I don't know," he says, voice laced with wariness. "The coveted Brass Bird has proven highly elusive. I'll bet you anything that this year's prize goes to Clifford Nolan again, posthumously—his dirt-file antics were never exposed."

Carl leans forward to assure him, "You're *in*, Mark. How could you lose?"

Manning grins. "The Partridge committee consists mainly of old-school editors and academic journalists. I don't think they quite approve of reporters blowing up their publishers, even under the most compelling circumstances."

As they all share a laugh, Roxanne cranes to glimpse someone past Manning's shoulder who is being escorted across the dining room by the host. A quizzical look wrinkles her face, then she says to the others, "Odd, I just saw someone I thought was Arlen Farber. It isn't, though. But that reminds me: Whatever happened to the *real* Pavo Zarnik?"

"He was never in danger," Manning says. "The story we all heard a few months ago was essentially true—he was being brought from Switzerland to Chicago with the assistance of the State Department. However, Nathan Cain's anonymous buddy in the Pentagon managed to have the real Zarnik tucked away on a three-month cruise of the Greek Islands while his impostor assumed the post at the planetarium."

"What's he doing now?" Roxanne asks.

"He finally arrived here in the city last night, and I met him briefly this morning." Manning grins. "Right now, I assume he's walking up behind me."

The others exchange surprised glances as the host steps up from the crowded dining room with the man who looks like Arlen Farber. Manning rises from his chair, and the host tells him, "Your other guest, sir."

Manning extends his hand. The frizzy-haired foreigner shakes it, saying, "I am sorry to be so late, Mr. Manning, but I have made the most remarkable discovery, which I am eager to share with you."

"Not a tenth planet, I hope."

"Ah, *pfroobst*." He laughs at his own use of Farber's artificial dialect, already assimilated by the masses into the season's most hackneyed slang. "No, I have discovered that your fair city is not, in fact, inhabited by gangsters. No tommy guns." He smiles benignly.

The others laugh, rising to meet him.

Manning tells him, "Professor, I'd like you to meet my three best friends. First, this is Miss Roxanne Exner, an attorney. . . ."

Roxanne shakes Zarnik's hand, telling him, "What a marvelous tan, Professor."

Manning continues, "And this is *her* friend, Carl Creighton, a newly appointed attorney for the state. . . ."

Carl greets Zarnik, "A belated welcome to Chicago, Dr. Zarnik."

And then Manning says, "Finally, Professor, let me introduce my, uh, loftmate, Neil—" But Manning stops himself, pauses, and clears his throat. Taking care that his words are sufficiently loud and distinct to be heard through the noise of the room, he says, "Professor Zarnik, I'd like you to meet Neil Waite, my lover."

❏